WAYA'S CHOSEN
II

WAYA'S CHOSEN
II

THE COMPANION

PATSY DEPPE

TATE PUBLISHING
AND ENTERPRISES, LLC

Published by Tate Publishing & Enterprises, LLC
127 E. Trade Center Terrace | Mustang, Oklahoma 73064 USA
1.888.361.9473 | www.tatepublishing.com

Tate Publishing is committed to excellence in the publishing industry. The company reflects the philosophy established by the founders, based on Psalm 68:11,
"The Lord gave the word and great was the company of those who published it."

Book design copyright © 2014 by Tate Publishing, LLC. All rights reserved.
Cover design by Nikolai Purpura
Interior design by Mary Jean Archival

Published in the United States of America

ISBN: 978-1-63268-861-3
1. Fiction / Romance / Fantasy
2. Fiction / Fairy Tales, Folk Tales, Legends & Mythology
14.10.01

CONTENTS

PREFACE

M Y FEARLESS FRIEND taught me new and intriguing things, such as how to get what I wanted, when I wanted it, and how to get off scot-free. Through the winter months, my untamed friend had ideas that clearly led me to stalking animals. What I had not yet learned then was how to take their life. What I was learning was inappropriate, but it felt great. I could feel the taste of the kill each time, watering the back of my throat. It happened one night, but I didn't know if it was real or a mere dream.

It was late May and I was soaring through the forest, leaping over vast brush and dead trees while my welcomed friend taunted me until we came upon a young buck feeding itself. Stopping behind a tree limb heavy with moss, I glared at the deer, feeling my mouth water.

"Take it. You know you want to like I do," my head suggested. "I have taught you well, my friend." While I was hesitating, the buck noticed my presence and bolted. I, being the arrogant hothead I had become, took off after him without thinking, hurling over stumps and downed trees like they were nothing. But the buck was faster.

"He hasn't gotten off that easy," my friend whispered.

Anxious to learn how, I whined, "Show me." Without a wasted moment, my friend took the lead, and we took off after that deer like a bullet from a gun. I had never run so fast in my life.

The strength in my legs made the trees almost nonexistent, like a painted background sans the full moon. It wasn't long before I was on that deer again when he came around the tree into my sight. Leaping over the brush in the way, I bared my teeth and came down on the back of that deer, just missing the horns, sinking them into the soft flesh of its neck. Struggling, we both went down, but I held tight, draining his life while my fangs sunk in deeper.

"That's right, boy. Just little longer, and he'll be finished," my head snickered. When the deer stopped panting, I also heard its heartbeat stop. Getting to my feet, I paced around the thing just to make sure it was indeed dead before I sliced its neck open with my sharp fangs.

With the flesh exposed and the warm life running out onto the ground, the aroma of the sweet smell was calling me like a soft wind. Hunger-driven for the taste, I stuck my nose into the wound, biting down on the flesh and tearing it away. My head had been right so far when it told me we could do things out of the ordinary and not get caught. But the feel of the chase and the kill and the taste of the warm life-giving blood were incredible. Then I came to believe what my friend said about the others keeping such things for themselves. Swallowing a tender piece of meat, I licked the warm blood with the tip of my tongue from my jaws as I caught a faint smell of what I thought was smoke.

"Finish what you have first," my head woofed. Without further ado, I fed on the deer until I was satisfied.

Feeling proud of what I had done, I cleaned myself of the remains and was ready for home when I heard a voice calling to me—not my head though. It was coming from within the woods. It grew closer as my fear grew stronger, but my curiosity bound my feet from running as my tail hid between my legs. Staring though the darkness at the trees, I thought I saw movement with shiny eyes glaring at me. What stepped out from behind those trees into the moonlight was gargantuan.

Standing not more than five feet from me was an enormous wolf with a coat so grey it appeared blue or maybe it was due to the moonlight. The eyes were so black they reflected the light at me and the nose so shiny it glistened with moisture.

"He has come for your kill," my head rasped in my ears.

"Shut up!" I snarled, looking at the creature in front of me. "What do you want here?"

Sitting down on his rump, he sighed, "Do not fear me. I am Waya. I have been watching you for some time." Those large bubble eyes could have cut me like a knife.

"I have heard of you," I snarled.

"I have paid a visit in your dreams."

"So who is Sandseff?"

"He and his two sons are my friends. The legends told today say they are the forefathers. I have let that rumor ride for centuries since no one really knows but those who have the true books written in blood."

I was about to ask how he knew me when my head growled, "Do not whimper one word." Knowing it meant my new friend was lingering in me, I kept silent.

He caught my hesitation. "I know about your dark side. Come with me. I have something I would like to show you that I think you will be interested in." He rose to his feet, and my eyes traveled up with him until the moon hung between his ears.

"Where are we going?" I barked, feeling my nose wrinkle.

"See what the fool has to offer," my head beckoned.

Agreeing, I growled, "Lead the way." The animal raised his snout into the air and inhaled. When he turned to leave, I followed at a distance.

Through the silent night, like a mated pair, I kept up with him, leaping over fallen trees and creeks until we came upon the smell of smoke, before I heard the voice. I dared not ask where we were going in fear the creature might snatch me up by my nape. Not long, I saw the light of the fire through the trees. Waya stopped behind a large red oak tree covered in moss and sat down. I took the liberty of easing over closer to peer around the tree at an old man with long grey braids on his shoulders and a young boy with black hair and eyes, I assumed to be his grandson, sitting cross-legged on the ground in front of the fire. It reminded me of my father and Chief on those nights around a warm fire telling stories.

Tuning my hearing, I listened to the old Cherokee teaching his grandson about life. "A fight is going on inside me," he said to the boy. "It is a terrible fight, and it is between good and evil. The evil is a creature that has anger, envy, sorrow, regret, greed, arrogance, self-pity, guilt, resentment, inferiority, lies, false pride, superiority, and ego." He continued, "The good is joy, peace, love, hope, serenity, humility, kindness, benevolence, empathy, generosity, truth, compassion, and faith. The same fight could be going on inside you."

The grandson thought about it for a minute and then asked his grandfather, "Which will win?"

The old Cherokee replied, "The one you feed."

Realizing the story was in reference to me, I stepped back and faced the large wolf. "It's me, isn't it?"

"Yes," he replied. "If you look closer, you will see they are Jeremiah and you back when you were just a boy. You will need to embrace the darkness within to find the strength to combine both. Otherwise, that creature will take you to your death."

Staring at the old man, I whined, "How is that possible?"

"Like the old man said, 'It's a rage inside.'" I watched the fire flicker in his eyes when he continued. "You wolf's nature is kind and loving, but the companion in you will make you become the most powerful and ruthless creature you will want to know." He glared at me. "I chose you for a reason, Luther." No sooner did he say that than he, the old man, and the child faded as if they were never there, leaving me to wake up alone.

THE HUNT

I COULD NEVER TELL anyone about my fearless friend or that I enjoyed his company on those nights when I found myself trotting along in my wolf form. But one morning, I was carefree and soaring through a majestic forest covered in moss with singing birds, flowers, and thick, lush, wavy grass that felt like a carpet under my paws. The sun was trying to peer through the thick trees but was cut off by the heavy limbs that drug the ground with moss. To my right, through the shadows, were two more wolves racing toward me. They had stealth in their style, their noses high in the air, and their long slender legs in tune with one another. Their bodies were covered in shiny, thick fur from the nose to the tail. When they reached me, one at each side, we trotted in tune together, like a pack through the forest, hunting, searching for something. Only I never had a clue until a creature stepped from behind a tree into our path.

It stood tall on its hind legs with a broad chest and wide head under two long, narrow ears. The shiny nose sniffed the air when we came to a sliding stop on our rumps. *The two wolves that were with me moved closer inward for comfort*, I thought. But they began to lick the sides of my face with their warm tongues, lapping over my snout. I felt uncharacteristic with each touch of the tongues by dearly loving every stroke. It made me want more, and they gave in to my nudges of affection.

I was so busy being pampered that I had forgotten about the thing in our path until it spoke in a growling tone that nearly scared the hide off me.

"Well, we meet at last. I had hoped to see you a lot sooner, but now is as good as any. I see you love affection. Soon I'll show you its pleasure." It laughed, then turned and walked off into the vanishing sun. With my attention taken by the thing, so were the other wolves when I looked around to find I was alone. As the light grew dim, a bone-chilling howl rang out that made my fur tingle on the ends. With a whining woof, I turned-tail and run like there was no tomorrow.

When I woke up from the dream, I was sitting upright in bed feeling scared of the thing. "Only, it was a dream, right?" I asked myself. I had many of those dreams on my return from the fort, but that was the first with that creature in them. Other times, I was led into a devilish mischief of digging holes, of how to lie and then get what I wanted. I didn't understand what it meant with "we meet again," so I ignored the thought. But there were times when I felt devilish inside, only to push it away in fear of letting it get to me and liking the way it felt. And then there were many times I wanted to just let go and run with the wind, howl at the moon, or just get into mischief I knew would lead to trouble. My whole being yearned to be free out there with the others as each day passed, and it grew stronger.

With Kimmi in mind, I grabbed the covers, tossing them off as I leaned over to sit up on the side of the bed, glaring out the window and feeling the soft wind that came through. I was supposed to see her that day, so I quickly grabbed clothes, and then jotted over to the bathroom for a shower. When I was done and dressed in slouchy shorts with a half shirt and sneakers, I rushed down the stairs toward the front door. But before I could lay a hand on the knob, Mae yelled from the kitchen, "Luke, Tom's on the phone for you." I snapped a finger in the air and U-turned toward the kitchen.

I took the phone from Mae's hand, coming through the doorway. "Hello, Tom," I said as I stuck the receiver to my ear.

"Have you seen Daniel this morning?" Tom sounded unusually different but quick and to the point.

I was lying in bed in a hotel room with a young girl I had met at the lake not so long ago. She had shown me the pleasures I never known before. She was sitting over me, bare-assed as I was, when she leaned over and kissed me. Firmly taking her into my arms, I rolled over on top of her, and we made love again. What I didn't know was what was to come.

After a joke or two, he asked, "Can you come to the house right away?" His voice had changed.

Concerned, I replied, "Sure, Tom. On my way." I hung up the phone and run for the front door as I told Mae bye. I never heard her response when I went out the door and to the car in the driveway.

It had begun to rain when I rolled into the driveway and parked, finding Tom and Mac outside with Jason in rainsuits. I hopped out, then sort of skipped over to see what was going on. Tom seemed angry when he turned around and saw me.

"Damn it," he swore, looking up the road while shoving his hands into his front pockets.

Stopping at the corner of the porch, I asked Jason, who was pacing, "What's up?"

He stopped pacing without looking up, moaning, "Willa called me this morning and said Daniel didn't come home last night." He glared down the road before pacing again.

Confused, I asked, "Does that mean what I think it does?" Jason nodded yes and nothing more.

Thoughtless, I grabbed Tom by the arm and turned him around in a jerking motion to face me.

Gritting his teeth, he said, "Yeah, Luke. It does." He coughed, pulling a cell phone from one of his front pants pocket. He dialed a number and waited for only a second or two, then said, "He's on the loose. Get Ben and the boys together." He puts the phone back in his pocket.

Mac stepped in, asking, "Do you two want to join the hunt? We've got to find him ASAP, Luke."

"Is this for real or a test?" I grunted.

Jason stopped pacing, grabbed me by the arm, and said, "I know you don't know him like I do, but he's in trouble right now. I know I joke but not at times like these; so please." His eyes watered and his grip tightened.

Gulping hard, I asked with a shaky voice, "Can we find him in this rain?"

"We're sure as hell gonna try. Y'all comin'?" Tom contested, stepping toward Jason's Ford.

I saw Jason motion yes when he released my arm. Tom turned, went to the passenger side of the truck, and grabbed the handle. "Well, let's go, boys. Jason, your truck was built for this," he said, opening the door. Mac left us and went inside. Jason shook his wet head and scurried over to the driver side while I jumped in the back just as the engine came to life.

"Okay, Jason, let's ride," I yelled, slapping the top of the truck with the palm of my hand. He put the old Ford in gear and began to drive in the direction that Tom had mentioned.

The rain stung my face and arms, but my mind was on why Daniel had ran off. God, I hoped he wasn't doing that call-of-the-wild thing. "Please, Daniel. Don't, my friend," I prayed in silence. Jason was right when he said I didn't know Daniel as well as he did, but I had come to like both as welcomed friends.

I braved the stinging rain as we sped along in search of any trace of Daniel while thunder rolled off in the distance. It didn't take long for the rain to become heavier, with a storm building and lightning striking in the sky. When a clap of thunder awoke, the truck vibrated, making me sit down with my back against the cab, listening to the wet pavement under the tires.

I wiped water from my face when I noticed two other trucks rounded the bend of the road behind us. They kept their distance, but I could see several heads sticking up over the cabs. I slid over to the passenger side and leaned over to the window.

Tapping on the glass, I asked, "Where we going right now?"

"Up over the mountain," Tom replied, grinning and pointing his finger toward the windshield. "It's going to be a hell of a ride, so settle in." I nodded and faced the rear of the truck in thoughts of why, how, and when it happened.

My thoughts were trying to reason why Daniel would do such a thing when I heard the commotion up front. I half turned to look through the back glass and windshield to see a large dog run across the road heading north.

I heard Tom almost scream at Jason, "That looks like him. Floor it, kid!" I watched Jason's hands grip the wheel while he stepped on the pedal, and the truck picked up speed. Grabbing the side of the truck bed, I rose to my feet and glared over the roof, ignoring the stinging rain. I tried to get a glimpse of the animal when the other two trucks roared past us. They split up just at the next fork in the road. I slid down with my back to the cab in thoughts of Daniel and me when I first met him and Jason on that chilly morning.

My mind was clouded when Tom opened the sliding window, startling me. I half rose in a turn to stick my head inside.

"He may go to the park first, then up to the Hollow. We'll start there." He turned back to face the road.

"Where's Mac?" I kind of yelled.

15

Tom widened that smile. "You'll see him in about…now." His grin widened when he looked over Jason toward the driver door. My glance followed his finger, and in that instant, around the curve ahead of us was a wolf hauling ass like it had fire on it. Not realizing who it was, I stared.

The brute was so quick that it didn't stop when it slid around the rear of the truck, losing its grip and falling into a roll. But in the same instance, it grabbed a hold with its back feet, and leaped up, covered in red mud. Plowing through the red mud, it came up along Jason's side of the truck.

Jason rolled down the window for Tom. "Looks like he's headed for the park first," he said with a point of the finger. When the wolf sort of growled, it turned toward the woods and was gone. I watched Jason's eyes, knowing he too was in dismay.

"Why is he running anyway, Tom? He needs our help right?" I stuttered.

Tom turned around in the seat and looked me in the eyes. "As we talked about at the fort, when you first became fully changed, you felt this need to run with the wild in you. We told you three that we refer to it as 'call of the wild.' You are carefree, and there's a hunger that pulls at your senses. It tells you to come and see, to be as free with it always. It's soothing to you, but you have to fight the dark hand of temptation."

"This temptation, Tom, is it stronger than the deer at the fort?"

"Much more than you can dream of when it leads and you follow, like if you lead a horse to the water when it is thirsty. Better yet, a drug. And if we can't catch him soon, he'll become savage with little or no way of turning back." Dropping his glance, he turned back in his seat, facing the road.

I felt my heart sink as a lump came into my throat. I swallowed hard with the thought that I could possibly lose a friend to the need. Bitter with anger, I whirled around and sat down with my back to the cab and lightly cried out, "Great Spirit, what'll happen to me? If I'm this huge thing they have raved about, how will they stop me?"

Out of nowhere, my head cried, "I am your companion, and they aren't." Shaking it off, I thought of Jason and quickly looked back in the window into the rearview as his eyes water. He must have thought the same thing as well. We spent the day searching for Daniel but coming up empty.

Night found me with my wasted mind scattered when the truck came to a sudden sliding halt that threw mud up over the side. Grabbing the side rail, I leaned over to see several wolves guarding one over another along the north side of the road. In the distance, I felt others watching me from the trees, waiting.

I placed a hand on the necks of the two wolves at my sides as I stared at the young man in the truck. He was, as father had said, magnificent. We stepped back, fading into the dark when he glanced our way.

Tom yelled for me, getting out of the truck, "Get the rope." I got up, retrieving the rope I had been sitting on and jumped over the side.

Jason came to my left as we walked toward the animals. "We have visitors out there."

"Yeah, I noticed them too." I never looked over my shoulder, feeling my back being bored into.

There were many others, I gathered were clan members, that I could see on our approach to the animals when some began to change back to human form the closer we got.

I swallowed hard when Tom stopped and said, "Come here, Luke. You and Jason should see this." He kneeled down to Mac, who was lying on top of one while the rest circled around us in a tight form.

"Tom, this is not him. Daniel is a mixed color," I said, kneeling down by the thing, hearing it whine like a pup.

"Right, but he'll not interfere anymore. This one is a scout for someone." Raising a hand, he said, "Hand me the rope." I gave Tom the rope, and he tied the four paws together.

With my companion's sly brain, I thought, *Poor thing*, with a feeling that I wanted to turn it loose.

I was so into my own thoughts of releasing the animal that I didn't notice Mac had changed to human until he placed a hand on my shoulder and said, "I hate that you had to see that, Luke, but it was for the best so you could understand. I think Tom told you why?"

Being testy, I said bitterly, "So when no one's around twenty-four-seven, then what, guys? We're alone."

Raising both hands, Mac backed off and said, "I see your point. We'll talk later."

The animal had just been put into the back of a truck that had arrived when Tom came to my right side.

Putting an arm around my shoulders, he said, "He'll be fine now, kid. We're taking him to Whitecloud's for the night. Daniel will be okay till morning, you'll see." I sighed heavily, staring at the animal only to think of Daniel having to wait until morning. Acknowledging, we got in Jason's truck. When they dropped me off at home, I hurried upstairs to shower.

After the warm shower, I dressed in pj's, then laid in the bed, listening to the ticking of the clock in the kitchen downstairs. My thoughts pictured Daniel back at the fort when we were having the time of our life after he accepted my apology for hurting his sis. I began to wonder what would happen if I ever had to fight one of them out there. What would it be like? Then my mind wondered back to my youth when I wanted to be carefree like the wolf and run wild. I rolled over on my back, staring at the ceiling while rain splattered the window, sending me to sleep. But my night had been restless with the dreams of the two wolves in the forest on our hunting spree where we shared a kill together.

Morning brought a bright day with the rising sun that hit me in the eyes. I quickly got up, dressed in sweats and a sweatshirt, then hurried down the stairs and out the door to the car. I rushed out to Tom's where I found everyone ready to resume the search for Daniel.

As soon as I got out of the vehicle, Tom yelled, "Luke, you come with me, Jason, and Ben." He headed to the Ford F350. Jason and another boy, who were carrying a large amount of rope, tossed it in the truck. We all climbed in while Tom took the front seat to drive. Everyone else had taken their rides. Soon we broke off into four trucks that went in four directions. Tom headed north.

Jason and I were sitting with our backs to the cab of the truck with another guy, an older man around twenty-five with a large build and long black hair tied back. He was standing up, looking over the cab with his short shirt flapping in the wind while his shorts whipped at his legs and his sneakers sort of laced up.

"You think he's okay, Luke?" Jason asked. "He's been out all night alone with those things. I wonder if he had dinner last night." His voice was growing shallow.

"He's fine," Ben said, leaning over.

I looked into his dark eyes and asked, "You've done this before?"

He replied just as I grabbed the side and stood up with him, "Yes. But this is only the fourth time for me. It's fun but not when you see a friend in need lose to a battle of feed."

"What do you mean the feed?" I asked sharply.

"It means that Daniel needs to fight the urge to hunt for the kill. If he follows the call to kill, it could mean he'll become a savage. The nature of the wolf is to hunt in packs. Their nature is kind, but, when in fear or pushed, will become a ruthless creature in order to protect what is theirs. I have seen those who died

19

protecting one another." I was shocked by what my ears heard and my heart heavy with the thought of Daniel having to fight for survival when I thought we were for the good of the land.

The paved road we were traveling soon turned into a dirt one when the truck made a sharp left turn. I quickly looked down through the window and saw Tom on the phone. He dropped it in the seat and grabbed the wheel with both hands, and the truck sped up. I leaned over the side to see if I could see anything up ahead, and what I saw was a large mixed-color wolf hauling ass. I watched Tom race toward him with a heartfelt gaze. I was so busy with the view that I didn't hear Tom yelling at me until he opened the sliding glass window.

"When I stop, you three need to change and catch him. He's going wild and needs our help," he said. He turned back to the thing up ahead and was on the animal's flank with dirt flinging from its feet as it tried to get away. He had to be running at least fifty miles an hour.

"Hold on," Tom yelled. Everyone braced when he turned the wheel and then slammed on the brakes. When we came to a sliding stop it nearly flung us from the back.

Ben didn't hesitate and was the first out of the truck, yelling at Jason and I, "Now you two." He changed into a handsome brown wolf with white scattered in the fur and red tint over the ears and amber eyes. When Jason leaped over, I followed after we watched Ben take off in search of what we thought was Daniel's wolf. I looked at Jason and he at me, then we changed into our wolves and set off in search of Daniel.

❧❧❧

Coming to, I didn't know where I was or how I had gotten there. The last thing I could remember was being in the hotel with Jada, a well-busted young woman with dark hair and green eyes, I had met at the lake. I wonder what Willa thought when I didn't come home last night. My vision was a blur, and the place smelled like a cave that had torches on the walls and one table that I could make out sitting near a door. I was sitting on the dirt floor with my hands tied behind my back. Now, was it from a drug or was it my imagination playing tricks? I sort of grinned, trying to play it off in my head. Or was it my newly acclaimed friend?

"Well done, girl," I heard a woman say. Even the voice was real, making me giggle a bit more.

Jada replied, "Thanks, Grandma."

I was unable to see who the woman was, but the voice said, "He'll do just fine, won't he, Cole?"

I heard footsteps on the floor come closer and stop. "Oh yeah, him and that skinny one Jason." The vision squatted down in front of me, placing a hand under my chin and forced me to look at the face when he said, "I can't believe you were so easy, Daniel."

Struggling, I snapped saying, "Tricked was more like it." I giggled, letting the dream continue not knowing how real it actually was.

"Give him another round. It won't take much more before he takes hook, line, and sinker," the woman said. By the time her words were out of her mouth, I felt a sting in my neck, then a burn before I fell into the dream world again.

In the thick of the trees, birds were singing and frogs were crocking when I found Ben nosing the ground for a scent of Daniel. Jason was on the opposite side of me doing the same. I took a whiff of the air, and we scouted the area for a fairly short time, finding nothing and believing Daniel had vanished into thin air. I wasn't looking when a two-legged form came into view from the darkness right in front of me. It was neither man nor beast. I felt my hair rise and tingle on my back as I stared at the thing before me. "What the hell are you?" I asked myself. I

21

didn't care to know when it turned and vanished in the darkness of the trees, leaving a howl and bringing me back to what I was supposed to be doing.

"Daniel. Got to be him," Jason cried, taking off in a run.

"Wait," Ben shouted as he took off after Jason. Feeling mischievous, I darted the way the cry came from when I lost sight of both.

I heard talk before the pounding of heavy feet on the ground, so I picked up the pace. Before I made the clearing ahead of me, Ben came by in haste with an animal hot on his tail and nipping at his feet.

"Daniel, "I whispered in confusion.

"Run, damn you," Ben screamed as he passed by. "It's not Daniel, Luke. It's another scout."

Something inside my soul took over, and I yelled, "Like hell if I run from it. I'll run to it." I was not about to be pushed around by those things. The thing in me growled, and we took off as fast as those four legs could go.

With the fur high over my neck and claws digging into the earth, I rushed toward the beast in front of me. The thing in me wanted to hurt the animal I was chasing, so the harder I tried, the faster we went. Damn, I was good and liking it. The feeling growing inside was the master of disguise with strong legs and a willing mind, making me like it even more. "But how do I tell someone about it?" I grunted and whistled to myself.

"You don't," it said in my head. The sensation was strong by the time my snout reached out, catching the tail of the beast after Ben.

Crunching down with dire force, my teeth hooked the tail, and it cried out the same time a cry of pain came from the woods. *Shit*, I thought. *Jason is in there.* I knew what the howl meant: he was hurt. Not wanting to release the tail, I twisted it, hearing the bone break, and with great pain, I released the tail, tasting the blood. I licked my lips, tasting the bitterness on the tip of my tongue, then swallowed the sweetness down the back of my throat. Jason quickly came to mind. I made a three-sixty turn, heading back in to look for him.

Just in the cover of the trees, I listened for the cry, which had become a whimper. I trotted off toward the cry where I found Jason still in wolf form, lying on the ground and covered in blood from bites all over the body. I stopped when Mac's wolf came through the trees, running like a mad dog toward us.

I dropped to my belly in a lying position, placed a paw on Jason's shoulder and said, "I'm sorry, bud." He whimpered in response, closing his eyes and passed out. I felt bad for not being there when he needed me, making my eyes watery in suspicion of myself.

Mac was human when I looked at him again, sprinting toward us, yelling at the downed man, "Change, kid, now, if you can." The last word came out the time he knelt down next to him, placing a hand on his side. I watched Jason slowly become human again, but the bites were all over his body. Some began to fade while others just bled out. My instinct was to lick them clean and make them better.

"Change, Luke, and give me a hand here," Mac said, reaching into his side gear. I sat up on my rump, and with a low growl, I quickly changed to my human form. Mac had pulled out some bandages to cover the wounds by the time I returned to help.

We had just wrapped Jason's waist when Tom and the rest of the clan cleared the trees. Tom never stopped when he changed to human form, and strode straight to Ben. In anger he shouted, "What happened here, Ben? You were the lead for them. Speak up."

Ben sucked it in and said, "I had a scout hot on my ass that Luke trailed, giving me a chance to turn when Jason cried out." He sighed, dropping his glance to the ground. I listened to Ben explain to Tom what happened while Mac got his feet. I was feeling Tom's anger rise when Mac told him to cool down. The conversation suddenly stopped altogether when a form passed by.

Thinking it was another of the clan boys, I didn't look to see who it was.

All talk ceased to exist, and an eerie feeling came over me. The shadow went straight to Ben, stopping between him and Tom. Regardless of who it was, Tom backed away with Mac standing behind him, leaving Ben to face it alone. I was unable to see clearly, but the shadow didn't speak right away. Instead, it raised an arm overhead that came down with a hand that slapped Ben's face.

"Damn," Ben wailed. "I'm sorry." He quickly rubbed his face with both hands. The sound even hurt me. *Ouch*, I thought. The form that looked around Ben to me was Paulene.

Bewildered, I asked, "What are you doing out here, girl?" She gave Ben a piercing glance, then stepped around him and Tom.

She knelt down by Jason on the opposite side of me in tears. She dabbed her eyes a bit with the edge of her black shirt and said in a teary tone, "I'm one of you. He's mine and I love him." She let the tears roll down her face as she leaned over Jason and kissed his forehead.

"So you're one of the two females in our group?" She shook her head yes and said nothing else while she brushed back the hair from Jason's face with a hand. I sat back on my heels and watched how she cared for him in a tender way. A feeling came over me and I felt anger for myself at the thought of what I could do to her. *What the hell is wrong with me?* I thought and shook it off.

Mac moved down to Jason's legs, knelt down, and said, "Luke, I need a hand here." He lifted Jason's legs under the knees while Paulene moved back so I could get to his shoulders. I grabbed him under the arms and lifted him with ease. Funny, but it was like lifting a feather to me. Paulene walked with us, placing a hand on his chest. Jason moaned in pain as we carried him to the F350 and placed him the bed.

Tom was standing at the driver door and yelled, "If you're going, let's go." He got into the driver seat, slamming the door. I hopped in with Jason and Paulene, who held his head as we took off to Whitecloud's. The others stayed behind to continue the search for Daniel.

Sizing Up

IT WASN'T TOO long before we arrived at the old man's place where he was standing on the porch, smoking a pipe and waiting for our arrival. Tom parked and hopped out while Ben and I got out the rear to lower the tailgate. Tom came to the rear of the truck, leaned in, and grabbed Jason up like a twig, tossing him over his shoulder before walking across the lawn. He approached the house and went up the steps in one long stride, across the porch and into the door that Whitecloud held before going inside himself. I slumped toward the porch and stopped at the bottom of the steps, staring up at the door with the thought of the thing I was out there for and my feeling that was damn good. I finally pushed the thought aside and went in the door.

Tom was just coming out of the bedroom when I stopped in the hall. He stared at me like he was furious, but I only got the cutting glance until he went into the front room. I hurried into the room to find Mac excusing himself. He nodded as he passed by me and gently closed the door. Luther was sitting on the bed next to Jason, who had a sheet over his waist. I noticed that a silver pan of water was already by the bed when he took out a rag, then rung it out and began wiping the blood from Jason's bitten and bruised face. Paulene was sitting on the opposite side of the bed, holding Jason's hand. Her eyes were red and wet from tears.

"How is he?" she asked with a teary voice.

"He'll be fine. Just give him a bit of time for now." He soothed her. "It was his first encounter out there. He'll catch on, Polly.

Maybe you can teach the ways and give him hints." He softly spoke to her while finishing the dressing. When he was done he pulled the sheet over Jason's shoulder as he rose from the bed. Excusing myself, I followed the old man outside.

We had just gotten out on the lawn with Tom and Mac when I heard Whitecloud say, "I believe we have a killer on the prowl. We haven't figured out who yet. He seems to keep avoiding us in the chase, so we need your help. Your sense of smell and hearing is intense."

Tom shifted his stand to the left and crossed his arms when he said, "You also have the build for speed in a chase, but you'll have to be careful because we don't know how to deal with him. He's smart, keen, and he knows it. Above all, Luke, you're a beginner."

I thought of the thing I saw in the woods. "I believe that thing has been following me around lately." I sighed, giving him a passing look.

Tom moved his hands to his front pants pockets and said, "Yeah, that's the one. He's been roaming around awhile but keeping out of sight. We just need to find out what he's up to."

"How am I supposed to do that? More along the lines of how do I do it and not get caught?"

"He's got a point," Whitecloud agreed.

"How's the search for Daniel coming along? I mean I have one friend down and one friend lost. How can this possibly happen to them?"

"Don't let this turn to anger. It will finish you without your knowing it," Tom said. "Be the happy-go-lucky kid you were six months ago."

"If they only knew you had a new friend in town. You're better than they ever will be," the thing in my head said. I grinned at the thought, then excused myself, going back inside. I found a recliner and sat down. It only took a few minutes to drop off to sleep, bringing a dream with it.

I didn't know where I was, but it wasn't the same dreams as before. I was standing in a large room, like a sitting room with a sofa, one chair, and a door. The walls were a dark grey with a mud-packed floor. The air was cool and as inviting as the scent that curled under my nose. I tried to speak, but the only thing that came out was a bark. Curiously, I went to the door and grabbed the wolf-headed handle, giving it a pull up. When the door opened, it was light outside.

I stepped outside to an enormous yard filled with lush green grass and evergreen trees. The morning was met with a gray, wet sky about to rain. I watched lightning as it ran across the sky in all directions, bringing a roll of thunder with it. I walked off the porch to the gravel driveway that had no end and turned around. I was facing an awesome two-story frame house with huge windows, a porch swing, and a front door like an iron gate standing half open.

Then the voice came from behind me and said in a whisper, "This can be yours if you want. Join me and let me show you." It trailed off.

Startled by the sound, I swallowed hard and asked, "Who are you and what do you want?" I didn't even face the voice.

In a snarling tone, it replied, "My name is not important, but like I said before, I am your companion. I have shown you petty things, but come and let me show you what you really want." I felt a furry thing take my hand and pull me. Effortlessly, I followed the thing I couldn't see. It was like I was floating through the air into the dark when I lost the light of day.

I slightly woke to a dog barking in the distance but quickly went back to sleep and the dream.

When I stopped moving, the full moon had risen. Like the beast I was, I let out a howl as I changed into a thing other than my wolf. I was growing in size. Oddly, I liked the feeling, but the body was strangely different. I was half man and half wolf with four legs under me and my upper body was my bare chest with two large arms and mighty hands that ended with long, shiny black claws.

"This is what you think you should be, and it could be if you want it to," the voice said.

"How do you know what I want?" I asked with a growl in my voice. I heard the low, unidentified growl and swallowed hard.

In the mist of the darkness, I heard a scream, and someone said, "Hey, wake up please."

I opened my droopy eyes to see the tube with a woman sitting on a bed talking to a man. I closed my eyes as I rolled to the side and instantly went back to sleep and the dream.

I was me again, standing on the porch of the house, overlooking the valley. "What in the hell happened? Am I dreaming now?" I whispered.

Again the voice said, "Yes, most definitely."

Uptight, I shouted, "Show yourself." In the dim light, a shadow came toward me. The closer it got, the more it resembled me, but it began to change into a mighty wolf on two legs, thick with fur, a long shiny snout, long fangs hung over the bottom lips, and the blackest eyes staring at me below the long ears of the huge head. I found myself not afraid by the view but consumed by it.

It leaned down into my face, and with hot breath, it said, "You are what you are. Come…be with me. We can go places, do things no one else can, and no one will stop us." It stood upright and howled into the night. Like a calling, I did the same and together, we cried at the falling moon.

The next time I awoke was when Luther checked to see if I were okay as he placed a hand on my forehead, and I thought I saw Ivan walk by before I dozed off again.

I was my wolf, running like a mad dog through the woods, but I had my companion by my side. It was fantastic with the wind in my face, my ears back, and my nose in the air. We were going nowhere specific. I had yet to learn the name of my new friend, but I liked his moves and the way he did things. I was drawn to him like a glove to a hand with each passing moment. We cut through the trees into a clearing that led to a cliff where we came to a sudden stop.

Twenty feet on the other side, the trail continued, but we stood there, staring at it. I looked over at my companion in wonder.

He saw me staring and said, "Someday soon, you'll make that jump with me." He came over and nudged me in the neck with a soothing rub of his nose, then began licking the side of my face. The tongue was warm and wet with comfort as it crossed my nose to the ears. It felt good to be pampered by another. My every being loved each pass of the tongue. I sighed and sat down to let my friend pamper me all he wanted to, but my feelings were growing stronger to be with him and his pack. I closed my eyes for the longing to come quickly.

The next time I opened my eyes, I was standing in front of the house. I saw Willa outside on the porch with Kimmi in the swing, laughing and having fun.

"Willa, I wish to thank you for the help," I heard Kimmi say.

"You're welcome. It gave me something to do other than my own."

"The first snow will come soon. The air is colder today," I said as I joined the girls on the front porch.

"Yeah, it is chilly today," Willa said.

"You all want something to drink?" I asked, going to the screen door.

"Not me," Kimmi laughed.

"What's so funny?" I asked, reaching for the screen door.

"You are covered in mud on your rear end." Willa giggled. I looked at my backside, finding it covered in red mud.

Looking at Kimmi, I said, "Do you mind too much honey?" I grinned.

"Be right back." She got up and went inside to get me a pair of shorts while I sat down on the steps and waited in silence.

It wasn't long before she came out the door. "Go change." She tossed a pair of black shorts at me. I got up and went to the side of the house as I pulled the shirt off, then changed into the shorts. I heard a long range howl as I pulled the zipper up on the shorts.

"I think it's time," my companion moaned.

"Time for?" Willa asked as both the girls stood up. I knew it wasn't me that spoke, so I played it off and shrugged my shoulders.

"Something comes," Kimmi said.

I leaped up onto the porch, reaching for the door. "Let's go inside. Willa, will you stay for now?"

Stepping up to the door, she replied, "Sure. That was kind of spooky." I held the door for the girls, then followed them inside where I went to the window and peeked through the curtain.

Staring out the window I could see a huge thing that was half man and dog. Spooked, I jumped back and closed the curtain. I wasn't really afraid, just curious.

"What's your problem?" Willa asked, giggling. I sighed heavily just as the front door was suddenly slammed into and the girls screamed. When the thing hit the door again, it made the handle rattle. In a moment of silence, there was a bone-chilling feeling before the huge thing came crashing through the door and into the room. It stood upright on four legs with the two arms over the chest. The dark eyes sparkled when it let out a growl.

It was part man and part wolf, snarling and growling with short stubby fangs, hanging over the lips and drool dripping from them. My instinct was to charge the thing because I didn't want to be there, I wanted to be with my companion. I changed into my wolf with my companion's help. Only I was a different sort of wolf.

"Let me help you, friend." I felt a sinister presence enter my body before the thing charged.

I leaped over the sofa in front of it. It stopped alright, but the huge arms reached for Willa so quick that the claws opened up the same time they opened her up at the waist. She dropped to the floor with a crash, and Kimmi screamed at the top of her lungs. The strange thing was, when I looked at the claws, they were mine, and it was I who had done the damage with my friend's help. I didn't even feel sorry for her. I felt incredible, and no one could stop me. When the house began to shake under my feet, I woke up as I hit the floor.

I rolled over on my back and found Tom standing at the back of the chair, with it tilted up.

He grinned, making me angry when he said, "That was some dream. Now about Daniel. We got word short time ago."

I stood up and rubbed my head, then asked, "Where about?" I let the anger drop.

"He was seen in the same area as before," he replied, sitting the chair down.

Mac came into the room, yelling, "Y'all comin'?" He never stopped or looked back as he passed by.

Following, I said, "Not now, but thanks." My whole being called for me to go, but I stopped at the door and watched the men get in the Ford, close the doors, and drive off.

After the taillights vanished, I went in and found Paulene sitting on the side of the twin bed with a damp rag, wiping Jason's face. With sorrow and regret, I faced Paulene, who looked up at me with a wet face and red eyes.

"Would you mind if I stayed?" I asked with a shameful tone.

"He would like that. Sure," she cried softly with a sniffle. I looked around, finding a deep-seating high-backed chair nearby. I sat down and waited with the thought of the dream and how I had felt until Daniel came to mind that was still on the loose.

I must have dropped off to sleep because Whitecloud was shaking my shoulder when I opened my eyes.

"Come. Your help is needed now." He sounded urgent.

I jumped up from the chair, finding Jason still in bed with Paulene asleep next to him. I left the room quietly, closing the door behind me. Following the old man outside into the night was an awaiting black four-wheel drive Ford sitting on the grass with Mac in the driver seat. Whitecloud took the front while he pointed for me to take the back. I leaped over the side in one swift move and settled down just as Mac drove off.

We were out in the middle of nowhere when Mac slammed on the brakes, bringing the fast-moving truck to a screeching halt, tossing me to the side where I hit my head. Cursing under my breath, I looked over the side toward the front just when a dark form came from the driver side of the woods, crossing the truck's headlights. I barely caught a glimpse of it, but it looked like a wolf. Uncertain, Mac put the truck in gear and continued on about fifteen minutes before stopping in the vicinity where Jason had been hurt. Grabbing the side of the rail, I jumped from the truck and went to Whitecloud's side while he stared out over the ridge of the trees. In my defense, I wondered what he was staring at since I could not see or hear anything but the whispering from Luther.

After several minutes, Luther turned to me. "Your wolf is needed tonight for Daniel is near and in trouble. He is in need of you. Go now and good luck." He placed a hand on my shoulder and squeezed gently.

I was stunned at his request, so I asked, "What do I do when I find him?"

He placed the other hand over his heart and replied, "You will know what to do when the heart speaks. Go now." Without question, I moved away from the man—changing as I went to my wolf form—feeling so abnormal with becoming a totally different animal. With the change finished, I faced the night in a trot to recover Daniel.

I was creeping along, sniffing the ground with the voices fading behind me until I came to a small clearing, catching a scent of something unknown. There was a tiny scent of Daniel drifting on the soft wind. I inhaled deeply, but there wasn't much except for the chilly air. I heard a cry or moan that made me stop, sit, and listen for more. It was almost undeniable to refuse, so I stood up as the moaning called out for me. The call in me told me to go, that it was my nature to follow.

"You know you want to," the voice told me. I took a step forward, but before I could take another, I was rushed and knocked off balance.

I rolled twice, then gained my ground with my feet back under me, turning to face the thing that hit me. It rammed me from the side again—before I could get a good look—sending me through the air to land on my side. The next time I gained my ground, I dug my long claws into the soft earth. With my sense in order, I faced the thing that was standing in my face with its eyes reddened and glowing. I could see it was Daniel with his teeth bared and the drool dripping from the black lips. Feeling that warm and confident sense of my companion, I faced the creature.

His nose wrinkled, showing his fierceness with ruffled fur matted around his neck and high along the back. His ears were laid back as his face came closer, making it hard to hurt him in any way. His eyes showed me they didn't recognize me, because he instantly snapped at me, catching the edge of my fur near the shoulder. I stood my ground as I felt myself gain strength from the inside.

"What are you waiting for?" The voiced asked me.

"What am I supposed to do with him?" I asked myself. I didn't know, but my wolf part took over and with a huge, heavy paw, knocked Daniel over on his back when he came charging. He rolled once, then came up snarling with his nose wrinkled, blood dripping, and teeth showing with the fangs dripping saliva.

"It's time to join me. Come, let me guide you into being a mighty warrior," my head told me.

"Yes, I'm ready now." I whimpered with a snarl of my own.

My wolf and I prepared while a crowd had gathered nearby. "God, please don't let Kimmi see this." I crouched down like the animal I was and began to snarl and growl to warn of my intentions. The fur around my neck ruffled, standing up along my back, tingling at the ends with the wind. Even the short and curly ones between my eyes narrowed when they rose. With my teeth bared, the fangs began to grow at unnatural lengths, and my nose wrinkled. The strength in my legs became unnerving, my jaws felt like steel traps, my claws became iron, thickening at the base, curling into the ground at the tips, and lastly, my feet widened for stability. When it was all finished I was ready with ears back, listening to the thing inhale before he came at me.

I didn't want to hurt him when we rushed at one another, so I just leaped over his back. I was slow on the turnaround when he came back in full force, catching my ear between his sharp teeth. Feeling his teeth piercing my flesh, I did nothing but sit there, wailing in pain while he tore it down the middle. He wasted no time in returning.

"Get off your ass and do what you're good at," the voice said.

"I can't," I whined.

"Yes you can and you will. Don't let this wimp stop you," my companion said, who was right, and I knew it. I gathered myself, losing my feeling of sympathy.

I quickly faced the wolf of Daniel and charged the oncoming beast, meeting him face to face in the air, snarling and snapping at each other's fur or throat or whatever it was we could get a hold of. He finally caught me at the base of my neck in the left shoulder. I felt the bite sink in as his teeth pierced the flesh, letting the blood come to the surface, sending the sting from the burning bit through me like no burn I had ever felt, even in the agonizing change to become what I was.

"What are you waiting on?" The snarl came at me.

"Not a damn thing, my friend," I snapped, dropping to my belly, and rolled over on top of Daniel, releasing his grip.

I quickly got to my feet, and faced him with anger of my own. He had blood all over his mouth as his tongue reached out to lick it off. I smelled my own blood as it dripped down my shoulder.

Daniel faced me again as I did him. We were about twenty feet apart. He had no idea who I was or why he was there. "God, help me," I prayed.

"Don't pray. Take his life and prove yourself," my companion lashed out.

"Fine," I snorted. Cringing, I dared Daniel with a snarl as we made our rounds in the circle. Daniel's eyes were blind to what had happened as he steps back growling. He takes a charge at me, catching my right jaw between his teeth with a snap, sending pain through me when his teeth tore in, peeling back the hide. When he whirled around to face me, so did I. The time had come to do what I thought I was supposed to do when he returned to finish the job.

The taste of my own blood was bittersweet, but the wolf called me out again. I quickly got to my feet as Daniel came at me again.

"Damn, Daniel, I don't want to hurt you," I growled at him. He didn't hear, baring his teeth and showing his pink gums with black spots.

"That's it Daniel," I slurred under my breath. Lunging at him, he bit into my shoulder again. My companion didn't wait for permission when he took off running with Daniel hanging onto my shoulder.

I couldn't stop, but then again I didn't want to, as I ran with my new friend in the lead. I was anxious to see where he took me, which wasn't long until we hit the first biggest pine tree. Daniel went wailing, taking flesh off my shoulder with him, leaving a gap about one inch deep and three inches long. I stopped long enough to lick my wounds and turn around. But when I did, he was already coming at me.

Grunting, my friend said, "Give him a run. Lead him away from the eyes of others." Angry with rage, I snorted and dug into the earth, making my legs use the muscles they were made for.

Daniel tried keeping up with me, but I was fast and growing faster. I stopped suddenly and looked back to make sure he was still with me. I stepped behind a tree until I saw him top the small hill. I leaped over him, and growled with a dare, nipping at his flank. He turned on me instantly. My wolf was a mere obstacle when Daniel and I charged and tangled in midair, snapping at one another. I saw the crowd in the distance as the two of us went at it, sending fur and blood into the air as we tore into the flesh. We went at each other like mad dogs for a long while, until we began to tire. Soon, I found my need to end the war with him. I didn't want to hurt him, but he was taking it out on me with my fur and flesh.

I leaped over Daniel's back, catching him by the nape, and took him down to the ground. I was larger and knew it as I placed a massive paw on his nose, keeping him pinned to the ground. I could see his fur pulsate under the jaw from his heartbeat. I didn't know what else to do when I bit into Daniel's jaw and liked the sensation of doing so, tasting the blood oozing from inside.

"Well done, my friend," my thoughtless mind said with a growl.

I heard a voice on the wind whisper, "It is time to take him down. You can do it." When I released the hold on Daniel's jaw, he jumped up, snarling with blood oozing from his wound and whirled around.

When Daniel charged, I ducked, making him leap over me and without cause or realizing what I had done, I grabbed him by the throat, and with a whip of my head, we went to the ground.

❀❧❧❀

I was running with my friend in the woods toward the clearing that led us to the cliff. Stopping short of taking that daring leap, I sat down with my companion, staring at the cliff on the opposite side.

"Soon, my friend." He gave me a tender nudge, and we continued on our journey back the way we came.

✻✻✻✻

I was thoughtlessly being led into misery of the devilish kind when my fangs found their way through the fur to the flesh. Breaking the skin, they pierced through to the life-giving blood of Daniel's jugular. With every beat of his heart, my fangs sunk in deeper.

Blood splattered my face from the gashed and torn skin of the flesh that opened wider from his struggling and allowed my fangs to sink in deeper. I felt his heart pulse with every beat, pushing the warm, thick, bittersweet blood into my mouth and down the back of my throat. Gulping long and hard, it tasted…good. With my jaws locked, Daniel was wailing from the pain, but I didn't give in. I was losing sight of what was real.

Soon, Mac and Tom came over to us and tried to pry me off Daniel, but the blood, the taste, and the smell had me fixed to him.

There was no stopping as it called to me, "That's it, Luke. Show him who's boss around here. Take what you can before they get you. Remember to save me some, just a tad will do." I wanted more, so I bit harder into his neck, squeezing out the warm liquid that was thick and sweet. I closed my eyes to the outside world and let it puddle up in my mouth, then slide down my throat.

As I laid there with jaws locked, I opened my eyes to a man I thought was Whitecloud approaching me. It was when he knelt down and placed a hand over my nose that I nuzzled into the warm palm.

I whined like a pup when I heard him say, "Luke, let him go. You're killing him, son."

Like a rude awakening from a dream, I thought, "Good God, what was I doing?" Instantly, I snapped out of the place I was and realized what had happened.

I let Daniel go and stood up on all four paws to face the crowd. Looking down at Daniel, who was in pain, had dark-red blood oozing from the wounds on his neck that I inflicted on him. Tom and Mac began tending to Daniel while I watched unsure how I felt right then. I had no excuse for my actions to tell anyone, not even myself. Dropping my head, I walked off, changing to my human form, ashamed of what I—my companion—had done. That was what I felt: shame. I fumbled my way back to the truck in the dark where I climbed in the back and sat down. There, I pulled my knees to my chest and crossed my arms to lay my head on while I cried myself to sleep.

After I was sure Luke was out of sight, I had Tom help me with Daniel. From the actions of the young man, the legend was calling when I noticed puncture marks in his neck. Pulling back the collar of his button-down, I found needle marks in the jugular.

"Someone has made it a point to introduce him to his evil side," I told the brothers, leaning over my shoulder.

"Damn him," Tom cursed, standing upright.

Mac knelt on the ground. "They sure ain't wasting time for the newbies, are they?" I looked around and thought of Luke with a soft prayer that he wasn't called out by the legend.

"Let's get him to my place, fellas."

Dawn was beginning when Whitecloud, Tom, and Mac found me in the truck. The old man placed a hand gently on my shoulder to wake me. I raised my head up to face him quick enough, but my thoughts were scattered as I tried to make sense of what happened to me. Tears had come and gone, leaving only the memories.

"Luke, there's no shame about your nature when temptations such as these are calling to you. You have to push it away, or it will devour you. You have to think of it as 'would I or not' as the blood takes you to the point of no return. It nearly did Daniel as you saw. I hated that you had to do that, but it was necessary to stop him. It was also a good situation for you to learn the ways of the wolf and what it means to be chosen. Come now. Daniel is headed to my place." I could only nod at the three men when they got into the truck. A cool wind blew over me like a hand touching my face, seemingly knowing my thoughts.

The truck came to life, and we started moving toward Luther's home, with my mind looking back at the view only to wonder. "What the hell took hold of me out there?" The shame continued to haunt me, even after Whitecloud told me not to. If I could do that to Daniel, what would happen to Kimmi if I got angry enough with her? We finally got to the house, and the truck stopped. I heard the doors open and close. I just sat there alone in the truck until they went inside.

I finally composed myself after a half hour, jumped over the side of the truck, and hit the ground, staring at the red home. Dragging my feet over to the porch, I made my way into the house and into the room where I found Daniel sleeping while Della cleaned the wounds on his neck. His face was bruised around the eyes and jaw, but they were slowly vanishing. Della looked up with warm eyes and smiled when I stopped at the bed. She raised a finger to her lips so I wouldn't speak, not to wake Daniel. I nodded to her, then left them as I walked out the door, through the front room, passing everyone who was talking, and out the door of the kitchen to the car. I headed for the lake with the most painful feeling in my gut.

I was sitting at one of the tables, staring over the water, pondering what I had become and how I could feel so good about my actions with no remorse. When I felt my back was being bored into, I turned around with my back against the edge of the table, letting my arms dangle over the edge. Looking into the shadows, I found Kimmi standing there in a blue satin pantsuit with her hair high off her neck. When she came to me and sat down at the table, I didn't move.

"You are sad, yes?" She asked as she searched my eyes. I didn't know if I wanted to hug her or just cry. I did neither when she turned around and faced me. How could I have told her what happened? Did she know? I wondered, pulling her to me so she could rest her head on my shoulder as I tenderly held her. I knew she had to hear the pain in my pounding heart. I just held her in silence with the thought of her not knowing of my secret until I finally told her I needed to get home.

WITNESSED

T HE NEXT DAY, Daniel was healed and back home with
Willa after accepting my apology.

❧❧

Sitting at the kitchen table across from Willa, feeling better after
the ordeal, I was stressed over how I was going to tell anyone
about my head talking to me. The last things I recalled were being
with a young woman in the hotel, the sort of dream that talked
to me, and the sting of something in my neck. My problem was
I liked the warm evil feeling it gave me. Even though I forgave
Luke for his intentions, my other me wanted to kill him that day,
and I couldn't stop.

❧❧

After spending the next two days at home alone in fear of myself,
I had a necklace made for Kimmi while I was unable to tell her
what had happened. Hell, I couldn't even tell my father. I sighed
heavily, thinking of how I once found it hard to digest, and yet
there I was with my thoughts in shambles because I just didn't
know. What I did know was I couldn't tell the two people I loved
about myself.

With that, I rose from the sofa, dashed up to my room for a
shirt, light jacket, and my shoes. I headed back down and slipped

out the backdoor into the foggy morning toward the Charger sitting on the lawn. I was tired of being cooped up looking at four walls. I quickly got in and started the engine. I leaned back on the seat, wondering why I wanted to be more of what I was with the strong sense to hide it. Putting the car into gear, I drove out to the reservoir.

I crossed the bridge into the entrance of the lake to find the place vacant, except the bare trees and singing birds. I parked the car, got out, and walked over to an old wooden table. I was about to sit down when I felt a presence behind me. Smiling and knowing it was her, I turned to look at Kimmi, who was standing in the shadows in a white silk pantsuit with her black hair dropping over her shoulder in a plait.

Her lips glistened from the gloss when she asked, "What brings you out on a day such as this?" She came toward the table.

"Change of scenery and you?" I asked, sitting on the bench.

She stopped just out of the upcoming sunrays. "Please listen to me." Her voice sounded sincere. "There is coming of something." I turned around on the bench and leaned back on the table's edge, facing her.

When she started toward me, I tried to stop her with a raise of my hand and told her, "You shouldn't come out in the sun." Hell, that didn't stop her, and I wondered what she had in that head of hers when she stopped in front of me with her back to the sun.

Her soft eyes sparkled as she bit her bottom lip, then she began to smile, and said, "I wish to do something if you approve." Watching the pale skin turn a slight pink from the sun and before she could say anything, I picked her up and put her on the table top out of the sun. She was so light.

"Thank you." She sat crossed-legged on the table as I sat down on the bench in front of her. There was a strange sense of needing to know about her and Cole or if it were true that she had seen what happened.

44

Kimmi didn't get upset but did become distant. Her face lost expressions as she faced me. I felt stupid with guilt and should've been ashamed, but I had to know.

Placing my hands on her knees, I said, "Kimmi, talk to me. Don't keep me shut out because of him." I pleaded with softness.

Sighing, she said, "It's hard to tell someone something when they don't believe." Like the bat that hit the ball, I thought of how she could have known how true that was.

"Tell me and make me believe, Kimmi. I have a lifetime to listen to you."

"So be it, Luke." She sighed. "It took place after the fact of Cole, Jess, and I."

"Chase and I were out one evening while the moon was at its fullest and high in the sky. We were just messing around in the dark woods, like kids do. We came to hear loud voices close by, so we went to investigate. We came upon a field with a house and people out front just on the opposite side. Chase chose to climb up into a nearby tree as I stared from the ground. Due to the moon, there was enough light to see what was going on.

"At first, a man came from the house. He quickly waved at something in the woods to the back. I saw a dark towering form come toward the house as a woman came out to the man. By the sound of it, they were arguing. The thing had made its way to the corner of the house. It waited with red eyes while it watched the two. The man's back was to us until he turned around to wave for the form to come. I was shocked to see it was Cole. I took cover so I wouldn't be seen, and watched the large wolf slip up behind the woman as she tried to talk with Cole.

"In horror, Chase and I watched as the beast, silent and cunning, rose up on its two hind legs, and took the woman by the waist with its huge jaws. Using her like a ragdoll, it tossed her around before letting go overhead into the air. Her screams were never heard when she hit the tree, crumbled down through the branches, and landed with a hard thud. I gasped for I knew she had no life left in her. I let out a soft cry I thought no one heard. But Cole swung his head around and saw us. In a terrified state, I snatched Chase from the tree, and we vanished into the night. The following day, I tried to warn Luther of what I saw, but due to our relation and what we are, it was hard to convince them of it. Some time passed before, Cole caught me out alone, and that was when he hurt me.

"With a falling tear, she said, 'I wasn't looking when I walked right into his arms. I was sky-watching my birds.'"

With my attention on the rise, I asked, "Hurt you? How?"

"He grabbed me with both hands, shaking the life out of me, and said, 'I would pay for what I did,' then struck me across the jaw with a hard fist, breaking my bottom jaw.

"Now you see why I'm afraid of him and why I don't speak of him? He's a killer, ruthless and evil."

When Kimmi dropped her head down, I rose from the table, reached over for her, and pulled her to my chest. I held her while the tears rolled down her face.

Soothing her, I said, "We should go to Whitecloud and make him listen to you."

Muffled, she said, "How, Luke? I've tried, but I've no evidence to prove it. Oh well."

Using both hands, I pushed her head back with a tilt and said, "He knows a way. I promise you that." I dried the tears from her face with a thumb. When she smiled, I picked her up and carried her to the car. I phoned ahead to let Luther know of our coming.

We found Luther and Mac seated on the porch in the chairs dressed like twins in relaxed jeans, a tee shirt, and sneakers. I stopped the car, got out, and quickly rounded the hood to help Kimmi out. I closed the door, took her hand, and we walked to the porch, stopping at the foot of the steps.

Looking up at Luther, I asked, "How's it going?"

His dark eyes showed concern when he replied, "Fair to middlen."

46

Taking Kimmi by the hand, I told her, "This is Whitecloud." I pointed toward him. "My great-great-grandfather."

Surprised, she said, "Finally, nice to see you, sir." She made a tilt of the head at him. He leaned over with an outstretched hand that she took.

With a light shake, he said, "Kimmi, good to meet you too."

"Over here, we have Mac, a good friend." I grinned, pointing a finger at him.

"Afternoon, Kimmi," Mac said, reaching for her hand as well.

Taking his hand, Kimmi softly said, "Same to you."

"Shall we continue inside for her sake?" Mac asked, standing up with the old man.

"Yes. Thank you," I agreed. Hand in hand, we followed them into the house, through the kitchen and into the living room.

Whitecloud sat in the large recliner, Mac sat in the high-backed rocking chair, and we sat on the sofa.

When Whitecloud spoke, it was directed at Kimmi. "Ms. Kimmi, why have you come to see me today?"

"I've spoken to you on the phone about…" She left it drift off.

I knew why she stopped. "Say it, Kimmi—the name." I nudged her.

She looked into the man's face and said, "Cole, sir."

"What's the reason he brought you here?" He asked. I could see that Kimmi was nervous, so I took her by the hand.

"As I told you once before, I saw what he had that thing do to his wife that night."

Mac leaned forward in his chair. "Again, Ms. Kimmi, is there any way that can be proven?"

Her gazed dropped to her lap. "No. But Luke thinks there may be a way you can." She returned her glance back to the old man who glared at me through those dark eyes.

"What might that be, Luke?" Mac asked with raised brows.

"Easy, Mac," Luther said. "Yes, I do, and it could be dangerous, but if you insist." Kimmi became silent as she thought it over.

When Kimmi's hand trembled in mine, I looked at her for her answer.

"What will you do to her?" I pried the old man.

"Nothing, but put her to sleep, then to see the ancestors." I knew of them and the dream world.

"How long will it take?" I asked, giving him a cutting glance.

Mac leaned over and replied, "Two hours…could be two days. It depends since there's no time."

"If indeed she tells the truth, then there's no problem, but if not, that's another thing," Whitecloud said. "Come with me a minute, Luke. Outside please." I nodded, and told Kimmi I'd be right back. We rose, then went out the kitchen door.

When we stopped on the porch away from the ears of Mac and Kimmi, he faced me with a bit of tension in his expression.

"Is there a problem?"

He quickly looked into my eyes. "If she agrees to this, you will have to protect this home and her body. She will become a spirit form and will need a body to come back to. Understand?"

"Yes, sir. I fully understand. How long will it take? I know about the out of body, but will it harm her not being Cherokee?"

"No, she'll do fine as long as she is willing to go," he explained. With that thought in mind, I acknowledged with a nod of the head, then we returned to the others.

We found Mac and Kimmi in conversation when we entered the room. Kimmi was laughing and Mac was explaining the trip they were about to take.

As soon as we sat down, Kimmi looked at Luther and said, "I'll do as you ask for I need to get it off my chest, and Cole needs to be punished for his crime. I have nothing to hide." She finished with good intentions.

Placing his elbows on his knees with his chin cupped in his hands, he asked, "You are sure?" Nodding yes without pause, she placed a hand in mine, and I gave it a tender squeeze.

With a nod, Luther said, "Return tonight prepared." Again she nodded.

Curious, I had to ask, "Will she be by herself?"

"Heavens, no." Mac laughed. "I'm going with her. She'll be fine. See you tonight." I had become as nervous as Kimmi when we stood up and thanked them. Mac rose, and him being the man he was, escorted us to the door. I took Kimmi out to the car and got in. She mentioned the reservoir just as I closed the door.

With the sinking sun, the entrance came into view, so I pulled into the lot and parked. Hurriedly, I got out and went around to the passenger side where I helped Kimmi out, and we walked to the nearby table.

Sitting down, Kimmi said, "Luke, there's something that I've been holding back."

I had a strange feeling inside. "Okay, what is it now?" I fashioned a worried smile. She took my hand, placed it between her breasts to the heart and pressed hard. I felt the faint beating inside through the cold skin of her chest.

With a hand on mine, she whispered, "This heart will always beat for you, now and forever. It burns an eternal flame that was lit by the fire of desire for you." I took her face into my hands and, with tender loving care, kissed her gently on the lips.

"If you'll sit right there for a minute, I have something for you." I reached into my pocket, pulled out the small red box, and gave it to her. Her eyes glowed as she took it from me.

Slowly, she pushed opened the top and reached inside to retrieve a baby-blue turquoise and silver-wrap necklace. She rolled it over in her hand to find her name on one side.

Watching her smile, I said with anxiety, "Now, flip it over and read to me what's on the other side."

She stared at it for a time, then flipped it over and read, "I have found something called love, and without it, I can do nothing." Kimmi's hands dropped into her lap as tears swelled in her eyes. "You love me, yes?" She wept softly.

"Yes, I do. I have for some time, but it took me going to Canada to really know and understand it." What I really wanted to say I couldn't.

With a smile and wet eyes, she said, "And I love you." She grabbed my neck, kissing me on the cheek.

Returning the favor, I said, "Come on. Let's get you home and ready for tonight." Without waiting for a reply, I grabbed her up and rushed her to the car, then drove her home. I went to Mae's for dinner, then killed time watching some tube before returning to take her back to Luther's.

I didn't waste time in getting Kimmi out to Luther's where we met him and Mac on the porch. Together, we all went inside where Kimmi and I sat down on the sofa once more.

Luther sat on the arm and looked down at Kimmi. "Young lady, are you ready?" he asked.

She appeared to be more ready than ever in her quick answer. "Yes, sir, I am," she replied.

Standing up, he said, "Let us prepare then." He motioned us to follow him. I looked at Kimmi, who looked back at me, and sighed. We rose from the couch and followed the two men, who headed toward one of many doors in the home.

Behind one of the doors stood a heavy steel door that Whitecloud effortlessly opened with one hand. It made no sound as he and Mac went through it with Kimmi tugging at my hand. Through that door, we went into another bedroom where Luther had walked to a huge black antique walk-in closet that looked like a self-sustaining decor. The design on the door was a symbol of a bird.

"What does the symbol of the bird mean?" I asked, tracing it with a finger.

Reaching for the wooden knobs, Luther said, "Freedom; out of body." He opened the huge doors, pushed the hangers aside, and reached behind the hanging clothes to a door in the back. I heard a click, then a door opened up, letting light come through.

He stepped through and was gone. Kimmi, not hesitating, pulled my hand as she followed him through the door.

Stepping through the doorway into a narrow hallway, I stopped and stared at the lit torches hanging on the walls. Mac followed us through, closed the door, and walked by with a nod. I returned the nod as we followed him into what looked like a cave. But it was more than a cave with a rocky-dirt footpath that led down into a long, dark passageway that appeared to lean in toward us. I thought the doors we passed were real until I decided to open one and found a brick wall behind it. The walls became hardened mud with rock, and if you looked at them just right, they seemed to move. The air became cooler with a sudden draft, and Kimmi's hand trembled inside mine.

"Where will this take us?" Kimmi asked, looking up the walls.

I heard water just as Mac replied, "We're deep within Black Mountain."

"The air is cold here," I said.

"Yes, it grows colder." Kimmi sighed, tightening her fingers around mine. We finally stopped in front of a massive black iron door that stood pushed open. With a tilt of his head, Mac went inside, then Kimmi and I followed.

The room was bare, except for three cots along the walls, dimly lit track lights in the corners of the room, and one table with a chair. Whitecloud was seated by one of the cots in a high-backed wooden chair with the small wooden table near it. He flagged Kimmi over to it while Mac took one of the others. She nodded, dropping my hand as she proceeded over to sit down on the cot's edge.

"You ready?" he whispered, taking her by the shoulders and laying her back.

As soon as her head made contact with the pillow, she whispered, "Yes." Placing both hands across her stomach and locking the fingers, she watched Luther reach for a small bottle of white substance from the table. Uncapping it, he poured a tad of the powder into his hand.

He turned to Kimmi and said, "Child, this will not hurt you." Kimmi was unable to respond when he lifted his hand, and quickly blew the powder in her face.

"What the hell…" It trailed as she fanned her face with both hands, stirring the powder.

I leaned against the doorway, watching while she became groggy and her eyes began to droop. Settling down, Whitecloud ran his hand over them to keep them closed.

Looking over his shoulder at Mac, Luther asked, "Are you ready?" He turned in the chair.

I looked over to the second cot opposite Kimmi and found Mac lying with his hands behind his head.

"Sure," he replied. Whitecloud went to Mac and done the same as with Kimmi. Soon they both were asleep.

"It is time," Luther said, looking up at me. "Go now, my son, and safeguard this place. Find Tom and Ben. They will help you. Hurry now." He fanned me with a hand. I gave him an acknowledgeable bow as I turned away only to stop outside the door and watch as he dusted himself.

When he was asleep, I closed the door, then made my way out of the cave to the room where we went in and found Tom already there when I came through the door to the living room. He was poached in a recliner with his feet up, laid back, and hands tucked behind his head. I saw him eye me as I came in.

He smiled, sitting upright in the chair. "I assume they're off to wonderland." He said it in such a way I had to laugh with him.

"Thought you may need some extra hands for a couple days, so I got Ben and his buddy Nathan, Nate as he likes to be called, to help out. I included," he said in a cool brainy manner.

"Where are Daniel and Jason during this time?" I asked, looking toward the kitchen.

I heard him scratch his stubby chin and say, "For Kimmi's sake, they were not told."

"Thank you very much for keeping Kimmi's safety in mind," I said, looking back at him.

He rose from the chair with the reply, "No problem, Luke." I nodded and we headed out to the front porch where we found the weathered rocking chairs and sat down.

I had just laid back in the chair up when Ben came racing from the south side of the house, breathlessly shouting something we couldn't understand. He stopped at the steps in front of us to catch his breath, his shirtless chest shining from the light sweat drizzling down between the breasts.

Pushing damp hair from his face, he looked up and sputtered, "We got glimpse of it out back, Tom."

"Heading?" Tom asked, standing up, pushing the chair against the wall with his legs.

"West when I saw it just now," he replied, leaning over, grabbing his knees.

"Get the truck and find Nate," Tom said with a deep voice, licking his lips. Standing up, Ben acknowledged him, then took off in a run as he called for Nate. I heard him tell Nate to hurry up and come on as the truck came to life.

I jumped up when Tom pulled the inner door closed after locking it, then dropped the key into his front pants pocket as the Ford truck came around the house. Stopping in the front yard, Tom stepped off the porch toward the driver side as Ben's feet hit the ground. The two of us got into the back with a younger fellow who was tall, slender, with short hair, light brown eyes, and a muscular build. He had an odd jagged scar under his right eye down the cheek. He was shirtless, wearing shorts and sneakers. With Ben and I standing up and facing forward, Ben popped the roof over Tom's head to announce we were ready. We roared off into the night like it was nothing.

I had Ben on the right and Nate on the left of me, and we were facing over the cab when I noticed how defined the jagged scar was.

I guess he knew I was staring because he asked, "How's it feel to be part of the team?" The curiosity showing in his eyes and grinning like the ass I believed he was, I watched the wind blow hair all around his face, slapping at his neck. Ever since the ordeal with Daniel, I had begun to hate myself. But even then, I had to admit, I was enjoying the fact that I was a brute.

"I'm getting the hang of it," I grunted. But the fact that I liked my companion better with each passing day was stronger.

Leaning on the cab, he said, "I'm sorry to hear about your friend Daniel. I knew him when we were in early teens. We graduated together, but he and Jason were a pair when they got together." He heaved a moment, then said, "I lost a friend to the need, uhmm…about three years ago now."

"I'm sorry to hear that," I whispered. There was no time for him to reply when the corner of my eye caught a wolf racing toward the field. No one saw it coming until a larger beast crossed our path. It had my attention to the fullest.

"Do it now, Luke!" Tom shouted through the window before bringing the truck to a hard stop and slinging me out.

By the time I went over the side and hit the ground, I had changed into my wolf, but Ben and Nate were done when I came through. Looking at them, I suddenly thought they looked like ants. They seemed so small, but I had to let it go for time was of the essence. Feeling eager and overanxious with an I-can-do-this attitude, I leaped over the truck and Tom's head, which stepped out. When I hit the ground, I was ready to a run, digging my claws dug into the soft earth. My companion had been right about one thing, I could become unstoppable. I liked the thought as I raced out over the field, leaving the others behind.

I was anxious to find that thing, losing my sense of knowing those behind me. I was ready to rock. Too ready, I thought.

"Hey, wait for us," Ben yelled. He was right, so I slowed my pace, and they caught up to me, coming up on my right flank, but Ben wandered off to sample the dirt.

I heard Tom, who had joined us in his wolf, say, "Look to the right, over there."

I stopped while Tom caught up on my left and Nate on the right.

Ben came roaring by not looking where he was going. "Why are we stopping?" he asked as his snout looked over his right flank, not seeing the beast that came from the trees. Tom yelled at him but not soon enough. Ben ran full speed into the thing.

Ben and the thing rolled for a minute, then came to a stop and got to their feet as they faced off. Before Tom or I could get there, the enormous beast lunged at Ben as he turned and tried to dart off, took him by the waist, sinking his teeth deep inside. With Ben wailing in pain, the thing picked him up, and slung him over our heads. I felt the pads of my feet and claws dig into the earth when I heard Ben slam against a tree. The bark crumbled under him as he slid to the ground and lay motionless. I watched in terror, feeling no pity. I lay in a crouched position ready to take off when the other thing ran off into the woods. The howling came as a taunting call.

"Don't even think about, kid. You'll die by it," Tom said. "They're luring us out." He came toward me, staring out over the valley as he began to change to his human again. "We need to see about Ben first. We'll get it later." He turned toward where Ben landed. Nate and I followed after we returned to human forms.

Ben was his human form when we arrived but doubled over as he groaned in pain. I noticed two compound fractures right away on the left leg and left forearm with both having the bones showing through.

Kneeling down, Tom asked, "Ben can you hear me? It's Tom."

"I'm sorry, guys," he stuttered, gushing blood through his lips.

"Don't talk now," I said, placing a hand on his shoulder.

Tom had been looking Ben over for additional wounds when he said, "We're going to have to pick you up and carry you to the truck." Ben nodded with a heavy sigh, then moaned as he placed a hand over his stomach.

Being informative, Tom said, "Kid you have many broken bones." He gave me a quick glance and said, "Luke, you take Ben by the upper body while Nate and I get his legs." Getting into position, Tom looked at me, and nodded. We lifted Ben, yelling in pain and hurriedly got him to the truck where Nate and I jumped in with him while Tom took the driver seat. The truck came to life, and we headed to the House of Pain. That was what I called it for that's where we would go when in pain.

It didn't take long to get there with the way Tom drove. It was a miracle we didn't roll over when he bought the truck to a U-turn stop right at the front porch. He leaped out, went up the steps very quickly for a man his age, pulling the key out, and inserted it into the door. Nate and I took Ben by the arms and legs from the bed, went up the steps and through the door that Tom held open for us.

Pointing a thumb, he said, "Through here." We followed him into a small room with a twin bed and one window. It was the same one that once held Daniel. We got Ben in the bed while Tom left to get a pan of water. We removed the clothes from Ben before Nate took off outside to scout the place.

It was a mere few moments when the door opened and Tom entered carrying a silver pan of water and a box of bandages.

"You can go out now. I got this," he said, putting the pan of water on the nearby table, then reaching over to turn on the lamp.

With a dry scratchy voice, I asked, "He will be okay, won't he?"

Sitting on the side of the bed, he replied, "That tree did a job on him. His back is broken, and I'm not sure." Feeling helpless and biting the urge to cry, I left the room to return to the living room where I flopped into the large fluffy recliner. I leaned back and closed my eyes not realizing I dropped off to sleep.

I felt a cold touch on my arm that I tried to shake off. Again, it touched me, and I tried to shake it off. The third time, I slowly cracked open my eyes to see Kimmi's face. *Is this a dream*, I thought as the picture became a blur.

"Luke, I'm back," the voice whispered. It was her. I jumped to my feet like a rabbit, grabbing her in a hug with her face muffled in my chest. I didn't hear what she was saying until she pushed back to look up at me and smile.

I kissed her on the head and asked, "Well, how'd it go?" I was so anxious to know the outcome.

"It was odd, but they were nice enough to me and helped explain the time with Cole that night."

Impatiently, I sighed, and said, "Well."

She began to laugh a bit when she said, "They used my body like a portal, taking me back to Chase and I when we heard the voices. Whitecloud and Mac were there too." Looking at up me, she said, "It did not hurt me in any way, but it was funny to watch them float in and out of me like a ghost." Her tone became distant when she said, "After Whitecloud saw, he turned to me and bowed his head, asking for me to forgive him." Turning away, she continued, "I did, Luke. I didn't think I could when he wouldn't listen, leaving me feeling betrayed. Then I thought he was like Cole and didn't care. Forgive me, Luke, for I felt hate for him."

Stepping in front of her, I took a finger, placed it under her chin, tilted her head back to see her eyes, and whispered, "Now he knows, and you're back here with me, and that's all that matters." I kissed her muffled reply.

She broke the attempt, saying, "It was like I was in a nightmare when it happened. Whitecloud was watching as it happened. Oh, Luke, he saw. But most of all, he believed. Thank you," she cried.

When Luther came through the door, he seemed upset but relieved at the same time when he said, "I'm sorry for not hearing you before, Kimmi." Walking past us non-stop, he went through the kitchen door with Mac on his heels. I took Kimmi by the hand and did the same in curiosity, forgetting Ben for a moment.

Going out the door, Kimmi and I stopped on the porch while Luther sailed off—not taking the steps—to where Tom was standing. Mac took the steps but stayed in close pursuit. They stopped in full view of Tom to talk in a whispering tone.

I knew something was up when the old man strongly told both Tom and Mac, "You two know what needs to be done. Bring him here! Go now." I heard him say using a sharp tongue with the two men. They accepted what he said, then left without saying anything.

"What will you do to him?" I asked when he came toward us and stopped at the base of the steps.

"You don't worry about that. He'll be dealt with accordingly," he said, looking around. "Come, let's check on Ben." The old man came up the steps and went into the house. Once again, I took Kimmi's hand and followed him through the door toward the room with Ben.

Leaving Kimmi on the sofa in the front room room, I was on the old man's heels when he opened the door and we went inside. Ben appeared to be asleep when I stopped at the foot of the bed. Luther sat down on the side, placing a hand on Ben's forehead.

Dropping his gaze, I saw tears fall down his cheek. "Damn."

Stepping closer to the old man, I asked, "What's the matter?"

He looked up at me with wet cheeks and said, "He's gone." He slid a hand under Ben's back and rolled him over on his side. I could see two breaks in his back protruding at the lower end just above the tailbone and an enormous bruise at the base of the neck.

Stuttering, I asked, "Does he have family?"

Laying Ben down, he said, pulling the sheet over his head, "Yeah, they're out on the reservation. I'll go today with the news." He said nothing else as he tended to Ben, so I left them alone, and returned to Kimmi, who was lying on the sofa.

I sat down with her, and she rose to a sitting position, placing a hand on my cheek. "You are sad, yes?" Her thumb traced the cheek where the scar had once been.

Looking at her, I knew I couldn't hide the tears when I said, "I just lost a friend in there." I began telling her that we had been out exploring when he tripped and fell off a cliff, breaking his back. She listened with understanding, but I wished I could have told her the truth of his death. The day fell into night when she finally said she was ready for home. I was thankful for her warmth and kindness in times of sadness, but I wondered if she realized the scars were missing. I took her home and kissed her good night, then rushed home to Mae's where I went to bed without a shower and cried myself to sleep.

Inhuman

I T HAD BEEN nearly two weeks since the thing with the Ancestors and Ben's death, and I still hadn't found the guts to tell Kimmi what I was. It haunted my every being in the day while I was awake or at night while I slept. I had yet to find that strength and confidence in myself. I was headed out the front door in sweats with a tee shirt, light jacket, and sneakers after Luther had called to wake and tell me that Cole had been found. He asked if I wanted to join them at the cave near the top of the old mountain. I knew the one he meant since Jason and Daniel had told me so much of it. I agreed.

I took the Charger already sitting on the lawn, then drove out to the dark narrow road that was buried behind the massive trees. I began the drive up over the hilly side of the mountain toward the top, wondering about myself and Kimmi when or if the time comes. The deep thoughts scattered when I arrived at the dead-end of the road to a ledge at the mouth of the cave, wondering if anyone else had arrived yet or were they already inside. I parked the Charger, grabbed my sunglasses from the dash, put them on as I opened the door, and got out. I walked around to the hood of the car, tracing it with a hand before leaning back on it with the sun rising over the horizon like the red dawn it was. I stared at the dark opening of the cave in thought of what was to come.

The tranquility of the morning didn't last long when the sound of a vehicle came to my ears. Turning around in time, I saw Tom's red Ford top the hill followed by the old man's blue jalopy.

When they passed me I noticed a cage—a steel barred cage, containing Cole. He was in his wolf form, foaming at the mouth, and howling like the hell he came from. The truck stopped at the mouth of the cave, and Whitecloud parked behind them. He got out as Tom exited his truck. They spoke a moment, then Tom returned to the truck and proceeded toward the opening in the side of the mountain. When the truck vanished and the taillights disappeared, I heard the old man yell at me to get in the car for us to go. I quickly got in, then eased over to him, and stopped long enough for him to get in the passenger side. When he closed the door, we entered the mountain of darkness.

Inside it was dark and murky with a narrow dirt road that sloped down deeper into the mountain. I thought that the dark mud walls were well maintained with drawings of large wolves. Whitecloud pointed to a left fork as we came up to it. I veered off to an even more narrow way, but that led us into an entrance that opened up into a parking lot well lit with lights and torches. When I parked near the Ford, Whitecloud, at his age, was fast to exit the car.

I wasn't as silent as I got out and asked, "What is this place?" I looked it over, finding no exit except for the way we came. Luther made no reply as he walked over to a closed door where he reached out, pulled the silver flap up and pressed a silver button on the side of the wall. I heard nothing, but suddenly the door slid open into a pocket in the wall.

On the inside, there was a large room with aluminum card tables and chairs, but what caught my attention was the huge cage in the right corner of the room where Cole was placed. His appearance was nasty with matted hair and foam all over his face. His paws were blood covered with broken claws. He snarled through the cage at us with his unseeing eyes. He was so inhuman that I wondered if he was the one at the lake that night when I first came back. "Did you toss that poor animal into the water?" I silently asked myself. I found I was not afraid, just cautious of him for my intuition was to be the same. I knew I had to keep that under wraps because it was for me and only me.

I was staring at him when Tom said, "Be glad it's not you, Luke."

I looked at him strangely and asked, "Why is that?"

"The plans won't be easy for him," he said, coming to my side. His jeans were blood covered at the legs as I glanced down at them.

"What will happen to the one that did the actual killing for him?"

"Cole won't talk. He's taking that with him, I fear," Whitecloud said, approaching from the rear.

I turned around to face him and asked, "How could he become so inhuman? I mean what happened for him to turn that way? Who turned him?"

I watched his eyes travel around the room to me. "There may be a wild one among us."

I sort of grunted when I said, "You're kidding again, right?" I laughed. "You're as much of a joker as Jason is.

"He has a sinister past, Luke, beware of him," Mac said as he approached us. His jeans were also bloody and dirty when he stopped next to the old man.

"Funny you say that, Mac, but who is he?" Glancing at the shorter brother, I said, "Besides, I saw a shadow in the woods just the other day."

"That is odd," Tom said. "You just take care out there. They know what you are, and they'll try to get to you any way possible." Everything became silent when the thing in the cage roared and growled at us, grabbing the bars of the cage and shook it with vengeance.

When the thing stopped its overbearing hateful noise-making, I glanced at the old man and asked, "Does anyone stay down here with them till they do whatever?" I waved a hand in the air.

"Yes, we have patrol," Mac said. "Why? Do you want to be a part of it?"

"Probably not a bad idea," Whitecloud spoke freely. "Maybe keep him calmer than you two have made him, Mac." Laughter lightened the room but only for a short period.

"Poke fun people but the time comes." The thing in the cage roared as it half turned to a man.

"Again, Cole what do you mean by time?" Tom asked, approaching him. Cole suddenly reached for Tom through the bars with hairy claws. Tom was just out of its reach but the tip of the sharp jagged claws caught and tore his shirt. Cole began to laugh in an evil, cunning, and deep tone.

I took the step toward the creature that was once a man and, in a mocking tone, asked, "What's so funny, Cole? You like to laugh at yourself maybe?" I instantly felt brave.

Snarling, he said, "No, Luke. But soon, you'll be in here with me. There's something out there that's waiting to sink its teeth into you."

I took another step toward the cage when I grunted, "Who may that be?" Feeling my fingers curl into the palm of my hand, I stopped.

"You'll not know till it's ready for you to join us; ha, ha, ha," he laughed with a raspy voice.

"Enough. We'll see about that," Whitecloud said. "You've threatened more than your share of people here." He went to the cage, out just out of arm's reach, and said, "Your time comes now. Mac, get it for me please." Mac left the room quickly while I watched the old man's eyes redden for the man in front of him.

Cole continued to mock him until Mac returned with a tiny bottle of blue liquid and handed it to Whitecloud.

Taking it, he told us, "I need your help, boys." Mac and Tom quickly changed to wolves while I stood there not sure what to do. Cole listened to every word we had to say like he was going to tell someone.

Luther noticed and said, "Luke, stay as you are and go to the cage. When he tries to grab for you, grab his arm as it comes from the cage. Hold him tight because he'll struggle against your efforts." I gulped hard, then nodded an understanding and stepped closer the cage.

Feeling that brave sensation inside, I began to mock Cole to make him angry. I took a step forward, not actually understanding just how quick he really was until his hand fanned me for the neck. Like a movie, I felt my hand grow in size as I reached up and caught his fist midair in the large palm of my hair-covered hand. Gasping, I was as surprised as the others from their glances, especially Luther. Yes, Cole struggled with violence as I twisted the arm toward the cage. From his constant struggling, the thing wailed as I broke the arm in the twist. The bone in the forearm sliced through the skin, spewing blood onto my chest.

When Cole slid to the floor, Luther hurried to the cage and opened it while Tom and Mac stood guard. The old man stood on the other arm, grabbed the thing's jaw with one hand while he pulled a handheld tool that looked like a pry bar from the pocket of his overalls. He shoved it between the teeth breaking two in the process and opened the mouth. With the jaws opened enough, he popped the cap off the bottle with his teeth and poured the stuff into Cole's mouth. It only took a moment for Cole to begin wailing and jerking around violently, so violent that the arm I held came free. He tried to lash out at Luther, but he became droopy and passed out.

Whitecloud stepped out of the cage and closed the door. He stared at me for a moment, then to the thing that was once Cole and sighed. "We can leave him for now." He secured the cage door with a brass lock, then dropped the key in his pants pocket as he backed away.

Feeling the vibes from Luther's glance, I asked, "How long before he wakes?" I waited for more than I got, knowing he had something on his mind from the look in his eyes.

"He should sleep until morning at least."

"What has happened to him?" I asked, puzzled.

"It's a long story from many centuries ago," Luther said, walking toward the door. "Let us go for now." Opening the door, he went out, and we all followed, leaving Tom to turn out the lights and close the door behind us. Even though no one mentioned my change, I could tell Luther was endowed to know.

Outside the cave entrance, we found Nate and another young man with dark hair and eyes who was in shorts and sneakers. He was broad across the chest and taller than me. I stopped where Nate was standing, and Luther got out while I was about to ask of the young man.

But before I could, Nate said, "Come meet Luke, Stan." He waved a hand at him. The fella came in a sprint to where we stood while Luther and the other two walked off, talking among themselves.

Tom and Mac followed me toward my truck where we stopped to talk about what happened with Luke.

"I assume you agree when I say that was of the legend," Tom whispered.

"And it happened so sudden, didn't it?" I sighed.

"Let's hope that is all there is to it," Mac implied.

"Not with what has happened lately with him—getting into trouble and stuff. You both know what is about to happen," I groaned. They both knew as well as I that trouble was on its way.

When the man stopped next to Nate, he towered over him and me like a giant and said with a deep husky voice, "I've heard much of you, Luke." He stuck his hand out which I accepted.

His grip was strong, and I said, gritting my teeth, "Same here."

Releasing the hand, he apologized. "I don't know my own strength sometimes. I'm still getting the hang of being a wolf thing." He laughed and his eyes sparkled.

"It's only been two years. You'll catch on," Nate grunted, jabbing him in the side. "Besides, Luke's gonna need a trainer." He gave me a sly glance.

I was about to respond when Luther came up to my side and asked, "Will you come stay for the night?"

"Sure, why not." I half laughed. We told the men good night and Luther got into his truck. I got into the Charger and followed him down the mountain to his home where I found a small room beyond the kitchen.

It was only a small one with one tiny window, a twin bed with a sheet, a blanket, and a small pillow laid on top. I grinned as I lay in the bed and took myself back to Kimmi. Why did I do that to myself? Because I could, I guess. I wanted to feel her embrace again. The soft smooth touches of her hands were persuasive. I dozed once, and was about to fall to sleep when I heard the loudest and nosiest bang outside. When someone cried out, it shook me awake to think of Nate as my first thought. They needed help, so I jumped from the bed, ran toward the kitchen, and out the backdoor.

I stepped outside onto the porch, tuning to the wailing of Nate as he called for help. I run to the car, jumped in, then made a dash out to where he and Stan were. When I arrived, I didn't see them at first, and there were no lights.

Rolling down the window, I heard Nate call, "Over here, Luke," he said in a teary voice. I looked around, and found him half sitting, half kneeling on the ground just out of the car lights in front of something just over the side of the hill. I pushed the gear into park, leaped out without killing the engine, and took off running.

When I got to him, he was already sitting with his legs straight out on the ground with Stan's head in his lap. He was crying as I knelt down, and from the low moonlight, I could see Stan's throat had been sliced open and he had bled out from the blood seeping into the ground.

"Nate, what happened here, bud?" I asked in lack of understanding.

He sniffled, trying to compose himself, and said, "Well, Stan was checking the cave as usual, so I went one way, then I heard him cry out." Ben's tears began to fall as he said, "I came running only to find a beast standing at the mouth of the cave with Stan by the throat dangling in the air before tossing him on the ground here. I didn't see everything, Luke. I'm sorry," Nate cried heavily, letting tears fall down his cheeks.

"It's okay. I have a pretty good idea what happened." I patted his shoulder in comfort. I stood up facing toward the entrance of the cave. "Cole, you son of bitch," I cursed under my breath. I left Nate sobbing and walked into the cave.

When I got to the bottom parking lot, I found the door to the room broken from the inside, and lying against the wall. Stooping down, "Impossible," I whispered, running a hand over the crumbled door. I rose and stepped through the door only to find the cage torn open and Cole gone. I looked down with a nod. "Shit." I sighed under my breath.

"Damn it," Mac said, stopping at the door way.

I whirled around about the time I heard, "I knew he was wild but not like this," Tom said from behind Mac as his head appeared over his brother's shoulder.

"Don't you mean *aggressive*, Tom?" Luther said, joining the crowd. "I now believe that what Cole has gotten into is the cause of this."

"You mean like in the old books? The legendary books?" Tom moaned.

"Yes. We had hoped it no longer lived within us," Luther sighed. "This is why it was told they become savage."

"I understand what Kimmi meant when she said, 'He hurt her.' I wondered how he could just knock her around and break something. Now I know." I gave the man a glance. "I think I'll head out for a bit." I turned to leave.

"You do that, and check with me later," Luther said to my back as I cleared the broken doorway. I nodded an okay, then left the room, dragging my feet back out to the top.

I walked the sloped rocky road in silence, thinking Cole was not a man any longer. I stopped at the mouth of the cave to tell Nate I would see him later, but there was a small crowd with them. Whitecloud pushed by going to them and began a death ceremony for Stan. What I saw right then was a ghost wolf rising from the body of Stan that became a star and vanished into the night. I looked up at the red moon as it tried to hide the death. I bowed by head and said a prayer before heading home where I rushed through the front door, up the stairs to the bathroom, and showered. I wanted to wash off the evil I had touched from Cole as I scrubbed my skin to a rosy pink. Done, I got out and went to my room where I dressed in pj's, then went to bed for a dreamless sleep.

I can't say how long I lay there in the bed when I woke the next day, but the sky was grey and cloudy. I got up and walked to the closet where I stood in front of the mirror, staring at the faded symbol on my shoulder resembling a tattoo. Finished with the exam, I rummaged through my clothes where I found jeans, a black button-down, and sneakers. After dressing, I looked at the untouched bed. Another day, I laughed as I quickly straightened the covers. I grabbed the comb from the dresser and combed my hair back tying it with a leather band. I thought of Kimmi as I realized I hadn't seen her for a couple days. I heavily sighed at the thought of last night but soon pushed it away when I saw the sun crest the window as it cut through the clouds. I grunted as I made my way downstairs to the kitchen where I found Mae at the table... alone.

She was smiling when I came through the door. Her face was happy as she picked up the cup in front of her and took a sip. I gave her a return smile, and noticed she still had on her nightgown and housecoat. I went to the sink and got a glass from the cabinet for water. I took the glass to the table and sat down with her.

I looked into her warm eyes and asked, "Where's Joe at?"

She blinked as she said, "He joined the search for that creature Cole. He got wind of what happened with the kid." She sighed. "Joe's the kind of man that hates and despises a killer for no reason."

"Mae, are you sure he did the right thing by going out there?" I asked softly. She smiled, picked up the cup, and put it to her lips.

"I need to ask you something please," I said politely.

Glaring over the rim, she said, "Sure, son. Ask what you must."

I leaned on the table's edge. "What can you tell me about our legends?" Mae raised her eye brows and smiled as she leaned back in her chair.

Staring into her eyes, I would have sworn they appeared to change colors as she began to talk. "It was told many, many centuries ago that it caused us to become more than anything we knew. It can be a drug-like thing and once induced into the veins, you soon become it—not the other way around. The wolf inside becomes the most undesirable thing—the dark side of the person." She paused, taking a sip from the cup. Sitting the cup down, she continued, "It combines the two into one to make a different breed of man. The dark side is an evil demon." She licked her thin lips and said, "Does this answer some of your questions? I hope so."

"Can Cole, and those like him, be a wicked and brutal beast with no consciousness?"

"Oh yes. How long he has been that way is unknown. Cole was once a sweet kid who would help anyone in need."

I sit back in the chair and said, "Thanks, Grandma." I rose from the table, went around to her, and kissed her forehead. I went into the living room, taking the glass of water with me and sat down on the sofa, leaning back into the cushions. I found the remote and turned on the TV when I should have gone to see Kimmi instead.

I dozed off until I was awakened by a hand on my shoulder. I didn't see who was standing in front of me when I tried to open my eyes.

"You think you could give us a hand?" A voice asked before I saw the old man.

"Sure, but what is it you need me for now?" I asked, coming from the grogginess of the nap.

I heard the old man sigh as he sat down on the sofa next to me. "A young lady has been missing for a couple days now, and Ivan fears she has been kidnapped."

That comment made me sit straight up on the cushion as I faced him. "Kimmi," I shouted, uncontrolled.

"Yes. Ivan called and said she went on her walk the day before last and never returned."

"Where?" I asked, sliding to the edge of the couch and rubbing my eyes with both hands to clear my vision.

"Go see Ivan. He can tell you more. We will get ready here. Get going before the storm approaches." He patted my back.

"Thanks for letting me know." I got up, went out the front door, and stopped on the lawn to inhale the air. Smelling nothing but clean air, "Storm? Right," I grunted, going to the car and headed off to the Creed home.

MISSING

WHEN I ARRIVED, the house seemed deserted, so I quickly parked, then leaped out running over the lawn, leaping over the steps to the front door, and knocked. When the door opened, Casey was standing there with eyes as red as the satin slim-fitting dress she was in.

Sighing, she stepped over the threshold, grabbed my neck and said, "Thank God."

Slipping my arms around her thin waist, I returned the hug and asked, "Ivan and Mollie?"

Releasing her hold on my neck, she stood back looking up through tear-stained eyes and said, "They're in the den waiting for you." She moved back through the door, letting me step in. Dabbing at her running mascara with the handkerchief, she closed the front door. With tears gathered in her eyes, she grimly smiled. "Excuse me, Luke." She turned and went upstairs. I was headed for the den at the same time I heard her door close. I reached out and opened one of the den doors and stepped through.

I found the man and woman both sitting on separate sofas as I came in the door, and my first thought was that they must have been arguing from the looks on their faces. Mollie jumped to her feet so fast that she was like a blur before stopping to give me a hug. I thought her skin was as cool as Kimmi's when I returned the favor.

After her trembling subsided, she stepped back and asked with a shaky voice, "Would you care for anything?" Her once green eyes were red from crying, with her mascara running over her jaw.

Unable to control the anger, my companion lashed out and said, "Sure, Mrs. Creed, the one most thing I love."

Not knowing my behavior until Ivan stepped in and said, "Where the hell are your manners, boy?" He rose from the sofa with a stabbing stare thru those grey eyes.

Feeling the regret come over me with a sly comment, my companion said, "Don't let these fools intimidate you like that. Stand your ground and be a man. You are a man, right?" Swallowing hard, I apologized for my rudeness.

"Damned fool," my companion roared at me. Mollie accepted it, then left the room in silence. After she closed the door, I went to sit on the sofa facing Ivan, who had returned to his seat.

Finally after moments of silence to gather my thoughts, I looked up over at him. "Tell me what's going on, Ivan, with Kimmi. Who took her and why did you wait two days to say something?" Despite my anger of loss, I calmed down enough to lean forward and place my elbows on my knees with my chin cupped in my palms.

Taken by my choice of words, he said, "Kimmi's a bright young girl. She knows her dos and don'ts when she goes on her walks. Mollie and I thought nothing of it as she does stay out late with her night creatures. It was night before last that I had Casey check on her when she didn't come in for dinner. Casey came to us and said that Kimmi's bed had been left undisturbed for two days. So, before Mollie and I left for work, I called Whitecloud for help. I'll be the first to admit I was glad he said you would be here," he continued with a shallow tone.

Looking past him to the sun riding the balcony, I asked, "Where does she usually go when she's out during the day?"

Dark clouds covered the sun when he replied, "She told us she was headed out to the dark forest for awhile."

Feeling my forehead slightly wrinkle, I asked jokingly, "Dark forest?"

With the surprised expression on his face, he said, "She hasn't told you." I glanced at him with a shake of the head.

Sighing deeply, Ivan leaned back on the cushion when he informed me, "There's a path at the edge of the woods out toward the back of the house." His finger pointed toward the balcony. "Find the trail, and it'll lead you deep into the forest where the mountain slope will steepen greatly, so be careful of slides. Look for the dense clearing with fallen timbers that have a green lush cover over them. It will be dark from the magnitude of towering trees, but once there, you will find the trees thick as molasses, old as the earth itself, and as large as time. The ground will be covered in hunter green grass as thick and plush as the cushion you are sitting on now. You will find plants of all sizes and beauty scattered throughout. But the one most impressive thing is the wildlife. It welcomes you with open arms. I know this from our many visits out there." He leaned forward when Mollie came in carrying a tray.

After she sat it down on the table, he licked his lips and said, "If you go, please take care when the trail continues up the mountain. The terrain is rough and rocky with large boulders ready to tumble at any time. The trail eventually narrows and ends at the top." Standing up, he said, "A storm comes. Help us find her." Tears fell from his eyes as he turned away from me. I got up just as Mollie handed me a glass of water.

I took the glass from Mollie's trembling hand and walked over to the double doors to look outside. The birds were pecking at one another while sitting on the railing. Vast clouds of dark grey were rolling in as the sun was starting to set. The thought in my head asked, *Where are you?* I took a sip of the water to wet my dry throat.

Mollie came over to me and opened the doors. "Please hurry before her trail is lost," she said with a pleading tone.

"I will, Mollie. I promise." I kissed her cheek, and needing no invitation, I walked out onto the balcony, grabbed the rail with one hand, and leaped off over, hitting the ground facing the mountain.

I began to walk along the edge of the grass until I found the small narrow footpath no wider than my foot. I didn't need a flashlight, so I looked around to see if anyone was visible. Not seeing anyone, I changed into my wolf form that quickly picked up her scent. I trotted up the mountain trail, following it breathlessly until I came to the clearing as Ivan had said. "My God." It was stunning. I sat down on the lush grass only to sink from my weight. My vision picked up deer and other wildlife stepping from behind trees into full view. They were not afraid but instead, invited me in. I stood up in fear when a skunk came running over to me. Squirrels and raccoons gathered on the fallen timbers to watch. Owls echoed from the overhead tree branches.

The skunk stopped at my feet and I looked down at it. It was rather a large fellow but impressive when it sat up on its back legs and reached out to me with black paws. I hesitated a moment. Then it began to squeak at me, moving its paws up and down. The raccoons began to insist as they waved with their paws. Intuition told me to lower my snout. When I did, I was greeted by the two small paws of the skunk when it placed one on each side. They felt like human hands with a tender, velvet touch. I can't say how long I stood there, but it came to an end when lightning struck in the sky. As soon as the light flashed and left so did the animals, leaving me alone, and back to what was at hand.

I took a quick sniff of the air, finding nothing right away. I placed my nose flat on the grass inhaling until I came up with a faint scent of something unusual that made me stop and look toward the top. The scent continued on up the path toward the top, but so did hers. With fog closing in and the oncoming smell of rain, I needed to move faster, so I started a sprint. It was so dark that I had to use the wolf's senses to guide me. I adjusted to the darkness and finally reached the top of the mountain.

Stepping from the cover of the trees, I felt large droplets of rain hit my head, which were becoming heavier from the scent on the wind that had begun to blow. "Shit," I whined.

With a snarl, my companion growled, "Leave her. She is just a nothing."

Shaking off the temptation from head to tail, I shouted, "Like hell. Why don't you leave me alone?"

"You don't really want me to, I can feel you, remember," it replied with a woof. "Besides, what will you do to the thing that took her?" I stopped suddenly as if I had walked into a glass wall. It was right. What would I do when I caught the culprit?

"Come. I will be your guide and help you as I did with that boy." Being led astray like a child, I followed my companion.

We quickly paced the clearing till we came across a large deep hole in the ground that angled off with no end. With rain growing closer and her scent shallow, I passed the hole and continued to walk the ridge. Stopping at the west edge of the mountaintop, I thought I heard a faint cry on the howling wind in the tree tops. I also heard a weeping from the nearby ridge before I saw the red eyes following me. Relying on my senses, I raised my nose to the air and drew in deep, letting the smells fill my senses. As I exhaled, a scent drew me to her, coming from the north. While my companion had wandered off, I continued north over the mountain.

There was no trail or footpath to follow, so I slowly traveled up the side of the slope. I again stopped as I heard that same faint cry. "Where are you?" I cried before the booming thunder that would drown out anything. Rain was starting to become a mist instead of droplets. Fog was thickening as it set in on the top of the mountain. "If I didn't hurry, I'd be lost and fall into a damn hole," I moaned to myself, and hurriedly began again. That's when I nearly fell into a hole I didn't see. "Oops," I cried when I slipped.

Careful now, I thought, recalling what Ivan had said. I could smell her, but with it was that sweet familiar smell too. I felt my mouth foam as it began to water. "Stop," I told myself, but it was luring me before I came to my senses and noticed the rain had become stinging sprinkles. Shaking my coat of the water, I slipped off into a hole. My paws began grabbing at the edge and raking at the top of the soft earth to gain a hold. I had all four paws going at the same time, but the earth gave way to my efforts. Finally, I got a good grip with my hind claws.

With all my strength, I hung on to the earth as I began to climb my way back out of the hole where I sat down on my rump and sighed. "Careful," I said to myself. *I bet if it rains hard or long enough, it wouldn't take long to fill one of those up*, I thought. Continuing, I approached another clearing where I stopped to get another whiff from the rising wind. Then I heard the cry, but I could only see red eyes from the trees. When I glanced around, I saw I was surrounded by them. They made no advance toward me as I stared at them.

"Who are you and what do you want here?" I shouted, wondering whether they or it could hear me.

I never saw the figure with the voice that said, "It's not what but who they want, Luke." My first thought was Cole, but then it couldn't be.

"You are?" I asked very rudely.

"Beware, kid. I will come for you."

"How do you know me? Show yourself," I shouted, wondering how it could hear me while I was my wolf. The eyes faded with an unseeing figure, leaving me wanting to know how it knew me. Kimmi was first, so I quickly picked up the scent again and crossed the clearing into the trees as lightning strikes flashed. The rain stung my eyes, making it hard to see, and I knew the mountain would give way in a slide from the rain. I had to hurry, so I picked up the pace.

I could hear voices of the clan in the distance as they made their way up the hill on the far side. I was hoping they would hurry when I heard a cry for help. It was faint and soft when it echoed. I started to dash off when Cole stepped from the trees into my way. Strangely and without resistance, I instantly became my human form to face him. He was in a rain outfit with a hat that covered his face. The brim of the hat underneath the rain cap dripped with rain runoff.

I wasted no time in speaking my tongue. "What the hell do you want here?"

"Get him!" My companion yelled in my head, which I ignored.

"That little girl there is mine, kid," Cole rudely claimed as his head rose to face me.

"Why, Cole? 'Cause she refused a bum like you, who wanted her only to use for sex. Hell, I wouldn't have you for that either. When are you going to just leave her alone?"

"Come on, let's take him." I felt my hands inching to make a fist but passed it off again.

"She'll be mine since you won't take her." He slightly changed under the raincoat when lightning struck, then like the creep he was, he turned with a laugh, and ran off.

"That's just pathetic. You need some enticing to get the job done," my head told me. "Later on when you're alone for a spell, I'll show you." I shook my head to rid myself of the voice and continued searching for Kimmi.

With the rain coming down in sheets, I couldn't see, so I took cover under some thick trees with foliage and lay down. While I waited, I drifted into a dream to see Kimmi waving at me from the top of the valley ridge, so I waved back. She turned and ran off toward the trees, giggling like a school girl. Ah, she wanted to play hide and seek. *Okay, let's have some fun,* I thought as I walked to the edge of the trees. I called out to her, but no answer came back. I began looking up into the trees to see if she had slipped up into one, but no, she wasn't there either. Becoming a tad frantic, I called to her again and she dashed into the darkness to fade. There in the distance was a light that was getting brighter, but when it glowed and started to bounce, I realized there was no getting past. "Kimmi," I cried out, only to hear someone calling me.

I awoke to Tom and Daniel squatting down and staring me in the face. I noticed the rain had stopped to a light drizzle and the sun had risen. I got to my feet and found my jeans soaked from the wet ground, so I stripped them to the boxers.

"How long you been here?" Tom asked with a sneer, looking at me with his own damp head of hair and shirtless.

"Not sure. It was still raining though. I couldn't see anyone but Cole."

"Cole?" He intruded before I could finish.

"Yeah, he stopped me once to have a chat."

"You ready to continue?" he asked with a confused expression. Without saying anything, I shook my head yes and set off again on foot.

"You may want to change. It's works better," I heard Tom say as I walked off. I just waved a hand at him and Daniel, changing to the wolf once more.

There was mud everywhere as I paced back and forth, trying to regain the scent of Kimmi. Damn, it was gone and I had to start anew. I stopped, raised my nose to the sky, and drew in deep. The many smells that came storming in made me slowly exhale and find a faint scent of her, which took me through the trees into a small clearing. Once there, the scent grew, and I took off into a full run as fast as possible on the soft wet earth, paying no heed to Tom's warnings of a possible slide.

I heard a cry that echoed but couldn't get a clear fix, so I paced the trees first, going in circles as I made a smaller circle, hoping to land where she was. When the circles grew smaller, I found the deepest hole in the ground where I heard another whimper. I peeked over the edge, but it was so dark that I couldn't see anything. Not even the vision of the wolf. *Oh shit, not again,* I thought when I felt several trickles of rain hit my nose. I sit down and let out a howl so loud it scared me. It was nice to know that others replied in return.

I quickly changed to my human, but the ledge of the hole was so slick and lose from the heavy rain that I nearly lost my balance. I saw some of the larger trees leaning over the side as if they were about to fall. I lay down on my belly and leaned over the edge of the hole that was hard enough to support my weight until the ledge began to slide. "Shit," I swore as I jumped up and moved away to keep from caving in. I could hear the running of feet like the water below and got the sense someone moving around down there.

❧❦❧

I tried hard to let whoever was overhead know that I was down here, but after struggling to stay above the water, had taken its toll. "God, how I wish Luke were here," I whispered, scrapping at the mud walls. "How can I tell him what happened?" I moaned as my head went under again.

❧❦❧

Suddenly, a figure swooped down then back up over my head. The birds arrived and knew Kimmi was there. I looked up just as the male flew down to me and landed on the ground not more than three feet in front of me. I froze as he sat there and stared at me through those dark eyes, his long beak clicking together while his talons dug into the ground. Did I fear them? Yes, but with respect.

I squatted down and said to the bird as if he understood, "You know, don't you?" He turned, walked to the hole, leaned over, and squawked. The sound echoed, but then I heard the cry climb up and out with the faint sounds of splashing water. The male motioned with a claw, then took flight and came together with the female. I leaned over toward the edge while they stayed within range overhead. It wasn't long before Tom and the group came over the top of the ridge with thundering feet splashing in the mud.

When Jason knelt down by me and let out a sigh of relief, I was never so glad to see someone right then as I was him.

Crawling closer to the edge, he asked, "Where is she?"

"The hole, but it won't support me," I said, pointing, getting up on hands and knees. "Be careful." As soon as his hands hit the ground, it began to slide. His face turned to terror when he had no time to back away, and he went over the side with it. Sitting back on my heels, I waited to hear the splash. So did Tom when he rushed over near the opening to see. He looked at me through those dark questioning eyes, and I nodded a yes.

"Damn," he swore, getting up and moving to the crowd.

I got to my feet and made my way over to Tom, keeping to the firmer ground. There were many young men and women in the crowd that I had never seen before. The ladies were rather cute, but my interest was in Kimmi.

Standing at Tom's side, I asked, "How we going get them out?" I didn't see the huge amount of rope they towed up the mountain side until he yelled for Nate to bring the rope.

Tom looked the area over, then said, "Only one way that I can."

Seeing the large amount of a two-inch-wide intertwined rope, I coughed and asked, "That is for what? There's nothing to tie it to." I glanced over the ridge of trees that sat back fifty feet or more from us. What trees there were, were too far away or apart from them and the hole. Or it could be that the rope was too short. A large raindrop hit me on top of the head right then and ran down my back. "Shit," I swore in silence.

With a grunt, Tom said, "Hold on, Luke. You'll see how we do it." He looked over his shoulder and called for Nate again.

He came to us with an abundant amount of rope on his shoulders like an anaconda was wrapped around him with the head trailing. Stopping in front of Tom, he pushed it over his shoulder, and let it fall to the ground. They began to pull it out, making knots in places until it was fully outstretched and looked like a knotted pine tree's limb. Tom paced the rope, lengthy cutting it into three sizes.

After the last cut, he stood up placing his hands on his waist, and looked at me and Nate. "I need for you two to change and stay right where you are."

Nate stepped to my side just as I asked, "For what?"

"Just watch," Nate replied with a laugh. With my uncertainty in mind, we did as Tom asked and changed into our wolves.

He called for Daniel, Paulene, and Mac to come help as well. Paulene went to the ledge while the three men got two pieces of the rope and pulled one to each side of Nate and me. I stood fast as Tom came around tossing the rope over my back, reaching under my belly, pulling it tight, then up around my neck fashioning a harness. I watched with astonishment while Mac did the same to Nate. Daniel held tight to the last piece to keep from sliding. Once they were fastened, I felt like a horse ready for the field, but Tom and Mac took the third piece, running one end through a loop in our harnesses, looping us together, then making a knot. Mac took the other end with Daniel and pulled tighter. It was a bit short for the hole.

Tom stepped in between us, grabbed the harnesses and pulled back tightening it around my neck, bringing my head up higher, and Nate coughed from the motion.

"Step back one step, boys," Tom whistled. Taking the step, I sunk into the soft ground but stayed afoot. I swallowed hard when Tom asked us again to make the backwards step. That time, it was enough when Mac shouted stop. I watched him toss the other end down into the opening to Jason and Kimmi. Tom released the hold on Nate and me to go to the ledge, yelling at Jason to take the rope. He stopped suddenly when the earth gave way to his weight, and he moved back, letting Paulene take over for him.

There was no reply at first, so Paulene called down again. I fine tuned my hearing to hear Jason say, "Yeah, honey, but hurry.

In a soft tone, she said, "Take the rope and wrap it around yourself and Kimmi." I patiently waited while my heart began to pound like the large raindrops hitting my head and nose. I looked over at Nate, who shook his head to remove the water. I finally felt the rope being tugged on; then I heard Jason say he was ready. "Thank God," I whispered to myself just as Tom came into view.

Placing a hand under our necks, he grabbed the rope, and said, "You two start walking forward those trees but slowly. It's going to take much effort on the soft edge to maintain them."

With a snort, Nate and I nodded, then began to pull the rope tight. I felt like the power of the horse was in me, but once the rope tightened, it became heavy from the weight of both people. I never thought Jason was so heavy.

It became harder to pull when the softness of the ground gave in pulling on the rope.

I looked at Nate when he said, "I'm not as strong as you, Luke." Then the bark followed.

With a whimper, I told him, "We can do this, and so can you." I extended my claws, sticking them into the soft ground. Tom was like a mighty engine when he groaned, and pulled on the ropes. The ground shifted suddenly under our feet, and we began to slide backward with the mud. The hole was giving way and enlarging from the wetness. I could hear the mud hit the water below.

Crouching down closer to the ground and digging in, I cried, "Steadfast, Nate. Pull."

Feeling the rope bearing down on my neck, Tom yelled as he changed into his wolf, "This is not happening." He grabbed the middle of the harness with his teeth and pulled with us.

Nate whined, "God, I'm trying." Then he slipped and fell, sliding with the rope toward the opening, nearly knocking Tom down with him, but he leaped over the fallen boy to keep steady on the ropes. When they tightened around my waist and neck, I didn't give way but growled with anger, pulling harder on the growing heavy rope. "Great Spirit, I call to thee. Please help me." Oddly enough, the strength came from the companion.

They were at my mercy as I called for strength again, and it replied, "I'm here." It was on me to pull them to safety. Even with Tom's help, they were heavy as hell. I heard the others rustling with Nate to get him up on his feet, but I didn't have the time to watch, so I hadn't noticed when he regained his footing and was back straining on the harness. The ground being wet gave in too quick as we strained to keep the ropes, even when we began to slide backwards again, fighting to keep our traction.

"Dig," I yelled, fumbling, and nearly losing my footing in the mud.

"God help us, Luke," Nate whined. "The earth is sliding from under us."

I knew we were about to lose the battle, until Tom yelled, "Stop, you two." Like a timer Nate and I stopped, letting the ropes hang tight while he changed back to his human.

Nate and I were staring at each other when we heard mud rustling feet at the edge of the hole, then Jason called for Paulene when I felt the rope slack. Impatient, I turned just enough to see Paulene take Kimmi's limp body from the hole and carry her to the fire where she laid her down on a blanket in front of a fashioned tent. She was all I had on my mind when I felt the harness being removed by Mac with the help of another man of mid-twenties with black hair and brown eyes. He was half dressed in shorts, a half shirt, and sneakers.

"Change before she comes to, kid," Mac said, petting my neck. I was actually beginning to enjoy the feel of my four legged creature.

Being respectful, I did as Mac asked. But when I turned around in my human form, I came face to face with Ivan standing there.

"You saw?" I asked in desperation. He nodded yes, then turned and went to Kimmi's side. I joined him at the makeshift tent of tree limbs and blankets, sitting against a massive tree trunk in between the roots above the ground. There was a fire nearby with several others around the area being attended by other tribe members.

I sat down against the trunk of the tree, reaching over, warming my hands from the fire when Jason sat down near me with a heavy thud. Looking over at him, I saw his clothes were soaked and covered in mud but he had a blanket around his shoulders with hair stuck to his face.

"Take this." He offered me a blanket.

"Thanks a heap." Taking the blanket, I opened it, and put it around my shoulders.

"She was barely conscious when I got to her. I hope she's okay, Luke," he said, leaning over a tree root.

A shadow stopped between us and the fire. "She'll be fine," Ivan said, handing me a hot cup of coffee, then one to Jason. "She's just drained from fighting with the water down there and needs to rest. Since it's a long trip back down the mountain in the mud, we'll leave in the morning." He sat down near the fire with us in his long sleeved shirt and slacks.

"Ivan, You need to know I believe it was Cole who did this to her." I looked into his diamond white eyes that I had never seen before until then. He sighed, saying nothing, so I got up and found another blanket for myself, then found a distant place to be alone in thought while keeping an eye on Kimmi.

The nights were cold on top of the mountain at that time of the year, at that altitude. It certainly turned out cold that night, so I settled down not far from Kimmi with my legs crossed and watched Ivan go over to Tom and Mac. While they talked, I watched Paulene and one of the tribe girls go in and out of the tent where she was. Ivan came back, grabbed a blanket from the ground, then sat down outside the tent, and leaned back on a tree trunk. The night took form and the wind began to blow in a low howl bringing a bit of cooler air which smelled of rain. *Oh well*, I thought, shivering a little as I pulled the blanket closed. It didn't take long before I wore down and began to drift off to a dreamless sleep. Leaning back on a tree, I pulled the blanket tight over my head.

Since my companion had ventured off, I didn't know how long it was before we were awakened by the sound of yelling voices. Coming to, I found the blanket soaked from the heavy rain. I could hear Whitecloud telling everyone to hurry. Tossing the blanket, the wind hurled it from me like our makeshift huts that went to hell as it rushed over the top of the mountain like a dark angry spirit. What people were standing were being tossed around like twigs. We bunched up together around Kimmi and Ivan, who were inside the tent, to keep them safe.

It was only a matter of moments when Kimmi began to stir around, and I heard her ask, "Hey, what's going on out there?" She stuck her head out of the tent, the same time Paulene pulled her back in. Pursuant, Kimmi pushed back through the opening and yelled out, "Where am I?"

I rushed over to her, and she asked, "Why are you here? Where are we anyway?" She took my hands into her cold ones and said, "Rain...here...now? Luke, where are we?" Pulling on my arm, she said, "You'll freeze out there."

I knew I could keep Luke warm, but how could I have shown him? There was only one way.

Pushing her back inside the tent, I soothed her and said, "I'll be fine, Kimmi. You stay there; be safe. The storm will pass soon I hope." I watched her smile before I grabbed a blanket and shielded myself between the tree and tent that sat in the groove of the two huge roots.

Balancing myself from the growing wind, I sat down at the base of the tree with the blanket the precise moment Kimmi rushed from the makeshift tent, pulling a blanket with her as she came to me. I was stunned as I watched her struggling against the wind for someone who was so light footed. She held fast to the mighty wind until she stood in front of me. I looked into her cool blues while opening the blanket for her. Smiling she tossed her blanket over my shoulders, then commenced to place herself in my lap and wrapped the blankets around the both of us. Snuggling against me, she felt as cold as the outside and faded back to sleep. Watching others cover themselves with blankets and tree limbs, I covered my head from the heavy rain, praying it would soon stop.

Through the night, it rained like hell with raging winds of at least forty miles per hour. I could hear timbers cracking and falling limbs crashing to the ground. I held Kimmi close, covering our heads with the blankets for little to no safety, but I wished. Finally, it stopped as fast as it started with the rising sun peeking through the fast-moving clouds onto the wet blanket. I pulled the blankets off us, listening to the voices that carried up over the sides of the wet hillside. Kimmi sat back looking up into my eyes with a cool touch to the cheek, then got up without question and walked off. I just watched her for a moment and wondered what she had on her mind, mixed with the sounds of the tribes people gathering the belongings of what was left. I noticed Ivan was even helping when I realized I had lost sight of Kimmi, so I rose to go find her.

She hadn't gone far when I found her standing at the entrance to the hole. She didn't face me when I stopped next to her.

"How did I get here and why?" She sighed heavily.

Surprised, I said, "I thought you might tell me that."

Facing me, she rubbed her neck and said, "The last thing I recall was sitting in the gazebo working on some macramé when I felt a sting in my neck." She placed a hand over the left side of her neck and continued, "I was so blurry eyed I never saw who picked me up before I passed out." With a sharp tongue, she said, "That creep." She bit her bottom lip when her eyes met mine.

I gathered she meant Cole when I said, "Don't worry about him. I'm here." I kissed her muddy forehead and whispered, "We should go now." She nodded in agreement.

Hand in hand, we walked toward the crowd when she suddenly tripped on a stick protruding from the ground and hit the wet dirt. The hard fall caused her to slide about ten feet from me. Even more mud covered when she stopped, I heard her grunt with laughter as she rolled over to get up on her knees. Laughing myself, I ran toward her, but before I could get to her, the earth shifted again, giving way into a slide. Taking Kimmi with it, Luther saw her coming and tried to grab her. Missing, she slammed into him. He lost his footing and went down, taking several others of the group with them down the side of the mountain. The sudden motion of Kimmi's fall quickly sent the saturated mountain into a mud slide.

Trying to hurry down, I slid several feet, just missing some trees, and hitting the boulder behind one. Feeling my shoulder crack from slamming into it, I rolled over onto my back, paying no attention to the people yelling, until the hill tilted over a small cliff. Unable to stop, we went over the cliff like a waterfall. Hitting the soft earth with a slpash, back first, I saw one of the biggest trees taken by the loose mud, pulled from its roots, and come down with the slid. Someone yelled to look out, and Whitecloud was one of the first to see it heading toward him and Kimmi.

Vigorously clawing the red clay, I tried to stop, but I was too far away to help when the enormous tree flashed over the top, taking two people while I ducked and watched Whitecloud. In slow motion, he leaped toward Kimmi who was just a few steps ahead of him. Grabbing her in a roll, he placed himself over the top of her just as the huge tree went sailing down over the top of them. I saw Ivan, Jason, and several others duck, but some didn't when it took them leaving a path of destruction in its tracks. Demolishing four more trees like a demolition crew, it caused one to tumble over and crash. I heard Kimmi and several others scream, but then there was nothing. Only the sliding mud for another hundred feet or so.

I forgot the pain in my shoulder when I leaped to my feet, sliding. Making my way through the limbs and over the roots of the tree, others shouted for those who were okay. Tripping over the last limb and falling face first into the mud, I heard Kimmi laugh.

Crawling out from the cover of the limb, I heard Luther ask Kimmi, "Child, are you okay?"

Slowly raising her eyes to Luther, she sighed. "I tripped as you can tell." Then she smiled, trying to make light of what had happened.

Getting to my feet, I asked Luther, "Are you alright?" He smiled with a nod.

Breathless and laughing, I asked her, "Oh, honey, are you okay?" I brushed at her mud-covered face.

"Yes, I believe I am," she murmured. "Laugh if you must, Luke."

"Should I carry you the rest of the way?" I asked, suppressing the laugh.

Tilting her head back, I saw her blush. "Well, it would be nice of you." As mud covered as she was, I picked her up with ease as if she was made for my arms and started down with her giggling like a school girl.

We reached the bottom of the hill on solid ground where I found Mac, Tom, Daniel, and Jason, but Paulene was nowhere to be seen. Placing Kimmi on the ground, I walked her to the passenger side of Ivan's awaiting Mustang. When she stopped to face me, she placed her arms around my neck in a hug. I returned the motion, placing my arms around her waist. So with one arm around her, I opened the door with the other to let her sit down. Closing the door, I leaned in the window to wipe her nose off with my forearm, then gave her a soft kiss on her muddy lips, staring at the tears in her eyes. She returned the kiss with shaky lips and trembling hands on my cheeks.

Ivan got into the driver side, reached for the key in the ignition and gave it a turn when I told her, "I love you. Go home and get cleaned up."

Placing her lips against my cheek, she whispered, "And I love you, Luke Winterset." Then the car came to life with a roaring engine. I stepped away from the car when Ivan put the thing in gear.

Watching the Mustang drive away, Jason yelled at me, "Come, Luke, let us go home as well."

"Right behind you," I shouted, glaring up at the mountain side. I could have sworn that in the farthest corner was Cole standing there staring back at me.

I said it loud enough I knew he heard me. "If you know what's good for you, you'll stay away from her." I turned and joined Jason and Paulene in the Ford that took me home.

BEACH PARTY

IT HAD BEEN a couple days since the event at the mountain, so I quickly dressed in shorts and a tee shirt, then called early enough to find out how Kimmi was doing. Mollie answered and said she was fine and that she was still asleep. I thanked her, and hung up. After a light breakfast, I called Willa and asked her to do me a favor. When I told her what I wanted, she readily agreed. I also mentioned that if she had to get with Paulene, I would like it done by Saturday. She said she could handle it. I thanked her and hung up, not knowing Willa had already met Kimmi, whom I was taking to meet on Friday.

Willa hung up the phone and turned to face me with a grin. She sat down on the sofa next to me and told me of Luke's plans. I was so excited, but I had to keep it under wraps. With that in mind, I told her I wanted to make plans of my own, and she agreed to help as well. We would make it a night to remember.

I felt good inside because I was about to help make one of Kimmi's dreams sort of come true. I called both Jason and Daniel next to ask for their help, which they seemed really anxious to do.

The days passed so slowly until it was finally Friday. I leaped from the sofa, rushing out the front door to the car and got in reaching over for the key in the ignition. Excited, I backed out of the drive and headed out to the Creeds where I eased into the drive and parked. I opened the door, leaped out, and rushed over the lawn toward the porch. Leaping over the steps onto the porch, I walked to the front door, and knocked like a nervous school boy. Kimmi must have been standing there, because she opened the door rather fast, catching me staring at her in a nicely dressed baby-blue gown. Her hair was up in two pony tails that hung over the sides of her face and down the chest. Her face was plain with only a touch of pale rose lipstick on her thin lips.

I found my voice and said, "Hey, sweetie"—and kissed her forehead.

"You want to come in, or shall we go?" She slightly whispered.

"I think we should go." I grinned.

"Okay, then." She came outside, closing the front door behind her. I took her hand, leading her to the car and helping her inside. I closed the door, then hurried to the driver side and got in, I smiled at her as I turned the key.

We arrived to find Jason's truck in the drive, and Willa came out the door in a half-assed run to give me a hug as soon as I stepped out of the car. She was dressed in a pair of white hot shorts, tank top, barefoot, and red curls up in a ponytail. I should have been ashamed when I thought what I could have done with her.

"Willa Browning, this is Kimmi," I said with pride. Willa reached over and gave Kimmi a hug.

"Thank you," Kimmi whispered.

Willa grinned as she took Kimmi by the arm. "Come with me. You need a break from this thing here." She poked my side as they headed for the house. I watched them go in just as Jason and Paulene came running out the door.

❦❧❦

When Willa came rushing through the door with Kimmi by the hand, they passed me, giggling down the hallway to Willa's room. The scent Kimmi left behind was enough to *almost* make me go in after her. The thought was unspeakable, and if Luke knew, well…I left it at that, knowing I couldn't tell anyone about my thoughts; at least not the ones I've had lately.

❦❧❦

They both appeared to be anxious about something by the time they stopped where I stood. I stared at Jason's attire of shorts hanging on his hips, no shirt and barefoot. Paulene's was a nice green pair of shorts, a tight tank top revealing the breast over the top, and flops.

"Hey, what's the rush, you two?" Jason was smiling like he just got laid. Paulene was about the same.

Breathless, Jason said, "Its official, Luke."

"That is what?" I asked with a grin, folding my arms over my chest. Jason hesitated, but Paulene jabbed him in the ribs.

"We are now engaged to marry, Luke," he blabbered out as he stood tall.

My brows rose as I began to grin. "Serious? Are you for real? Paulene, is he?" I asked without a breath.

I saw Paulene blush as she said, "It's true, and we would like you to be the best man for it."

"I'm honored, but have you set a date yet?"

Placing his hands on his narrow hips, Jason said, "Why hell no, not yet. We just got engaged here."

"Why haven't you asked Daniel to be best man? He was your friend before me."

He became jittery as he said, "He refused and said to ask you. Cool, right?" I was about to say something when Daniel came from the house, waving his arms like a mad man.

He was flushed in the face, and grinning like the ass he was when he stopped in front of us, breathless.

"Daniel, what's the matter?" Paulene asked.

"I think I'm going to steal Kimmi from ya, Luke," he said, inhaling.

"I don't think so, bud," I said, dropping my arms and grabbing him in a bear hug. Jason jumped him from the rear, and we hit the ground rolling in a playfulness wrestle for a spell. I was feeling boyishly cool, even when Paulene joined in. I won't deny I didn't like what I saw when she leaned over. She was definitely that of a tomboy with the body of a woman. The dream flashed back at me, so I stood up, brushed off the dirt, and left them to venture inside to find Kimmi and Willa.

I found them in Willa's bedroom at the dresser, so I stood back from the doorway to eavesdrop on their conversation. Peering through the crack in the door, I saw Willa combing Kimmi's hair as she talked about me. I overheard this conversation between them.

"How long have you known Luke?" Kimmi asked, staring at Willa through the mirror.

"Many years, girl...when he was here as a child," Willa replied, with a brush in her hand, stroking Kimmi's hair.

"He was here before now?" Kimmi's trembling voice asked.

"Sure. When he was a kid, he lived here with his dad, Sam. His mom died here too." Willa let the long hair slide from her hand like silk.

"How? Was she sick?" Kimmi asked, bemused.

"No. She gave her life for him at childbirth. He should have told this to you." Willa took another down stroke on Kimmi's hair.

"It must hurt too much for him, yes?" Kimmi asked. I don't know what possessed Willa to do what she done, but I watched the view with eagerness.

Willa stopped with the hair brushing and turned the chair with Kimmi in it to face her. Leaning over to Kimmi, Willa said with an even tone, "Don't be angry with Luke when I tell you that I love him and have for a long time. When he came back a man and not a boy on those wobbly knees, well, I don't know what you have, but don't you ever hurt him. Understand? He's been through a lot not only with you, and he'll not have far to go if you do." Willa stood up as she looked down at Kimmi, who gulped hard as she pushed back in the chair. With a tender smile, Willa said, "But you know what? Now I'm glad he has you, for you have brought him life as never before. You are good for him, Kimmi. Now let us finish that beautiful hair." Willa swung Kimmi around to face the mirror as I turned to leave them alone with the girl talk, and thinking Willa never told me that she felt so passionate for me. I guess I should've known the day she showed up at my door after the car wash.

Outside, I found Daniel and Jason still wrestling while Paulene was on the sideline watching, so I joined her.

"Is she ready yet?" Paulene asked as I stopped at the car and leaned over on the hood.

"No, not yet." I laughed, dropping my head. "They are doing that hair brush thing," I said with a chuckle.

She walked over, leaned on the Charger's hood, and asked, "Have you told her?"

My heard jerked up to face her when I said, "Tell her what? How do I say it?"

"You know she'll find out some day."

"Yes. But would she believe me or leave me? She might think I'm a crazy man or something." The conversation was interrupted when Kimmi and Willa came out the door.

Kimmi's hair was the first thing I saw. Multiple strands of tresses laid over her head and shoulders like a rainbow with ribbons tied at the ends, leaving the streaks dangling by her eyes. Smiling, I knew Willa had worked her magic when Kimmi came to where I stood and rested against me, running an arm around my waist.

Placing an arm around Kimmi, I said with a smile of appreciation, knowing how Willa felt toward me, "Thanks, Willa."

Crossing her chest with both arms, she cued, "Anytime. I love her hair."

I looked at Kimmi and asked, "You ready?" She nodded yes, so we said our good-byes and left.

Kimmi had a strange glow about her as I drove her home, while she fidgeted in the seat.

Being nosy, I asked, "Hey, did you two do the girl thing, and talk about me behind my back?"

"I think you know we did." She turned to face me. "She loves you, yes? So how do you feel for her, Luke?" I was taken by the question but I answered with truth.

"I do love her but not the same as I love you. Willa has been a friend, and I'll not do anything to ruin that relationship. Please understand how I feel for you. I knew she had feelings for me, but I didn't realize they went that deep and since we are being open; I have been with her. I won't hide it, I love her in my own way. I find it harder with each passing day to say no to you." She made no sudden reply, so I kept my eyes on the road in thought of what she would possibly have to say.

With my eyes on the road I heard her turn in the seat making a little sniffle before she said, "Luke, look at me please." I slowly faced her.

With a trickling tear, she said, "Thank you for your honesty."

"Does that answer your many questions now?"

She leaned over, kissed my cheek, and whispered in my ear, "I do love you."

"And I love you," I told her, reaching out, taking her by the shoulder, and pulling her to my side. We chatted till her home came into view where I stopped at the front door and helped her out. Giving her a kiss, I told her to get ready for a special night on Saturday. She kissed me good night with a grin before going inside, and I went home knowing that Paulene was right. The time was coming that I would have to tell Kimmi about myself, but for now it was as is—a secret.

The night crept by until it was finally Saturday. I spent the day lounging around the house, waiting for the right time when I quickly dressed in shorts with a nice tee shirt and sneakers. I combed my hair back, tied it with a leather band, then took a fast look in the mirror at myself. Satisfied with my looks and anxious, I hurried out the bedroom door, went down the stairs and out the front door to the car, and drove as quickly as possible out to the Creed home. I made sure to pick Kimmi up by 7:00 p.m. as I told her. When Kimmi opened the door, she was wearing a full-length light blue sundress with the necklace I gave her hanging around her neck. She was so excited she was trembling with it. I laughed at her, and she smiled back.

I got her to the car, sat her down, then hurried to the driver side, and got in. I reached for both the door and the key at the same time.

"Where are you taking me? It's hard to contain myself," she asked as I leaned over for the door.

"It's special tonight. I cannot say," I told her, closing the door. She trembled more as the excitement grew, making her teeth chatter too. I started up the car, and pulled out the drive. With the full moon shining through the windshield, we headed to the lake.

It was silent when we crossed the bridge into the entrance. With no cars in sight, I wandered.

Kimmi turned to me in the seat with a grim look of confusion. "Why here?"

"You'll see." I brought the car to a stop, then got out, and went around to help Kimmi out. We walked to a table near the water in silence. She had just sat down when Mollie and everyone came roaring from all around the area. Some lit lanterns while others had flashlights. Some brought food and so on. Kimmi stood up to me with surprise on her face.

"What is going on, Luke?" She asked as her hands went to her face.

"Surprise, Kimmi," Everyone said at once, making her eyes water.

I took her face into my hands and asked her, "You remember when you said you wanted to be able to swim and have fun like others." She nodded.

"Well, this is my way of giving that to you tonight. No sun to harm you here. No hiding from it."

Trembling, she asked, "Why?"

"I missed your birthday, so tonight is our night—just me and you." She smiled as a tear fell, and I wiped it away. "None of those either."

She nodded, putting her arms around my neck and kissed it, whispering, "Will there be dancing?"

In one swift move, I had her in my arms, swinging her around. "Is this good?" I asked, kissing the top of her head and let her slide to the ground just when soft music began to play and smoke filled the air since someone built a fire. I took Kimmi by the hand and pulled her away from the crowd.

We stopped at the water's edge, with me staring at her in the moonlight, thinking how radiant she was right then. Dropping the glance, I slipped out of my shoes, stuck my toes in the water, and asked, "Shall we go for a swim?" I nudged her with an elbow.

She looked up at me. "I have no suit." She looked around me, then back at the water. "Skinny dipping?" she laughed.

I shook my head no and told her, "I thought you'd say no." I called Willa over to us, dragging Paulene with her.

Willa stopped in front of us and wow, she had a narrow waist with wide hips and full breasts. She had worn the green two-piece suit with a white beach towel around her waist while Paulene wore a two-piece white suit with a see-through robe around her.

"Yes, Luke," Willa said sweetly. "She needs the box?" she asked, staring at Kimmi who blushed.

I winked at her and said, "Yep." Paulene didn't ask as she took off, but it wasn't long before she returned with a square white box with a pale-blue ribbon tied around it and handed to her. Kimmi took the box with excitement and sat down in the sand like she had a new toy.

She sighed as she slowly pulled the ribbon free and opened the box. Her thin lips curled upward as she reached inside and removed a navy-blue two-piece swimsuit.

Surprised, she jumped to her feet, taking me by the neck and whispered in my ear, "Where do I change?" She trembled when I placed my hands on her hips.

Willa pulled the huge beach towel from around her and said, "Turn around, Luke." Obedient, I turned my back to the girls, who surrounded Kimmi so she could change. While she changed, I stripped down to my trunks as well, listening to the *ooh*s and *ahh*s.

It wasn't long before I heard Paulene say, "Turn around now, Luke." I faced the girls with my own excitement growing as I watched Kimmi being unwrapped like a gift when the towel was pulled free. She was so gorgeous in the suit that hid very little of the firm breasts and legs. She didn't have to ask how I thought she looked—she could see it in my face.

She came running and jumped into my arms. "Thank you, thank you," she said, planting kisses all over my face, wrapping her legs around me, and bringing back the sensational feelings of our first night at the lake.

"You're so welcome, girlfriend," I said, giving her a hug. Willa and Paulene winked at me as they made their way back to the crowd, leaving us alone. With Kimmi so full of life, I wondered what dark secret she held.

I looked at the water. "Ready?"

"Carry me, Luke. Please." She snickered. I would have readily carried her anywhere. I held her facing me and waded into the cool water.

I was at waist high when I stopped, and put Kimmi down. She clung to me for a short time, then dove into the water without a word and disappeared. I was waiting for her to surface when something grabbed me by my ankles. My first thought was that it was Kimmi being playful, but the grip was much too firm that I was pulled under. At first, it was too dark to see, but soon I saw the face of Willa, Paulene, and Sam in front of me. Sam! I sucked in water from the sight. It caught me off guard, and I surfaced so fast I lost my breath.

Sam came up next to me. "You okay there?" he asked, grinning like an ass-eating briars, and patting my back.

"Sure, but where's Kimmi?" I asked in a coughing manner. I looked but didn't see any Kimmi. Then I felt the arms come around my waist and the fingers locked.

Placing my hands on top of hers, I faced Sam. "What are you doing here? Our last phone conversation said you were going to Iraq."

His eyes glanced at Kimmi. "You should ask the young lady there." He motioned with a finger.

Feeling devilish, I asked, "Which one?" I gave a sly grin.

"The one hanging on to you for dear life." He laughed with the others who had joined in.

I felt childishly odd right then and asked, "The jokes on me, ain't it?" I gritted my teeth into a smile.

I felt the squeeze when Kimmi said, "Yes, love. This time, it is. You've done so much for me it was my turn to surprise you. Does it make you happy?" Kimmi's tone was so unnatural it made me shiver.

"Yes. Very much so," I replied, pulling her around in front of me and kissed her lightly on the lips.

Turning to Sam, I asked in a daze, "How long you been in town?"

He made a goofy grunt as he said, "Couple days"—letting it roll off his tongue.

I licked my lips and chuckled, "That long, huh? We should hang out then, tomorrow maybe."

"Sounds like a deal. Will your young lady be joining us?" I looked at Kimmi who did the double take at me.

"Well," I groaned.

"Well what?" she asked in return.

I bit the laugh and said, "You want to spend time with me and Sam tomorrow?"

She glanced at Sam and began to smile as her eyes twinkled. "Sure would. I would love to get to know your dad." She sneered.

"Good, then it's settled. Let's head up to the table. I'm a bit hungry," Sam said, turning toward the bank and waded out. I followed after Kimmi jumped on for a piggyback ride.

The picnic table was lit up like a Christmas tree with foods of all kinds to be seen. What got my attention was the sound of a small truck engine getting louder and louder that soon drowned out the music.

When it stopped, I heard someone from the crowd say, "It's here."

Kimmi whispered in my ear, "Luke, what's going on out there?"

"I haven't an idea," I said, letting her slide to the ground as we turned like all the others to watch. Flashlights ran to the darkness, lighting the truck up as a lift gate came down.

My eyes, as well as all the others, grew when a humongous crate, the size of myself, was sat off the small flatbed truck onto a black cart with four huge wheels. Sam came to me and put an arm around my shoulders as we watched like all the rest. The cart was pushed by people over the soft sand, having no trouble until it stopped at the table. It was well sealed from top to bottom with shrink wrap and tape. Three men turned and headed back to the truck, got in, and left, leaving the crate and cart. The air filled with whispers louder than the people who stood around staring.

Sam and Daniel pulled knives from their pockets and began cutting the wrapping, then slowly opened one side of the massive crate. When the flap hit the ground, sand flew everywhere, but we all continued to stare at the crate while someone went inside. The crate tilted when the man came out pushing a smaller square table with a two-tier cake with all kinds of candles on it. I heard the crowd gasp.

"Whose is it, Luke?" Kimmi asked.

"I don't know," I fibered, shrugging my shoulders. While the crowd tried to figure things out the sound of a helicopter came into hearing range. The cake was forgotten when the attention was turned to the approaching sound.

Two lights, one red and one green, made their way into view when they topped the trees. With the wind from the blades, things were being wiped around, mostly the sand, but there were *oohs* and *ahhs* from the group.

"Incoming," someone yelled from the astonished crowd. I rushed over toward the crate to cover it the same time Willa came to help. We pushed the cart back inside the crate and closed the door. Bright lights came from the helicopter, filling the sky and lighting the beach as it made its way to the ground. Kimmi ran over, grabbing me by the hand, and we moved away as the chopper came down to land. When the large blades finally stopped, a man got out.

I watched in amusement when Sam hurried over to him, shaking hands and hugging one another as if they were best friends. They walked toward the rear of the thing and faded out of sight. "What the hell is this doing here?" I mumbled to myself.

I heard Kimmi's teeth chatter before she asked, "What is that thing?" She began to tremble.

"It's a navy helicopter," I told her, wrapping an arm around her shoulders, giving her comfort.

"Whose is it?" Jason asked as he and Paulene ran over to Kimmi and me. Again, I shrugged my shoulders.

"Let's just see," I said in a whisper of puzzlement. Everyone was silent while we watched and waited for what happened next.

A loud rumbling noise came from the rear of the chopper about the time I saw Mollie and Ivan plow through the crowd, stopping next to Kimmi and me.

"What's happening?" Mollie asked, bewildered.

"Beats me," I replied, feeling everyone thought I knew the answers. Lights came from the rear of the helicopter, but it was too dark to make out what it was. They went around the opposite side and faded. Not long after, the pilot returned to the helicopter, then started it up again. Everyone braced themselves as it rose out of sight, but where was Sam? I began to feel something was oddly strange in the silence. Off in the dark, a round light began to make its way slowly toward the table. I could only hear the crunching of the sand underfoot.

I was still learning to adjust my senses to the sight, sound, and taste of the wolf. But the thing that came into light at the table had Sam sitting on it. When it stopped, he got off the shiny black seat of a new black-and-silver Harley motorcycle. My eyes widened with the gasps from the crowd as they gathered around us.

I began to stutter as I tried to ask, "What's going on, Dad?"

He smiled as his eyes toned to a warm color. "You too, Luke," he said.

"What is me too, Dad?" I was puzzled with curiosity.

"Why ask why? Just live with it. Besides, you're gonna need something to chase me with tomorrow." He laughed aloud.

"There's only one Sam and two of us. Now how's that work?" I snickered, looking around.

Sam faced the ground and laughed as he turned around. Another man came into the light, pushing a red Harley bike to the table.

The man was tall and stout with broad shoulders and light brown hair and eyes. He wore black shorts, a white tee, and sneakers. He stopped at the table and dismounted the bike.

He glanced at Sam and said in a husky voice, "Evening, Sam." He reached over and patted him on the shoulder.

Looking over at me, he said with a soft smile and very deep voice, "You are Luke, I presume. You look just like him." He looked over at Sam, who was grinning.

I nodded yes, then said, "No way!"—my eyes tearing and my mouth dropped opened.

"Yes way," Sam chuckled, glaring at me. I felt Kimmi tighten her hand in mine and whispered in my ear.

I looked at Sam and asked, "The cake?"

"Oh yes, that's for the young lady behind you. Come now, it's late, but it's here. Happy birthday."

"Thank you, Sam," she muttered in a weak tone of not sure what to do.

Sam broke out into a laugh as he said, "It wasn't me. I just helped with it."

Kimmi's mouth dropped open as she looked at me, "Luke."

I was just as surprised as she was when I said, "Not me, honey. Sorry." Both of us were in confusion as to who made the appearance happen when no one moved as they looked around at each other. Puzzlement was going among the group since no one had said a single word.

Suddenly, Ivan came forth, pulling Mollie with him. I could see Casey and Chase standing in the distance of the dark. I waved at them, and they returned the same. The man and woman stopped at the table to face Kimmi, who was bewildered by them.

Both in tune together said, "Happy birthday, Kimmi. From the family."

Kimmi gasped as her eyes watered, ran to Mollie, and wrapped her arms around her neck as she cried, "Thank you, both." She glanced up over Mollie's shoulder and smiled at the two in the dark. They waved back as they turned and walked off.

I could no longer hold back my tears as I watched Kimmi's fall. Sam came to me with a hug that I returned readily.

I could smell his scent as I laid my head on his shoulder and asked, "Why have you done this tonight?"

He sighed as he pulled me tight, "You may be a man, Luke, but you'll always be my son. It's time I treated you as one." He sighed, and then told me about the day I called Willa with my plans. What I didn't know was Kimmi was there at the time. Willa made this happen, but it was Kimmi who had called Sam and told him to please come. He agreed to the plea.

"Thank you." I sighed, tightening the grip around his neck.

"You're welcome, son," he whispered, returning the favor. I can't say how long we stood there, but I loved every minute of it.

I began to notice his scent, realizing that my senses were becoming more sensitive as I began to wonder if he knew what I was.

My train of thought was broken when Kimmi asked, "May I?" I looked to see she had a camera in hand.

Turning with an arm around each other's neck, Sam replied with a grin, "Sure thing, young lady."

I composed myself and faced Kimmi with a smile as she took several pictures of my dad and me.

Sam in turn took a couple of me and Kimmi together. Time had proven how much I loved my father as a child but more as a man when I stood back and watched him with Kimmi. Willa had outdone herself with her magic, and I was grateful. I rejoined the party, until everyone finished. After we cleaned the place up, we all headed home. I took Kimmi home, and then told her I'd pick her up later. We kissed a long good night before I left and went home for the night. My night was dreamless by the time I did get to bed around 2:00 a.m.

RECALLING

I ROSE BEFORE DAWN the next morning to shower then dressed in blue jeans, a flannel shirt tucked in, and a black belt and boots. I combed my damp hair, ran down the stairs and out the door to the car. I hurriedly picked up Kimmi, who was exquisitely dressed in a velvet, full-length red-and-gold gown with a V-cut front and back and long sleeves with diamond-cuts at the wrists. Her hair hung loosely placed with combs and two sapphire studs hung in each lobe. She was as excited as I was to see Sam for the day. I helped her into the car, then raced out to the old man's place.

The sun was just peering over the rim of the mountain by the time we arrived at Luther's where he and Sam were sitting in the rockers on the porch drinking coffee. I parked behind the jalopy where I had the door open and nearly falling out to rush around and help Kimmi out of the car. Hand in hand, we walked to them where I could see they were taken by her view. I saw Sam's mouth water, even as he held back, making my head sort of swell.

"Morning, old man," I said, stopping at the base of the steps.

With a snarled grin, Sam asked, "Which one?"

"This one of course," I said, pointing to Whitecloud.

He may be old but not blind as his brows raised high at her. "How do you do, Ms. Kimmi?" he asked in a downy nature.

I watched her cheeks dimple when she replied, "Very carefully, sir." To please Kimmi, both men, being the men they were, rose from their seats in a bow.

Sam's eyes glared at me. "She could teach you a few things, Luke," he said, sitting down.

"That—she can," I said with a leer, placing an arm around her waist.

Luther crossed his legs with a grunt when Sam asked, "You ready for that run?"

"Sure. Where are the bikes?" I asked, glancing around.

Sam looked at Whitecloud then me. "I never meant that run. The other one, if it's okay with the lady?" He winked at Kimmi, and my heart went into my throat like a lump.

Right then, I knew what he meant, and I shook my head with a slight no, so Kimmi didn't see. He replied with an eye, making me swallow hard for he was just about to give me away.

Luther, catching the moment, finally said, "The bikes are around back."

A heavy burden lifted, letting me sigh. "We need to talk anyway." I looked into Sam's understanding eyes. He nodded, and I left Kimmi with the men, going around the house to find the bikes under a tarp. I pulled the tarp and brought them one at a time to the front. On the last trip, I found Sam on the lawn and Kimmi seated in his seat. I bounced up on the porch and kissed her while Sam took the black bike and sat down on the seat. Taking the red bike, we fired them up and rode off toward the east.

I followed Sam, letting the wind take me to a world of my own until we got to the gorge. A place where I nearly died as child and hadn't visited since my return. What was his reason for going there then was uncanny. Stopping on the shoulder, we got off the bikes, and I looked out over the ravine, shading my eyes from the sun. Sam was quite for bit while he took a long glance at the mountain.

Sam faced me with sad eyes and said, "I assume you have spoken with Jess?"

Going toward him, I replied, "I have, yes. What's wrong, dad?"

His eyes searched for the right words before he said, "When you met Jess, did he tell you the whole story about what happened that night or just his part?"

I wasn't sure how to answer, so I told him what I was told. "Jess told me he and Jay crashed into you that night, pushed you off the road, and how he tried to stop Jay but failed to listen."

His eyes said a lot but not of what I was about to hear from him with my own ears. "Son, if I could have gotten my hands on both of them, I would have killed them right where they stood that night." I saw tears in my father's eyes before he wiped them away. I knew about pain, but it did not compare to what he had to say.

"Talk to me, dad," I pleaded.

Sam swallowed hard, then said, "The Ludlows had time after time threatened to kill you for the life of Nettie. Deep down in my chest, I had always feared it."

"It was the last day of summer, and we were heading back home from our last swim before we left town. We were with Jack and Jason when it had started raining, and it was dark and very late. You and Jason were just tots in the back seat of the Charger."

That was where I got the feeling that there was something sinister about the car.

"Jack and I talked about my leaving with you, where I would take you for safety, and how long did I think before Jay would just give up on me and you. Jack was a good man and father to Jason. I was more than angry the night he died. He was one of my closest friends other than Tom and Mac. We were talking when I noticed a bunch of bright lights coming up on us fast in the rearview. I sped up a little so it would go on and pass, but it just hung back there, blinding me with those lights. I moved over to the shoulder even, but that was to no avail."

"Why did you not talk to me about this?" I read his face as he looked for words to make me understand. I felt a little resentment growing.

"Do I detect resentment?" Sam cursed under his breath. "Well drop it, because I was alone with a motherless child and hurt from her death with the thought of losing you as well that night. I couldn't endure the pain then, and I didn't want you to have to either." He looked over the horizon as he placed his hands on his hips.

"With the road wet and all, it was easy for me to lose control of the car as we spun around in the middle. When we stopped, we were facing crossed way in the road, and that truck coming at us. I tried to start the engine but the car had stalled. Jack and you were in the passenger seat when it hit and pushed us over the side into the ravine. We rolled two or three times I guess, before we finally stopped. I gathered my surroundings and realized we were upside down with the wheels spinning overhead. I heard the truck stop, but I didn't hear any doors open or close. I looked over at Jack, who was slumped half in the seat and his neck was broken with his head hung over his shoulder. I think his back was too."

I felt he was reliving the night in his mind when he faced me, and put his hands in his pants pockets.

"It's just that night when I looked for you and Jason over the seat, I couldn't see either of you. So I panicked as I vigorously tried to unfasten the seatbelt as quick as I could. Then there was the smell of gas, making me work harder with a belt that wouldn't come lose. When that didn't work, I fumbled for my knife around the dash and finally found it. I cut the belt free, then fell hitting my head. Feeling the warm blood drip over my eyes, I quickly reached over and yanked on the door handle till it opened. That's when I heard the truck's tires spin on the pavement, squealing off into the darkness, leaving us for dead. When I rolled out onto the grass, I was dazed and hurt. My nose was bleeding, my hand bled from the glass, and the split over my eye. At that particular time, I thought I had lost you. I tried looking around when I saw what I thought was a white glow, I think."

His eyes narrowed when he stopped momentarily to gather his thoughts as a painful expression came across his face.

I felt anguish for him. "Dad, why was Jess never tried for attempted murder?"

Sam's mouth somewhat curved when he said, "The elders saw to it that he was banished only to stay on the reservation for his remaining life. Jay is yet to be caught."

"Finish telling me what happened please. What was the glow you saw?" I began to think he was dazed and confused to the point that he was out of his mind when he hit his head. The sun slid down the mountain ridge, leaving us in the dim light. Sam dropped his gaze as he turned toward the ravine. I heard him huff.

"I don't know. It came down and pulled you and Jason from the car. I tried to stand, but my left leg was broken, so I began crawling with my elbows digging into the earth. But it left before I could get to you. Both you and Jason were laid out on the grass of the shoulder. Jason was okay, but you…I thought you were dead when I felt no heartbeat or pulse. The cuts on your head and neck were deep, covering you in blood. I began yelling at the gods for letting it happen. I cursed the spirits to hell for my anguish, but after awhile I composed myself.

"I had tears in my eyes and anger in my heart for I knew you were dead. Somewhere in me, I found an inner thing that made me stand up. I picked you both up, one in each arm, and walked with a broken leg to Whitecloud's. When I got to him, he offered help, but I just left you two there and went home—the home I built for Nettie, the home you were born in."

When he paused, he faced me and asked, "Want to take a little ride? It's just a short distance to the place you were born."

Of course I was willing to go. We quickly got on the bikes and drove north about five miles. Turning off onto a narrow tree covered dirt road, Sam led me over a small hill into a clearing. I found a huge willow tree shading a pile of rubble overgrown with weeds inside a picket fence and a small pond. Stopping the bike, I was mesmerized by the view of why the house was not standing. Getting off the bikes, Sam walked to the fence and stopped, placing his hands on his hips when he began to speak.

"I bought a fifth of whiskey on the way, stopped at the shed out back, got a can of gas, and went inside to the kitchen. There I sat the can on the floor while I sat at the table with the bottle of whiskey, which I drank in its entirety as I made plans to burn the house down with me in it. The bottle was so I didn't feel the pain so much."

Breaking in on his story, I cried, "You didn't mean you were going to...?" I let it trail off. I felt tears in my eyes as they watered. I sniffled.

"Yes, yes I was. You were gone, and Nettie was gone. I had nothing to live for any longer. I had the gas can sitting at the table with me, so when I was done with the bottle, I tossed it at the fireplace in the front room as I reached for the gas can.

"Starting in the kitchen, I poured gas all over everything, then down the hallway to our bedroom, the bed, your room, and finally I stopped in the front room, staggering from the whiskey in me. I drenched the sofa and myself, then dropped the can to fumble for the box of matches I had stuck in my boot so they wouldn't get wet. I prayed for forgiveness as I pulled the tiny stick from the box and effortlessly struck the match. Letting it burn down to my fingers, I tossed it onto the sofa, and watched it smolder like it was going out, but it took no time to flame up. I watched the slow fire roll off the couch onto the floor and ease across to the curtains. It raced its way toward me, but I stood fast as it inched closer to me. Smoke soon took over, and I began to pass out. Just before I completely lost consciousness, I saw that glow again, and I swear I felt it take me by the arm and pull me from the fire.

"The next day, I still didn't know you were alive when I woke up at Luther's place. I rose from the bed to find he had put a splint on my leg. I found I had slight burn marks on my arms, and there was something else. Long slender fingerprints around my arms just below the elbows where the thing had taken hold of me. I shook it off when I stood up, and got my balance. With my wife and child both gone, I only had one thing in mind as I stumbled out into the hall toward the kitchen. I wanted death more than anything.

"I stopped in the small doorway and found Whitecloud at the table with his back toward the door as usual. I leaned on the wall when I heard him chuckle as if he were reading the paper or saw something funny. But when he turned around in that chair, I was no longer able to support myself when I saw you in his arms. I slid to the floor in disbelief of the view, right there in the doorway. I cried as I thanked the Great Spirit for your life while I watched Luther stitch your wounds and clean you up."

I wiped my tears as they flowed freely while Sam took my shoulders with both hands and gently squeezed them when he said, "Now, Luke, tell me. How do you tell a child with no memory of it, or better, how do you explain it so they would understand?"

I thought I completely understood until my dad said, "When the headaches came, I was hoping they would pass, but they didn't, so here you are. I was so hurt from your mother's death I didn't know where to even start with the heritage thing. I will say this, son: I hope you never know the feelings of what I endured in life."

I turned to Sam not as a child or a man but his son, and took him around the neck in my arms, hugging him hard and long as a son would. "I love you, Dad," I muffled, nudging my head into his shoulder.

"I love you too, son," he said, pulling me closer. I felt a sense of relief with the tears I couldn't hold back while they flowed like wine onto his shirt. Moisture gathered under my cheek as I listened to his heartbeat mixed with mine. He knew what I was, and I thanked God for that. After a time, we composed ourselves, got on the bikes, and headed back to Whitecloud's with the thought that someday I would return to see what that monster held.

The old man's place was coming into view when I saw Kimmi run off the porch toward us, but in the same instant, I saw a brown wolf charge at her from the woods. When Sam looked back at me and nodded, I thought the only way to get to her was to change to my wolf, only I chose not to. Gearing the bike faster, I raced time with every beat of my heart until she happened to turn around. Her hands went to her face when she screamed in horror just as the thing caught a corner of her gown on the pass. When Kimmi tripped over the gown, it drug her across the ground until the gown gave way, letting the beast continue into the woods. I heard Sam yell over the noise of the bikes that he would tend to her and that I should go after the thing. I roared off into the darkening trees where I last saw the thing vanish. I can't say how long I simply drove around looking for it, but it had given me the slip, so I turned the bike back to the house.

I dropped the bike at the porch as I jumped off, taking the steps with one leap, striding over the floor, and into the house where I found Sam and the old man in the living room. Kimmi was on the sofa, covered with a blanket. I sat down with her, and took her cold and tender hand from under the warm blanket. Whitecloud rose, excused himself, and left the room to me and Sam.

"She'll be fine soon. It was the shock of what she saw," Sam said as soon as Luther was gone.

In a mere whisper, I said, "I just hadn't told her yet. I don't know how to, Dad."

"I know, son. It's hard to tell someone something that she'll never understand. You will have to tell her eventually."

"Did mom know about these things before her death?" I asked, raising only my lids at Sam.

"Yes," Whitecloud replied when he came in the room carrying a tray toward the sofa.

When he sat it on the pine coffee table in front of the sofa, I saw it had a silver teapot with one cup. "This will help her," he said, pouring the warm liquid into the small cup. He handed it to me as I looked up at him, taking it with shaky hands. I lifted her head gently with one hand and put the cup to her lips with the other. I tilted the cup slowly as she took it in. With the tea gone, I put the cup back on the tray, then let her head rest back on the pillow.

"She should rest now. She had an uninvited guest. Let's go out onto the porch for now," he continued. I rose from the sofa, kissed her forehead, and followed them outside into the cool night.

The two men sat in the chairs while I stood, leaning on one of the porch pillars. Our conversation was heating up. I gulped hard as I faced Sam and said, "I know, but how do I tell her, Dad?"

No one heard Kimmi come to the door until she spoke, "Tell me what, Luke?" I turned around to see her standing at the doorway in a cotton flannel robe and white socks on her feet. She was totally out of her attire, but I found her breathtaking at the moment.

"It's a family secret, and I'm not sure I'm ready for you to know, okay?" I said, giving both men a daring plea. She looked hurt as if I didn't trust her enough.

I took a step toward the door and whispered, "Honey, look at me." I placed my hand on the door. "You once asked for my patience. Now I am asking for yours. Please, please give me time. I am still looking for the right words to tell you." She opened the door and stepped out where I took her to me, placing my cheek to hers.

I whispered in her ear only for her to hear, "Just a little more time please."

She placed her cold hands on my hips. "Then time you shall have," she said with an undertone. With that, we spent the rest of the time with Sam, who agreed to stay until after the harvest which was the following day. We talked till midnight, said our good-byes, and I took her home. I went to Mae's for a quick shower and dressed for bed where I began to dream a dream that would make any man suffer, but I was hooked to my companion.

"Luke, wake up." I felt a warm wet thing on my face, so I opened my eyes to blurry things in the room. I rubbed them, but still the view was blurry.

"Luke," a female voice called out in the dark.

Sitting up on the side of the bed, I asked, "Who are you? You're not the companion."

"No, but I am here with you. It's time you have some fun. Come now. I brought a friend."

"Please do," another female said with eagerness. Unable to stop, I rose from the bed and was taken by the hand of the ones I couldn't see.

"You wish to reminisce with your father. Then you'll love this and will remember it for a long time to come," the companion growled. I liked this fellow more and more when we walked through a narrow doorway and stopped.

I had no clue where I was or where we were going but it was a misty dark and blurred visions around me. I soon felt a pair of hands on my chest that slid up to my neck, then down over my shoulders. I shivered from the feeling when they stopped at my waist.

"Let's remove that confining thing." Tugging at the shirt, the female sighed softly, running a hand underneath to my nipple, and gave it a tender pinch which I rather liked, sighing from the pleasure.

I reached for her but she quickly moved away and said with a gentle laugh, "Not just yet."

A pair of hands gave me a gentle push forward when I asked, "Who are you?" I stumbled forward in the dark, reaching for anything to grab.

Sighing, the female replied, "They call me regret." The voice coming from behind me pulled on the shirt again. I stopped only to feel hands roaming my body from neck to back to front and then special attention to the groins. Enticed, I gladly removed the shirt and let it drop. Next, I was taken by the hand again, being pulled forward a few steps, then suddenly pushed backward. Gasping in surprise from the push, I fell backward onto a mattress, running my hands over the softness of silk and lace.

Unable to see, I lay there in the silent darkness until a tiny light began to glow from god-knows-where in the room. But I didn't care when a woman with auburn hair and green eyes stood over me in a sheer robe with nothing hidden.

Smiling, she said, "A handsome one you are." She removed the robe, revealing a set of full breasts with a silver ring in each of the nipples, a thin chain around the waist, and curves in the right places. She grabbed my knees, and with a sudden pull, she spread them with ease and stepped between, running her hands up my thighs to the waist of the boxers. Hopeless to the pleasures, I laid there while she teased parts of my body with her wet and warm lips that I thought had no feelings. What I didn't notice at first was a second woman had joined us.

She had dark brown hair with many curls, and a diamond in her nose and bottom lip. She eased up to my neck, licking it, and the ear, making her way down to my chest where she laid over me and bit my nipple with a tease. I gasped from the suddenness of the move but moaned from the pleasure of it.

After I caught my breath from the tingle of the bite, I asked her in a groaning whisper, "Who are you?"

Licking the tingling nipple, she whispered, "I am sorrow, my friend." I felt like I had been drugged when the room began to whirl around me. Nothing else mattered, and I didn't care while the sensations sent me to new heights of pleasure. Even Willa couldn't have been as sensual as those ladies were. All I knew was I couldn't tell anyone how it felt or how I felt, but I was lost to the ways of a woman right then. The pleasure they brought were unmentionable, and I loved every minute of it. That was every man's dream, and I had one of the ladies in each arm while they caressed me and themselves. That was when I woke up.

I sat upright in the bed with sweat dripping off me, needing a shower. When I got up, I noticed my shirt and boxers were missing. "Impossible," I groaned, grabbing clean ones from the dresser. But, the feeling of pleasure was still there. Rushing to the bathroom, I made the water hotter than usual to wash off the feeling that I had come to like. I was beginning to like things too much, but those were supposed to be only dreams. After the shower, I returned to bed at 4:10 a.m. with no more dreams.

OBSERVED

I T WAS STILL early by the time I got out to Luther's to help in the field. Sam was still sawing logs, so I joined the others in gathering the early crop of sweet white corn. I had just cut an ear when I felt the eyes on my back. In an instant, I knew who it was before I spun around to see Kimmi coming toward me in a cute calf-length yellowish dress, wearing a hat and flops. I smiled at her, shaking my head for she had never dressed in such a way. Truthfully, I was growing to like her attire instead of those long gowns.

She stopped in front of me, looking up from under the hat and asked in that special way of hers, "Can I help?"

I shook my head in disbelief at first, then asked, "Know how?"

She bit the tip of her tongue and said, "No. But you can teach me." She grinned.

Surprised, I chuckled, "Seriously, Kimmi."

"Yes. If I am to be with you, then I want to know all that you do."

"Well then, come here." I waved for her, stepping toward a stalk with her trailing along. I shook the feeling we were being watched.

We had been watching the boy Luke in the field when the girl showed up. I squatted down while Jay stepped behind the tree toward me.

121

"Times acoming, Cole, she'll be yours soon enough, but I want that boy, you hear." He snapped with force in his tone. Not sure if it was fear or the man himself, but I agreed with a muffled yes.

I momentarily watched Kimmi before continuing what I was doing after the feeling passed. Kimmi wasn't aware of it. If she was, she played it off well.

When the sun had finally gotten too much for Kimmi, she left her corn on the ground where I picked it up when I finished the row I was working on. Wiping my brow, I faced the barn--a two-story red-oak frame house--with a rusted tin roof and a large window with two shutters open over the double doors leading into the barn. Walking toward it, I could see hay bales double stacked on the second floor. Inside, hay was scattered all over the place, which was not unusual. Like all the rest, it was tall with tools, carts, bags, and things for the market that would come soon. They were things that took place to make monies for the people of the tribe. I finally found the cart with the other corn and dropped the bag in with them.

I walked out of the barn and was looking at the old place in thought when I felt someone or something staring at my back. I thought it was Kimmi at first until I looked and found no one there. With the feeling gone, I shielded my eyes to see across the pasture. I got a sudden chill and brushed it off until I turned toward the house and bumped onto Tom, who had snuck up behind me.

"Damn," I swore under my breath, facing the big man. With a little growl in my voice, I said, "Why do you do that, Tom?" I laughed.

His lips curled up. "What's that?" He cackled.

"Sneak up on people," I said, stepping into the warmth of the sun.

"Well, if you keep your senses tuned, I wouldn't, would I? I keep you on your toes." He was right when times caught me off guard.

After we got our wits back together, I faced the ridge in thought of what I saw earlier. I covered my eyes to get a better look.

Tom stepped next to me and covered his eyes as he looked. "You see something out there?"

"Yeah but...well...I've had this feeling of sorts, and I can't put a finger on it. It's like I'm being watched, or would that be being followed?"

He nodded his head as he replied, "Yeah, it's been coming and going here lately. We'll catch him in time." He sort of looked down at me since he was taller than I and said, "You should get on home now."

"If you insist." I grinned.

"I most certainly do," he chuckled, grabbing me around the neck, playfully horsing around a bit before heading toward the house where everyone else had gone already.

I stopped at the porch to speak with Whitecloud, who was taking it easy with a cup of coffee and his pipe. He was sitting back in his overalls, long-sleeved shirt, and work boots.

I leaned on the rail and said, "It's almost finished." I whistled, aiming to mock him in a joking manner.

Pulling on the pipe, he let the smoke slide through his lips and said, "Thank you."

"Where's Sam?" I began to laugh. "Cutting logs still?"

"He is. Now get out of here for awhile," he said, fanning his hand.

"Well, if you'll excuse me then," I said with a laugh as I walked to the car and got in. I waved as I left them on the porch.

With the radio playing, my mind was lost until I had to stop at a light facing a 4x4 Ford on the opposite side of the road facing me. When the light changed and we crossed the road in the middle, I looked up at a dark blue Expedition with dark windows. The driver's side window was down, revealing a male with short black hair, light brown eyes, and about my age, looking down at me. The look he gave me was no doubt as if he knew me. *Not possible*, I thought, wondering who he was as I watched the vehicle fade out of sight in the rearview. I shook it off, because I had a date waiting. I mashed the pedal and hurried toward home where I rushed in and showered.

After the shower, I ran across the hall into my room where I rambled through the closet for a nice pair of jeans and a dress shirt. Finding both I went to the dresser to locate under clothes. After dressing rather quickly, I looked at myself in the mirror on the closet door. Looking back at me was a nice young Indian man with long black hair and dark eyes. The vision that came out next to it was a mild-colored wolf with amber eyes. When I noticed that my left eye had a slightly different sort of tint to it, I leaned into the mirror. Unable to tell for sure, I passed it off with a shake of the head, found my boots in the closet, and put them on.

Fully dressed, I felt good but odd at the same time. I grinned to myself at the thought of how long it really had been since the last time I had been out. It was with Kenna and a buddy of his about seven years ago. Hell, we were kids when we went to that dance in a barn. Ever since then, I had not been so well dressed for going out. I combed my wet hair and left it hanging, left the room, and took the stairs two at a time till I reached the bottom, and yelled at Mae I'd be back later. I didn't hear the reply as I closed the front door behind me and headed for the Camero.

The drive out to Kimmi's was fairly nice, even as I went up the hilly road and into the drive where I parked near the old oak tree. Killing the engine, I got out, walked up the steps to the front door, and knocked softly. Casey opened the door, nicely dressed in a bright red full-length satin dress with short sleeves at the forearms, a split up the left leg to the knee, and her hair up with the ends dangling at the neck.

Her brows rose as she whispered, "Oh, you look nice, Luke, but she's not ready yet."

"Thank you, and that's fine," I said, stepping in the door. "You're looking good yourself." I stopped to give her a peck on the cheek.

"Well, thank you," she said with a blush before closing the door. I started toward the den when she took me by the arm, tagging along with her heels tapping the floor.

We stopped in front of the double doors as I reached for the knobs, and Casey dropped her hold on my arm. I turned the knobs and push inward, making the doors swing open. I went through the door toward the first couch.

"Where's Chase these days?" I asked, sitting down on the sofa.

"He's away for awhile," she answered as she flopped down the opposing sofa.

"When will he be back? He has been gone for some time now, hasn't he?"

"He's only been gone a few days now. He should return in a month or so."

I glared at her with a smile. "I'm being noisy, but where is he?" I teased with a wink.

"Damn," she snapped. "Gone to see the Marswaye. Happy now?" She growled as her eyes narrowed.

"Testy, are we? I'm just funning, kid." I leered at her before sliding back on the cushion.

"Evening, Luke," Mollie said from the door. I rose from the sofa at the statement and her heels tapping on the floor.

She was well dressed in a hunter-green and lace evening gown at calf-length. Her perfume was nice, not too sweet. Her hair pulled back with combs revealed an emerald earring in each ear and finally the emerald pendant on her shoulder.

"Evening, Mrs. Creed. You're looking good."

"Thank you, Luke. Where is Kimmi?" she asked, looking around for her.

"Not down yet," Casey softly replied.

"Speaking of Kimmi, where is Ivan?" I asked, looking over my shoulder.

"He too is not ready," Mollie laughingly said. "Talk about women." She came over and sat down on the couch with Casey. Talk was small while we waited for Kimmi and Ivan.

We had just ended a conversation when the den door opened slowly and Kimmi stepped in wearing a form-fitting full-length black and white cotton dress with one strap over the left shoulder, her black heeled shoes tapping the wood as she came toward the sofa and me. Her ears had two diamond studs in each lobe. Her hair was pulled from the front and fastened in the back.

My heart fluttered like butterfly wings when I said, "You got it going on, lady." I couldn't help myself when I whistled at her.

Blushing, she said, "I'm glad you like it. Willa loaned me the dress, and Casey helped with the rest."

"Willa did right by you, and Casey you're good," I groaned with pleasure. "Thank you," I said, facing Kimmi whose petite body I took into my arms and of whom I kissed the top of the head.

I pushed back looking into her eyes and asked, "Ready?"

"I suppose I'm about as ready as I'm gonna get." She sighed, putting an arm around my waist. I placed one over her shoulder, and we walked to the front door. Opening and closing the door, we walked off the porch to the awaiting carriage for tonight. I took her to the nicest little hideaway restaurant Mae told me about, where the lights were dim and we could be alone.

I drove up to a small place just west of town and recognized it after numerous times on my way to somewhere. It had a blinking green-neon sign that read *Back Forty Diner*. I parked up front near the doors, and quickly got out to rush around to help her out of the car. We stood at the hood, looking at the four steps leading up to the double glass doors that had two large windows with beer signs and other stuff. Below the glowing neon sign, it read *open*. Kimmi's hand was vibrating inside mine.

"You okay?" I asked, looking at her. "You're trembling."

"Just a bit nervous," she whispered. I squeezed her hand gently as I led her up the steps to the door where I pulled it open and followed her inside.

The inside was dark at first, but then it became brighter. The place was busy that night, and the hostess was a young black woman in a blue shirt with short sleeves, dark blue pants, and black shoes. She greeted us, then led us to a corner booth in the back were the lighting was dim. The booth was fairly large with a flower center arrangement. I seated Kimmi and then sat down next to her.

"What will ya'll have to drink?" the young woman asked.

"Tea for me," I said, facing Kimmi, who didn't know what to say. "What do you want to drink honey?"

"Water," she finally announced. I looked at the lady with a smile, and she nodded with agreement, then left.

I turned my attention back to Kimmi, who was busy looking the place over with interest.

"Oh, Luke, this is great. Thank you very much," she quickly said with zest in her tone.

"You're more than welcome, and I thought I would treat you," I said, sliding closer.

She looked toward me, then over my shoulder, and said with a slight smile, "People are beginning to stare." She dropped her gaze to eye level with me.

"Don't let them bother you," I replied to her, taking her hand and never looking back. "They are as I once was: curious of what they don't know." She seemed more at ease with that, and we talked until I began to feel eyes on me. I turned around to find Sam standing behind me with arm on the back of the booth.

My expression told a hundred stories while I sat there and stared at him in disbelief once again.

He waited patiently while I found my tongue and said, "Have a seat, Dad."

He sat down across from us and said, "I thought you'd be here, couldn't find anywhere else."

"What brings you out tonight?" Kimmi asked.

"Giving thanks with you two." He looked at me as he said, "Above all—you."

I felt a sudden warmth inside. "Thanks a lot, Dad. I'm glad you're here with us." The hostess came around and took Sam's drink order, then vanished again. Talk was about him, and when he was leaving, until I felt that odd and strange presence again.

I sat back in the seat, looking around, but I still saw no one unusual. Only a blonde-haired girl from town came in with little to nothing on in way of clothing as she passed by wearing a miniskirt that stopped just under her butt cheek, a shirt that hid nothing, and heels. She walked past us while staring at me as she made her way to a nearby table. I spied on her as she sat down at a table with the man I had seen earlier that day in the Ford.

"Luke. What you looking at there?" Kimmi asked, putting a hand on my arm.

"Oh nothing. Just thought I knew that guy." I looked back at Kimmi, and she smiled.

Sam laughed out as he looked back at me and said, "Not anything to imagine, is there?"

"Well now!" Kimmi proclaimed aloud, causing us to break out into a laugh just as the waitress finally came to the table to take our orders.

She was a pale teen with light brown hair and eyes, wearing a white shirt, navy-blue pants, and black shoes. Pulling out her notepad, she asked, "Are y'all ready to order?"

"Shall we order now? Are you hungry yet?" I asked, holding the menu up.

"Yes, but I feel out of place here," Kimmi implied.

"That's because you've never been to a place like this. You'll get used to it," I said, patting her hand.

She sighed in a whisper, "Okay, then. I guess we should order." She looked at Sam, who grabbed his menu up, then glanced through it only to lay it back down with a grunt. I smiled as I opened the menu, then slid closer to her side to discuss what we wanted.

Kimmi settled on the small chicken platter with a side salad and water, whereas I chose the ham and turkey double decker with chips, a pickle, and Pepsi. Sam grinned and took the works: a ham steak platter with mash potatoes, some other veggie, and tea. Afterwards, dessert was a banana split for Kimmi and I. Sam had a slice of apple pie with ice cream. The night went well until Kimmi became silent as if frightened of something. Both Sam and I looked at each other, shrugging our shoulders.

Facing her, I whispered in her ear, "Honey, what's the matter?"

Inhaling, she whispered, "It's nothing to worry about. I just feel strange for some reason."

"Other than that, you feel alright?" I asked, raising my hand for the check.

"Yes." She smiled as the teenager came to the table.

Sam took the check. "It's on me tonight," he said as the young girl left.

"Thanks," I told him as we slid out of the booth and headed for the door. With the meal over and the check paid, we left the diner. I helped Kimmi out to the car, and told Sam I'd see him before he left. He agreed with a hug and told Kimmi good night, and we parted ways.

The reservoir was coming into sight, and Kimmi wanted to stop before she went home, so I pulled across the bridge and parked. I helped her out, and we went to a table near the water where I sat with Kimmi straddled between my knees as I sat on the tabletop.

"Luke, I wish tonight and all others could go on forever like this," she said as I pulled her back on me.

"I do too, and I'll spend what time I can to make it as long as possible for you." Deep inside, I was longing to tell her the truth.

She placed her arms across my knees. "Yeah, I wished." She giggled.

I had a sudden urge come over me. "I'll be right back," I said, jumping up and ran to the car.

I stopped at the driver door the same time I heard her shout, "Hey, where are you going now?"

I opened the door as I replied, "Be right there. Hang on." I got in and tuned the car, so the headlights would shine toward the table.

Kimmi flinched at first as she shaded her face. I turned on the radio, found an all-night station with soft music, and turned it up loud where we could hear it. I went back to the table where Kimmi was and held out my hand. She just sat there not knowing what it meant.

I smiled and said, "Take my hand and come with me."

She cringed, sighing. "To where?"

"Take my hand, and I'll show you." She hesitated, then placed a cold trembling hand in mine, and I pulled her to her feet. She made a giggling sound as her feet drug the sand. She followed me as we moved away from the table.

On the opposite side of the table, I stopped and pulled her to face me. She looked a bit tense as she asked, "Here? Now?" She laughed.

"You just hang on a minute and see." Slowly I took her by the hips and moved her body close to mine, taking her left hand to my right shoulder as I placed the arm around her waist and said, "Don't move it."

Her eyes looked at me, surprised. I took my left hand into her right and said, "One dance. Please. I've longed to hold you since we never got to at the beach that night." She watched my eyes for a time before stumbling. In a moment's time, we both went to the ground, landing in the sand and began rolling with laughter.

"I'm sorry." She laughed, rolling to face me with sand all in her hair. She laid her head upon my chest while I placed a hand on her back.

The thought that crossed my mind was devilish, but I said, "Someday soon." I put the other arm under my head and stared into the starry sky.

Listening to Luke's heartbeat, I wondered if I could ever tell him about the real me, if he would laugh or leave. Magnyss said it was forbidden to tell anyone the truth. That was why my mother was killed.

She felt enticing like the dream did, but I pushed it aside while we watched the clouds cover the shining stars. Soon a far off rumble of thunder brought a lighting strike from the west. The clouds moved in faster, so I got up, helped Kimmi to her feet, and brushed her off. Instantly, I felt someone was watching us. Kimmi instantly looked off toward the direction but said nothing.

I watched the two playing in the sand like his father and mother used to do when Nettie was still alive. The only thing that lingered in my head was revenge. Somehow, someway, I was going to get it. It was a shame that Sam didn't come with them. I could've finished it in one night. When they noticed my presence, I backed farther into the trees and left.

I picked her up, rushing to the car, and closed the door. I took her home, gave her a kiss at the front door, and told her good night. I returned to the car with a feeling I was being followed. Unable to see anything in the dark, I got in the car and went out to see Daniel.

I arrived at Daniel's place around 10:00 p.m., parked, went to the door, and knocked. Willa opened it with a surprised faced followed by a smile. She had on a tan see-through nightie with a housecoat. Her hair was up in a bun or something.

"Bedroom," she said, standing on tip toes to peck me on the cheek.

Looking her up and down, I sighed and said, "Thanks." I went through the living room, down the narrow hall two doors down, and found him in his room playing on the Xbox.

"Hey, Luke. How the hell ya doing?" he quickly asked when he looked up from the game he was playing. His attire was that of boxers and no shirt, sitting on the floor in front of the small TV.

"Good for now. How about yourself?"

"Should you ask that?" he said with a soft giggle in his voice. Daniel geared the control for the racing game he was playing while I sat down in the chair nearby. I watched for a while, not realizing I dozed off while Daniel raced on.

I didn't know where I was or going, but I thought I saw Kimmi in the distance.

I called, "That you? Oh, I see now. Your hair gave you away." The moon lit the dark sky, and I could see she was wearing a black gothic sort of full-length gown that flared at the bottom with a purple trim that went up over her breast in a heart shape and trailed off in a shear high collar.

Lifting a finger to me, she sighed, "Come here."

I watched her slide one shoulder of the gown off as I asked, "Why are you here?"

She faced me and said, "For you, my love." Then she let the gown drop to the ground.

In the dim light of the moon, she was totally nude with a thin chain around her waist and a horseshoe ring in her navel. With full bust and nice curves, she began to walk toward me. I felt I was being pulled toward her.

"She wants it as much as you do. Go to her," my companion devilishly snarled.

"Here, let us help you." The women from the prior dream took my hands and pulled me toward Kimmi, who was sitting on a blanket in the middle of the thick forest. The trees closed in on us the closer I got. I couldn't resist the temptation of the one I loved. Yes, I wanted her badly, so I stopped at the edge of the blanket, and with the help of the two women, I was stripped of my shirt and shorts, and left standing there. I felt unstoppable when I knelt down to Kimmi and laid her back on the blanket, kissing her neck, her cheek, and finally her thin, quivering lips that invited me in.

She moaned softly with every warmth of my kiss and I with every touch of her hand that was like a fire. We caressed one another for several minutes, finding all the right places until she took me by the shoulders, rolled over on top of me, and nipped at the already tender nipple, sending me to god-knows-where, and the same to other side. There was no stopping us that night when I rolled her over and took a soft nipple into my watering mouth, giving it that longed-for, wet sucking kiss. Her moans of pleasure told me she was ready and so was I.

Running a hand down over the soft stomach, listening to her soft moaning, I touched her thigh with a velvet touch, then positioned myself between her soft, cool awaiting legs.

She arched her back with pleasure and sighed. "Please, don't stop," she moaned. The sight and sound of her drove me and my companion over the top. I leaned over and kissed her wet lips while her hands fondled my nipples and sides, moving down my back to my buttocks. Not able to bring to myself to stop, I reached down between her legs the same time the two other women knelt down beside me.

The ringing of a phone scattered the dream and brought me to life. I sat upright in the chair only to find Daniel was gone, and the ringing was that of the movie on TV. I rose from the chair and stumbled through the doorway into Willa coming from the bath.

"Well, look who's up: sleeping beauty."

Unable to deny the feeling that crossed me, I stared at her and said, hoping she didn't notice, "Morning, Willa. Where's Daniel at?" But she did and come to me, vigorously taking me around the neck, kissing me hard.

❦❦❦

I had been following Luke around at my father's command. I sneaked a peek through the curtains of the small bedroom at the two in the hallway. I couldn't tear away from the view when Luke grabbed the redhead in a way half lifting her off the floor. She clung to him like a lost lover after she dropped the robe right there.

❦❦❦

"She wants ya, you know. Go get it," my head called. In a heated moment, I grabbed her around the waist, and lifted her off the floor. Dropping the robe, she clung to me while I carried her into the bedroom where I pleased myself in lust. My companion, raging all the time in my head, forcefully used Willa in a way I didn't like, but couldn't help but give in to.

When it was over a short few minutes later, Willa lay in bed, watching while I dressed, feeling proud of myself for taking control with the evil thought that my companion was right. I was arranging my shirt and pants when Willa rose from the bed.

Coming toward me, she sighed, grabbing and slipping on a robe to cover with. "You know she'll find us out."

Fastening the belt, "There…is…no us," I implied.

"Then what was this?" she cried.

I half laughed, unable to stop when I said, "What do you think?"

Gasping, she said, "You bastard. She'll know."

Facing her with a laugh, I said, "Who do think she'll believe?" I could see the fire in her eyes when she raised her hand to strike me. I caught her wrist, forced a kiss, crushing her lips to mine, then shoved her on the bed before leaving. Making my way outside, I felt the impulse heighten when I took control like my companion said.

I was standing by the car when Daniel came into the driveway, parked, and began laughing when he got out. I followed him to the trunk where he opened it, got out two bags of stuff, and took them inside.

"Where ya want em, sis?" he sort of yelled down the hall.

Willa yelled from the room, "Just leave them on the table." I waited for her to rush out and tell Daniel what happened, but she didn't, and it left me wondering why.

Dropping the bags on the kitchen table that was located in the middle of the mobile home, Daniel and I headed for his room.

"You game for a race?" he asked, rounding the corner of the door into the room.

Stopping in the doorway, I asked, "When?"

"Now," he responded with gusto.

"Sure. Why not." I shrugged my shoulders in an okay fashion. It sounded good at the time, and it wasn't like the dream of Kimmi or the moment with Willa. Whatever was happening to me was anyone's guess, but I liked it even more after that smooth move.

After lunch, I told Daniel I had fun but it was time I headed home. We said our good-byes, and I left. The two-lane road was vacant while the sun was setting low behind the trees. I was moving fairly fast when suddenly I thought I saw a figure that appeared to look like Cole. The shadow appeared, then disappeared behind the trees. I lost track of what I was doing to watch where it drew back till I could no longer see it. I was so caught up in it that I didn't see the oncoming car. Before I nearly hit it, the horn blew, breaking my attention span, and I slammed on the brakes. Coming to an abrupt stop in the middle of the road, the Dodge, had also stopped on the shoulder of road.

Getting out of the car, I noticed all the windows were dark tinted. I walked over and reached for the door about the time it opened, revealing a young girl in the driver seat. She got out of the car, and I noticed she was in her late teens with blonde hair and brown eyes. It was the same girl from the diner. Her dress code was somewhat better with jeans and a sweat shirt.

"I'm sorry, I didn't see you. I was playing with the radio knob," she claimed.

"Are you okay?" I asked, assuming she was.

"Yes, thank you." She seemed a bit confused as she looked around.

"What are you looking for, and maybe I can help."

"None of your business," she snapped.

I was taken with the comment and said, "Fine. You okay?" I spoke with sharpness in my tone.

"Yeah, just shaken some." She got back in the car and slammed the door. She glanced at me, then started the car up and drove off without another word. I thought for a moment of how rude she was. Staring out in the direction I came from, I stopped at the car door as I felt eyes on my back.

I kept watch at a distance as Dad asked, and he was right to claim Luke would make a good addition to the clan. I wondered if he even knew what was happening to him. Apparently that Daniel had not spoken to anyone about his ordeal either. With a half laugh, I left Luke to his adventure.

I didn't turn around. I just got in the car and went home where I readied for bed early in the evening. From the accursed dream of Kimmi and the force I put on Willa, I had been tired when I lied down and closed my eyes. Counting the ticks from the clock, I found myself in a dream again.

It was extremely dark. Even the moon could not penetrate the thickness. I felt that I wasn't alone, so I turned around, pressing my back up against the large gate. I felt a warm soft breath on my face as I strained to see into the darkness. I heard a low growl as a figure appeared to take form in a smoky haze. Walking toward me on its two hind legs, I felt threatened when it stopped and leaned down to face me with no face.

In a growl, it asked, "How did it feel to take what you wanted when you wanted it?" Something touched my waist about the time the long, narrow, sharp claws reached out for me, missing my neck by a mere thread, leaving the breeze they made behind.

Sitting upright in bed screaming, sweat was rolling off me like rain, making my hair stick to my face. I sighed just as a knock sounded on the door. I shook my head to gather myself. "Yes," I said in a weak voice.

"Is everything alright in there?" Mae whispered through the door.

I smiled and replied, "Just a bad dream. I'm fine. Thank you."

In a misty tone, she asked "You're sure?"

"Yes, ma'am," I said, lying back on the pillow. I heard her as she turned and left. Rolling over, I got out of bed and went to the window, finding it dark and raining. Looking over my shoulder, the bedside clock showed 3:00 a.m. and thought how I really needed to see Whitecloud about the dreams. I returned to bed and to a dreamless sleep.

ILLUSION

T HE NEXT MORNING, I decided on sweats, a short-sleeved T-shirt, and sneakers. With my hair braided down the back, I headed out the front door and into the early morning's cloudy grey day. I didn't stop as I made my way around to the shed and to the Charger inside. It reminded me so much of that movie *Christine* that it fascinated me. What was once my Dad's, was now mine. I finally made it to the large doors of the shed and stopped. Sighing with anxiety, I reached for the handles.

I pulled the doors open to reveal the car sitting alone in the dark. I went over to it, placed my fingers on the hood, and let them slide along the cold metallic thing to the driver's door handle. I opened it slowly, then sat down on the soft seat. In an instant, I looked up and swore I saw a thing, a figure or something, cross the doorway of the garage. I waited, but there was nothing more. I reached out and closed the door, then started the car and let it come to life for a minute. Taking a moment, I stared out the shed doors, and let my mind wander back to my hidden friend before I went to see the old man.

Mac was on the porch smoking a pipe when I arrived. I waved as I got out and went toward him.

He yelled as he raised the pipe, "Whitecloud's in the barn." He pointed.

"Thanks, Mac," I said, raising a hand to him. Walking toward the barn, I could see the old man stacking corn. I stopped at the door to watch until the light from the dim sky at my back casted a shadow inward.

I saw Whitecloud smile as he glanced my way. "Come on in and help. Don't just stand there."

"If I must," I said with a groan, not really wanting to. I went over, grabbed an armful of corn, and placed them in the rack with the rest. We finally cleaned out the small cart and headed out of the barn where I stopped to close the doors while Luther headed on in.

As I turned around, Kimmi was walking toward me, waving a hand in the air. Like in a movie, she smiled, tugging at her soft-blue, full-length satin gown that tapered her legs. Half running, half walking to me, I grabbed her around the waist when she got close enough, and softly kissed her cool quivering lips. She returned the favor when she placed her hands on my face, pressing harder.

"What brings you out here?" I asked, pulling my head back to see her eyes.

"Your grandmother. I called, and she said you were out here." She dropped her hands to my shoulders. Watching Whitecloud heading off to the house, I saw him wave when I noticed Kimmi's scent and liked it. Bringing the reminder of the dream, my heart began to rush.

"Come with me," I whispered, grabbing her by the hand, not thinking.

"Where to now?" she shouted. Trying to run, the tapered gown nearly tripped her, but she quickly got control as she lifted the gown above her knees. I swear those legs went all the way up…. I laughed to myself, headed for the barn and out of sight.

Inside the barn, I flipped Kimmi around to face me and gave her a long kiss. She instantly returned it as she eased her hands around my neck, finding their way underneath the braid of my hair. I so longed to have her, but it would have been inappropriate somehow.

"Inappropriate? Like hell," my head said with laughter. Ignoring the voice, I found her skin exceptionally cold. But wasn't she most of the time anyway? The kiss ended too soon when I took her by the hand and led her to the ladder that went up to the loft.

"What's up there?" she asked with a baffled look, taking hold of the wooden thing.

With a sinful grin and that warm devilish feeling, I replied, "Privacy."

"Alright," my companion growled, "It's time you took her." She grabbed the ladder and placed a foot on the bottom step. Due to the gown's tapered shape, her other foot couldn't reach the next step. She looked at me and I up at her with that same sinful grin. I knew better but couldn't stop thinking about it.

"Need some help?" At a loss for words, she nodded yes. I reached out and grabbed the hem of the gown, giving it a slow tug, and pulled it up to her knees. She took hold it at the hem before heading on up. The thing in me had to stare as she went up the ladder.

My imagination went wild, seeing the smooth pale legs under the gown that led to baby-blue silk underclothes. I quickly dropped the gaze when she reached the top and crawled up onto the flooring. When she looked over the edge, I grabbed the ladder, and stepped up onto the second step. It squeaked from my weight while I climbed on up and peeked over the top at the hay scattered everywhere. Kimmy was standing at the window, overlooking the mountain range. She was just out of the sun's reach when I came up behind her.

"It's beautiful up here," she whispered. A soft wind blew through the loft and her scent came to my nose, causing a sudden surge of sinful fire.

"Yes, I know. I like coming up here, but now its better," I said, taking her by the arm, and turned her to face me.

Her eyes shimmered from the glow in them. Suddenly, I had a passion to hold her as if I were going to lose her, or drop her off the ledge. I slipped my arms around her smooth body and pulled her to me, until she stepped on her gown, tripped herself, and landed in the scattered hay.

Rolling over, she looked up at me, and said, "Now what?" She laughed, unknowing what my companion had in store. Those eyes called me to her, and I dropped like a weight down beside her. She reached for me and I leaned into her as she wrapped her arms around me with one under my arm and the other around the neck. My stopping her had become nonexistent as my longing for her grew. I laid out flat, taking hold of her in a way that was soothing and tender as I slid closer to her.

With her tender body underneath mine, I placed a leg upon her thighs with my knee laying on her hip. I put an arm under her neck as my other hand roamed her back, and finding its way to her chest. I crushed her lips to mine in a frenzy, holding her tight from struggling. At first she gave in, but then she began to resist my efforts. The smooth silk hid nothing from my hand that crossed the firm breasts under her gown, and gave them a tender message. I wasn't sure if she moaned from the pleasure or the way I was taking her, but I flamed with desire. Her teeth bit at my lips with a painful nip, leaving a blood trail and I liked it. *Damn, I liked it.* I didn't know, but the feeling was something I wanted more of. I reached down, grabbed a handful of her gown, and pulled it to her waist. Her hand reached out and struck me across the jaw. The coldness made me sigh, but that didn't stop with what I was about to do when I reached for the zipper of my pants.

Struggling against me, I heard her whimper, "Luke, please stop." With my companion leading the way, I didn't want to as I tore at her gown.

I never thought they could see me while I watched them from the rafter overhead. But what Luke was about to do to that young girl was unacceptable. I made my way to the flooring and eased over toward them. Spotted by the young girl, I placed a finger to my lips in hopes she understood—which she did. I grabbed my son by the nap of the shirt with one hand, the waist of his pants with the other, and with force, pulled him off the girl. It may have been too much, when he rose off the floor, and landed on his back three feet away with a thud. With a quick glance at the young girl, I made my getaway to the opposite side of the loft to watch.

I heard Kimmi gasp before I hit floor. Quickly sitting up, I faced Kimmi who was in a kneeling position, but there was nothing else in sight.

"What the hell did you do just now?"

Looking at me in fear, she cried, "It wasn't me. I swear." I didn't know if I wanted to believe her or not, but there was surely something wrong, and I couldn't explain it. I felt she had the ability to do such a thing and was lying about it.

Sitting with my head propped in my hands, peering through my fingers, I whispered, "I'm so sorry."

"The accusation or for what you tried to do just then?" she cried.

"Both, I fear."

"What is happening to you? You've changed lately."

"I don't know."

"Oh, but you do, you storyteller." My head laughed.

Ignoring the comment, I said, "I was raised with dignity to have respect for women. Even if you are different, you are still a woman that I want more than anything." I looked up at her with hay all over her hair and a torn gown across the front. Rubbing my jaw, I mumbled, "I don't want to be like Cole, but I don't know what happened just now." With that, I meant I didn't know what pulled me off her. "I can't bring myself to harm you. If, someday we wed, then that will be a whole new story." She crawled over to me and sat back on her heels.

With her face in front of mine, she took her hands, placing one on each cheek, and tenderly kissed me. Sitting upright again, "I thank you for being a man, a good one too," she said as a tear fell. "I have dishonored myself for I knew what I was doing, but I had not the ability to stop. I have wanted you since the day of our lakeside. Please forgive me." She bowed her head as if in shame.

I quickly put a hand under her chin and raised it to face me. "Don't be guilty for wanting something such as sex. It is a natural thing, but it is a desire that has a strong hold on those who will let it control them."

"And you like it all too well, my friend," my head growled.

"I am glad that whatever it was stopped me for I was about to dishonor not only you but myself. I love you dearly with more passion that I can say. Harm will not be seen by me to you." I thought it was the truth at the time.

She grimly smiled and said, "I too love you. Thank you for being what you are, and that is human." She rose to her feet and stuck a hand out for me. I took the offer and got to my feet, brushed the hay from her as she did me, and gently grazed the mark on my jaw. Looking at the gown, she tore the remaining piece off to match. Ready, we went back down the ladder and toward the door.

I watched in tears, knowing the boy had no clue what he was up against and knew that Luther apparently hadn't talked to him either. After they left, I vanished into the wind with heartfelt agony of what was to come.

We went out the barn door hand in hand, walking toward the house where we found the old man with a pipe sitting in a rocking chair on the porch. When we reached the porch, I stopped and looked at Kimmi. "I need to talk to Whitecloud about some dreams I been having lately."

"If it's okay with you, I need to get back home. Casey and I have a hair day." She blushed lightly.

I kissed the top of her head and replied, "That's fine. I'll see you later this evening then."

Turning to leave, she replied, waving as she went, "Okay, bye now."

"Come on, and let's talk over coffee," Whitecloud said, rising from his chair toward the door. I jumped up on the porch and followed him into the kitchen.

I seated myself at the table while Luther gathered two cups and poured the coffee, then brought them to the table and sat down.

Placing his hands together, he asked, "Tell me now, when did they start?"

Looking into his dark eyes, I replied, "They've been coming on for some time, but lately they've been really horrid." I hesitated because I didn't think he would believe me. I sighed, biting into my lips. "How...,"

"Talk to me, Luke," he said, leaning onto the table.

I searched for the right words when I said, "The thing...the figure...in them walk on two legs, upright like a man, but I can see no face when it comes to me."

Whitecloud asked with interest, "Luke, are you sure of this?" His face showed a bit of fear in his eyes.

"As sure as I can be. I mean, they're starting to happen often when it was just now and then. What are they?" I cried, "What's happening to me?"

"It sounds like your dark side is expecting something. I know you don't understand these things," he said, picking up the cup to sip at the hot liquid. Replacing the cup on the table, he asked, "Have you seen anyone strange around here?"

"Recently, I saw a someone or something that looked like Cole just yesterday."

I saw the old man when he tensed and his grip tightened around the cup. "Where was he when you happened to see him?"

"I was headed home from Daniel's when it made me nearly hit another car." The phone rang suddenly and Whitecloud rose to answer it. I sat patiently, sipping at the coffee.

When he returned to the table, he had an odd look upon his face. He didn't sit down as he placed both hands flat on the table, and looked at me with a sigh.

His eyes softened when he said, "That was Ivan Creed." Before he could say anything else, I jumped up.

Standing upright, Luther waved a hand in the air and shouted, "Hold your horses now, Luke. Ivan said he thought he saw Cole hanging around out there."

Leaning on the table, I stared at him, asking, "Are you sure, old man?"

Luther stood up taller with a reply that sent a chill over me when he politely said, "Not only him, but he has a friend close by."

Pushing the chair under the table, I told him, "I should be going now."

I was at the screen door when he said, "Take care. They're waiting and watching your every move out there."

Pushing through the door, I replied, "Yes, sir." Letting the door close, I leaped off the porch toward the car. I got in and impatiently roared out of the driveway.

The day was still young when I arrived at the Creed's to find Casey sitting out in the gazebo. She jumped up with excitement while Kimmi came through the front door in a white gown with blue lace. Kimmi leaned on the car door and took my hand just as Casey hugged my neck. She quickly turned to Kimmi and grabbed her in a hug with a tender kiss on the jaw and Kimmi kindly returned it.

Hanging onto Casey's neck, Kimmi faced me, asking, "What brings you here? I thought you had business with Luther."

I was being mischievous when I said, "Well, I thought I'd catch you off guard with your hair in curlers." I winked. The three of us broke out in laughter. I didn't want to upset Kimmi any more than she already was, so I kept it to myself till I talked to Ivan.

Casey pulled at Kimmi's hand and said, "Come sit with me."

Kimmi grabbed my hand. "Yeah, come on," she said, pulling at me.

Dragging my feet, I said, "Okay, just for a little while. I need to speak with Ivan."

"Okay, in a while." She laughed aloud. I had just sat down when the clearing of a throat from the doorway made me look up to find Ivan.

"I have to see Ivan now," I said as her eyes followed me to a standing position.

I kissed her forehead about the time she said, "Okay."

"I'll be back." I walked across the yard to the front door and looked back to see her blowing kisses before I went inside.

I followed Ivan, who was handsomely dressed in a dark blue suit with a vest and tie, to the den where he seated himself on the sofa nearest the balcony.

"You are heading to somewhere special?" I asked with a snicker, sitting on the smaller sofa.

I saw him slightly grin. "Whitecloud tell you I called?" he asked with cause.

Puzzled, I pushed back on the cushion and replied, "Yes. So what did you see?"

He looked up into my eyes, then said, "Well, I thought I saw something or someone that looked a whole lot like Cole hanging around out back last night."

In a kind manner, I asked, "Kimmi know?"

"No, and I'll not tell her. That girl has been hurt enough by that bastard," he swore with an undertone of hate.

"She told me of the two men that came in on her, but I stopped the moment she said they tore at her clothes. What I'm trying to ask is she still... a virgin?"

❧❧❧

The day of our first encounter played in my head when I stepped from behind the tree toward the two girls in the gazebo. I had brought along a friend, in wolf form, who wanted to see firsthand what was about to happen and would hopefully join me in the raid. At first, they were too busy talking like little girls do. We were no more than twenty feet away when Kimmi happened to cut a glance over her shoulder.

When the screaming started, I yelled, "Run, David." We hauled ass, knowing Luke and that man would be to their aid.

❧❧❧

Ivan had just finished the statement when a scream broke from outside that sounded like Kimmi. The both of us scrambled to our feet and ran out the double doors to the balcony.

Right outside, I leaned over the rail to see the front lawn where Kimmi was lying out on the ground, facing the back of the house. Casey was lying across the bench in the gazebo. I focused my attention on Kimmi when Ivan yelled for Casey the precise same time he took the rail and leaped over.

Following pursuit, I leaped over, and yelled in a run, "Kimmi!" I got to Kimmi's limp body, knelt down, took her by the head and shoulders, and rolled her over onto her back. Thank god, she had only fainted.

"Kimmi, honey, you hear me?" I said, patting her cheek. "Honey..."

"Bring her inside, Luke," Ivan said, picking Casey up. He headed for the house while I picked Kimmi up. At the front door, I stopped to look over the way at nothing. I felt a deep fear he was waiting for something. I walked through the door, then kicked it with a soft foot, gently closing it behind me.

We carried the girls to the den where Ivan placed Casey on the sofa while I laid Kimmi on the loveseat. Mollie came through the door just at that moment with her hands going to her face in fright.

Ivan spoke before she screamed out, "They're fine, honey."

"Thank God." She coughed, placing a hand over her chest. In a short sprint, she went to Casey first. After all, she was their daughter. She made sure she was okay, and then came over to Kimmi.

She eased down on the little couch, placing a tender hand to Kimmi's forehead. "Kimmi," Mollie whispered. When she didn't respond, Mollie spoke in a language I didn't know, but the tone was soft like the words.

"What did you just say to Kimmi?" I wanted to know.

"I just said, 'Honey, wake up now,'" she respectively replied.

I nodded with understanding, and asked, "Do you think she'll teach me this language of hers?"

She smiled and replied, "Someday, I hope." She gave Casey a glance, then Ivan, who also nodded.

Shortly, both girls began to stir around.

Casey was the first to wake, and Ivan reached over to her, when she began to struggle, until she realized who he was. Kimmi screamed out as she bolted upright with her eyes blind. I took hold of her hand but got slapped by the other. I drew back from the sound, not from the sting it inflicted.

"Kimmi," Mollie shouted, reaching for her hand. Kimmi struggled against both of us as she fought in her sleep.

"What is wrong?" Casey asked. She waited for no answer when she rose from the sofa and went to Kimmi. Her move was quick and silent like in a movie: instant. Mollie moved just as quick when she rose from the seat for Casey to sit down.

"Kimmi, it's I," she soothed her, taking Kimmi by the shoulders. Then without a warning, she raised her hand up and came down with a stinging slap across Kimmi's cheek.

Kimmi inhaled as she faced Casey, who cringed and said, "Sorry."

"It is okay." Kimmi's response was gentle. I felt a sense of joy as I took Kimmi's hands into mine. She looked at me and smiled, sort of.

"What happened out there," I asked, rubbing her hand gently and staring at the red mark that came to her face from the slap.

I reached for it when she cried out, "It was that creep Cole."

"Yeah. He and something that resembled a wolf," Casey implied. Ivan looked at me as I did him. "Are you sure?" Ivan asked. She nodded yes, but Kimmi began to tremble.

"Hey, what's wrong?" I pulled Kimmi to me in comfort.

"That thing out there was like nothing I had ever seen before. It was ugly as hell. It had long arms with long narrow fingers that had claws on the ends. The face was not recognizable. Cole called it David, I think." The room fell spine-chilling silent as a sinister howl rang out over the range. Everyone looked at each other. I felt time was approaching to an end with Cole, somehow. There was no other incident while my stay was great, but soon it got late, and I had to leave for home. I stopped at the door, kissed her, told her I loved her, and left.

WARNING

I was standing out on the balcony adoring the sun when the phone rang. Mollie answered and said it was for me. Thinking it was Luke, I hurried inside to the table where Mollie stood. Taking it rather quickly, I stuck it to my ear and said, "Hello." The muffled voice on the other end that spoke, was not Luke's, but a female. I didn't know who she was, but she told me something, hurting me dearly.

When she was done, all I could say was thank you, and hung up. I never told anyone who it was or what the conversation was about, hoping that Luke would tell me himself.

It was the last of winter, and snow was making its way down, sticking to the ground while I sat on the couch watching the tube. I was thinking of how calm it had been over the past week. Hell, even Willa had kept her silence. Right in the middle of the Blue Lagoon, Luther called to tell me there had been a sighting. Accepting the fact, I rushed out with Jason and Daniel to the north ridge to do an area check on things.

Jason suddenly stopped and said with a snort, "There's something strange over here, guys." Finding him funny, I trotted over to take a whiff of the ground and air.

Coming up with very little, I woofed, "There is, but it's not a scent I have ever come across before."

"Hey, over here," Daniel barked, who took off to examine the trees near a mound. Jason and I trotted to where he had wandered off to in search of whatever it was he found.

Stopping at the mound behind one another, we raised our noses to the air, drew in deeply, and let it out slowly.

I tasted an odd taste in the back of my throat. "What is it, bud?" I asked, sucking in the smell again. With a woof, Daniel moved to the side, revealing an enormous print in the snow from a two-legged creature.

"Man, what made that?" Jason whined, leaning on me.

"I think I've seen these in my dreams," I huffed.

"What are they then?" Jason whined, nudging me again.

"Honestly, I have no clue, and Luther's not sure."

"Well then, let's explore," Daniel said, taking off in a trot. Jason agreed, following. I nodded with agreement, looked up over the mound, and slightly inhaled before joining them.

The three of us trotted up the mountain a ways and stopped where the prints vanished into thin air. I looked over at Jason, who was sniffing the ground. I inhaled the air again, then let it out slowly. Jason stuck his shiny nose in the air and inhaled.

His nose flared out as he asked, "How do they just disappear like that?"

"Maybe the aliens got it," Daniel's snarl replied.

I growled a grunt, "Be serious for once, will you, two?"

I heard his suppressed laugh as he said, "I was just funnin', Luke." The laugh was getting louder.

He was right. It was time we took time to have some fun again.

"Let's stop here and head to the lake for awhile. Sound good?"

"Right now, in the snow?" Daniel whined. "Hell, I'm all for it, being hot blooded," he howled, then began digging in the snow, and it coming up over his back, falling on top of his head.

Sticking his snout in the snow, Jason woofed, "I concur."

I let out a little bark, "It's settled then, let's go." I began to walk with small steps while the two caught up with me. We picked up the pace and trotted off the mountainside toward the lake.

We changed to our human forms just short of the reservoir entrance. It was remarkable that after we returned to humans, we had on the same clothing. That came with what we were—nature's creation. Composed to humans, we crossed the bridge to find Willa and Paulene sitting at one of the snow covered tables, chatting. Getting that go-to-hell look from Willa, I played it off.

"Hey you three," she said as we approached the table. "Why are y'all here?"

I stopped in front of her as she straddled the bench of the picnic table, dressed only in black jeans and a thin white shirt tied at the shoulders under a thin jacket. If only my mind didn't know better, I stared at the round firm breasts that tried their best to climb over the top of the shirt. Paulene, on the other hand, had on a white jacket with a blue slouchy shirt and jeans.

She asked as she planted a kiss on Jason's nose, "You hanging out with these characters today, sweetie?"

"For R and R," I replied with a daring stare at Willa. She jumped to her feet and grabbed me around the neck in a hug.

"Well then, how about a swim?" she whispered low in my ear while pressing her breasts to my chest. "I'll get you sooner or later." I could feel the warmth of her skin as the things raged over the top.

I placed a hand on one hip, held firmly, and said, "Well, I don't know." Squeezing harder, she moaned from discomfort.

"Come on, then," she said with a tempting glare. I knew what she was trying to do, and I released her.

"That's right, don't let that bitch make a fool of you," my head warned.

She stood back and with a tease, pulled the thin jacket off, and let it fall to the ground. Using both hands, she pulled the other shirt to her chin and stopped. The breasts that jiggled under the bikini top were crying to be stroked. Swallowing hard,

I stayed back from the urge to place my hands upon them while she struggled with the top and me staring at the breasts. Finally, it came over her head, and she tossed both shirts on the table. Shimmying down to the ground with the jeans, she revealed a skimpy white bikini. Looking over her shoulder while she picked up the jeans, she winked, then tossed them on the table, and took off in a run toward the water. I stripped to my trunks and headed for the cold murky water.

I dove in, going deep before I surfaced to face the blonde-haired girl from the restaurant. Her black suit was strapped over the shoulders with her eyes glaring at me, and my first thought was *Why is she out here in the cold?*

"You, are you following me, lady?" I asked in a demanding tone.

"Why would I do that mister?" she snickered.

"Well, who's your friend here, Luke?" Willa asked, coming over and placing a hand on my arm.

I didn't get the chance to say before she replied, "I'm Jada, and you are Miss?"

"A friend of Luke's is here," Willa replied, squeezing my arm and implanting the nails.

I felt tension build in Willa's touch, so I asked, "Tell me, Jada, why are you here today?"

With trickery in her tone, Willa asked, "Luke, you know this girl?" I knew Willa was looking for something to tell Kimmi to get me into trouble, or at least try.

"No, but I have bumped into her," I replied, shaking Willa's grip when I thought I heard my name being called. I turned to see Mac on the bank, yelling at me, his hands waving in the air.

With my own treachery, I kissed Willa on the check and whispered, "Gotta go." I went toward Mac's yelling to hurry the hell up.

By the time, I stopped at the table, Mac said, "I need you to get the other two and come out to the house. We have a problem." Without any questions, he turned, got back into Tom's red truck, and left. I turned to the lake and looked for Jason, who was backstroking, and Daniel was talking to Jada. I yelled at them twice, getting their attention, flagged them in, and told them of Mac. We excused ourselves and left in a sprint. We didn't have far to go when we walked up into the drive to find Tom, Nate, and Mac standing on the porch waving us in.

When the others stopped at the steps, I was the last to bring up the rear. I walked past Mac, who was entering the house, and asked, "What's up, Mac?" He made no reply as we followed him into the living room where he sat down in the large recliner. Tom and Nate stood near the fire place.

"How was the cold bath?" Nate grinned.

Laughing, I told him, "Damn, you missed out."

"We have a problem. He's back," Tom interrupted as he began pacing the floor.

"No questions?" Mac's tone was shy of a whisper.

"So we know who it is, but what does he want now?" Daniel asked.

"Does Ivan know?" Nate intruded.

"Not yet," Tom replied. "We're not sure just what to say."

"Wait a minute, Tom. I was out there not long ago, and Ivan said he thought he saw Cole hanging around one evening but said nothing to Kimmi. You think he could be after her again?"

"It's possible," Mac said. "I hear you thought you saw him too."

Leaning forward on the cushion, I said, "Yeah, well, I wasn't sure then, and I'm not now. I haven't seen the whatever since."

"Well, you got any ideas as what to do about him? Do we wait or go after him?" Jason chimed in.

"We wait, because we're not sure what he's up to," Tom said. "He is their leader, or he's one of the first hands to the leader."

"And if we see him doing what?" Nate sneered. "Run or chase?"

"You had better run, kid," Tom said. "You've seen what he can do—what he is capable of." He sat on the arm of the chair with Mac.

155

"I just want you guys to take care out there till this sticky situation can be dealt with," Mac said. "Meeting adjourned. Now get outta here." I didn't know about Nate, Daniel, or Jason, but I shot out of there like a shot from a gun. Rushing home for a quick shower, I dressed in jeans, a sweat shirt, and sneakers afterward. Taking off to see Kimmi, I ran out the front door, sliding across the yard to the car.

I drove the ice-covered road with caution until I pulled into the driveway and parked. I saw Kimmi out in the gazebo working on something as I got out, so I sprinted over to her. When she stood up and waved, her arms appeared from under long-tapered sleeves of the navy-blue form-fitting gown with an open V-cut down the front below the cleavage of her full breasts.

"Hey," she shouted with eagerness. With the gazebo only a few inches off the ground to keep the rain from running in, I stepped up on the edge with a near slide.

"Oh shit," I swore, catching myself on a post.

Kimmi quickly grabbed me by the arm with both hands as she began to laugh and said, "Steady now."

"Thanks."

"Anytime, come and sit down." She anxiously pulled me by the hand to the bench seat and sat down, facing the house where she had been working on a macramé plant holder.

We were in an offhand conversation when Casey came out the front door in a red full-length form-hugging dress in matching heels. Stopping on the porch, she grabbed and snapped open a red umbrella in one move before coming across the yard. Stepping up on the edge of the gazebo, she stopped, closed the umbrella, and looked at us as she went to sit down on the other side of the gazebo.

Facing out over the valley, she said, "I hope I'm not intruding on you two, but I had to get out of there."

Her glance went over my shoulder when Kimmi said, "You alright?" She noticed Casey's face shadowed a horror look.

My sense of smell picked up the presence before Kimmi and I looked behind us. Finding Cole about three hundred feet away in the shadow of the trees, was as if he were waiting for something. With the wetness of the hat running off the brim, he tilted his head up, and we met eye to eye. My blood rushed to my face as anger came forth, and my fingers curled into my palms.

Kimmi didn't react as I thought she might when I rose, and her hand grabbed my arm.

I looked into her tear-filled eyes. "Please don't, Luke. I feel something isn't right. Don't go," she cried softly.

I had no time to reply before Casey shouted, "No, Luke!" Trusting in their instincts, I looked back up at Cole, who was smiling that daring grin. Apparently, he knew not to come any closer when he turned tail and left.

With a whisper, he implied, "Soon, she'll be mine again, and I don't pay heed to threats, boy." I couldn't see him, but my ears perked up, waiting for more, but it was silent.

In an instant, with that warm, ambitious tingling feeling, the time had come for Kimmi and I to talk alone.

I looked at Casey with a plea and said, "Can we borrow your umbrella for a while, please?"

"For what, Luke, you're going somewhere?" she asked, looking around at me.

Winking at her, I said, "We are indeed."

Kimmi looked at me with a tilted head and said, squeezing my hand, "In the wet snow? Now?"

"It'll be more than that if I have any say," my head growled, making my superiority grow.

"Yes. Let's talk in private," I said, leaning down to kiss her forehead, taking in her scent.

Kimmi smiled at Casey and asked while going toward her, "Well, can we?"

"If I really need to, okay." She handed the umbrella to Kimmi, who then gave her a kiss on the cheek. She stepped toward the edge of the gazebo and opened the umbrella. I went to her and took her by the hand as we stepped off the edge, and into the slushy snow.

We walked to the rear of the house and entered the woods by way of the path, which Kimmi quickly found. She hurriedly pulled me by the hand, leading me in, and we rushed up toward the hidden forest.

"Slow down. There's no hurry," I said before slipping on a slick surface and my feet went out from under me. I let go of Kimmi's hand as I went down in the red-covered snow. Kimmi began to laugh when she turned to face me. With a nod, she came over to give me a hand. I took her by the hand, but instead of me getting up, I simply gave her hand a tug that pulled her down to me. She dropped the red umbrella as she landed on top of me. I tried to fight back the thought of Willa when Kimmi made contact with me, losing the umbrella, which rolled down the path.

Kimmi sat up, straddling on my waist. "You're going to catch your death of cold." She leaned in, placing both hands with palms down flat on my chest, and said, "You are funny."

My hands slid up her thighs to her waist when I said, "Is that right?" Grabbing her firmly, we rolled once more, and I was on top of her.

I felt the moment was perfect and so did my companion when he said, "Don't waste time playing with your woman. Give her what she is longing for."

I let go of her waist, took her hands, and pulled them up over her head as I laced my fingers with hers. I held her like that, watching as she bit her bottom lip, then smiled. When she began to struggle, I shook my head no. I leaned over to her and our lips met, but I paused, not going any farther. I began to tease her and she began to squirm under me. What I could have done to her right then was evil and thoughtless when I crushed my lips to hers. I was vigorous and hard, but damn it felt good when I pushed my tongue between her teeth deep into her mouth.

With a laugh, my companion snarled, "Do it. You both want to. Let her have it. You know the feeling. Please, do with her like what you did with Willa."

Pulling back from me, pressing hard in the snow, Kimmi whimpered, "You're hurting me." The comment made no impact as I forcefully raked at her clothes with one hand while holding her with the other.

❦❧❦

I waited as long as possible before following them up the path. I had sensed a difference in Luke that was unnatural. I stood back out of sight and watched him force himself on Kimmi. Knowing I could do nothing myself, I rushed home and phoned Luther.

❦❧❦

I was losing touch of reality the more she struggled under me, feeling the sensation of her while ignoring her pleas. Sliding my hand over her breast to the cut, I slipped my fingers in and began pulling the zipper down. It didn't give in right away before she managed to free a hand and cut me a slap across the jaw with her nails that opened me up. Releasing her hands, I took her face and softly kissed her.

Feeling the oozing blood, I said, "Now who has the upper hand?" I laughed, sitting upright.

Hitting me in the chest with both fists, she said, "Well, I don't know." She struggled, pushing at me. "What's gotten into you?" I could hear the bitterness in her tone.

"Does she not feel sensational between your thighs?" my companion said.

Yes, she did—more than I wanted to admit.

"I'm sorry. I don't know what's happening to me." I got to my feet and offered her a hand, which she surprisingly took.

I didn't want to tell Kimmi of my friend just yet, so I apologized for my rudeness. She didn't have the chance to reply when a figure stepped from the trees in front of us. When Kimmi saw Cole, she gasped and fainted right then. She slid to the ground before I could catch her. Knowing she was unharmed, I faced the beast with an eternal hate, leaving Kimmi where she was for the time being.

From somewhere deep inside, I snapped with vigor, "What could you possibly want here?"

He half growled and said, "There's only one thing I want and you know what it is. Since you weren't man enough to do the job at hand just now, give her to me, and I'll be on my way. You'll not see me or her again. Jess was right when he claimed her." With the thought of what he meant to do, I felt myself start to change, but his remark made me stop.

"Do it and die, kid," he said with ridicule, slightly changing into the thing he was at the cave.

"Not her. I'll die for her right now if I have to," I said with hatful indecisions.

"Get him, Luke. Show them who's boss," my head ragged me.

My egotism was about to get the better of me, wanting to rip the life from the thing. In a standoff, I didn't hear the footsteps behind me until the voice spoke.

"No, you don't," Whitecloud snapped, making me spin around.

"How did you know?"

Cole turned to run but Tom caught him by the throat from behind. "You in hurry?" he snarled.

Looking over at me, he said, pressing in on Cole's throat, "Check on Kimmi."

Squatting down at her side, I implied, "She just fainted from the sight."

Lifting her limp body, I heard Tom say, "Take her home. We'll deal with this for now." I never looked back when I acknowledged with a nod and got to my feet. Leaving the scene, I heard Tom's fist plow into Cole's gut, and him groaning.

I stumbled down the mountainside from the moist ground but kept my footing as I quickly carried Kimmi home.

Approaching the house, I yelled, "Somebody, open the door."

Casey opened the door and her jaw dropped. "You bastard," she yelled as she stepped aside and let me through.

"Calm down. She just fainted," I said, walking past her.

"What did you do to her?" Casey questioned while closing the door.

"It wasn't me," I said, taking the stairway toward Kimmi's room.

"How not you? I saw what you did out there." Casey, hot on my heels, rushed around me at the top of the stairs, and stopped at the door. "What happened if you didn't do it?" she growled, not realizing I had not harmed Kimmi, even if the intention was there.

Pushing past her, I said, "So, you're the one that informed Luther of my whereabouts?" Going to the bed, I gently laid Kimmi down.

Facing Casey's horror-struck face and feeling guilty, I explained Cole had showed up again.

"What'll dad say?" She sniveled.

Placing both hands on her trembling shoulders, I soothed her and said, "Nothing. Now listen, calm down. Get me some water and a wash cloth to clean her with." Casey took off for the requested things while I turned back to Kimmi. Reaching over, I slightly opened the front of her gown to reveal more paleness of her firm breasts. My fingers were inches from the zipper below her cleavage. Taking that daring step, I reached over and tugged on the tiny thing until it came down below the breasts and snagged. My hand itched to reach inside the opening and caress her breast.

"No!" I told myself.

"Oh yeah, let's have a look," my head said.

"Leave me alone," the wolf in me growled.

I had sat down on the side of the bed when Casey came in, carrying a pan of water, and put it on the bedside table with a rag.

I grabbed the rag and wet it before she said, "I think I should be doing that?"

Ignoring the statement, I wiped Kimmi's face, then handed it to Casey and got up. "I think you're right."

Snatching the rag with haste, she screeched, "Get out of here!"

"Take care of her." I leaned over and kissed Kimmi on the forehead.

With bitter force, Casey snapped, "Get out!" I left the room in silence, headed downstairs, and outdoors to face Ivan, who was standing at the base of the steps.

He was dressed in his work clothes for the day, and his eyes were covered in grey contacts. I caught a glimpse of Mollie getting out of the car. I stepped out onto the porch, wondering how they knew.

Ivan walked past me toward the door. "How are you doing, Luke?" Stunned, he said no more. I nodded.

"She'll be back to herself soon," Mollie said.

I whirled around and asked, "How did you know?"

Smiling, she replied, "Casey called." From her expression, Casey didn't tell her everything, leaving me puzzled.

I had no explanation when I asked, "How can I stop this reprisal?"

"Come inside. She'll be looking for you." Ivan stopped at the door while I faced his back. "There is only one way, but your people are not like that," he whispered in an uncommon tone.

"Are you saying…?" I left the subject drifting.

"Yes, death becomes him."

"And Kimmi?" I groaned.

"She is learning the ways and yet has so much affection to give. She's a true forgiving being." With nothing more, he continued inside while Mollie and I followed.

Casey was standing at the base of the stairs when Ivan and I came by. She told me Kimmi was dressing and would be down soon. I thanked her and she went back upstairs. I went in the den with Ivan, who was sitting on the loveseat. I sat down on the sofa and waited patiently. It wasn't too long until the doors of the den opened and Kimmi walked in, revealing a clean face. Wearing a snug black-silk pantsuit and shoes tapping the floor, she came toward me.

Gloomy, she sighed, and said, "I'm sorry. My actions were unacceptable today." She sat down next to me while I waited for the war of words to begin.

When it didn't come, I took her hands into mine, feeling them tremble somewhat. I gave them a tender squeeze.

With admiration, I said, "Look at me." I reached out with a forefinger and tilted her head up by the chin when I said, "Everything will somehow work out. I don't know how, but it will. Please hang in there. That man wants you as bad as I do, or he wants to see you fall on your ass. Excuse my language, but it's true." I pulled her hands into a curl and placed them against my chest.

Her innocent eyes looked at me in a forgiving way, with tears. "I could go back home till it's over."

"No," I stuttered. "You can't run from him like that. Let me see what I can do first, please," I begged her.

"Luke, please tell me what to do when I feel I'm a problem to you." Her voice quivered and tears fell from her eyes.

Watching them through the window, I felt my fury growing at what Tom and Luther had done. Even with a broken arm, I trapped and killed a rabbit. I was going to use it as a warning until I thought I could use the girl instead. Having my bow and arrows with me, the rabbit could be used for bait.

Sighing, I hugged her, and we leaned back on the cushion. Something hit the window of the double doors to the balcony, making all of us jump.

I rose to my feet, eased over to the balcony door, and looked through the glass. Not seeing anything in the dark, I reached for the knobs, and slowly opened one. Finding a dead rabbit, I bent over and scooped it up to find its neck was broken.

Ivan walked up behind me and rested a hand on my back. "Damn," he cursed under his breath. I placed the rabbit on the deck when Kimmi came rushing toward the door. I stopped her with a hand before she saw the dead animal.

"What is it? What happened out here?" Her tone was as unnerving as the hand she placed on me and shoved. I didn't move as she tried to get by me.

She leaned over to get a glimpse as she said, "Please, Luke. I have to see," she beseeched. I dropped the arm and moved aside to let her pass as she stepped out onto the deck.

When she stopped just outside the door, she gasped, raising both hands to her face. In a whimper, she stumbled backward toward the doorway. I rushed and caught her before she fell backward inside the doorway and eased her down on the floor.

Crying, she said, "It's him. I just know it." Her whole body began to shiver. Glancing at Ivan, who was staring at us, made a gesture of his head toward the couch. I picked Kimmi up, who was sitting on the floor with her feet under her. She took my neck in her arms and I carried her to the sofa where I laid her down with a pillow when Mollie came in.

She went to the sofa and sat down next to Kimmi, taking her to her breast like a mother for comfort. They talked while I fanned Ivan outside toward the balcony.

"Cole?" Ivan said as soon as his foot touched the deck.

I faced him by saying, "Yes. He wants her so bad it's hurting him from the inside. He's become inhuman, and I fear for her life."

"Huh?" he said. "Luke, if it were okay with you, would you mind if she went back to the Marswaye?"

I was interrupted when Kimmi chimed in. "No. I refuse to, Uncle," she screamed at him from the doorway where she had been eavesdropping. I went to her, took her hands into mine, and tried to make her see.

"Once, you yourself told me you would be safe. Remember? Please," I implored, but she pushed by and came out onto the balcony.

"No. I'll not leave you again. Remember?" she cried as she flipped around and pulled on my shirt with her fists.

I took her face into my palms and tilted her head back and told her, "I do remember for I am the one that said it." Ivan had walked to the doorway only to stop when an owl's hoot rang out, and echoed into the night. Spooked, a deer ran from the ridge to the other side and vanished into the woods. *Hunters*, I thought.

The girl was in perfect view when I pulled out a short arrow and placed it in the bow. It was for short range when I pulled back and released it. I saw it make contact before she went inside and they closed the doors. I left them with a calamitous warning of my implication.

"Inside," Ivan said, fanning a hand. I heard Kimmi sigh when she pulled away and went inside toward the sofa while I helped Ivan secure the doors.

I had just locked the doors when I heard Kimmi whisper in a tone of anguish, swearing under her breath, "Oh shit." Then Mollie gasped as I turned around. She was off the sofa in a rush to Kimmi, who was looking down at herself when she stumbled, and fell to the floor on her knees. Then I saw the blood when it appeared near the right side of her suit. In shock, I took to her in a run as if in slow motion. I raced to her side, but Ivan got to her first, rolling her over to get a closer look at the wound. In her right hip area, a small arrow had made its way into her flesh.

"Damn it!" he cursed under his breath. He began to tear strips of the suit to make a bandage to stop the blood. "It's deep in her side and from the looks, it's embedded in the bone," he whispered. Using some of the clothing as a rag, he wiped at the wound where blood oozed out. My heart sank, but at least it was low instead of high. I felt that was just a painful warning for now and fought back the tears.

"Help me, Luke. Carry her to the lab, and let's remove that tip," he said, breaking off the wooden end with a snap. He quickly rose to his feet and headed for a large door opposite of the hall.

"Will she be okay?" I said, wiping tears.

"She'll be fine. Now come on and shake it off. He's threatened her before, just not to this extent." I sighed, then gently picked Kimmi's body up off the bloody floor and followed him through a set of huge wooden doors that Mollie had opened.

The passage was a dimly lit steep set of eleven steps that lead to another room. Ivan opened the door and flipped on the lights so I could see through the doorway. I stepped inside a room that looked like a lab. Two oblong lights hung overhead, a metal table stood in the center of the room, and all the things that went into one. Mollie placed a blanket on the table for me so I could lay Kimmi down. I placed her so her wound faced upward to the overhead light. I backed far enough away to see the blood had left its mark on my shirt as well.

Through gritted teeth, I sniveled, "No, this isn't happening." Tears filled my eyes and I actually began to see red.

"Luke, stop for Kimmi's sake," Ivan implored, stepping in front of me. Knowing he spoke the truth, I pushed the anger aside.

With a nod, Ivan said, "You can stay if you like."

I looked at him as he turned to the table and said, "I'm not leaving her, so I guess I'll be staying." I wiped my eyes and moved toward the wall with my back against it so I could watch.

"Fine, then," he said, reaching for a pair of gloves. I watched him put on a white pair of rubber gloves, then took a pair of scissors from a steaming pan. Cutting away the side of Kimmi's pants, Ivan revealed the open wound in her side.

Adding a bit of pressure to the wound, I saw a shiny tip of a metal piece protruding from the top of the hole in her side. Sighing, Ivan took the tiny scalpel Mollie handed him with one hand and one hand steady on the wound.

I was appalled and made the comment, "Surely you're going to give her something for the pain first or at least keep her asleep?" I found myself pressing hard against the wall.

"You have a lot to learn about her." He looked at me, then began to cut at the flesh on Kimmi's side. Mollie gently blotted the blood with cotton gauze while Ivan cut deeper into the wound, making my stomach turn with it.

I watched with dismay as he slowly and gently inserted two forefingers into the wound and looked up at Mollie when he bit his lip. Mollie quickly handed him a tool that looked like pliers from the tray. I felt sick but couldn't look away when he inserted it into the wound. With a swift tug, out came the blood-covered tip of the arrow. I noticed a small dark patch on Kimmi's side below the wound when Ivan cleaned away some of the blood, making Kimmi slightly moan. Mollie got a thread and needle from a cabinet and handed it to Ivan, who inserted it into Kimmi's side and stitched her closed. After the four stitches were done, Ivan washed up in the sink opposite the table.

Turning to me with a white towel in his hand, he said, "We should leave so Mollie can clean her up, son."

"You call me your son? After what has gone on between us, Ivan?" I said with panic in my voice.

"I can and will. No matter what you two have gone through. It was no fault of either. Now, let's go upstairs, and Mollie will call when she's done." He firmly took me by the arm, turned me toward the doorway and pushed me up the stairs, through the wooden door, and into the den where he closed the door behind him.

Ivan was silent when he went through the den door toward the stairway. I went on out onto the balcony where I watched the sun rise into a new day. *A new day of what?* I swore with an undertone and tear-filled eyes. My thoughts were of Kimmi with her smiling face and those eyes of blue. The one thing on my mind was evil, but the feelings I had for her were like a heavy hand squeezing the life from my heart, making it ache and hard to breath. I leaned on the balcony rail and stared out into the woods, not seeing what seemed like hours, before I heard Mollie call for me. I jumped to her call and ran down the stairs.

When I walked through the door, Kimmi was bathed and dressed in a long blue cotton nightie. Her hair was still wet from the washing and spilled down over the table, nearly touching the floor. The streaks slid through her hair like white silk or cream in a black river. I walked to the table and stood looking at her as if she were dead. Her breathing was a bit shallow. I sniffled as I wiped my eyes.

"She's fine now, Luke," Mollie soothed, placing a hand on my back.

"Can I?" I asked Mollie, tracing Kimmi's chin with a finger.

"Sure, she wouldn't mind."

I swallowed the lump in my throat and said, "Thanks, Mollie." I gently picked Kimmi up and carried her up the stairs, through the den and to her room where I laid her down in bed on fresh sheets. Covering her to the chin with the white blanket, I found the high-backed chair in the corner again. Sitting down in it, I stayed through the night.

I was awakened when Mollie softly knocked on the open door and came in with a change of bandages.

She stopped at the bed and said with a smile, "She is looking good and her color is nice."

I rose to my feet and glanced at Kimmi, who seemed at peace. I opened the doors to the rising sun and stepped out onto the balcony, watching the day arrive.

Watching a deer slip into the shadows of the morning, I heard Mollie call for me, "You can come back in now."

"Thank you," I moaned and turned around as she went out the door. I went to the bed and sat down, watching Kimmi sleep for a while. She seemed so at peace, that I hated myself for what I had nearly done to her. I traced the once scratch marks before rising and kissing her on the forehead. Not wanting to wake her, I went back out onto the balcony.

The birds swooped down as soon as I stepped out, and landed on the rail to study me as I did them. When their heads began to bob, they moved along the rail, squealing and stretching their necks to look past me to the door. Looking over my shoulder, Kimmi was sitting up on the side of the bed. Moving aside, they flew past me, through the door toward Kimmi, and landed on the bed. I watched while she soothed them, pulling a treat from the bedside table, and acting as if nothing had happened the night before. Leaning against the rail, I watched her talk to them as if they knew each word she said and what they meant. After about fifteen minutes, they took flight, soared past me toward the trees, and vanished. I looked back at Kimmi, who was staring at me. I smiled as I stepped through the doors toward her.

I took the few steps to the bed, knelt down in front of her, and took her hands from her lap into mine, making her slightly groan.

Bubbling with anxiety, I asked, "How do you feel?"

"I'm sore," she whimpered, reaching for her side.

"I know, honey, and I'm sorry." I comforted her with reassurance, telling her Mollie had already been in to change bandages and cleaned her up with a fresh pale-green cotton gown. It opened at the neck in a *V* with long sleeves.

She took my face into her hands and said, "Why are you sorry? You did nothing wrong."

Through gritted teeth, I said, "Have you forgotten what I tried to do to you and look what happened last night?" She looked at the side of my face with the scratches she made and bit her lip.

With a stern tone, she said, "Look here, you." Her hair fell over her shoulders as she pulled my face up to hers. "Not your fault. Casey told me you brought me home when Luther arrived. It was bound to happen and it is I who should leave."

"I love you and that's all there is to it." I sat back on my heels and changed the subject. "Do you know how to drive?"

"Yes, doesn't everyone?" she replied, yawning. "Why change the subject?"

"I think you should rest now," I said, watching her eyes water, and got to my feet.

With a painful groan, she leaned over onto the pillow and said, "Maybe just a bit longer."

Grabbing the blanket, I said, "I love you." I leaned in, gave her a hug, and covered her shoulder.

I heard her moan, "I love you too." I left her with a kiss on the forehead, closed the door, and made it out to the car. I went home for awhile to shower, have a late breakfast, and even caught a nap.

RED-TAILS

OVER THE FOLLOWING week, while Kimmi healed, she mentioned her birds and their protectiveness of her. I was rather curious since they tried to behead me the first time we met. She made me promise that if I took her out to the creek where we first met, she would tell me the whole story of her, the birds, and Cole. Of course, I agreed with eagerness, to know how Cole and Jess escaped them... untouched. I arose that dim morning, quickly showered, then dressing in jeans, a sleeveless shirt, light jacket, and sneakers. I found my comb in the dresser and combed my hair back, tying it with a leather band. Looking at myself in the small mirror, I had been waiting for Kimmi to mention the missing scars on my neck and cheek. I ran a finger over the place they once appeared. Did she notice the things were gone or maybe she didn't want to upset me again? I smiled, left the room, slid down the stairs, and out the front door to the awaiting Charger.

Arriving in the driveway, I parked and baled from the car in a hurry, trotting up to the front door and knocking. I waited for a spell until Mollie opened the door in her green night gown with robe.

"Morning, Luke. Come in," she said, moving aside.

I walked past her toward the stairs when she said, "She's still asleep." Just as I put my hand on the stair rail, I stopped and faced her with a smile. Her knowing smile and nod said okay.

"Thanks, Mollie." I slowly took the stairs till I reached the top landing, eased over to Kimmi's closed door, and pressed my ear to it. I didn't hear anything, so I reached out for the knob, placing my hand on the cold metal thing, and turned. The door didn't squeak on the hinges when it opened with ease. What I saw on the bed was a sight to see.

Kimmi was fast asleep with her hair cascading over the side. But nestled down in the center, next to her, were the two birds, in a silent wake. I wanted so bad to laugh out, but I held it in. Staring as I stepped backward, I backed right into Casey, who was standing behind me.

"Peeping tom," she whispered in a laugh. I felt embarrassed but had to laugh with her. The giggles awakened Kimmi, who was lying there staring at us. I looked at her and her at me. Smiling, she glanced at the birds as she rolled over, got out of bed, and opened the doors, letting the birds escape into the early morning.

Turning from the door, she grabbed the robe at the foot of the bed, and put it on as she came around the bed, letting it drag the floor. Her hair was a mess of tangles when she stopped to glance in the vanity mirror and began to laugh at herself.

"Morning, sleepy head," I said, laughing with her.

"Stop that, you two," Casey said, yawning. "I'm leaving now." She went back to her room and closed the door.

I faced Kimmi, who was pushing hair back from her face. "Let me dress. I'll be down soon." She slid across the floor on her bare feet, out into the hall, and softly kissed me. She turned and went back in, closing the door. With nothing else to do, I made my way back downstairs to the front yard.

I had been watching a fox play in the underbrush when Kimmi pulled open the door. She stepped out onto the porch in a black loose-fitting dress with silver hems at her calves.

Staring at her from the neck down, I gasped from her view, "Good God."

"I'm sorry, hon. Am I overdressed?" she asked, looking down at her bare feet.

"You are already beautiful and have no need for extra." Watching her blush, I said, "Grab your shoes, and let's go if you're ready." Waving, she stepped inside the door, and retrieved a black pair of canvas shoes. She slipped them on before coming off the porch to me where I picked her up, carried her to the car, and placed her in the passenger seat. Closing the door, I leaned in, and gave her a soft kiss on the check.

Grabbing my chin with two fingers, she whispered in my ear, "Come on, get in." Looking into her sparkling eyes, I grinned with agreement. Anxiously, I slid over the hood of the car to the driver side, got in, reached for the key, and started the engine. I closed the door, put the gear into drive, and headed toward the creek.

During the drive, Kimmi was exceptionally quiet while staring out the window. I found myself wondering what she had in that head of hers when I started a conversation about the two hawks. "How did you get the names for your birds?"

She looked up from under those long lashes and wrinkled her nose. "Are you really interested, Luke?" she asked in doubt.

Being honest, I said, "Yes, I am. I want to know all there is to know about you. You did promise."

Sighing deeply, she said, "Well, the birds were given to me by the Marswaye, but the names came from the Spirit Trees."

Feeling that inner laugh rumble from below, I said, "A tree gave you those names." I tried not to laugh.

"Yes. Her name was Sheree."

"And where are these trees?" I asked childishly. I saw her gently bite her bottom lip when she sat back in the seat.

"When I was a child my parents took me to an island called Simons. Late one evening, I wandered down along the beach, watching the sinking sun with the place to myself. I picked up seashells along the shore until I wandered into the trees. Being a child, I was frightened to find several trees that looked like a woman's body attached to the bark. I was captured by the sight, so

I went over and placed my hands upon one. The bark was so soft to the touch, almost like the hawk's feathers. As I walked around it, tracing the bark with my fingers, I noticed the figure unfold its arms and open its blue eyes. Startled, I stopped in my tracks when it whispered my name."

I watched the smile cross her face at the thought and wondered how true the story was.

"I looked around, thinking someone else had called for me, then it called to me again. Not sure what it was, I just stood there, taken not only by the bark's softness, but the soft whisper of the tree. It told to me that two birds would come to me and that I should name them Hawkloun and Talwheana. They would bring me comfort and good luck. I spent most of the night talking with Sheree. By dawn, I was back home and in bed before the others rose. It wasn't long after when I lost my parents, and the birds were given to me by Magnyss a year later. They were my friends, my companions when all seemed lost, and I was alone. When I become an adult, I found out those trees were spirit trees." She fell silent as she turned back in the seat and stared out the window into the night.

I didn't what her to stop there. "Their food, what do you feed them? I saw you pull something from your pocket once. What was it?"

Turning her head, she looked out the windshield. "It is a small sort of oval fruity treat called tangelo." Kimmi appeared to have something else bothering her. The rest of the ride was in silence.

I drove through the entrance, then parked and got out, dashing around to give Kimmi a hand out.

"You think it'll work today?" she asked as soon as her feet hit the ground.

I gently pulled her to me as I looked into her eyes and smiled. "It will today, sweetie." I kissed her sweet, inviting lips. It ended too soon when the birds overhead announced their arrival.

"They're early," she said, glancing over my shoulder.

"It's time you tell me exactly why they guard you so." I took her by the hand and faced the trail.

"I tried, but you once interrupted and stopped me." She squeezed my hand as I tugged on hers to come and go with me. We headed up the trail with me, watching the hawks that had landed on one of the limbs of a nearby tree to watch. I felt as if they mistrusted me somehow. Hell, I didn't trust myself much lately when it came to my companion. The rising sun made me hustle in order to shield Kimmi from its rays, so I picked her up.

Gasping, she said, "Well now." She took me by the neck. I began to sort of trot up the path to the top with the birds following in silence.

We topped the trail where I stopped and let Kimmi slide to the ground. We began to slowly search for the tiny path that led to the creek. It had been some time since I had come back to visit. I didn't know how long it had been since Kimmi's last visit, but she found it soon enough.

"Here it is," she said, pulling at the tall weeds to reveal the tiny trail. I hurried over to her, took her hand, and we slipped into the grass behind the tall trees. It was like we were hiding something and continued down the trail toward the clearing.

Even though the day was chilly from the coolness of winter, the sound of trickling of water came into hearing range. I hurried over and sat down on the cold ground, and leaned back on a willow tree. Kimmi placed a hand on my shoulder while she sat down next to me.

Sighing, she said, "Oh, Luke, it's been awhile since my last visit here. The water is even a bit slower than I remember."

"Do you want to play in it?" I laughed out and didn't know why.

The birds landed on the opposite side just as she replied, "No, but they might." Biting her bottom lip, she said, "I've wanted to tell you about them and how I came across Cole again."

Leaning forward, I asked, "Are you sure you want to talk about *him*?"

"Yes, and I think it's time you knew how the birds met him too." She sighed.

"Okay, we have all day then." She slid down to where she could lay her head in my lap and see the sky. I brushed hair from her face as she began.

"Dawn was just beginning while I stood on the balcony to my room, calling for my friends to come. When they arrived, they landed on the rail, eager about something when they began pacing back and forth and looking toward the back of the house.

"I paid no mind to them when I said, 'Morning, you two.' Of course, they can't talk, so I had grown to understand their many tones when they squawked. When they began to dance, I knew it was for their treats. Pulling it from my pocket, I peeled the tiny fruit and gave each a slice while they followed me around the balcony. We made a game of this, but the female, a soon to be mother, began to become frantic, so I glanced over at Chase, who was entering the house. He had gone to see the Marswaye awhile at their request. I was daydreaming when a knock sounded upon the door.

"The birds fluttered and I turned to the doorway as another knock came. 'Who is it?' I asked, entering the room toward the door.

"'Casey. Can I come in?' she asked through the door.

"'Sure, come in.' I unlocked the door for her and she stepped in the room still in her burgundy night clothes and housecoat with slippers.

"'Can you do me a favor?' I noticed her hair in disarray.

"'If I can. What is it you need?' I stood staring at her. She went to my vanity and sat down, looking at me through the mirror.

"'I see you need hair work. How would you like it done today?' I asked, going to her, and placing my hands in her damp hair that was just hanging there, sort of lifeless.

"'Oh, Kimmi, what can you do with this mop today?' Talwheana stepped through the open balcony door and stopped to watch through the mirror as we watched in return.

"'Are you in need of hair work too?' I jokingly asked the bird. The bird flapped her wings, then hopped onto the bed rail at the foot.

"'What's going on with you? It's getting close, isn't it?' I talked to her as though she were human. She squawked and flapped her wings in dismay. I felt a sudden presence outside, but I paid no heed as I continued to talk with the bird.

"'Are you bedded yet?' Talwheana tossed her head up then down for a yes.

"'Good.' I sighed. One might have thought I was crazy, talking to a bird that was once considered senseless.

"Casey stirred in the chair and said, intruding upon our conversation, 'Kimmi, my hair please.'

"Ignoring the present feeling and returning my attention back to the head of hair, I said, 'If you are in that much need.' I laughed at her.

"I had just picked up the comb and began to comb her hair when a gunshot rang out, making Casey and I scream. The birds went to screeching in the silent morning to warn of danger.

"The door swung open, and Mollie raced in, yelling, 'Is everyone alright in here?' Then continued on out to the balcony with the birds. Casey and I replied yes and that we were fine. Mollie made sure all was well, then left us to our business.

"After braiding her hair in one strand, Casey thanked me, and left the room to me and the female, who was attentive to cleaning her wings. I had told Ivan of the upcoming chicks and he agreed to make a box for them.

"Looking at the swollen belly, I said, 'I have a bed coming for you and the little ones if you like.' She stopped her piercing glare like she knew what the words meant. I spent the next few minutes talking to her until a soft knock came on the door.

"I glanced up just as Ivan came in with a large brown wooden box, more like a crate, with the help of Chase and put it in the corner of the room near the window. Mom watched the whole time in concern until they put the box down.

"Wiping his hands on his pants, Ivan said, standing back from the crate, 'There are limbs, grass, hay, and etcetera for her bed.'

"'Thank you so much,' I said, not moving when the bird squawked as she left the bed. Slowly landing on the floor, Talwheana walked toward the box in caution.

"She checked every nook and cranny of that crate, then flew up to the opening on top, which was a big hole. She tilted her head so she could peek inside, then jumped down into the opening. I could hear her moving around inside the thing. It was silent for a spell, but then she suddenly came out of the hole, and back to the bed where she began pacing back and forth, bobbing her head.

"'What?' I asked, not sure of the meaning. I had never seen her act that way. But it wasn't for me. She wanted the male to check it out as well. He came into the room, landed next to her, and together they walked in circles around one another, then he flew to the crate.

"Like the male he was, he paced the crate for security before hopping up to the top where he dropped inside for a bit. Finally, he came out to the top and landed with a squawk. The bird stopped and looked at me then the box—back and forth a couple times.

"'I see. You are ready for her in there.' The bird bobbed his head yes. I went to the dresser and gathered up some soft lining for the inside. When I rose to my feet, Talwheana wasted no time going inside the box. I noticed the day vanished, so I had a simple dinner of grilled cheese with a salad, then readied for bed.

"'Good night, you two,' I said, turning out the lights, before I pulled the blanket up over my shoulders.

"Several days passed before the eggs were laid. After three weeks, one morning, I heard a chirp. I was awakened by a soft cry. *What is it and where was it coming from?* Groggy and not realizing what it was, I got out of bed, facing the window and the upcoming sun. I shaded my eyes, but the chirp came again. Then it dawned on me—the box. I ran over to the box to find the eggs had finally hatched. It had been eleven days since Talwheana laid three of them. Hawkloun was pacing by the doors, which meant it was time to hunt food for them. I ran over and opened the doors for him. He quickly took flight, spreading his wings to full length as he soared higher. When he disappeared, I returned to the box to check on the chicks.

"They're cute as hell, wobbling around in the nest while Talwheana moved about them. They were hungry in their cries for breakfast, but there was one that didn't look so well, and I hoped it wasn't sick already. But I watched in amazement how she cared for the tiny things and cleaned the nest, tossing out the dung. In no time, the male was back, landing on the bed. I moved away so he could enter the box with a large beetle for Talwheana. I left them alone while I dressed and went downstairs.

"The following weeks, the chicks had grown and had been taught to fly. Since it was time for them to be back in the wild, I watched them as they headed for the woods. The little ones were growing fast and would become like their parents. I waved and yelled, telling them good luck, until I no longer saw them. I turned back into the room and closed the door. I felt sad but happy at the same time as I got dressed, then went downstairs."

Stirring from sitting so long, I asked, brushing hair from her eyes, "Now, is all of this true about your red-tails and the little ones?"

She rolled her head to my waist. "All true, especially the little ones who are now grown and have families of their own. It's also how I came to meet Cole for the last time."

"I was out on a cloudy day with the little ones in flight, but I soon lost track of them. I quickly ran through the trees to look for them if possible but instead of them, I saw Cole. I ran head on into his arms. He grabbed me by the shoulders, laughing this awful laugh while I struggled to get free.

"He made the sly remark, 'You need a man to take you to the moon and I'm here just for that.' He reached for his zipper, groping himself.

"Trying to get free, I told him, 'There are plenty of others places to stick it.' He slapped me across the cheek, then back handed me across the jaw, sending me to the ground. Tasting the blood from the broken jaw—that you already knew of—I wiped my mouth with the back of my hand. Cole wasted no time in dropping his trousers to finish what he and Jess started. I saw the shadows of the birds come over the tress in a silent predatory soar. Cole never saw the oncoming birds before they hit him on the top of the head, taking hair with them, opening his neck and across his shoulders. I was on my feet and out of his reach before he hit the ground and blood splattered on us both. They returned, taking more of his flesh off his back and down his legs, before leaving again. He passed out and I ran like hell."

Kimmi fell silent with tears in her eyes. I was so caught up in the story, I never saw the birds leave until they came back and Kimmi watched them.

"Luke, when I left Cole that day, I was hoping he was dead." Sitting upright, she moaned, "Is it so wrong to wish for one to be dead?" The question sent me for a loop, not knowing what to say.

I gently wiped away the tears, replying, "It's getting late. You ready for home yet? My leg's asleep."

Sighing softly, she said, "Do I? Can't we stay here?"

"I wish. Come, let's get you home."

Not catching her in time, she grabbed me around the waist, "Come here and kiss me." She quickly pressed her lips to mine while her hands found the back of my head and pulled me tighter.

My hands eased around her waist and pulled her tight, returning the motion. She moaned in pleasure, pulling tighter on my neck from the intent. I had a growing need to drop her to the ground when my hand slid over her buttocks and squeezed. My head called to take her when her hand moved down my back to the waist and the goal to continue.

"Stop please," I whispered, pulling away from her grasp.

"Please, Luke. Do you not want me as I do you?" she said in desperation.

"Oh yes, but not now. Please."

She came over, looked me in the face, and with those crystals, she asked, "What would happen if I were no longer pure? Would you still love me the same? I love you and I cannot stop the desire for you."

Like a slap in the face, I asked, "You are still a virgin?" I sighed in agony for my love for her.

She licked her lips and said, "When you stopped me the first time about Cole and Jess, you probably thought I had been raped. But see, I wasn't. If it had not been for Casey, I would've been." The birds were out feeding when they came in."

Swallowing, I asked, "The Lake?"

"I'm an affectionate person who has longed to be loved and to return that love. I thought that was what you wanted. You see, we are a loving tribe."

Taking her face into my hands, I said, "Then I'll not take that one virtue that is most important in a woman."

"Oh but you can, and you will in time," my head said.

Kissing her forehead, I said, "Listen, I love you more than anything I have ever known, and I will always have to pull back before I do something we both may regret." She kissed me on the cheek with a smile and nodded okay. I lead her from the trail and took her home before I took myself home to a cool shower.

PLAYBACK

T HE REST OF the week passed with me helping around the house, asking about the thing called the gorge. I was told it had a nasty reputation and recalled what Sam had said once. Well, it was finally Saturday, and I had agreed to meet Daniel and Jason at the lake, even though it was still icy from the late winter. About noon, I crossed the bridge into the lot and parked the bike, watching the others already there and wondering if they knew any more about the gorge than I already did. I knew Jason had poor feelings toward it since he could remember that tragic night. I got off the bike, grabbed my towel, and walked to the table where I dropped it with theirs. I shimmied down to my trunks, took off running and hit the cold murky water.

I was midway into the lake when I surfaced about where Jason was standing waist-high in water.

Daniel came up on the other side of him. "What took ya so long?"

"Hey, guys," Jason managed.

"Question: Do you all go to the gorge?"

"Woo, the Black River?" Jason said. "I don't like it, but it's an awesome racetrack."

"You can't be right in the head." Daniel chuckled.

Feeling the laugh, I said with a shake of the head, "Are you two even real? You joke about everything."

"If people didn't have fun or a joke, it would be a boring world to live in," Daniel replied.

"Joking is one thing, but the fun would be going down the gorge. Daniel you know this," Jason came back.

"When was the last time?" I asked in wonder if either actually had the nerve.

"Both of us. About a year before you returned," Daniel said.

"From the looks of you both, you stood there and looked at it from a distance. Correct?" If I read them right, it had been true up to when Jason's grin disappeared.

"Not exactly. We watched up close as someone else took the dare," he replied.

"Who was it?" I surprisingly asked and patted the top of the frosty water, looking around the lake. People would have thought we were out of our minds if they had seen us in there.

I looked back at Jason when he said, "Don't laugh now, but it was the two brothers in a dispute. Whoever won the race got the dispute. We were bystanders, you might say."

"Who won, Tom or Mac?" I asked, grunting and finding it unbelievable.

"Well," Daniel cited. I saw his eyes slightly rise, and through them, I saw a figure ease up behind me when I was jumped and pulled under by Mac.

We played under the darkness of the water for a spell, then surfaced together. Jason and Daniel were goofing off nearby.

Shaking the water from my hair, I asked Mac, "What the hell you doing here?"

He propped his chin in his hand, then smiled and said, "Let's see. It has to do with water and swimming." He hit the water with the back of his hand.

"Funny, are we?" I grinned, grabbing him around the neck, and took him under again. The fun was on then, but I wondered who won that race.

Around three, Willa, Jada, and Paulene had gotten there. Only the place was still empty except for us, the weird ones. The day was cold, and I wished Kimmi had been there too. I swam to the bank as Jada walked to the edge and removed the black beach towel to reveal a black-and-white two-piece bikini. *Nice*, I thought and was about to whistle, but decided against it. Paulene, who wore a gray full-body suit, dropped her towel on the sand.

I heard Jason call, "Hurry up, I'm cold, sweetie." I saw her blush as I stepped from the water and onto the bank where I found Willa at the table.

Wondering if she would even talk to me, I walked to the table, and sat down facing her. Her brown eyes stared at me as though she could strangle me.

"How'd you know we'd be here?" When she didn't answer, I grumbled at her, "You sitting out today?"

"Yeah, just today…not feeling good." Even her tone made it apparent she was ill. I felt bad about what I had done, but I had no way of explaining to her, and my head really didn't want anyone to know.

"Problem?" I sighed, leaning on the table.

She was quick to strike at my cheek and miss. "Not in the mood is all!" Her freckles wrinkled over her forehead, and silence fell over her again.

"Are you ever going to get over that?"

Those green eyes cut through me like a knife. "When hell freezes over or you're dead."

"She liked it. She's just not admitting it." My head laughed. I passed it off, feeling she was just upset, and finished the day with the crew, before heading home to shower.

I dressed in sweats, a light-blue sleeveless T-shirt, and sneakers. After combing my damp hair, I went downstairs and out the front door.

I kept to the darkness and watched Luke run from the house, anxious about something. My anger was overflowing with resentment and I didn't know how, but I wanted him to regret the night by my hand.

With an eerie feeling, I stopped on the front lawn as if I were being watched. When it passed, I ran over, got into the Charger, and headed out to the Creed's.

I rolled up into the drive, parked near the porch, and got out. I walked to the door just as Kimmi stepped out on the porch dressed neatly in a long black satin gown with long sleeves. She had always been so elegantly dressed, but what made her so formal, other than her skin? Anyway, I hugged and kissed her, took her by the hand, and walked her to the passenger side of the car to get in. I closed the door and dashed to the driver side, quickly getting in.

"We are going where?" Kimmi asked as soon as the engine came to life.

"I want to show you something that lies on this mountain." I put the car into gear.

"Sounds interesting." She quivered as she spoke. "So, what is it that has you in an uproar tonight?" She giggled.

"Not something usual." I smiled with a glance. Talk was the about the usual for us. I drove out of the drive and down the hill toward the gorge.

I stayed out of sight, watching the boy and girl until they left. I eased out of the darkness with the headlights out and followed the taillights of the Charger. My hands tightened on the wheel with anger. I whispered to myself, "Where are you going?"

I drove through town and up the small curvy road to the top of the lifeless gorge and parked on the shoulder. I got out, rushed to the passenger side, and helped Kimmi out. Standing at the hood, we stared into the dark, and the empty two-lane highway. I weighted the option of taking the chance of doing such a thing or passing.

Kimmi was staring over the mountaintop as if thrilled with the view when she asked, stepping closer to me, "Luke, why have you come here?"

"My father once told me about this place and its price for life. Not to mention that Daniel and Jason said it was a good racetrack. I thought since it was dark and the road was empty, we would ease down it."

"From here, it looks…evil. Let's not," she cringed. "What about the overlay of ice?"

"Yeah, Sam said it was a black, heartless, breathtaking, heel-nipping, winding, life-taking, and never-ending bottomless pit where I nearly died as a child. I lost my childhood memories of this place and The Black River that lies beneath it." I grew quiet as the words of Sam ran through my head and lightning struck in the distance.

I felt Kimmi's cold hand slip into mine. "I feel you have a need to do something wild and crazy. Shall we?" she asked in that cute way of hers.

"Sure, before it starts sleeting." Shaking off the feeling we were being watched, I took her by the hand, and helped her into the car. I glanced back into the darkness and saw nothing, so I got in. Easing onto the pavement, we slowly headed down the mountainside of towering black mass of ice over the red dirt road.

With the lights out, I put the shifter into neutral, and rolled off the shoulder in silence when Luke and that girl took off down the road. A silent black night and a slick road, I knew it was the perfect place for revenge. It took me back to that rainy night with Sam when I reached for the stereo and turned it up, letting the memories play over and over of that fatal night.

The night was black as coal except for the lights on the car. I took my foot off the accelerator and coasted for about a mile. The curves were narrow, then tightened as we went down. Some curves let the hood hit the shadows ahead of us before the rear could complete the bend. I wasn't afraid, I just didn't know the gorge or its reputation, but the view of the town below was awesome. I slowed down a bit, watching the headlights chase the sparkling red road of ice.

We were silent in thought and I didn't notice the speed until I heard Kimmi gasp. I looked down at the odometer that read thirty-eight, before pressing on the brake pedal to slow down.

"You okay over there?" I asked, grabbing her hand.

"Yes," she said with a nervous laugh. "It was a bit fast."

"I'm sorry. I wasn't paying attention." I gently squeezed her hand for comfort.

"Can we go now?" she asked as she began to tremble. I hadn't seen the thing come up behind me, till the lights came on.

I stayed back as long as possible, watching the taillights in the curves. When the car slowed down the last time, I was right on it, waiting for the right moment. Through the windshield, I saw Luke face the girl and knew it was time for payback. I flipped the on the lights and said out loud, "You're mine."

With so many spotlights, I was blinded when I looked up into the rearview mirror. I grabbed the wheel and began slowing down while I moved over for the vehicle to pass, but it stayed right on me. I felt I'd been taken back to the day when I was once a child with Sam. I gently mashed the pedal and speed up. But it wasn't enough when the thing rammed us in the rear. "Damn," I cursed under my breath. Droplets of sleet had began to hit the windshield, and Kimmi was softly whimpering in the passenger seat. I patted her hand and found it trembling fiercely.

When my sweaty palms grabbed the steering wheel, thoughts of my father's story rushed into my head again, and I fought to see the thing behind us as it rammed the back of the Charger. With the road becoming slicker, I had no choice but to try and keep control. My heart was pounding so hard it hurt my chest in fear of the inevitable while the lights continued to blind me. When the vehicle hit us again for the third time, I swerved but quickly gained control, knowing it was only a matter of time. On the last bump, I finally lost control, and the car began to spin.

I hung onto the wheel with white-knuckled hands as I yelled at Kimmi, who was focused on the ravine, "Brace yourself." That was all I had time for when the thing hit us in the right rear and began pushing us sideways down the road. Suddenly, it stopped, and roared off around us. The the night fell to an eerie silence for a short few seconds before the lights came on again. Kimmi screamed when the thing struck me in the driver side and stopped.

I stared at that kid through the windshield in a hated manner. I mashed on the accelerator over and over while gripping the wheel with both hands, waiting for him to make the dash that his father never did. But he didn't.

It revved up over and over, but it was too dark to make out its color. I could tell it was an offroad vehicle. The last time it idled, Kimmi yelled as the thing began pushing us toward the shoulder. I fought to start the stalled engine before we went over into the ravine and rolled twice. I heard the horn blow from overhead and the last thing I recalled was smashing my head into something when the steering wheel hit me in the chest, causing me to lose consciousness.

When I began to regain consciousness, I couldn't say how long we had laid there, but I realized I was still belted in. That was when I thought we were upside down. I could barely see Kimmi, who was lying with her head against the broken window. I saw blood drip across her face and the imminent bruise. I tried to reach for her, but she was just out of my grasp. With my head pounding and vision blurred, I fumbled with the latch of the seatbelt that was jammed.

"Shit," I cursed out loud. I struggled with it for a period before remembering I had a flashlight in the center console. When I got it opened and found the light, I turned it on.

One of my legs ached badly, but I shined the light toward Kimmi. Seeing through my blurred vision, she was still buckled in the seat, had a gash on her forehead and on her cheek, bleeding. In the silence, I laid there and remembered that this was the way I was supposed to die as a child. I wasn't going to let that happen again. And upon recalling I had a tiny knife in my pocket, I rummaged for it till I found it in my left pants pocket. I was dazed and confused some, but Kimmi was all I could think of as I opened the small knife, and began cutting the seatbelt off me at the waist.

Dropping to the roof, I realized we were wrong side up. I tried the door that was jammed. Turning my back to the console and with my feet, I kicked out the window and crawled out onto the ground that was heavy with freshly laid ice. I rolled over, facing upward, and noticed my nose was bleeding from the warmth of the blood running down my cheek. I rolled over onto my stomach and tried to get to my feet, but slipped from the steepness of the ravine. I laid there for a moment in tears because I couldn't reach Kimmi. That's when I felt the kick in my side, breaking ribs. Groaning, I rolled over and passed out again.

The next time I awoke, I was soaked to the bone from the sleet. Through tear-stained eyes, I saw it—the glowing light. I rubbed my eyes to see a blur, but the huge thing moved closer to the car. I had probably been dreaming when the second one came up behind it. I instantly feared for Kimmi as I tried to get to my feet again.

"Stop!" I yelled in vain when I slipped on the wet ground. Moaning from the pain in my leg, I watched the things as they got closer and closer to the car. I never got a clear vision because they were swift, and I thought Kimmi was a goner, but I still cried out hoping to stop them.

I rolled onto my back to let the wetness wash my face of the tears when I noticed I had a broken right arm, but I felt a wanting presence around me. I slowly opened my eyes and jerked from the sight of a huge white thing standing over me. It had a glowing white face with ice-blue eyes. I felt warm air from its nostrils when they flared open, but I flinched as it came closer to my face. I was too shocked to blink as I pressed harder into the saturated ground.

I thought I made out what I surely believed were wings on the thing as they spread open behind the animal, but the nose was too close to mine. I heard it snort, taking a deep inhale of the air and my scent. I blinked once when it lowered its face to mine and tilted it slightly to the right. It blinked twice. I closed my eyes thinking it was a dream for it could not have been real. I just laid there and let the cold sleet wash me, losing track of time and Kimmi when the pain of darkness took over.

In the darkness was a voice calling to me. I tried hard to see, but all I saw was a blur of things. Again I only heard the voice as it called my name. "Luke," it yelled. Feeling trapped, I couldn't move since my legs were numb and my head hurt. "Luke," the voice whispered. I couldn't see while I struggled with it, trying to open my eyes that could not see.

I felt a deep pain in my chest and moaned, "Kimmi, God, where's Kimmi?" I whined.

"Can you hear me?" the voice said, shining a light in my eyes. I tried to shield them, but my arms didn't move. I struggled to get free of whatever it was that held fast to my efforts.

"It's me, kid," the voice said.

"Okay, me who?" I cried, wanting so bad to move, but what the hell was I tied to? My eyes began to flutter but only in slits to see sightless visions.

Again I opened them, finding Tom and Whitecloud were there. My temples were pounding with pain.

"There you are," Whitecloud soothed.

I ignored him when I truly realized I was on a stretcher and strapped to it. I began to struggle with them, only to find them secure. "Kimmi," I uttered.

"She's alive, kid," Tom said, leaning over me. "Do you remember what happened?"

"Barely," I said, rolling my head from side to side.

"Later then," Tom said.

"Tom, I need to see her please," I whispered.

"You have a broken rib, leg, and arm. You don't need to get up," Whitecloud informed me.

"Please," I gasped, struggling with the straps.

"Help him up, or he'll break them," Whitecloud implied. Tom loosened the straps, helped me to my feet, and, with an arm around his neck, helped me limp over to Kimmi.

Ivan and Mollie were down on the ground on the other side of the car when I got there. Peering around them, I saw Kimmi on a gurney out cold. Her face was covered in blood, and her left leg was broken in two places when I saw bones had cut through the skin. There was a gash over her left eye in a well-rounded bruise. Mollie jumped to her feet and slapped me with hand that stung.

It left me unable to get mad at her for she had the right to be upset with me. I rubbed my cheek and realized Ivan was silent as he bandaged Kimmi's leg with a splint.

I released my grip around Tom's neck and dropped to the ground next to her with tears and cried, "I'm so sorry. Please forgive me." I looked Ivan in the eyes without a blink. "I didn't do this. Someone rammed us and pushed us over."

Tom squatted down by my side when he said, "You say someone rammed you?" I nodded yes as my temples felt like they exploded inside.

Through those white eyes, Ivan cut me in half and said, "You bastard. Casey told us what you did to this girl. Now, you don't come back to see her. And only then if she wishes." Swallowing hard, with tear-filled eyes, I agreed to their wishes as I watched them pick the gurney up and carry it over to the Mustang. With the backseat down, they put Kimmi in, and without another word, I watched the black car carry Kimmi away. Tom helped me up, and we went to his truck where I sat down in the back seat, lost in thought so much I felt no pain from the broken bones or the throbbing temples that seemed to vanished like Kimmi.

Over the course of the next two weeks, I healed fully. All the scars vanished as if they were never there, and I felt renewed. But I still hadn't heard from Kimmi or the Creeds of her condition. I longed for her embrace but I could only wait as asked. It didn't stop the fact that I dearly missed her. I still hadn't told anyone about the blurry things that night either. They would have only thought I hit my head too hard. But did I? Memories flooded back to the day Sam told me of the ones he saw in the gorge. What does that place hold deep inside? I dressed, went downstairs to have breakfast with Mae and Joe, then went to the living room. Crashing on the sofa, I spent the day and night watching TV. When I did go to sleep, I dreamed of Kimmi, those eyes, and the flowing black hair with the white streaks. I would wake myself up thinking she was there beside me.

BROKEN DREAMS

I T HAD BEEN another week before I received word that Kimmi had gone back to the Marswaye. Sightless of what I had become, I took the day and went to the lake while the misty rain showered down on me. I sat on the tabletop and looked out over the rippling water. With almost no feeling for the rain, it ran down my face and into my eyes, which did not see things as before. The only thing I saw were Kimmi's blues hanging in the grey dreary sky, behind the trees, or shadowed from the sun.

I thought I had found a friend, someone to talk to and be with or just to be around with, but all of that had changed for she was gone. Why did it have to be? I often wondered if she would return to visit her aunt and uncle. I tormented myself with thoughts of her, but the most torturous was when I spent the day at the lake. With my mind going back in time, I recalled the night she asked for that first kiss in the shimmering water. We moved around with the moon overhead, bathing us in its light to reflect from her hair as she turned to me. Her eyes were like diamonds looking at me. That night, I found her to be breathtaking in a swimsuit that covered nothing for the imagination I had of her then. I saw the beads of moisture run down her body like tears. When I held her close and felt her body swaying with the water, I knew I would never ever have the desire for another woman as I had for her. The problem was whether or not I could erase her face from my mind. I have dreamed of our first night together and the pleasure that would have followed. All of it was just a dream when it vanished into thin air with her when she left me there.

I wish I knew what I could have done differently to have kept her with me, but it's been some two months since she had gone. The days that passed were as long as the seasons. The spark that hit me when we first touched was unnerving. I was captured by the first smile, and trapped by it still. How could she have put such a hold on me and I not know it? All I really knew was, she had a powerful pull of beauty. I hadn't actually thought about it till then, knowing she would never come back and that I'd never see her face again. Since we've been torn apart, it left me feeling like I was in a horror movie played in slow motion. I had always been told that you never know what you have till it's gone. How true it is. "Where are you tonight?" I whispered, letting the tears drop, while the half moon slowly peeked at me over the trees of the lake. I finally got up and went home. I couldn't stand the cold without her any longer.

During the last month of winter, I let my companion take a stronger hold me, finding myself digging holes in the snow-covered ground, learning the art of telling lies, and letting someone else take the fall for my stupidity. The house on the hill stood vacant like the storm that came through the night. When I rose from the bed and went to the window, I saw a fresh snow-covered ground outside. "Does it snow where you are?" I whispered to the window. The pines were so full of green needles while others had lost their leaves that were blown around like the wind that carried them. My days were trying to run together while my mind searched for her face and I wondered why on earth was she someone I couldn't resist.

I dressed in slouchy clothes, but why? I would only sit in a chair and watch the day go by as the sun rises with grace, then shines down with desire and leaves with the times. I never ventured out to see friends. I seldom left my prison for I was alone in hurt, sorrow, and pain. My heart called to stop with each passing day. How could I or anyone, anywhere have feelings that way for someone? Was it even possible? Since she came into my life, I had come to see that anything was possible. "Where did she come from?" I often asked myself? "The paleness of her beauty came from where, how, and why?" I cried at the winds that blew. Guilt was what I felt, but I was told all my life to just go with the flow. Well, I did. And where did it take me? To a place I could not and desired not to return from A place that was cold and dark. I no longer wanted to be alone in the world where she left me. But I had no choice, I was bound by what I am.

One night I dreamed of her and me dancing on the sands of time—laughing, talking, and joking about a life together. Her face was as beautiful as ever, and her hair was as black as coal with the streaks flowing through it. I saw the moon peer up at us, then smiled in a way I'd never seen before. It felt as I did when she was with me. We danced so close while I held her close to keep her safe from harm. She wrapped her arms around me and held on tight. I saw fog as it began to roll in and thicken around us. I felt her become stiff and afraid of something. Her face looked shattered as she tried to scream but could not. I looked up to see enormous white hands and arms reaching out, pulling her away from me. I desperately tried to hang on, but the hands were too strong, so she was snatched from my arms into the darkness and vanished. I awoke with a startle to find the room was dark, and I was still alone at home in my room. What was happening to me? Will time really erase her from me? I rolled over to see the moon looking in on me, but I finally drifted back to sleep only to dream again. Again I woke up startled by the dream, feeling tears fall to the pillow.

Kimmi

I was sitting at the table in the conference room dreaming of Luke when Magnyss came in. Feeling my temper rise like it did the day I was forced to leave Black Mountain, I leaped from the table, overturning the vase of artificial flowers.

Magnyss stared at me a moment before he asked, "Are you still bitter with me for not letting you return to that boy? Or is it maybe you are growing inside and cannot tell the young man?"

Clinching my fist, my fingernails dug into my palms, and I replied with force, "Why will you not tell me what I am?"

Stopping me before I could continue, Magnyss replied, "You already know, my child. I know you have called forth the spirits for help."

Stomping my foot, I growled with real meaning and said, "How could you? You said my mother and father were the only ones that knew." By the time it crossed my lips, I realized just where I stood. The growl lingered in my head.

"Now that you know, will it stop me from killing that boy? No! I have seen those like him, and he is trouble," Magnyss said coming to me. I felt lost with nowhere to go and no one to turn to.

Looking in to his pale face and green eyes, I chocked down my angered pride of being self-sufficient and said, "How long do you think I will idly set aside and let you murder the man I love? Besides, if I am to become something ground-breaking, then what? Will I be like you?"

"Yes. And then some." Wrapping me in his strong arms, he said, resting his chin on my head, "You are the last of a dying breed. I fear for your life as I did your mother's. I refuse to let you leave here again. You must marry within your own kind." Feeling my eyes water, I began to wonder if I would ever see Luke again. I would have to find a way to bring him here…someday.

It was mid spring, and I was awakened by pebble sounds hitting the window. From the bed, I looked out the window to a storm going on outside. Hail was hitting the window while it chased the wind around and fell to the ground which was already covered in white stuff. I got up, moved to the window and stared out. Feeling a chill, I said in a whisper, "Is this how you live where you are? Is it snowing there? Are you hidden from it and safe, or are you out playing in it, with friends of your kind?" I cried to myself and wished I knew. I stuck my forehead to the cold glass, listening to the beating of the frozen rain.

I found the chair once again where I sat down, propping my elbows on the window sill and watching the rain drops fall. I thought of the time we spoke and how she said she was as pure as a snowflake. I guess that's as pure as it gets. How I wish she could have been there and let me hold her so she would be warm. Again I could only wish as she said one time, "That's what dreams are made of." The day raged on as the storm pushed through with the soft tap on the window. The droplets grew larger and began to fall like a waterfall to the ground. Then there was nothing but the coming of night when it started to chase away the clouds to the other side of the earth. I rose from the chair and went down stairs to the smell of food. I had not eaten for several days, so I had to keep myself strong in times of need. Returning to bed, I finally dozed off.

Coming from a run with my companion in a dream, he led me to dream about Kimmi and I. We were somewhere on a beach while the sun shone its warmth on us. Her face was as light as the sun when it reflected off it. It turned to a rosy pink, so I picked her up and carried her to the water's cool pleasure. She hung onto my neck, slowly lowering herself down. Her hair was that of black beauty, and it shimmered as it knocked the sun off when she ducked under the water. She slowly surfaced to let the water run down her slim body. I watched the chills running up and across her breasts. She held out her hands for mine and I reached for them but could not touch them as mine passed right through. "What?" I cried out and tried again. It was like she was fading away, so I hurried to her, but she disappeared into thin air.

How could I have let her go? Why did I have to? I could have kept her safe.

"That's what I'm made for," I shouted aloud, but no one heard.

The wolf standing at the edge of the water said, "She is nothing. Leave her be and come with me." It was the companion.

"How could anyone believe that now?" I cried to myself. I walked to the sandy bank and sat down. I was awoken by the sun as it glared at me through the window, blinking as it hit me in the eyes. I shielded my eyes from the yellow thing hanging in the window and got out of bed.

Finally, the first months of summer hung in the air with the trees and flowers blooming with the warming temperatures. Dew covered the day as I walked out the front door. I had decided on jeans and a pullover tee shirt. I stopped in the sun to let it shine on my face and wondered again what it was like where she was? Was it the same today as it was yesterday? Does it ever warm there, or is it always cold? I wished I knew how she lived in such a cold region. I have found many days in the past when I wish I could go visit her, but I don't want to ruin her life again. I did hope that she would find the happiness she wants in her world for I shall not in this world without her.

"Shut up with the whining. I've heard enough," my companion snapped at me.

"Go to hell," I cursed, grabbing my head with both hands.

Did I really want to keep doing this to myself? Yes, I had done something stupid that hurt her, and I was sorry. Kimmi's blue eyes could satisfy any man's need. Her embrace and kiss were untouchably ones to remember. I wiped the droplet of tear from my eye as Mae came out the door to where I stood.

Putting a warm arm around my waist, she squeezed. "I hope time will ease the pain for you. It's been months now that she's left. I have lived many years and seen many, many things but not like what I've seen with you and her."

"How much longer can I hold on to her and feel this way? I long for her every day that passes. I see her in my dreams and in the shadow. I fear the heart will heal someday but the mind won't. It refuses to let go."

"You need to get out of here and go see your friends again. Call Daniel. Y'all go see Jason and Paulene. Just so you know, those two have set the date to marry." When she turned to leave, she said, "By the way, Willa called many times for you but you have refused to take any calls. Sam included."

"Have you told Sam why I haven't talked to him?"

"Yes, he knows about Kimmi leaving. Now, get out of here. This house has been your prison far too long now." She handed me some keys.

I looked at her, and she said, "Camero is in the garage." I gave her a kiss on the cheek and told her thanks, then watched her go back inside and wave as she closed the door.

It had been several months since I left Luke and that mountain after the accident at Ivan's request. Even though I had heard nothing from him, it was time I returned. So the Marswaye had been summoned for a conference at my request. They were sitting in their high-backed Victorian chairs, in their black suits while I stood in front of Magnyss after our bitter argument. He had refused to let me leave the walls of that home and return to the mountain in the states and to the man I loved. I glared into his evergreen eyes, knowing he was never going to change his mind. I bit into my bottom lip, then swallowed hard, the blood that pooled inside my mouth and my hands turned into fists.

I had more anger raging in me right then than I would've probably ever known. With tears streaming down my face, I turned away in haste. With a stomp of the foot, I stormed out of the room, letting the door slam behind me, only to catch my dress. I didn't stop as it tore, and I ran down the corridor to the front door where I grabbed the knob. With a swift twist of the wrist, it opened. I stepped through it, out onto the porch, into the fading sunlight, the howling winds, and heavy snow. The storm had been brewing all day from the cloud-covered skies.

I stepped off the steps into the frozen snow and howling wind, making my way out the distance of two hundred yards before I dropped to my knees in the snow. The wind carried my hair like a kite as the snow fell around me and the once wet tears were frozen sickles on my cheeks. I looked up to the sky as I raised both arms outward and began praying to the Great Spirit to hear my plea and come for me. "I have never been touched by one such as him. I cannot and will not live without him. Please hear me; hear my voice on the winds. If he could only hear me, I know he would come. I want him to know how I love him. Good-bye my love."

Feeling that the fathers were watching from somewhere, I dropped my arms, rose to my feet, pushed back the hair from my face, and brushed off the snow from my dress. I turned toward the door which I came from, only to see Magnyss standing there. I sighed heavily, and walked toward him and stopped long enough for him to step aside and let me in. I dearly loved him, but right then I deeply despised him. I walked past him without a word to Mollie who was standing behind him. I ignored her pleas as I went down the hall to my room where I would stay, haunted by the dreams of my love, waiting to perish in this life. But...would he come? Would Mollie get to him in time?

Staring through the windshield of the car, I gained my thoughts and left the driveway, heading anywhere for the time being. I guess the drive would have been good for me. I didn't want to see things where she and I had been. I avoided those, but I could still see her sitting there in the passenger seat, looking out the window. I saw her face in windows and the clouds. Her eyes glared at me from the trees as the winds blew, and swayed as she did when she walked. How do you get over something as quick as that? Something, somewhere would always remind me of her. I could feel my body growing weak for her sometimes at night.

I was so far in thought I didn't see the vehicle coming at me. The headlights looked like her eyes as they glowed from the moon. Tears filled my eyes and began to fall. I wanted to follow them to wherever they took me.

"Look Out!" a voice in me said. I looked up in time to see the car right in front of me, drifting over into its lane. I braked hard, swerving to miss the oncoming car, but there was no shoulder when I began to spin in the road. I spun out of control, going over the edge of the ravine and sliding down the side as the earth gave way to the weight of the car. The last thing I recalled was the tree when I hit my head.

Somewhere in the mist, I heard voices getting louder. I couldn't tell because my head was heavy, and I couldn't lift up to see what was going on. I thought I couldn't move my legs and arms. What happened was done so quickly, I couldn't feel my back. The car seat was holding me upright against the steering wheel in a pinned position. I couldn't remember what happened to me, but I tasted blood, and it was mine. I tried swallowing to wet my dry throat, but blood was the only thing I tasted. Unnerved and uneasy, I saw a light off in the distance, beckoning to me to go with it. Should I have gone before I blacked out again?

I can't say how long I was out, but loud voices rang in my head, making me look to a shadow of a vision. I began to see the movement, but it was only a blur. It closely faced me, and I swear it looked like a wolf, a white wolf with blue eyes. *Impossible*, I thought to myself. Then it vanished into thin air. After a short minute or two, I felt my head move, but it wasn't me doing the moving. I heard a loud ripping, gunning noise that made my head hurt even more, but I couldn't see what was going on.

My eyes refused to fully open for me, but what I could see were through the slits in them. I barely made out what looked like the picture of a man leaning toward me and saying something. I couldn't hear when my ears began to ring.

Then I heard a voice clear as day say, "Hang on, Luke. Help is here." There were so many of them talking that I was wondering who kept saying *hang on*.

"Hold on to what?" I tried to ask. I felt my left arm being touched as someone pulled on it. Then a stinging burn coursed through me. It wasn't long before I began to fade and my eyes closed to everything going dark again.

When my eyes began to flutter, I began to see outlines of things. I heard whispers as I tried to open my eyes slowly at first because they hurt. Blinking rapidly, I tried again to see more, but the shadows were unrecognizable. So who were they? I thought, *Were they people, or was that a hand in my face?* I thought I heard someone talking, but I couldn't tell what was being said. It sounded as if they were in a box somewhere. It was muffled, or was it my ears?

I tried to raise my left hand to my head, but it wouldn't move. *Okay, what's going on here?* I thought as I tried to sit up. When that didn't work, I felt strapped down, and began to struggle with whatever had me bound with no results. I felt hands on me, and I became agitated and furious.

"Easy now," a male voice said, patting my shoulder.

When I did find my voice at last, I demanded, "What the hell is going on?"

"Easy now," the voice sighed as I felt hands under my shoulders and the restraints released around my wrists.

Someone helped me to an upright position in a bed, so I could see things as they came into focus. The first thing I thought I saw was Sam.

"Sam? Dad, that you?" I choked up.

I felt a hand on my shoulder when he said, "Yeah it's me, son."

I stuttered when I asked him, "What happened, and why are you here?"

He sat on the side of the bed and asked, "You don't remember?"

"The last thing I recall was that tree." I rubbed my head with the other hand to find a few stitches. The left arm had a cast on it, and there was a cast on the left leg also.

"One among many you slammed into going down the ravine," Whitecloud said. I looked around the room as I followed the voice to find he was seated in a chair at the foot of the bed.

"You are either lucky or you had a guiding hand." My eyes were clearing, and I realized I was not at a hospital but at Whitecloud's place.

"How did I get here? The other car? What happened to it? I think I missed it. I tried to." I began to sputter.

"Tom is fine. He called me. We went down, and got you out of the…," He trailed off.

"It is a twisted piece of metal." Sam finished for him.

"I don't care about the car as long as Tom is okay."

"What were you thinking, Luke?" Luther asked.

"It wasn't because I wanted to. My thoughts were elsewhere, old man."

"Kimmi," Sam asked.

"Yeah, I couldn't help it, Dad." I looked at him and said, "I'm sorry about the car."

"That brings me to a question I need to ask: what do you have against cars? You have had a Ranger for years without accident, and you get here." he laughed.

"I don't know what happened, and I am sorry. Okay," I snarled.

He brushed my cheek with a thumb, saying, "I know the feeling. I've been there, remember."

"How long was I out?" I inquired, looking at the room of people.

"I have kept you under a week so you would heal quicker. The arm and leg will be healed soon, but the stitches will come out tomorrow," Tom said, coming into the room.

"Thank you, and I am sorry," I said, peeking at him through half-opened eyes.

With a grunt, he said, "For what? You didn't hurt anyone but yourself, kid."

"The way I feel right now is that I didn't try hard enough."

"You don't mean that, and you know it. You're hurt and upset, but it will come to pass soon. Rest now, you need it," Sam said as he kissed the top of my head. I watched as they left and the door closed behind them, wondering if they knew the feeling I had inside.

I spent the following week at home, healing, loafing around the house, watching and waiting to hear from her, at least once more. Sam had gone back home after a couple days to return to work. Willa came by at one time when she heard from Luther about the episode with Kimmi. I apologized for being rude and for what I had done to her. All in all, we became friends again but nothing more. Daniel offered the use of his Camero until I could manage to get another for myself—an offer I accepted. Jason and Paulene were welcomed company when much of it was needed ever since I was laid up in thoughts of her. I wished I could have told her I dearly loved her and maybe even asked her to marry me. But I couldn't, she wasn't there with me. The thought of marriage consumed me over the following weeks until she was nearly faded as a dream.

ALASKA

I WAS DREAMING WHEN I found Kimmi and I sitting at a table at the lake. She reached over and nudged me, then said, "Swim?" She slid off the tabletop and walked to the water's edge. Pulling her long hair back from her face, she secured it with a blue lace ribbon. Being a tease, she knew I was watching when she let the dark green gown slide from her shoulders to the ground, revealing a full-bodied, skimpy-cut white suit. She smiled as she looked back at me. I knew she was teasing when she stepped into the lake, sending the chills up her arms, but she didn't stop there.

Leaning over and letting the suit crease her buttock, she smiled and said, "Well, are you going to join me or not?" With a wink, she let her hands slide up the sides and over her breasts. How could I have said no? I jumped up from the table, shredding my shorts to the boxers, then tore off the tee shirt, and ran for the water.

The water was cold on my face when I lunged to life but found Willa standing there in front of me with a glass, waking me up from the dream. "Get off your ass, and get into the water," she chattered.

"What the devil did you do that for?" I asked, wiping my face. I had fallen asleep at the table where I had gone to the reservoir with Jason and Daniel. It had been several months since I last saw Kimmi, and yet I still dreamed of her, wishing I could forget the touch, the smile, the hair, and most of all, the eyes. With summer in full swing, I looked at Willa, who was still standing there in a pink bikini and smiled. The day was young, so I jumped up as she took off, chasing her to the water and grabbing her around the waist as we fell in. When the day came to an end after sunset, I went home, quickly showered, dressed in shorts, and went shirtless.

🐾🐾

I was sitting on the side of the bed with Kimmi in her weakened state. Staring at her pale face, I knew she was dying. She said she would rather die than stay here if she didn't get to leave or see Luke again.

Taking her lifeless hand into mine, she said in a lifeless tone, "Please…Mollie, go to him. You know him. I…I…don't care if you lie to him. I don't have much longer…" Sighing, I composed myself, wiped my tears, and rose from the bed. I had to go for her sake. But…would he listen after what I done to him? God I hope so.

🐾🐾

Feeling hungry, I hurriedly went down to the kitchen, finding the paper plates and some chips. I made myself a turkey on wheat, grabbed a glass of water, then went into the other room where the TV was already playing a Boris Karloff movie, *The Mummy*. Sitting the plate on the coffee table, I grabbed the remote and flopped down on the sofa. Searching for something a little more interesting, I came across the newer sequel of *The Mummy*. I settled on that and ate the sandwich only to grow tired by the time the movie was over. I turned off the TV, took the plate and glass back to the kitchen, and then headed upstairs to bed.

Through the shouting, I was suddenly awakened by pounding on the bedroom door. Mumbling, I rolled over groggy, "Who is it?"

"Mae. Please get up." She sounded frantic.

"What's the matter?" I yelled as I rolled out of the bed. My feet hit floor and I stumbled over, reaching for the knob and opened the door.

"Come downstairs quickly," she whined with tear-filled eyes. I let the door slide from my grip with a nod and turned to find the bedside clock read 6:13 a.m. and the birds singing. When Mae left, I rubbed my eyes, found my clothes from the night before, and dressed. All along I was wondering what the hurry was or what had happened. I combed my hair and raced down the stairs to the living room.

When I finally made it to the front room, I stumbled to a hard stop when I found Mollie standing there. After all the months that had passed, I didn't know if I wanted to rush over and give her a hug or stand there dumfounded.

"Hello, Luke." She sighed.

I thought I would say more than "What brings you here?"

Mae was sitting on the couch so I sat down by her. Mollie sat down in the chair near the window and her hair feel forward in a braid over her shoulder.

Clasping her hands together, Mollie said, "I've been sent here to ask that you return with me. The Marswaye have requested for your presence, and they sent me to get you. Here is the letter for you." She leaned over and handed me a pale-white envelope with a red blood seal on the back. I gently opened it, then removed the letter that read:

> Luke Winterset, You are hereby requested to appear in front of the Marswaye on the grounds of Kimlaye Creed. I have sent Mollie Creed to escort you back as soon as possible.
>
> Thank you,
> Magnyss

Looking at Mollie and Mae in despair, I asked, "What is this about, and who is Magnyss?"

She hesitated only a moment before saying, "Kim received a letter where she is promised to marry someone, but it didn't say who, only that she would receive another before her twenty second birthday." Mollie's eyes filled with tears, but my heart sank to the hurting point.

"Will you come back with me?" she supplicated.

I didn't feel the sadness. "I thought I was done with her when she has not called nor done anything to let me know she cared. So what are my options for not going?"

Exhaling that long-winded breath, Mollie said, "She has longed talked about you, has dreams of you when she calls out for you in her sleep. The girl loves you, kid. Now, get up and dress. You need to pack warm clothing for we leave tonight. That is your option." She wasn't so delicate in her statement.

"Hurry, Luke," Mae said as she stood in front of me. She took a hand to the side of my face and tilted it up to her. "I know you do. I see it still glimmers and you cannot hide it." There was a knock on the front door, and Mae went to answer it.

I turned my attention back to Mollie. "How long, Mollie?" I whined in desperation.

"She has never given up on you, and don't you give up on her," she cried through tears.

"I tried not to, for I have prayed she would return someday," I whimpered through my own tears.

Mae came back into the room with a young man, who was as pale as Mollie, with the same green eyes, long black hair, and well dressed in a black three-piece suit.

"Luke, this is Jock, Kim's lifelong friend back home," Mollie said as she rose.

"You are this Luke, yes?" he asked in the same accent, extending a hand toward me. I rose and shook his hand in return.

As I took the hand of the young man, images that flashed before my eyes were unmentionable.

"We must be hasty for time is wasting," he said.

"I agree," Mollie said. "Luke, please. I am begging you to come with me," she cried. How could I say no, or maybe why would I want to? After a great deal of consideration, I knew I wanted her back and from what Mollie said, so did Kimmi. I looked them over and nodded yes. Mollie ran to me, dropped onto her knees, and threw her arms around my neck in a hug. I returned it momentarily before I rose and dashed up the stairs to pack.

At 22:48, we boarded the plane in Ashville for Fairbanks, Alaska. I was nervous as hell, because I didn't like to fly. Apparently, Jock caught the hesitation and pulled a small bottle from his jacket pocket, then poured two tiny white pills into his hand.

"Here, take these. They will calm the nerves," he said, dropping them into my hand.

Looking at the two pills, I said, "Will they make me sleep?"

"Huh." He chuckled. "No. They are just to relax you."

"Thanks." I took the pills with the soda I had. Mollie had made arrangements for travel from Fair Banks to Point Barrow then finally from Nuwua to her. I wondered if she would still feel the same as she did months ago.

We were seated first class, I was seated in the middle of Mollie and Jock when I felt the plane shimmer as its engines started. The stewardess came along, telling everyone to fasten our seatbelts, so I pulled the belt tighter, almost too tight. Then the plane began taxing down the runway as the engines became louder. I gripped the arms of the seat until my knuckles were white and the lights outside the window were almost a blur when the plane left the ground air born for the long ride.

It was past midnight when I glanced at my watch while Mollie and Jock whispered to each other.

After a moment or two, I finally asked, "Why did she do it?"

Through moist lips, Mollie replied, "When she left you that night, she thought you didn't love her. She wanted to see you one last time in her life before she passed on." Mollie abruptly stopped, then glanced out the window.

Stunned at what I heard, I prudently asked, "What the hell did you just say?"

Looking back at me, she said, "She dies from a broken heart Luke. There was so much love between you two. Talks went between her and Ivan for a week before we left, but she wanted to call, only Ivan refused that request. She told me and Casey on the day she left that she'd have no life without you since no other captured her like you did." Mollie's tone dropped to a near cry when she said, "But then after a while she wanted so badly to come back, only Magnyss refused that request upon others from prior experience. There is one other thing that you probably should know about."

Sighing, I said, "Well…"

"Magnyss is not the sort of man you want to make angry. Just watch yourself while you are there, okay?" I nodded yes, and Mollie grew silent for awhile. I didn't know what to say either, so I sat in silence. Jock I thought was a middle man, but he too had no words, so I leaned back in the seat in thoughts of Kimmi and this Magnyss. When we made a two-hour layover in the O'Hara lobby in Chicago, I took the liberty to scout the place. I didn't venture far for fear of getting lost or separated from Mollie in such a huge place. I had never or ever would again see one so booming. I was so glad when we boarded our other flight, and I finally went to sleep.

I was sort of dreaming of Kenna and my home back in Patten when Mollie stirred in the seat. I gave her a glance when she turned to me. Her expression was of confusion, I thought. Finally, she spoke, "I'm curious about one thing. Would you have asked her to marry you if you had known she was going to leave?"

Caught by surprise, I answered, "I didn't know I had a time limit to ask her. But yes, I would have for it had crossed my mind." She sighed as I reached over, giving her a hug. Feeling the coldness of her brought flowing thoughts of Kimmi with it.

Releasing her, I said, "If it's all the same with you, I need to ask her in my own way.

With a soft smile, she replied, "I understand, and yes, it is fine with me." She patted my hand.

Watching snow fall onto the wing outside the window, I had to ask like a child, "How did you come to be as you are?"

"That's a long story in itself, but each shadow person holds a special place in the heart. It's like a dormant being lying in wait for the right moment to come forth. We are very affectionate people."

Rolling my head on the rest toward her, I grunted, "You speak in such ways I cannot comprehend."

Turning in the seat, she said, "Kimmi is a very special girl, and I hope she finds in her to explain her life in full to you."

Rapidly blinking, I said, "Funny, I wonder what it will be."

"Who knows? We each are different to the one we love." Jock stepped in. "Now swap places with me and get some sleep." I traded places, so I had the window to look out over the snow-covered wing and drifted off to sleep. Relaxed in thoughts, dreams brought her running to me.

She was so happy that her face glowed with it, and her eyes told on her. The sparkle was magical when she jumped into my arms and her tender lips found mine with a long, loving kiss. She held me tight, wrapping her legs around my waist and arms around my neck. Watching the falling snow—sweet and pure white snowflakes—they were as large as my hands. I slid her down to the ground, and the flakes covered her black hair in white. She leaned down, making a snowball, then threw and hit me in the arm, actually hurting me.

"Ouch, that hurt," I said as I felt the arm.

A voice broke the moment, "Good, time to get up now. You were out of it for awhile there. Must have been quite a dream."

"It was indeed." I sighed, looking up at Mollie. "We're in Fairbanks?" I asked, sitting upright.

"Yes. Time to head on out. Choey is waiting for us." I looked out the plane window to the ground.

Outside was a black 350 Ford double cab with six blue-eyed huskies in the bed. I looked at Mollie with a grin. "Are you kidding? Dog sledding?" I asked, chocked up.

"Thought you'd like that idea," she said. "Put these on." She handed me a heavy leather coat with a hood and some leather boots to wear over the shoes. I put them on while she waited.

"Now it's time to go, move." I got up and followed her off the plane to an awaiting six-team dog sled, fully packed and ready to go. I put the baggage in the back seat with me while Mollie and Jock rode in the front. Jock drove us out of the lot to the north side of town where we were to meet our guide.

Just on the outskirts of town in a small village, we met an Eskimo man named Choey, who was our guide for the rest of the way. I helped unload the team and watched as he quickly set them up. The dogs were a beautiful black-and-white mix and friendly as hell. They bounced around like pups until spoken to by Choey, who was a huge Eskimo with a broad chin, wide shoulders, and long arms and legs. I glared up at the seven-foot-tall man with a headband around his head of long black hair and who was well dressed for the trip. I didn't understand their language, but both Mollie and Jock talked with the man in his tongue while I waited.

I petted the dogs and got the feel of them, only it brought thoughts of me and my beast to mind. The biggest of the bunch sort of snarled at me, and I felt he knew about my companion.

After several moments, Mollie looked at me as she pointed to the sled, "We are the riders and they the team. Get in and cover up well. The harshness will only get worse from here out." With a soft smile, she said, "We'll make a short stop in Big Lake before we get to Point Barrows"

With sunshine and a little chill from the air, I grinned when I said, "But it's such a nice day and all."

The big man stepped onto the back of the sled and spoke to Mollie who nodded as she faced me. I knew the question before she asked and nodded. Getting into the covered sleigh, I slid down, pulling the hide over me as she asked. I lay back in the sled when the rocking motion began, which starts our trip over the vast harshness toward Kimmi.

The sleigh rocked while Mollie and Jock rode in the back, talking with the sleigh master, who called for the huskies to keep moving. The sleigh moved gently for a very long time, but then I noticed it picked up speed. I could hear Mollie and Jock chatter about that home of theirs. Relaxed, I wondered what it would be like there with her. To know the harshness of winter had to be unforgiving. Would I survive at all? Was it a one-way trip to her? Kimmi told me once to bring warm clothing if I ever came here. Quickly, I saw her point. The rocking of the sleigh became rougher the way it moved. Like a wondering fool, I peeked out from under the covering, over the tip up front, to the huskies riding on the front end of the long sleigh, and I began to laugh. I was pushed down with force on the top of my head, so I covered up and finally drifted off to sleep.

After seven hours of rough terrain, we made that short stop in Big Lake. I got out long enough to stretch my legs and use the restroom.

I was staring out west at the green color in the sky when Jock came over and said, "They call that an aurora."

"Wow," I moaned. Someone went to yelling in the background as a beige 4x4 came to a stop right in front of us.

"Here he is," another yelled. Looking back toward the wooded area, I saw a young man rush into the clearing, carrying a very young moose.

Gasping, I asked, "What are they going to do with it?"

Laughing, Jock replied, "It will freeze tonight. It has been lost from its mother. They will care for him until morning." Mollie called to us and said it was time to leave. When we began moving again, I thought of the young moose until I fell asleep.

I was awakened when I heard a loud call for the dogs to stop. When the sleigh stopped, I got up, pushed the covering off, and discovered it was still snowing heavily. I got out of the sleigh to face an enormous building of mammoth size and beauty. It tripled over the back with each level higher than the other. My first impression was that giants had to live there. I noticed the front doors held gold handles of lions-head knobs on two sets of double doors. The enormous windows were massive in colors of dark stain to keep the sunshine out. I pulled the large coat closed as I began to shiver from cold that was more than anything I knew. I focused my attention to the building that seemed to cover the whole island itself when I couldn't see around it. Ice and snow cracked underfoot as we walked to the doors setting on a concrete porch with four towering pillars holding up the roof. Going under the canopy, we stepped up onto the three steps, and across the porch. While the Eskimo man left, Mollie knocked on the door. I could hear it echo inside through the howling wind while we waited for the doors to be answered.

When the giant doors swung open, a young green-eyed girl stood there in a black silk pantsuit with a white shirt and spoke in a language unknown to me, but Jock and Mollie answered it. I knew then how Kimmi felt when she said she felt out of place. The girl moved aside, and we went in. Closing the doors, she spoke to Mollie who replied in the same language.

Turning to me, she said, "We will follow the young girl to the waiting chamber for awhile." Jock had taken the lead, while I just nodded to Mollie. We turned and followed the young girl down a cold, damp, and chilling hall of the building.

The twenty-foot ceilings contained soft lights all up and down the hallway that I could see. The floor was bare but lain with stones I've never seen before that could have been ancient. The walls revealed stones of great size and colors with murals of wolves and hangings of all sorts. Mirrors of all sizes and shapes and a scent of amazing purity. It was cold as hell, so I pulled the coat closer to keep the air from coming up at the bottom. When we stopped at a door half the size as the front ones, the girl opened it for us. When the door closed behind us, it didn't even echo.

The smaller room was lined with books and albums on shelves from floor to ceiling. The warmth was coming from a little fire in the fireplace in the wall near the large sofa. Of course, I rushed over to it, pulling off the gloves and sticking my numb hands over the coals. Shivering from the cold, I stared over the mantel at a clock that read 2:00 p.m.

Looking over at Mollie and Jock seated on the sofa, I asked, "What is this place, Mollie?"

She slid to the edge of the cushion and said, "This was once our home before we chose to live outside these walls years ago."

"The young girl, who is she?" I asked with a tilt of the head.

"That's Jewel, a mere secretary for Magnyss and the others," Jock replied.

Dazed, I gulped and said, "Others? Like him?"

"Yes. There are many others like Magnyss. You'll meet some of them while you're here."

Our conversation was interrupted when a knock sounded on the door. We all faced the door when the knob turned.

It opened, and the girl Jewel came in with a silver round tray that had a hot pot of steaming liquid, three cups, milk, and sugar. She put it down on the small table near the sofa while Mollie spoke to her before she left, closing the door.

Looking at Mollie, I said, "How long will we be in here? This room I mean?"

"Until Magnyss gathers the others and is ready to begin," Jock answered.

Confused, I said, "I thought I was here for Kimmi?"

Mollie shunned the question and said, "You are, but we do nothing here that isn't approved by them first. That includes Kimmi." She poured coffee into a cup, and took a quick sip. There was no time for more questions when the door opened and the girl spoke while waving us out into the hallway.

Mollie sat the cup down and stood up, returning an answer to the girl. Jock got up, and we headed out the door into the hallway again. Jewel lead us deeper into the building that was becoming colder the darker it got and whispers lingered in the distance. I had a hard time trying to understand what was being said. Again, we stopped, but that time we were facing a double set of white doors with a one-inch golden trim at the bottom. The young girl knocked once. In an instant, a voice spoke in their language. Jewel opened the door and stepped aside to let us in.

The room was an off-white set in stone with a high ceiling that opened into a mountain peak. The floor was covered in a white ancient stone with visible black streaks of a rare coloring that trailed over the walls. The first person I saw as we stepped inside the door was a man of many years in a black full-length coat that was tied with a black belt. His hair was short and black, his lips pinkish and thin, but his eyes were of green emeralds. He and the young lady spoke in their native tongue.

Mollie was standing next to me when she began naming the men and women from left to right. "Magnyss was the first but it was Bault standing next to him." He was a young man with black hair and green eyes and had the same paleness and thin mouth. "Kiest." She pointed to a tall and thin man with black hair and diamond eyes. "Bryce," she said, referring to a tall woman with long black hair and green eyes. "Unic." He was a shorter man with black hair and diamond eyes. "Leota." She was a young girl with black hair and blue eyes. "Last but not least, that is Huley," she said, referring to an older man with black hair, white streaks, and dark blue eyes. They were all well dressed in the same satin trench coats with suits under them.

Magnyss faced Mollie, and they spoke until he stepped off the top step off the breezeway toward me and stopped.

With an undertone the same as Kimmi's, he said. "Now that we have gotten that done, tell me, Luke, why do you seek to see Kimlaye?" His face was level with mine.

I stared into his green eyes and said, "I hear she's ill and has asked to see me."

"Yes, that is correct. But how can you cure this illness of hers?" he asked. "Not to mention, how will you deal with the one who is to marry her?"

I saw his eyes glimmer for a second and thought, "This man is going to make it difficult for me or he thought he was."

"What can you offer her that we cannot?" Bault asked, coming off the step to me.

Facing the room, I asked them, "You really want me to say this?"

"This is why you are here, Luke," Bryce said.

With an offset comment, I said, "Fine then. What if I wish to ask her to marry me before she dies here... alone?" I snapped, not realizing what I had said.

"Snappy," Bault said with ease.

"Do you truly think she will after what has happened?" Magnyss asked, leaning in closer to me. His scent rolled under my nose, and I noticed it was nearly the same as Kimmi's but a tad different.

Something in me right then said I should have killed that man where he stood, but I didn't know why at the time.

Shaken, I replied, "I do."

"Then let's see. Bring her here." Magnyss demanded, never looking at the room when he fanned his hand. Bault and Leota acknowledged the order and left the room.

Magnyss turned his attention to Mollie when she tapped his arm. They moved out of hearing to talk while I began to wonder what the place was and what these people where.

"You are brave to come here, Luke. Jock and Molaya have outdone themselves. No one other than we, have traveled here in these harsh times," Kiest said, rising from his high-back Victorian chair, and stepped off the porch to the bottom. Studying him, I said nothing while I watched Bryce come off the upper step to me.

When she stopped, I realized she was taller than I, making me swallow hard. Her scent was well noticeable but different than the other man's.

"There is something different about him, Magnyss," she whispered in a bitter tone.

The man glared at me, saying, "Yes, I know. He's invigorating, isn't he?" With a godly grin, he said, "I can see why Kimlaye has adored him so. His scent is unquestionably unique."

I knew I was an outsider, but I asked with a snap, "Why do you speak of me so?" Unable to withdraw, I held my breath in wait.

"You are strange here among us, and you have this tantalizing smell that goes through the roof. You can see what it has done to Bryce," Unic said from the comfort of his chair. Oh god, did they know about me? Did Mollie tell them? No one smiled the whole time I stood there while Leota and Ivan went to speak with Magnyss. He nodded to her, and she returned to the upper level with the others. Ivan stepped over and stood in silence with Mollie and Jock.

While everyone took their places, I noticed the green-eyed man staring at me, but no one spoke, so I took the leap of faith into my own hands.

"Where is Kimmi?" I solely demanded at Magnyss. "By the way, who is to marry her?"

I got the attention I needed then when Kiest answered, "We received a letter about a year ago saying Kimlaye was promised to a man in marriage. It never gave his name." Then he leaned back in his chair, crossing his legs left over right.

"We just received the second one today, and it named the promised one," Bault claimed.

I looked at the room and with a cheesy grin and asked, "What letter? Kimmi never said anything about a letter." I stared at the room full of people. The room fell silent, but I could hear my heart beating, and I knew they could too.

Magnyss came off the top like a ghost and stopped right in my face, to take a long draw of my scent, making his eyes light up. "She has become too weak to come here, so we shall go to her instead," he said, standing upright with his hands behind his back.

I didn't hesitate when I said, "Lead the way then." I stomped, feeling brave.

Magnyss tilted his head forward, then turned and walked out the room. We followed, leaving the rest behind as ordered. Mollie joined me in the walk to Kimmi when she took me by the hand.

The once dense hallway became longer and darker like we were going down into the depths of the ice that lay on top as cold as it had gotten. I hung onto my coat for warmth but soon released Mollie's hand and stuck my hands in the pockets, balling them into fists. Listening to our shoes echo as we walked, made a chilling sound. Magnyss finally stopped at a pale-blue door, grabbed the knob with long thin fingers, and opened it into a dark room with very little lighting. He stepped aside to reveal Kimmi in a bed and two women in white gowns with shear long sleeves and high necks. One of them was an actual redhead, and they were standing on the opposite side of the bed. Magnyss flagged them out as I rushed past them to Kimmi's side.

I sat on the side of the bed while Magnyss went to the foot, and Mollie sat down on the other side. I picked up her hand, lying on top of the blanket, but Kimmi didn't move.

Mollie pulled the other hand from under the sheet and checked her pulse. "It's weaker than before."

When Magnyss spoke in their language, Mollie went silent, and Kimmi remained motionless.

I leaned over to Mollie and asked her in a whisper, "What did he say?"

She looked over her shoulder at him, then said, "He told Kimlaye she had a visitor."

Not waiting for her to look up or answer me, I leaned closer to Kimmi and said, "Kimmi, look at me please. Listen to my voice. I'm here," I whispered. "Can you hear me? Follow the sound of my voice please." I felt a lump in my throat when she laid there lifeless. Mollie took a tiny light from her pocket and checked Kimmi's fading blue eyes.

"What the hell? What's happening to her, Mollie?" I stuttered in shock.

"She has given up and doesn't know you are here nor can she feel you as before."

I felt the hand barely move when she spoke, "Luke," her shallow voice said in a deathly tone," Am I dreaming again?" I had to let her know I was real and there for her.

Moving closer for her to hear me, I said, "No dreams, honey. I'm here."

With death facing her, she said, "Let me touch you to see if you are here." Her head rolled to face me while her eyes closed.

In desperation, not sure it would work, I rose from the bed, opening the heavy coat and pulled my shirt from my pants. Inhaling deeply, I reached for her hand and placed them on my chest. God they were so cold. I even thought they were colder than the first time I held them.

"Do you feel it?" I asked, shivering from the cold.

"Yes, it is warm, and it beats. It's real, but I can barely see you, and my eyes hurt."

"That's okay. I'm right here. I told you before that no matter if I lived or died, I'd be there for you. Remember that day?"

She gently slid her hands down my warm skin and said, "Yes." I wondered if she heard my teeth chattering. I felt the man staring at my back, so I sighed and sat on the bed.

"Well now, there is some kind of bond you two hold for one another," Magnyss said as he left the room, closing the door.

Mollie checked Kimmi again after Magnyss left, and her eyes filled with tears, "Thank God."

"How long before she can go home? Her real home," I whispered.

In a teary tone, she said, "Two days, maybe sooner. Time will tell."

Leaning over, I said, "I want to stay here with her."

Mollie rose from the bed and walked to the door where she stopped and said, "As you wish. Thank you for coming."

"I have longed to come for her, so thank you for bringing me." I never knew she adored me.

"How could I not help you?" She left the room, closing the door. I softly ran a hand over Kimmi's face to see if she was as real as she looked. I couldn't believe I was in that place she called home—a godforsaken place, like hell. I stayed the night because I refused to leave her side.

I was awakened the next morning by Kimmi's touch. She was standing at the foot of the bed staring at me where I had fallen asleep.

"Luke, please. I can't see well." The shear sleeve of the blue gown raked across my cheek again.

Quickly sitting upright on the bed, I said, "I'm here."

Steadying herself, she said, "Give me your hands." I reached for hers and our fingers touched. "They feel so good. Hug me," she said, pressing the palms to her cold cheeks. She pushed harder into the palm as I stood up, taking her to me in a long warm hug.

"How I have missed you."

"I didn't know if you would come," she replied, in a weak tone.

Placing my cheek on the top of her head, I confessed, "I'm ashamed to say, but at first I wasn't. I didn't want to cause you any more pain."

She quickly looked up through those half-faded blues and said, "I'm glad you did." A tear rolled down her face.

I wiped it away, and she asked, "Would you mind carrying me to the bath?"

"How about some breakfast first?"

"Do I have to?"

"Yes, you need to eat and get some rest so we can leave this place and go home."

She glared at me. "Home," she whispered under her breath. I nodded, picked her up, and she showed me the way to the kitchen with a real breakfast of ham, eggs, and toast. They didn't drink coffee, so I settled on orange juice.

The following day was like nothing had happened when it came to the letter. Kimmi and I were standing in front of the Marswaye with Mollie, Jock, and Ivan, talking among themselves as if I weren't there. Since Kimmi had not mentioned the letter, I came to the conclusion that I should. But I never thought my companion would step in.

Finally, I interrupted, "What about that letter now?" I blurted out. If silence could kill, it already did. I could hear the breathing of the Marswaye for the room was so quite.

Magnyss came off the top level and stopped in my face with his eyes leveled with mine. "So, you want to know who or why first?" He mocked with those green eyes. I didn't flinch but wanted to knock him down to size when my fingers curled into my palms.

He took a step closer, nearly too close. "You think you can?" He snickered, making me wonder how he could have known.

"I'm pretty good and you?" I lashed out to keep from getting rude. Mostly, it was to keep my companion at bay.

"Stop please," Kimmi shouted, putting a hand on my arm and shook her head no. I agreed to her request, never taking my eyes from him.

He looked down at Kimmi before he went back to the others, sat down in one of the chairs and called for Leota. "The letter!" he rudely ordered. The young lady left the council while the rest of us stood around, quietly waiting until she came back in the room with a letter. She handed it to Magnyss who opened the envelope and pulled out the paper.

Glaring over the edge of the paper at me and Kimmi, he read:

> Kimlaye Renee Creed, You are hereby promised to marry Lucas Ray Winterset. It is signed by George and Eliza Creed.

My mouth dropped open, and so did Kimmi's as tears fell from her eyes. Turning to me, she jumped into my arms.

"How can this be?" I asked the green-eyed man, glaring over Kimmi's shoulder.

He held up another envelope. "Your letter arrived this morning." He handed it to Bault, who came down and handed it to me.

I put Kimmi down as I took the envelope with shaky hands and sighed. I opened the letter and read:

> Lucas Ray Winterset, You are hereby promised your hand in marriage to Kimlaye Renee Creed. An explanation letter will follow. Please forgive me for not telling you sooner.
>
> Your father,
> Samuel Winterset

"What does it mean?" Kimmi asked.

"I cannot say." Feeling her being alarmed, I was at a loss for words but the *what, how,* and *why* lingered.

"What do you know about these?" I shook the paper at Magnyss.

Getting to his feet, his eyes glowed greener. "More than you need to know at this time."

Kimmi whirled around in front of me. "What binds your tongue?" she snapped.

"You will mind your tongue and your place!" He returned with force. I watched with reckoning while Kimmi never backed down or gave way to the man. I would have sworn they were related somehow, but that was a foolish thought even.

I stepped in front Kimmi, blocking the glare of Magnyss. "I will find out when we get home." Her eyes traveled up to mine in an angry glow when she nodded. With that settled, she and Mollie spent the rest of the day packing. Ivan took what he could and left the next day, leaving the bare minimum for us.

The day after Ivan left, Kimmi was well enough to travel, shining with anxiety and trembling with desire to hurry up. She had dressed in a full-length black velvet gown underneath a trench coat and hood while Mollie dressed much the same. I carried the bags out to the sled that waited outside, then rushed back in so we could excuse ourselves from the Marswaye. Magnyss was with Bault when I entered the chamber room and, Kimmi was talking to them.

While Kimmi and Magnyss spoke in their language, Mollie translated. "He tells Kimlaye to have a happy and long life with you. Kimmi replied that she would always for the life she has now. Thank you and good-bye."

I watched her kiss the man's cheek and his eyes softened. "You must keep her safe. She'll be vulnerable outside these walls and be happy together." I acknowledged while Kimmi rushed to me, taking my hand. Wanting to run like hell, I held back until we walked out the room and then ran like hell to the front door and out into the snow.

❧❧❧❧

I put my hands behind my back when the door closed after the boy and Kimmi had gone, ignoring the talk of the others in the background.

I faced the room for Jewel. "Bring the watchers." She rose without question leaving the room. I knew Kimlaye knew nothing of the boy's inner self because she had not the sense of sight yet. I faced the room of people who instantly became quiet when I cleared my throat.

"You are still unsure of the boy, yes?" Kiest asked, standing up.

Through clinched jaws, I replied, "Yes, but more of what he is hiding that he has not told her."

"I sense he's different in many ways but not as you do. But then Kimlaye has not told him either, has she?" Bault implied.

"I have yet to figure out what she's waiting for," I said as the door opened and Jewel stepped in.

The council and I faced the women that entered the room while Jewel left and the other two came to me. I faced them, staring into their eyes, knowing they both feared me with good right.

Sighing, I said with a forceful tone, "You are to watch her at all times, never losing sight of her, even in her sleep." I snapped my fingers in their faces.

Dropping their glance to the floor, they both replied, "Yes, Magnyss."

"Good then. If that boy hurts her in any way, you will tell me, yes?" I reached out, placing a hand under one's chin and tilted it to face me. Her eyes glared at me when I said with a bitter tone, "If he does, you two will pay the price. Understood?" Acknowledging the request, they hurried from the room.

I couldn't believe I had just come to a desolate wilderness to claim the love of a woman when I grabbed her up in a swing and we laughed out loud. She shined with grace as the sun lit her in a glow. The big man and the team were already there and waiting.

I let her slid to the ground and said, "It's time to go home."

Breathless, she replied, "Yes, and I'm so ready."

I grabbed her up, running toward the sleigh when Mollie came out the door. "I can see you love birds are more than willing to get out of here."

Breathless and ready, I replied, "Yes we are." I placed Kimmi in the sleigh and sat down next to her.

"Then let us get gone," Mollie said, getting on the sleigh.

Pulling back the covering, Kimmi said, "Get in and stay warm. I'll see you in Big Lake and at the airport." I kissed her, and got into the awaiting sleigh. I heard Choey yell at the huskies to get up. We began the trip to the plane that would take us home.

During the flight back, I realized I had lost the nervousness of flight. I also took the time to tell Kimmi about my accident. I told her the car was totaled and I no longer had one but Daniel being the guy he was loaned me his Camero. She seemed overly concerned but she understood and grateful that I was safe. We talked off and on until when we arrived at the airport where we met Ivan. He helped gather the bags and carried them to the awaiting Mustang. I dropped some in the trunk, then helped Kimmi get seated into the back passenger seat while Ivan assisted Mollie. Soon we were on our way out of the parking lot. I held Kimmi's hand all the way until we drove up into the front yard of my grandparent's home. I kissed Kimmi, told her I would see her later, and got out waving as the car drove out of the driveway. I went inside with Mae and Joe, telling them the whole story of the strange stimulating journey.

MOCKERY

SUMMER WAS LINGERING with a month gone since I had bought Kimmi home from the Marswaye, who was as vivacious as ever. I was in Daniel's Camero when I picked her up at home with a picnic lunch for later. We were on our way to lake when something seemed not right. She was overly silent, staring out the window of the passenger seat, and I dared not interfere because she had been through so much already.

Staring out the window, I couldn't help but wonder how I was going to tell Luke the truth when the time came. I guess he'll run like a madman. I knew I didn't have much time before the change, but I prayed that Luke would find it in his heart to understand.

With the fading sun, we crossed the bridge into the lot. I parked, got out and rushed over to help Kimmi. Grabbing the basket from the back seat, I walked with Kimmi to a table near the water under a shaded pine tree, but Kimmi made her way toward the water.

I sat the basket on the table and was watching her when I thought I saw an object cross the bank on the other side. Kimmi never saw it, and I wasn't about to say a word as I watched it run in the direction of the trees, thinking it was a dog. Pushing it aside, I observed Kimmi, who was bent over at the waist, pulling water up onto her arms. She made a fast glance and caught a glimpse of me watching while she reached for the belt, pulling the knot free. Still watching me, she slowly tugged on the robe. Thank god it was vacant.

"Damn it," I swore aloud. A tease she was when she disrobed and let it slide over her naked shoulders and down her pale back, dropping to the ground and revealing a black full-bodied suit. Watching her with eagerness, she bit her bottom lip as she leaned over at the waist. Scooping up a handful of water, she let it trail from her neck and over her arms, reflecting the fading light.

My pounding heart fluttered for I knew she knew what she was doing. Without any patience left, I jumped off the table, snatched off the shirt and dashed to her.

Without stopping, I never gave warning when I grabbed her around the waist, hitting the water and took her under with me and we came up splashing each other with the water.

Wiping her face, she said, "You seem a bit different somehow. Are you okay?"

With that uncontrolled devilishly sly feeling, I said, "I feel fine. Do I look okay to you?"

With jealously, I watched Luke and Kimmi in the lake from a distance. I had apologized for being rude and wanted to take him to me then because I loved him still. I never meant for him to die literally that day. I was so full of envy with what they had together I never heard the footsteps behind me. Someone grabbed me by the mouth to keep me from yelling, and in the dark, I couldn't see who it was when my clothes were torn from me.

I heard a deep voice whisper, "I won't be as gentle as Luke, but I'll take what I want." I was forcefully manhandled until I finally got the chance to yell.

I picked her up with delicate tenderness, knowing what my body and the companion cried for, and I knew it was just a matter of time. She was hanging onto me when a woman's scream or something came across the lake.

Trembling, Kimmi asked, "What was that?"

"I don't know what it was." Letting her slide to the ground, I took her by the hand, rushed to the bank where we grabbed our belongings, and got into the car. Bringing the engine to life, I shoved it into gear and spun out of the lot toward the other side of the lake.

With the high beams on, I rolled through the place in the near dark, looking for anything that could have made that cry.

I was looking to the left when Kimmi screamed, "Stop the car." The door was opened, and she was out before I stopped. I leaped out, following her through the darkness toward the beach with heightened senses. I smelled the blood right away and heard the distant running of feet. In the vicinity, I heard the moan. Picking up the pace, I looked and listened for anything. When Kimmi gasped and dropped to her knees, I dashed toward her where I found Willa curled up in a fetal position, naked and bleeding.

Squatting down, I said, "Get the towels from the car." Kimmi didn't ask questions when she leaped to her feet running.

While she was getting the towels, I took Willa by the trembling shoulders, and rolled her over gently to face me. I didn't know the extent of her injuries since it was dark, but what I could see was heart wrenching.

Placing a hand under her neck, I gently lifted her, pushing hair from her face, "Willa," I whispered, "who did this to you?" She tried to speak, but I couldn't make out what she said.

Kimmi came rushing back with her robe. "I know she's larger than I, but it'll fit." I carefully sat Willa upright, and Kimmi placed the robe around her shaking body, then quickly ran toward the water's edge and came back with a wet towel to wipe Willa's bloody face with.

Sitting back on her knees, Kimmi cried in a heart rendering moan, "Who could do this to her?"

Getting to my feet, I picked Willa up. "I don't know, but I need to get her help." I didn't know where to go or to begin. I didn't even think to call Daniel when we took her to the local hospital in town a few miles away. After several hours in the emergency room and after Willa was cared for, I called Daniel.

Kimmi had stepped outside for fresh air, leaving me in the room with Willa. She was bruised, cut, and had been raped. There were fingerprints around her mouth and neck where she had been held with force. I was holding her hand when she stirred around and began to blink, opening her eyes that were red. Swallowing, she tried to speak, but there was only a whisper.

Standing up, I said, "Don't talk," I kissed her forehead.

"Luke," she moaned.

I sat on the edge of the bed, "Do you...do you know who did this?" I stuttered.

Shaking her head no, she slowly licked her dry lips. "The voice said...the voice said it was going to take what it wanted." Tears began to fall. "I'm sorry."

Leaning forward, I said, "Sorry for what? You did nothing." I soothed her.

"I was watching you two when I was grabbed. I was jealous Luke. I'm so sorry," she said, swallowing. About that time, both Kimmi and Daniel came through the door. Daniel rushed to Willa's side like only a brother would and brushed the tears from her eyes. After a few minutes, Kimmi and I excused ourselves and left. I dropped Kimmi at home and went to see Luther.

When I arrived about daybreak, I found everyone outside, kidding around, and having fun. But I didn't find anything funny at the moment. I parked and went inside to find the old man sitting at the kitchen table, tapping his fingers. "What took ya so long?"

Taken by the remark, I dropped my head. "I been at the hospital in town." I sat down opposite him at the table.

He dropped the grin. "What happened?" I told him about the lake, Willa, and what she had told me.

Getting to his feet, he called for the others. "Make a perimeter run and be back here by dark."

"Y'all heard him. Let's go," Tom yelled. Without question, I got up and followed Tom, and we changed to our wolf. After everyone paired off, I was left with Tom, and we headed south.

We had our noses to the grindstone when I found a hint of something that caught my attention. Strange, but I liked it quite a lot.

"Hey, Tom, check this out," I woofed.

He trotted over to me, sniffing the area. "Sourly sweet," he barked. "Let's continue on." He walked toward the forest, raising his head to sniff the air. A brown and white wolf came charging out after him, but Tom bolted. But not in time when the beast caught him in the right flank. He sounded out in pain when both of them rolled to the ground, struggling to over gain the other. As soon as I felt all four feet and claws dig into the ground, my instinct called me out, and I bolted toward them. But the assailant dashed off, leaving Tom wounded.

I was on it in seconds, snapping at the thing and catching it in the side, filling my mouth with fur, but I had the hold. It shook with fierceness, taking us into a roll that only lasted a second or two until I got it down. It lay whimpering and whining like a pup as I laid my heavy body on top of it.

Tom was several hundred feet from me when I barked, "Hey, you hear me?" When there was no reply, I barked louder.

"Yeah, kid, just a minute," he groaned, changing to human form. When he got up, he walked with a limp until he sat down in front of me.

"Do what you do to get the others over here." Looking at where his hand was, I saw blood leaking from within the right thigh. I let out a howl that could have echoed into the next day. I changed to human and took a fist to the beast, hitting it right between the eyes and actually knocking it out.

"Damn, Luke," Tom whistled.

"Amazing, isn't it?" I knelt down in front of him, tearing the shirt over my head and wrapping the wound, never mentioning my friend.

It wasn't long till Nate and Jason showed up changing to their human forms as soon as they cleared the trees.

"Lord, what happened now?" Nate asked, running to us.

Without looking up, I told him, "That thing came out of nowhere and attacked Tom." I pointed a thumb over my shoulder. Nate went to see the wolf about the time Jason dropped down in front of Tom.

Cringing, he asked, "Damn, Tom. Did you bite back?" he joked.

Tom began to laugh when he said, "No. The sting sent me for a little roll." He tore at the pants leg, saying, "It burns around the wound."

Nate knelt next to Tom. "We need to get you back." Tom acknowledged while the three of us helped the big man to his feet.

Stumbling back to the ground with a groan, he grabbed his leg and slurred, "No time." Then he fell over.

"Christ," Nate cried, squatting down to Tom.

I watched him take out a pocket knife and asked with a sigh, "What's the matter?" He made to comment, cutting through the shirt and pants leg.

Dark blood seeped from the bite marks in the leg while Nate looked at me with narrow brows.

Wiping his bloody hands on his pants, he said, "Luke, I hate to ask but can you draw?"

"You want me to do what exactly?" I asked with a grunt. I knew what he meant, but that just didn't seem to be my style.

"You smell it like I do. Go for it," my head nagged.

"Work the wound and remove any poison, or he'll become something you haven't ever seen before." That comment made me wonder even more what the mountain had to offer.

"Time, my friend—time," the nagging continued. I slid down next to Tom while Nate rose so I could get at the leg.

With Tom's thigh in one hand, I knew he was in trouble when I reached in my pocket for a knife with the other. I opened it with my teeth, then gently cut a small slit into the bite pattern. Leaning over, I pressed it into my mouth and bit down slightly. With God as my witness, my fangs grew longer with ease as they slid into Tom's flesh, letting the blood spew a sweet enticing flavor onto my tongue.

"Keep going. A tad more won't hurt," my companion said with a ghastly growl. Wanting more, I bit deeper, taking what I wanted.

After four attempts of coming up clean, I inhaled deep, and then slowly let the air out. Jason leaned over to cover the wound with his shirt but not before I saw my own bite marks.

"I think that's it," Nate said as he placed a hand on my back before helping wrap the wound with Jason's shirt. I inhaled longer and deeper to catch my breath.

"Good job. Thank you. I don't have that kind of pull," Nate said as he sat Tom upright. Night came on with a shiny moon for a light. We settled down to wait for the rescue team, and I drifted off to sleep.

In a dark forest, I heard nothing but the steps of my own feet and the beat of my own heart. Where was I? There is no light to follow as I fumbled and stumbled my way about the place. Then a screech sounded out that sent dark chills up my spine, and the hairs on my neck rose like little wires as if I had stuck my finger in an outlet and got shocked. I stopped to listen, but all I could hear were footsteps that were not mine. Where were they coming from? They sounded as if they were all around me in a circle. I felt the chill when something came up behind me. Did I want to see or run? I didn't know as my palms began to sweat and they curled into fists. I felt myself turn around to face a beast standing on two legs, well covered in fur, and growling at me. I was frozen to the ground but I managed to take a swing at it. I missed, and its shiny claws came at me.

I jolted upright to find Jason grinning like the joker he was with his face in mine. He leaned back and said, "Man, you were having some kind of dream there. What was after ya?"

I grinned and asked, "What was I saying?" I thought the idea was funny.

"You never said a word. It was the loss of color in your face and the eye movement you had going on." His tone changed and he asked, "Did you see something unbelievable?"

His statement caught me off guard. "You might say that." Curiosity made me think he knew more than what he was saying.

I didn't hear the old man walk up until I heard him say, "Might could say what, Luke?"

Grinning, I looked up him. "Shit. I was hoping you could tell me."

He squatted down in front of me, pushing his straw hat back. "Talk to me."

I licked my lips, but I didn't tell him everything except what I wanted him to know. "I've been to you before about the dreams of dark things that walk upright on two legs." Gulping, I said, "What's going on with me?"

"Listen, I cannot say for sure what it is. So hang tight, and let's work on it, okay?"

With a make believe gloomy tone, I said, "Sure. It's not like I don't have the time to spare." Luther stood up, and Jason reached down, giving me a hand up to my feet.

I brushed myself off, watching Mac tying the paws together of the assailant with help from Nate and another older man I had never seen.

"Who is that, Whitecloud?" I asked, pointing at the ground.

He rubbed his chin. "An old acquaintance."

Being cocky, I half grunted, "I must have really knocked it out."

Knowing he already knew, he asked, "How?"

I raised a hand. "One hit and it went down."

"Brutal fist," he replied, but there was that all-knowing air about him that he kept a secret. I smiled for a moment, then took care of the business with Tom as we got him in a ride back to his home while the others took the other brute to a holding facility.

Mac stayed with Tom while he recovered. The thing that bit him was headed into a cave where Cole once was and I pardoned myself walking. I arrived at the mouth of the cave just as a scream echoed across the ridge that made my skin crawl with a chill.

"What the hell was that?" Nate yelled from inside.

"Beats me, I heard it once before."

I heard the footsteps before the voice. "First for me," Jason said, coming from the cave. "Erie."

"Something has everything in an uproar," the voice said from behind us. "There may be a gathering coming soon." I whirled around to face who I thought was Joey, only it was a tall thin man with long grey hair and old as time.

Nate made the introductions. "Luke, this is Daydreamer." My eyes traveled up the tall man, who had to be six foot eight, maybe.

"A gathering?" Was all I could say at the time since I was overwhelmed by the size of the man.

"One right off the top of my head, but it's not you he wants."

"How could I forget that?"

Leaning over at me, Daydreamer said, "Does she know you are a wolf...yet?"

Wondering how he knew, "No." I shunned the question. "Are you kidding?" I said through clinched teeth.

"No, I'm not," he snapped. Before I could answer, a howl sounded out from inside the cave. Oddly another came back in a softer cry.

"Are they talking to each other?" Jason asked.

"You know something? I think you're right," Daydreamer said, stepping back down into the cave.

A rustle of leaves caught the attention of the rest of us. A huge fast-moving form ran with speed and vanished across the range, leaving Nate, Jason, and I looking at one another in mystery.

"It was real, right?" Nate whined.

"Look at these, Luke," Jason said, stepping closer to me and Nate. The hairs on his arms were at new heights. Nate looked at his and so were they.

"I come for you, Luke," a bitter voice said out of nowhere. "The redhead was just a morsel. I wasn't as smooth as you, but I got what I wanted from her." The words rang in my head like a bell.

"You bastard," I cursed under breathed.

"Was it human?" Jason asked.

"That's what I want to know." Luther managed a huff, coming over the edge of the hill.

"What's going on?" Nate asked before a vulgar laugh broke out.

"He's mocking you, and it's only a matter of time before you two come face to face." Luther implied, going into the cave.

"Time will come, and you won't have to wait. You can show them what you are made of, and they can't stop us. You and I are growing to be something spectacular. Just wait a little longer my friend. It's coming, I promise," my companion said.

"Let's take care of this thing in here," Nate said. "Meanwhile, Luke, you go home and get some rest." I nodded and headed toward the house with the comfort of a bed in mind, but my companion wanted more until I pushed it off for the night.

The next morning, I rose to the smell of bacon and eggs. When the aroma of coffee lingered into the room, I swiftly dressed in shorts, a half shirt, and sneakers. Looking in the mirror, I didn't know if it were the room lighting or what, but my skin tone was a bit darker and my eyes were changing colors. "Damn," I swore in silence, grabbing a comb to put my hair back with in a rubber band. I winked at myself in the dresser mirror, then went out and down the stairs toward the kitchen where I knew I would find Mae sitting at the little table.

"Good morning," she said, sitting the cup down.

"Morning," I said, going to the fridge for the pitcher of orange juice and cabinet for a glass.

Sitting down at the table, there were a plate of fried eggs, bacon, grits, and toast. Looking up at her, she smiled that warm smile knowing how I felt. "I heard you come in late, so I made extra."

Leaning over the table, I kissed her cheek, and said, "Thanks, but I was headed out to see Luther. I'm sorry you went through all that trouble."

"I understand, and it's no trouble. Joe can have it later." I poured the juice into the glass when I asked about Willa.

"I hear she's fine and will be able to go home in a couple days." I thanked her, downed the juice, and placed the glass in the sink on my way out the door.

I drove up the drive, parked near the jalopy, and hurried in to find Luther at the table with a plate of sausage and eggs in front of him. He laid the fork down when I pulled a chair from the table and sat down across from him.

Mac was standing at the stove when he faced me, "What'll it be?" he respectfully asked, holding the spatula in the air.

Returning his grin, I gratefully replied, "How about just toast and sausage."

"I paid visit to the old ones during the night," Luther said. "The forms and dreams are shadows of mockery.

Mac placed a cup of hot steaming coffee down in front of me just as I asked, "They'll never return to what they once were, will they?" Taking a sip of the hot liquid and burning my tongue from the extreme heat, I quickly it put back down.

"No, Luke, they are forbidden here," Whitecloud said as he took a sip of the coffee. He sat the cup down and sighed. "Some of their clan's blood sizzles with venom which has burned into their veins with no way out."

I leaned over the cup and blew. "Tell me more of this."

Clearing his throat, Luther replied, "We call it a true poison. Once it enters the blood, it makes one an evil being. To cleanse the blood could cost the life of another, and no one truly knows how far it will go before they become cruel creatures."

Mac sat a plate in front of me with three slices of toast and four pieces of sausage. "Cole was poisoned long ago, around the time his wife died." He sat down with his own plate right of Luther.

"Thanks," I said as I got up and went to the fridge, pulled out the orange juice, then a glass from the cupboard.

I went back to the table and sat down where I poured the juice and we finished breakfast with small talk about Kimmi, Willa, and how she was doing. I relayed the message Mae told me when I sat back in the chair, rubbing my full belly.

"What about Kimmi? When will you tell her?"

"I still haven't thought of a way yet. I know it grows closer each passing day, but so is my fear of what she'll do."

"You'll find a way. It comes in many ways," the old man sighed.

"I hope so. I don't want to frighten to her away."

"When it happens, she'll understand. She is that kind of person," Mac intervened. I spent the day talking about the Creeds, why they were there, and how they became allies with the Indians. At dark, I called Kimmi to make sure she was fine before going home to a dreamless night.

ENGAGEMENT

AFTER FOUR DAYS of hospitalization, Willa finally got released so Daniel could bring her home. Over the month, it took her to heal from most of her wounds she still didn't know who did it. Her actions proved that she was a different woman in every way because she wouldn't let me touch her in a hug or anything. Daniel was the only one she trusted, and I couldn't blame her. I spent a lot time looking for any clues to who had hurt her in such a way. It left me with the thoughts of what Cole had in mind for Kimmi, pushing me to the brink of exhaustion.

I just laid in bed one morning thinking about what and how to tell Kimmi about myself but coming up with no solution. I truly felt she had earned her right among us when I rushed to get her out of that place and back with me. What I really wanted to do was give her a proper engagement. With that thought, I leaped out of bed and quickly dressed in slouchy clothes of shorts with a tee shirt. I called Willa and asked if she knew who made customer rings. She did, so I got the number and called the old man who lived on the reservation. He agreed to my request and said it would be done in two days time. I thanked him, then hung up and called everyone, asking that they meet me at the tavern where Willa worked, and that it was of the most importance. Everyone agreed. I left the bedroom in a state of haste, going downstairs to find Mae in the kitchen.

She was sitting at the table in her night gown with a housecoat over it. Her warm smile invited me to sit down with her.

"Morning," she whispered over the cup in her hand. The smell of banana pudding and apple pie covered the kitchen in aroma. I sucked in long, then sat down at the table across from her.

"Hey there, I need to ask a favor if I may."

With a wink, she said, "I'm all ears."

"I need a cake for a party on Thursday. Would you do the honor please?" I placed my hands on the table in a praying position.

"What sort of cake is needed?" She peered at me.

"Well, I'm officially asking Kimmi for her hand."

I thought Mae was going to fall out of the chair she was sitting in as her jaw dropped open. "Oh yes. I'll gladly do the honor." She was more excited than I was when I told her it was in two days.

She placed her hands flat on the table. "Then so shall your cake."

"Thank you so much." I got up and went around the table to give her a kiss on the cheek.

Time was quick when the day arrived. I hurried out to the reservation for the ring, then headed back where I spent the day with Kimmi out in the gazebo. Soon the conversation came up about going to the tavern.

"You look good today. We are going out to where Willa works. There is a party going on out there tonight, and you are coming with me."

Caught by surprise, she said, "Seriously? You want me to go?"

"More than anything, yes." Her face lightened up with a smile.

"Then I suppose I have no time to ready myself." She bit her bottom lip.

"Yes you do. Look at me." I laughed.

"Yes, I can see," she laughed at me. I took her into my arms and held her gently as I looked into her blue eyes, then pressed my lips to her soft sweet lips, tenderly kissing her. She was more important than anything else in my life. I wanted her eternally and from her actions so did she. Wrapping her arms around my neck, she pulled me closer into a hug. Releasing her, I stood up, and walked away as our hands slipped away to hurry home and shower.

I dressed in nice jeans with a blue-grey button-down shirt with the sleeves rolled up to the elbows and boots. I looked in the dresser mirror at my hair that was frizzy. I quickly combed it back and tied it there. I inhaled and exhaled while reaching into the top drawer and pulled out the little blue box that contained the ring. I stuck it in my pocket and went down the stairs to see Mae, who was finishing up the last of the two-tier white-and-blue cake with red roses around the edges. It was beautiful, and she had done her magic. So I kissed her and went out the front door to the car.

I watched Luke jot from the house to the car sitting out on the lawn. My rage for him and his father were mind troubling. Even the gorge didn't fix the problem, but he'll pay. And Sam will know the feeling to lose a loved one. "I hope he cries like a baby," I sighed lightly. When the boy left the yard, I followed at a distance to see where he went.

I had the strangest feeling I was being followed but I never saw anyone or anything behind me so sped up a bit just in case. I was always told to follow your gut instinct but I failed to that night. When the drive came into view, I roared up the hill, opening the door before I had it parked. I jumped out and ran across the lawn, leaped over the steps and slid across the front porch. I stopped, knocked on the front door, and patiently waited. The door soon opened and Casey stood there in a red evening gown. It was not as long as usual but it fit her well with her hair up in a ponytail. The neck of the dress was low cut in a U-shape over the top of the breasts. She had red earrings dangling from her ears and extra height from the heels she wore.

"Hey, Luke, come on in." She stood back as I came in.

I stopped and gently kissed her cheek. "You look nice tonight. What's the occasion?"

"Nothing special," she admitted with a blush.

I headed for the den while she closed the door and said, "She is still preparing herself."

I reached for the door knob of the den, looking over my shoulder. "I can wait." I turned the knob and swung the door open to find both Mollie and Ivan inside.

Casey walked past me and went to the sofa with Mollie and sat down. Mollie stood up in an emerald green gown with long shear sleeves, her hair up in a bun, and emerald studs in each ear. "Well, Luke, you are of the most handsome tonight," she gleamed.

"Thanks, Mollie," I said, feeling a blush in my cheeks.

Rising to his feet in a handsome black suit with a white shirt and no tie, Ivan said, "Come sit." He produced a genuine smile, and his hair looked perfect for some reason.

I had just sat down when Mollie said, "We want to thank you for helping Kimmi back to herself."

Feeling proud, I said, "You're both welcome."

"The Marswaye inquired about her today," Ivan said, leaning forward on the sofa.

"Why?" I asked politely.

"Her guardians have always kept tabs on her," Mollie whispered.

I didn't quite understand that statement as I rose to my feet, feeling a sense of anxiety. "Guardian," I snapped. "I thought you were her guardians after her parents died."

"Please sit down." Ivan addressed me. "She is fine and can tell you herself when time arises."

With a sense of a relief, I sat down, knowing Kimmi had a lot to talk about. When the den door opened and she breezed, she was wearing a satin navy-blue sophisticated gown.

The satin came just over the breast in a heart shape that ran under the arms and around to the back to a zipper—details that where revealed as she whirled around the room. Satin shear and lace finished the high neck and sleeves with beads. A belt went around the middle and tied in the back, leaving the rest of the gown to drag the floor behind her tapping heels. She had her hair up in two ponytails with the two streaks hanging at her eyes and barely covering two blue sapphire earrings in each ear. Her lips were covered in a soft pale rose lipstick and eyes in a pale shadow.

I rose to my feet in amazement as she came to me, taking her hand into mine. "My god, you are beautiful." I whistled a breathless tune. My heart pounding dangerously hard, leaving me with the thought it was going to leap from my chest.

"Thank you," she said, moving into my arms. With a hug she softly kissed me, leaving her scent and pulling my mind to the place it didn't need to go.

"Well, are you ready?" I asked, good-naturedly holding out my elbow.

She placed her hand around the crook. "I am indeed." With that, I escorted her out the front door to the awaiting car. I opened the door for her to sit, then gently closed it. Like a gentleman, I went to the driver side and got in. For a moment I thought the little blue box was going to burn a hole in my pocket before I could ask her. I started the car, and we headed out to the tavern.

I waited patiently while Luke and that girl came out to the car. When they left, I pulled from the darkness of the trees and followed. "Where are you going in such a hurry?"

Willa worked at a small tavern on the east side of the small town that bordered the mountain. She had made arrangements for it to be closed till Monday. It was late, and she had agreed to help me with the party, but so did Daniel, Jason, and Paulene, who would be there. Only Mae knew it was an engagement party. Kimmi said she liked the eighties music and was especially pulled to the softer songs. She got excited the closer we got, squirming in the seat of the car.

"Luke, how much longer?" she snickered, rubbing her thighs with both hands.

"What's the hurry?" I laughed at her.

"The last time you held me in a dance was the night out on the beach. I have longed for you to do it again. Yes, I'm in a hurry." She faced me with a glee, and her eyes glared. That made my head swell, but my heart burned for it since it was the one and only time I had ever held her like that.

I turned off the main road onto a dirt one until the small dimly lit tavern came into view. I pulled into the gravel lot where other cars were parked everywhere, but no one was in sight. I parked, got out, and was helping Kimmi out when I sensed a nearby presence. I turned to the tavern, pushing it off as I found it hard to hold my own anxiety to a minimum as we walked toward the tavern door. I could feel Kimmi's hand inside mine, shimmer like an erupting volcano. The closer we got, the louder the voices inside became. Kimmi sighed, and I watched her face when we stopped at the door of the tavern. She had become impatient, shaking her hands. I reached over and touched the knob, and she hissed at me, making me grin, and pulled the door open for her. Laughing, we went inside to the dim lights.

I sat in the dark watching the two go into the tavern wandering. My hands gripped the wheel with anger, listening to my pounding heart, cursing myself for not actually finishing the job right the first time that night. Mom was already beside herself, steaming with anger.

As we entered the tavern, we saw that the lights were low. The colored lights hung from the ceiling and over the bar on a spinning ball. Tables and booths lined the walls and down the center around the pool tables. People were sitting at the bar, in booths, or on the dance floor swaying to soft music. They paid us no mind as we entered the room.

"Whew!" Kimmi said, blinking from the light change. "I have not been to a place such as this. I think I am too formal, don't you think?"

"Come on. Let's find a seat by the back wall." I took her hand and sort of pulled her along as I headed to the darkest corner. We found Paulene and Jason in each other's arms in a corner booth with the light out. *How cute*, I thought. I looked for Daniel when I heard him yell from the dance floor at me. I found him with that girl Jada, arm in arm. I gave him a thumbs up and waved, and he grinned. I left it at that.

"Come sit a minute," Paulene said. Kimmi had taken a liking to her, so she went over and sat down with them. I pardoned myself, to look for Willa, who was at the bar.

I went over, put an arm around her neck—meaning nothing by it—then she instantly got up and slapped me. "Don't ever touch me," she screamed. She was wearing a black-and-white dress with thin straps, cut low in the front, showing her cleavage, and stopped at the thighs of her long legs.

The move caught attention from others but only for a moment when I said, "I meant no harm. I'm sorry. But how you've been?" People went back to doing whatever.

"Fair, I suppose," she replied, sitting back down on the stool as though she were in the dumps. When she turned on the stool to face me, she asked with bitterness, "Are you ever going to ask that girl to marry you, or you just goanna string her along?"

"Snappy, are you?" Knowing no one knew about the party, I said, "If you will excuse me, I have a date to get back to." I headed back toward Kimmi.

Kimmi and Paulene were in a heavy conversation by the time I got back to the booth. I flopped down in the seat with Kimmi and faced Jason, who was grinning like an ass. Paulene was nicely dressed in a black dress with short sleeves while Jason, on the other hand, was just Jason. He wore a pair of shorts, a nice tee shirt, and sneakers. His hair was at least combed back and was sitting with his arm around Paulene's neck while she leaned on him with her head resting on his jaw.

"I must say, I like your dress Kimmi," Paulene shouted over loud music.

"Thank you," Kimmi replied. It made me feel good to watch her and to know people were glancing at her when she thought no one was looking.

"If I can get a little help here, we'll move these tables out the way," Willa yelled over the music.

"Coming, Willa," Jason said as he rose from the table. "Be right back, honey." He kissed Paulene.

She replied, "Hurry back."

"You should go too," Kimmi whispered in my ear as she sat upright.

"I suppose so." I kissed her cheek and got up.

"She's mine while you two get lost," Paulene said, moving over to sit with her. Winking at them, I followed Jason.

I went to the pool table where Jason stood and grabbed the opposite end of the heavy table. Daniel took the center on one side and Nate on the other.

"I truly think your lady has found a new friend there," Jason said.

"Yeah, I think so," I agreed, giving a grunt as we lifted the table.

"Over here," Willa shouted over the music. She was standing near the bar toward the entrance. We carried the table with ease, weaving around people until we gently sat it down, then went to retrieve the other table Willa wanted moved. I was watching Kimmi when I bumped into Willa, who was bent over the table.

"Watch it," she yelled.

Being the ass of the night, I said, "I was, the other way." I laughed, but she unexpectedly tossed a pool ball at me. Luckily, I caught it with a left hand and a stinging ouch.

"Wow, nice catch," Daniel applauded.

"Come on, guys, get it moved," Willa teased, slipping up onto the side for a ride. We each grabbed a side and moved it with Willa over to the door with the other one.

"Happy now," Jason asked, dropping his end of the table to the floor with a thud. Willa wrinkled her nose at Jason as she slid off the table and went to the juke box. The rest of us returned to the table with Kimmi and Paulene while Daniel disappeared into the crowd.

Willa had selected a soft tune from jukebox for the first round, and I took Kimmi by the hand as Jason took Paulene, and we headed for the floor. It was a wooden floor but had sawdust down, so our feet would move easier.

"Now," Kimmi shouted.

"Hell yeah. Come on, girlfriend." I laughed. She slid out of the booth as I pulled her hand. I could tell she was nervous. I also felt a presence somewhere in the crowd, but I played it off and headed to the floor. When the lights gave way to the glitter ball overhead, they glimmered off Kimmi's gown.

I pulled her gently but swiftly into my arms with a soft and gently smile.

When she faced me, I said with pride, "Yes, right now, my love." She moved into my arms when her arms went around my neck. I was surprised, but I liked the feel of them there. Above all honesty, I had not really danced with a woman until then. Her head lay against my chest as she hummed with the tune *Slow Hand*. I knew it was high time to ask her, so I held her tighter than before but gentle as a dove. Her moves were exquisitely in tune with mine at all times until it ended.

When everyone started back to their seats, Kimmi thought she was too when she started toward the booth. I held her hand and pulled her with me as we headed for the bar. The slick floor made it difficult for her to resist.

Sort of stomping her foot, she asked, "Were we going?"

"Just come with me please." I stopped at the bar, faced Kimmi, and with both hands, I grabbed her around the waist and sat her up on a stool.

"Luke," she blushed.

I faced the crowd and waved my hands in the air. "Everyone, can I have your attention please." I had to say it two or three times over the music and talking until everyone and everything came to a stop. Even the jukebox stopped when Willa pulled the plug.

"What's up, Luke?" Tom asked, stepping from the crowd.

"I have a question that needs an answer, and there is only one that can answer it." I dared not look at her right then, or she would have known, so I played it straight.

"So ask it," someone shouted from the crowd. Mae came through the double doors behind the bar with Joe and stopped at the end as I turned toward Kimmi, who was a bit confused. I took both her hands into mine and looked her in the eyes.

She smiled with a whisper, "What's going on?"

"Kimmi Renee Creed, I wholeheartedly with honesty and every breath love you." I dropped one hand as I reached into my pocket and pulled out the little blue box and opened it. I turned it toward her, and her faced lit up like a light as her eyes became teary.

"Now, will you marry me?" I asked, getting down on one knee in front of her. The room gasped aloud, but instantly, it was speechless, and Kimmi looked at me with tears. The room felt tense as we waited for her answer. My heart pounded harder than ever as a lump came up into my throat.

Leaving the truck where it sat, I made my way down the hill and around to the back entrance undetected while everyone was watching the two at the bar. I found the darkest place and sat down to wait for the right moment.

In the dark, I came upon Jay's truck sitting on the hill, facing the tavern. Feeling the hood, I found it warm. Stepping to the edge of the cliff, I saw him sneak around the back of the tavern. My thought was he went inside to cause trouble for my son, so I slipped down to wait for his exit.

Kimmi slid off the stool, took my hands, pulling me to my feet, and looked up at my eyes. "Yes, yes, and yes," she cried. With trembling hands of excitement, I took the silver engagement ring with one diamond from the box, and placed it on her finger. I kissed her while the room clapped and roared.

She tightly hugged me. "I love you, Luke," she whispered in my ear.

"And I love you," I whispered back, watching through the mirror over the bar at Mae and Joe sit the cake off the cart onto the counter. I winked, and they stood clear while I turned Kimmi to face it. Still again, she cried with joy, and I was truly engaged to her. The date would come soon enough, but first, she needed to get over the excitement. I took her face to mine and kissed her wet, soft lips again.

All had went exceptionally well when the jukebox started back up, and I looked at Kimmi who was trying to keep from crying as she dabbed her eyes with a tissue.

Mae came to her side and gave her a hug. "Beautiful, just beautiful," she said as she became teary eyed.

"Thank you so much, Mae," Kimmi said, hugging her neck. Feeling that odd presence, I looked over the crowd in the dim light. Finding a man in a corner of the tavern, he was maybe forty or forty five, but I couldn't get a good look at him. *No one I had ever seen around before*, I thought, turning my attention back to Kimmi.

Tom came to the bar and looked at her. "May I?" he asked, holding out a hand to her. She looked up at me, and I nodded okay, and she took Tom's hand. They made their way out onto the floor.

I watched them with my heart filling with joy and pride, but the presence was strong.

Joe came to my side. "Congratulations." He smiled. "She is a lovely girl tonight."

"Thanks. Yeah, she is, Grandpa." I hugged him as he hugged me around the neck and patted my back. We made talk, but it was only in general before he went back to where Mae had gone at the end of the bar. I hadn't noticed the music had changed as I looked for Kimmi whom I didn't see. I became nervous when my eyes searched in the crowd only to find Tom was dancing with Willa. Then in the middle of the crowd, I saw Kimmi who appeared scared to death. When I saw the man from the corner, he had his hands upon her.

In a bit of temper, I made my way through the group to where Kimmi was and stopped with a huff. He had Kimmi around her wrist and held her as she struggled to get free. He reached out with the other hand, took her by the opposite hand, and pulled her to him in a rude and unruly manner. My hands curled tightly into fists, until I felt a hand on my arm. It was Tom, and he saw what was going on.

"You know him, Tom?" I asked.

"Yep," he replied with a hateful look in his eyes.

"Well, who is he?" I demanded with a shallow shout. My temper flared even more as I watched him slide his hands over Kimmi's back, holding her still. He was not what I would call handsome but nice looking with dark skin and long hair. He wore jeans, a black button-down shirt, and boots. His face was evil looking as he glared at me and Tom.

"Let her go," Tom said, stepping toward the man.

I heard a light whimper from Kimmi when he replied with a squeeze, "Why, she's takable, Tom." He grinned.

"No, she's not yours to take, Jay," Tom sprung on me. My fists hurt when they tightened even more as I felt a change coming on.

Mac came from the crowd and grabbed me just as I leaned in toward the man. "Not here," he said. "Tom can deal with him right now. Not you."

"That is my uncle?" I wept with hate.

Since all the attention was on Jay, I watched from the doorway in silence, knowing what I had to do was to avoid hurting Luke and his fiancé. I stepped back outside, closing the door without a sound and waited. I knew Tom would drag that bastard out for me.

"Indeed he is a rude and hateful SOB," he replied with vulgarity.

Tom went to the man, got right in his face, took Kimmi by the hand, and pulled her free. She came running to me with tears, frightened as hell, stumbling with fear, and buried her face in to my chest. I wrapped my arms around her, hugging and consoling her until I heard the table break.

I looked up to see Tom rise up from the floor where the man had apparently knocked him down with a fist. I could see his lip bleeding as he wiped it away with the back of his hand. His eyes narrowed as he went back toward Jay in rage. Taking him around the neck, he nearly twisted Jay's head off when he flipped the man over his shoulder. Jay landed on his feet, turned, and jabbed Tom hard enough in the side that both men went to the floor. Mac was about to intervene when a gun was fired. I swung about to see Willa standing behind the bar with a 22 pistol in her hand. The two men on the floor struggled to get up, but Tom was quicker. For such a big man, he grabbed Jay by the hair of the head and snatched him to his feet. Taking him by the neck with an arm, Tom drug him across the floor to the door where Willa stood with it open.

When Willa opened the door, I had already changed forms and was in a crouched position, ready for Jay when he came out. I heard her gasp, but she didn't scream, thank god. She followed my eye movement from the door to her and slightly nodded, biting her bottom lip. I listened to the approaching feet and readied myself when Tom came through the door.

Tom pushed past the woman with the man outside, then more or less tossed Jay out into the lot, and yelled, "I best not see ya back here." Then put his hands on his hips.

That was my cue with all the hate I had for him and his followers. I made my presence known when I rushed over in front of the open door, taking Jay by the neck of the shirt in one swipe, and disappearing into the night. Yelling like the creep he was, I never stopped until I made it out to the west range. As soon as I came to a complete stop, I let him think he struggled free. Facing me, he knew right away who I was and why.

"So you think you can stop me, Sam?"

Growling with an angered tone, "Change, and let's see." He knew what it meant since he was also a wolf. When he did, it was no time that we were at each other's throats. With the fur flying, I finally caught him in the side. Tasting his blood pool inside my mouth, I could have killed him, but I couldn't bring myself to do so. I let him go.

Changing to human, Jay swore, "You bastard. I will finish it sometime or another. Watch me."

With my own human form in place, I replied, "I can wait that long." I didn't wait for a reply. I turned tail and headed back.

With Kimmi's trembling face hidden in my chest, I was glad she never saw the thing. As for myself, I thought it was just one of the tribesmen.

"Please, I want to go home now," she pleaded with unsteadiness, leaning harder into me.

Pushing off what I thought I saw, I said, "Sure, babe." I took her hand and headed for the door where Tom stopped me.

Looking at the big man with a daring stare, I swore, "Don't even try, Tom."

⛀⛂⛁

After giving Jay a few biter points, I returned to watch Luke from the distance of the dark, knowing it was only a matter of time before it came out. After all, what was I going to tell him when I faced him with the truth once again after holding back?

⛀⛂⛁

He held up his hand. "Take mine just in case." He tossed me his truck keys, so I gave him those to the Camero and went out to the truck. I got Kimmi settled in the passenger side, and closed the door. Feeling the stare, I played it off until I could get Kimmi home, making the night end abruptly.

A Gift

IGOT THE CAR back the next day when I returned the truck to Tom, but the rude ending of our engagement party had brought much uncertainty with Jay Ludlow and his devious ways. My only concern was Kimmi because she was terrified of him. That's not to mention what she might have done if she had seen the thing, and I was grateful she didn't. It had been a week, and it was late Saturday afternoon when I decided to take Kimmi to the creek for a quiet day to ourselves. The warm days had me dressing in shorts, cut-off tee shirts, and sneakers.

I hurried downstairs, out the front door and jogged around to back of the house only to face Whitecloud standing by the garage door. Grinning under that straw hat, he tilted back his head as he leaned back on the door.

Surprised, I asked, coming to a stop, "What are you doing here?"

"Some of the tribes' folk brought you something, and I wanted to be the one to see you got it. I thought today would be a good day, don't you think?" He moved from the doors. "Have a look and then tell me if you want it or not." I stared at him, not knowing what to say or do. I took the step toward the doors in eagerness to find out and placed my hands upon the handles. With my fingers tightened, I tugged, and the huge double doors swung open with ease, squeaking on the hinges. But what was inside made my jaw tighten, clinching my teeth together.

Inside the doors where the Camero once sat, there stood a new Ford 250, 4x4 sidestep. Jason, Daniel, Nate, and other young man were working on the overhead lights on a black roll-bar behind the back glass. The color was that of a blue-black prism.

I was stunned by the sight when Daniel asked, "Well, whatcha think?" He waved a tool in the air with a grin.

"Where's ya tongue?" Nate groaned with laughter.

Luther put a hand on my shoulder and said, "Boys, he'll find his voice after a while. Finish up now." He squeezed my shoulder. "Let's have a look around." I nodded, still unable to speak, and followed him around the truck.

Starting with the twenty-two-inch aluminum rims, with tires, we made our way to the left. Two sliver steps laid under the passenger door, and two three-inch aluminum dual pipes rose over the back glass. Walking past the open door, there was CB antenna standing on top with the radio sitting on the dash. A silver four-inch steel guard rounded the headlights and grill. And last but least, the windows were quite dark with a lighter windshield. I thought I was about to cry when we stopped in front of the monster truck.

I felt everyone staring when Luther asked, "Well?" He dropped his arm to his side. After the final effort to find my tongue, I looked at the truck, Luther, and the boys.

I felt the grin coming on. "Oh, hell yeah!" Bubbled out between my lips, and I began jumping around like mad man. I grabbed Luther around the neck a tad rough, but I was so overjoyed.

"When did it happen?" I asked, standing back.

Reaching into his pocket, he replied, "Couple days after the party when Tom told me what happened." He pulled out a shiny silver key, tossed it to me, and I caught it midair. The gang in back had gone to yelling, Luke over and over, so I rushed around to the driver side and quickly stuck it in the silver keyhole, unlocking the door.

I grabbed the pull-up handle, and the huge door swung open with ease, letting the smell of new leather ooze out. I grabbed hold of the handles inside the door and seat, pulling myself up on the steps and inside. I sat down on the brown leather seat, feeling the soft touch sink under my weight. The carpet under my feet was black with a plastic runner on top. The dash and overhead cloth was a light grey in color, and a CD player sat next to a GPS. There were so many different types of electronics I didn't know where to start, so I stuck the key in the ignition.

With a five speed on the floor, I pushed the clutch in and turned the key. When it started, it snarled like a mad dog, but it had no problem coming to a full roar. I let it idle to watch the old man standing at the passenger door with a smile. I grinned as I listened to the dual pipes rumble and felt the vibration of the truck, making me feel like I had the power to do anything. The guys in back leaped out, running to the shed doors.

Jason stepped to the driver door and said with a grin, "It's ready when you are, bud."

I stuck out a hand to him which he took, and I said, "Thanks a mill."

"Anytime," he replied, releasing my hand and went with the others as they left the shed.

Rolling the passenger window down, I yelled at Luther, "Need a ride home?" He dropped his head as he began to laugh, opening the door, and stopped for a minute, grinning up at me.

I cannot say why I said what I did, but I asked with a teasing laugh, "Need a lift, old man?" Shaking his head no with a grunt, he grabbed the handles, taking the steps until he was seated in the seat, and closed the door.

Looking over at me with that ripe old grin, he laughed and said, "Let's go. I'm ready now." With uncontrolled laughter, I closed my door, pushed in the clutch, and put the shifter in gear. Releasing the clutch, I eased out of the shed, taking Luther home before going out to Kimmi's.

I eased up the drive in thought of what she would think of the thing. I arrived to find her sitting out on the lawn in a patio chair, dressed in a blue-grey sundress, under one of the many oak trees.

I parked and jumped out, running to her. Her eyes were as wide as the truck when she raised the sunglasses.

Standing up from the chair, she asked, "Where did you get that thing?" Before I could reply, she said, "Furthermore, how do I get in there?" She dropped the glasses back over her eyes.

Stopping in front of her, I placed an arm around her waist, pulling her to me in a hug.

"Whitecloud and some of the tribe got it for me. What do you think?" I asked with excitement.

I pulled her back, taking her by the hand. "Let's go see." She was a little reluctant but came anyway, stumbling across the ground.

I stopped at the hood, and she looked up at the massive thing and said, "It's nice, but why would you want one so big?" She walked to the grill and ran a hand over the bar while standing on tippy-toes. She tried to look up over the hood when I saw her lips curl into a smile. Instead, she raised the sunglasses to the top of her head, cutting me with those blue eyes.

Biting her bottom lip, she snarled, "Well, give me a lift, big boy." She took off in a slight run to the passenger side of the truck where I met her. I grabbed her around the waist just as she stopped at the door.

She slung her arms around my neck when I leaned in, giving her a tender kiss on the lips. Even though it was short and sweet, I reached up, and opened the door. I picked her up by the waist and sat her on the seat. I waited until she was situated and the seatbelt in place before I jogged to the driver side and got in, doing the same. When the rumble of the engine came to life, Kimmi squealed with laughter. I glanced over at her when I put the thing in gear and headed out to the creek where we first met.

Hidden in the darkness of the massive trees, I sat in the car, watching the young man with Kimlaye kidding around the enormous truck. I had loved her for years, but she was headstrong about wanting to be free and to explore on her own. After they passed me and were out of sight, I drove on up to see Ivan and Mollie.

I entered the park, found a place to park, jumped from the truck, and hit the ground running. Opening the passenger door, I took Kimmi by the waist, and helped her to the ground.

She looked around. "It has been awhile."

"Yeah, just a bit." I took her hand into mine and walked up the path, feeling the fresh air on my face. Taking in the smells of summer, Kimmi wandered off in the shaded areas before she got too warm. At the top of the ridge, we trotted over to where the thickness of the trees hid the tiny trail that lead to the creek. I took her hand, and we waded through the tall grass into the clearing of the creek that was as beautiful as it was before.

Kimmi went to the edge of the water, sat down, pulled her shoes off, and stuck her feet into the clear running water. I looked around, then joined her as I pulled my shoes off and stuck my feet into the cold water.

"Feels good, yes?" Kimmi asked, wiggling her toes.

"Yes, it does," I replied, sliding my toes under the little rocks at the bottom.

Kimmi oddly looked at me, "Tell me truthfully. Do you believe in what you see and touch?"

Unsure of what to say, I uttered, "As any other person would, sure, why?"

"I'm not really sure. It was something I felt I had to ask."

"Why do you ask such a thing?" I watched the shadows from the dimming light move across her face.

"It makes me wonder who I am truly. I mean I feel I have a difference in me."

I felt something was wrong right then. "Hey, what's this all about?" I asked, sliding over to give her a hug.

"Sometimes I feel I'm not right for you. The home you have here, the people love you. I'm just so different than they are."

"And that is what makes you special. Besides, I can't do without you now since you are my everything." The hawks overhead had become agitated about something that lead to me feeling an odd presence but it was nothing I'd ever felt before.

"We've a visitor approaching," Kimmi whispered, standing up. I also got to my feet.

In the silence was an eerie sound like the sound of wings flapping, growing louder. I wondered what the hell could make such a sound other than a plane. In an instant, I forgot when Kimmi gasped, and placed her hands over her mouth, making me look up to a shadow coming toward us. I stepped in front of Kimmi just as the tall stranger came into view.

Kimmi shook my hand loose and ran toward him, with me yelling, "Kimmi, no. Stop!" But it was to no avail. She went right to him, placing her hands up around his neck. He did the same, and I recognized him as her lifelong friend, Jock. He was dressed like Magnyss, in a long black canvas trench coat over a black suit.

After a time of talking, Kimmi took the man's hand and pulled him over to where I had leaned against a tree. She seemed rather surprised by him.

"Luke, you remember Jock, yes?"

Extending a hand, I said, "Yes, I remember. How are you?"

Taking the offer, he replied, "So, so I suppose."

A large black wolf and many others in a pack: The scene changed to a brutal beast of death and chaos in the near future. I released his hand, looking deep into his eyes, and he knew I knew. What he didn't know was the extent of his outcome.

❧⁓⁓❧

I released his hand when Kimmi asked, "How did you find me?"

Looking at her as if he could make love to her, he said, "Okay, Kimlaye. All I had to do was listen to the breeze that blew over the leaves that whispered from the trees, carrying the waves of your voice over the air.

With the jitters, she said, "Thank you. Now tell, Luke, why you have come all this way."

He looked from Kimmi to me and said, "I understand she is to be married and I wanted to see the man for myself who is an outsider. I know I didn't take the time when we first met, and for that, I am truly apologetic."

"And?" I quizzed.

"You are surely different, and Kimlaye loves the indifference in people. Please. I'm not here to cause a problem. I'm just a friend to her." He looked at Kimmi as if in wonder. The Marswaye have been buzzing ever since your visit there."

Kimmi placed both hands on Jock, turning him to face her when she asked, "Just what does that mean? I've not heard you speak as such before."

Feeling the tension, I said, "I hate to intrude, but does Mollie and Ivan know you're here?"

He took Kimmi by the shoulders and replied, "Yes. And I have brought you a gift that awaits your attention."

Kimmi turned a rosy pink with excitement when she shouted, "Shall we go see it now?"

"Yes," Jock replied, kissing her forehead.

I looked at the man when Kimmi took my arm. "Will you come with us, Jock?" she asked, taking his other arm.

"I'll be there. You go on." He turned, running off into the woods. "I need to explore for a moment," he yelled back.

"Well, shall we?" I asked, picking Kimmi up.

Flushed with excitement, she laughed. "Oh yes." With her in arms, I grabbed our shoes from the water's edge and ran down the mountain to the truck, and took her home.

❦❦❦

I rushed into the woods to take a moment for myself and release my mind of the visions I knew I could never tell her or Magnyss. He wouldn't allow Kimlaye to marry such a beast in a beast that would bring death to us all. I wondered how long it would be before she told him of herself and obtained the sense of sight of her own. I freed myself of the thoughts and rushed to the Creed's.

❦❦❦

Kimmi was so excited by the time I pulled the truck up into the drive and parked. Casey rushed from the gazebo in a full-length dress, nearly tripping. She was as excited as Kimmi was.

"Hurry up. Kimmi," she yelled.

"What can it be?" Kimmi asked as I jumped from the driver seat. Dashing around to the passenger side, she had the door open and waiting for me. Casey took Kimmi's hand as soon as her feet hit the ground.

"We'll soon see," I told her, heading to the front door.

We stopped when a voice yelled from the gazebo, "Over here, Kimlaye." We found Jock sitting in the gazebo, waving at us. Kimmi dropped my hand when she and Casey headed off toward him only to stop as if they had walked into a wall. I heard a bark that was followed by a whine.

Kimmi had begun to tremble, and she asked with caution, "Where is it?" She looked around as if in doubt of her ears.

"It is here." Jock raised a blue box for her to see. Again the whining came only to be followed by scratching on the box. Kimmi dashed over to it and sat down so Jock could place the blue box on her lap. She swallowed hard, placing her hands on the lid, then hesitated.

"Well, what's the problem, Kimlaye?" Jock questioned. She trembled as she slid her hands over the top of the box, sticking a finger under one flap and flipped up the edge. But when the top extended up all the way, Kimmi's eyes watered when a small white blue-eyed puppy popped its head up at her. It couldn't have been more than three months old, and it was so small. I watched Kimmi reach down into the box, lift out the squirming puppy, and place it in her lap.

The puppy whined and nudged at her hand for her to run a hand over its coat from the head to the tail as she soothed it. When it barked that little bark, her face glowed, and I knew her heart was captured by it when a tear fell.

Wiping the tears back, she asked, "How did you catch him so small?"

Jock half turned to face her when he replied, "I was out roaming one evening when I caught a breeze that carried the whine of this little guy over the trees. Sounding hurt, I hurried to find him. When I arrived, I found the mother dead and this one near dead. It wasn't yet ready to leave her, so I took him home and nursed him back to health. When I heard of your engagement, I thought it would be the right time and gift for you. He reminded me much of you with the blue eyes since they are very rare for the breed."

Teary, she asked, "Have you named him?"

Wiping the wetness from her face, he whispered, "No, that is your choice now. I left that for you."

"Luke, what do you think would be a proper name for him?" Kimmi asked as I seated myself next to her with Casey on the opposite side of me.

Sitting there, I stared at the pup with crystal eyes and thought about what Jock had said about him. After a few minutes I looked at her and said, "Since it has made a comeback for survival that shows he is spirited as you, I suggest the name be Spirit—a reminder of you."

Jock nodded and said, "Luke has a good point, Kimlaye."

"That is what it shall be then for you are right." Kimmi picked the pup up, and kissed its nose. "Spirit it is." Right then, it licked her in return.

Jock faced me with a grim look, and I watched his eyes when he whispered, "Luke, I meant no disrespect when I bought it here for her. My apologies." At least he was gentleman enough to say it.

"I accept. Thank you." I turned my attention to Kimmi. "Well, you are now the owner of an arctic wolf, and soon he'll become domestic, then what?" I surprised myself with that one.

But Kimmi was better when she said, "Then you will surely make a good playmate for him." She laughed, nudging me. But then the thought came: did she know really know?

I pushed it off when she said, "You asked for that, sticking your foot in your mouth." Laughter took over, and she screeched with joy. Jock and I fell into laughter when I knew I had it coming, and she was right. While Casey and Kimmi soothed the pet, Jock got my attention with a tilt of the head. We excused ourselves and stepped from the gazebo.

The front door opened to Chase. "Did I hear a dog bark?" he asked the time a growl escaped from the gazebo, getting his attention. Even more when it snarled. He took to running when he saw the pup's head.

"Let us take a stroll," Jock said, placing his hands behind his back, then walked away. I followed.

I tagged along until we were out of hearing range, and he suddenly stopped, facing me.

"I don't know what you have done, but I like it, and she's happy. She shines like the moon itself. So whatever it is, please don't hurt her."

I knew he saw. "You saw what?"

Swallowing, he sighed, "I'm more of a seer than Mollie, and what I saw was chaos and death."

"Don't let this fool lie to you. I will show you what you truly are when the time comes," my head growled.

"You have my word, Jock. I'll not harm her in any way. My heart couldn't live without her now, and I know you know."

"Yes, I saw the wolf, but you hold an odd presence with it. I see in your face that you tell the truth. Thank you. Now, when is this big day? I have grown excited to give her away to the man she loves."

Dropping the matter-of-factly conversation, I said, "We are having a hard time on that." Prying a little, I asked, "Why have you no wife?" Jock dropped his head and stared at the ground. His quietness felt strange when I thought I had hit a sore spot.

Jock finally looked up at me with pain in his green eyes and sighed when he began to speak. "I did once, a long time ago." He turned to look out over the East Ridge. "Caffe and I had been wed three years on that winter day in the village where we lived. It sat at the base of a steep mountain in the regions of the waterfalls. I was out hunting with several others the day she went into labor with our second child. It had been snowing all day for three days, and the harsh winter had been extremely hard that year on us all. The river valley had frozen over so thick it was hard to break through. With the side of the mountain thick with snow, it gave way to the tremor, sliding down the side and covering the village. Very few survived, but neither my mate nor two children did, and I have been alone since then. I cannot find the will to love another as I did her."

Jock swallowed hard and turned away. But I could hear the tears fall. I watched him wipe his face, then turn to me again with his eyes wet and red from the tears. "I'm sorry to have unloaded on you like that, but I've not talked to anyone about her death until now, which will be twenty years tomorrow." I felt honored he confided in me.

"One favor please: don't remind her. I don't wish her to be upset again at this time."

"I can do that." I agreed. Since he was into keeping secrets, I asked, "Jock, just what does Marswaye mean in your language?"

He smiled, and his eyes lightened. "Centuries ago, we needed a name for ourselves. The shaman came up with the name Marswaye, which means 'old ones.'"

"Kim never told me yet. Thank you." I knew I lied, but it was for me only.

"No, thank you." He looked into my eyes and said, "I want you to know that Kimlaye was once the apple of my eyes for many years, but she was a woman with her own heart, and she wasn't ready, so I never pressed the issue. I had never kept the secret of the death of Caffe. They were once best friends."

Concerned, I asked, "Has she not wanted to talk about her in passing?"

"She has, but I made it impossible in fear of hurting her myself."

"I am truly sorry for your loss." I consoled before we headed back to the gazebo.

The puppy and Kimmi were playing tug of war with a towel when we arrived. Casey and Chase were having a blast, giggling at them like school kids. Watching her from a distance, I had not seen Kimmi laugh like that until then, and it made her glow even more.

"Luke, the dog will bring her comfort for when you're not around." Jock sighed, standing next to me.

"Thanks, but I plan on being around for a long time."

"No, my friend, that's not what I meant, and you know this." He placed a hand on my shoulder at the time Kimmi came running with the puppy tugging at the towel, shaking its head, and growling at her.

In desperation, she cried, "I could use a little help here. He is strong for such a little thing." Then she lost the grip she had on the towel, and it went trailing with the puppy to disappear out of sight. My fine hearing could hear it growling from the back.

Meanwhile, I heard Casey ask Jock, "Are you a true Marswaye?"

"Well, let's see," Jock said in a joking manner. I looked around when I didn't hear the puppy any longer.

"Where is Spirit, Kimmi?" I looked around her.

"Look behind you," she giggled. I looked around to find the little puppy silently sitting right behind my legs. I reached down to rub the nose, and he licked my hand. The wet nose and warm tongue felt good. Jock pardoned himself, and with Casey and Chase on his heels, they went inside while Kimmi and I sat in the gazebo to talk.

Kimmi was so excited that her friend had come to visit, and she had a pet to keep her company at night till we were married. I didn't want to spoil the moment, but we needed to talk about the date. "Do you recall the first time I met you? "I asked, putting an arm around her shoulders.

She thought a minute, then said, "Yes, I do. Why?"

"The date," I said, looking down at her.

She smiled and faced me. "Oh, you mean that date?"

With a sly tone, I said, "I do."

"It was the eighteenth of May," Kimmi replied, looking confused.

"Yes. So what is today's date, dear?" I went on.

Studying a spell, she finally replied, "Then it is September 17."

"I've not seen you this happy before, so this will be the date of our wedding. May eighteenth is only a few months away. Sound good to you?" She grabbed me around the neck so fast I hardly had time to blink. I felt wetness on my neck run down to the shirt.

"Hey, are you okay?" I half-assed laughed. She was muffled, so I pulled her back to see she was crying. "What's the matter? I thought you'd be happy?"

"I am overjoyed now. I have waited and waited. Now it is here, and I can't stop the tears."

I pulled her to me while she wept, then began to tremble, so I asked in a sly tone, "So, I take this as a yes." She shook her head yes, unable to speak.

"Good then, we have time to make plans which we'll talk of later."

I had no clue we were being eavesdropped upon until Mollie asked from the doorway, "Did my ears deceive me?" Her voice quivered with excitement.

Unable to deny it, I replied, "No, they did not Mollie." I raised a hand at her.

"Hot damn," she said, clapping her hands together. When the door closed, I heard her tell Ivan, "Honey, it's in the making." My heart picked up the rhythm with it.

When it had gotten late and it was time for Jock to leave for home, he and Kimmi stood out by the gazebo and hugged, saying their good-byes. He made his way to the white Mustang in the drive, waved at everyone before he got in and closed the door. But when he drove away, Kimmi had tears. Even after he was out of sight she continued to stare down the drive. Spirit went over and licked the palm of her hand for attention. She smiled, reaching down to pet the head with one hand, and wiped the tears with the other.

"Will you be okay?" I asked, walking over to her and the pup.

Sniffling, she replied, "I'll be fine. It was a really good day for me. And thank you for setting the date that I've longed for." I gently took her into my arms, kissed her with tenderness, then walked her to the front door. I told her I loved her, then went to the truck and left for Mae's, feeling good about myself.

WATCHERS

THE FOLLOWING WEEK zoomed by with no dreams of my companion, but I still had that devilish warm feeling to do something wild and stupid. I wanted to be me, to do what I wanted for a change, even if it meant getting into some bad behavior. The night before while lying in bed, I watched the moon rise with all its glory and longed to be in the open to howl at it. Kimmi rushed into my head the next morning while I was sitting at the computer table staring out the window when I realized she had never rode on a motorcycle before. With that crazy feeling lingering in me, I quickly rose from the chair, dressing in jeans, a pullover tee shirt, and sneakers. Quietly, I went downstairs to the kitchen for the phone and called Kimmi to tell her of my plans to take a bike out for a ride. She agreed with eagerness. I hurried outside to find the ground saturated from the heavy rain of the morning, but at least the road was dry. I went to the shed and chose the black bike since it had the small pad on the back and quickly brought it to life, then zipped out to grab Kimmi.

I rolled into the drive and stopped at the porch where Kimmi was standing in a dark pair of jeans, a white tee, windbreaker, and of all things, sneakers. Her hair hung over her shoulder in a braid tied with a ribbon at the end. My jaw dropped from the view while she ran out to me, grabbed my neck and planted kisses on my cheek. That was the very first time I had ever seen her dressed that way. My god she was gorgeous, and I let out a whistle telling her the jeans fit all the right places. I rose from the bike, gave her a hug, then placed a ball cap on her head with the bill down in the back.

My head growled, "Damn, man, what we could do with that. You had the right idea to take her out away from everyone. What do you have in mind? Well, if you don't know, I can show you what she's made for if you'll just let me at her. You're a tough one to get to, but it'll come with time."

Snapping out of it, I stood back and looked at her, "Damn, Kimmi. You're looking good. But how did you know about jeans?" I whistled.

"I asked Paulene, of course." She grinned, lightly blushing.

I asked in a laughing manner, "You ready then?"

"I think so," she half mumbled. I picked her up and sat her on the sissy pad, showing her where to keep her feet. Tossing my leg over the seat, I raised the bike and started it. I reached back and took Kimmi's hands, placing them around my waist with her knees pressed against my legs.

"Now hold tight if you're sure you're ready." She nodded yes, so I patted her hands for assurance. I eased the bike forward, and soon we were off when we rolled down the drive.

I stuck to the back roads until we reached the Mountain State Park. Since Kimmi had never been there, it was her day for sightseeing. I found a parking spot just inside the entrance where Kimmi and I got off the bike.

"It's beautiful here." She exclaimed with excitement in her voice. I took her by the hand and walked over to a narrow creek that ran along the foot path of the mountain.

She looked at me, then squatted down when I said, "Try it." I half smiled. She reached over patting the water, then scooped up a handful and drank it.

"It's fresh and very cold," she said. "But it's good." She reminded me of a child in a woman's body who had never been outside in the world. I knew she was different, but I also knew she kept a dark secret as I did, or was it just my way of thinking? She scooped up a handful of water and tossed on me when I stooped down near her. Being caught by surprise, I returned the motion, making her fall back on her fanny, laughing.

❦❦❦

We were standing on a limb at the top of the tallest of tree, watching the boy with Kimmi when I said, "They're a very beautiful couple, aren't they, Jade?" I implied, never looking over at her.

I heard her when she leaned on the tree bark and replied, "Someday soon, Pearl, we'll have to let her go."

With a teary tone, I said, "That'll be a sad day in the making indeed." I felt a tear fall while we continued to watch them without further talk.

❦❦❦

Feeling that strange presence, I stood up and said, "Shall we?" I held out a hand that helped her up and brushed off the dirt.

"Oh yes," she finally said, looking up into the clouds. Hand in hand, we walked toward a sign that told about the park and the mountain before we made our way up the path.

Keeping to the shadows of the trees, we spent about twenty minutes talking about the things she saw until we stopped near a field. It was filled with pink flowering dogwoods and purple, blue, and yellow blooms. With the ground soft from the rain, she ran into the field, sinking with every step.

"My goodness." She sighed, kneeling down to a colorful flower and pulled it. "Some of these are called four o'clock flowers," she said, holding a purple one in the air.

"Why are they called that?" I asked, but my ears heard a slight flapping noise on the wind.

I turned my attention back to her when she said, "They close in the night, then some reopen at 4:00 a.m., while others open at 4:00 p.m." She reached down and pulled a blue and black one. Running back over the wet ground toward me, she giggled. "Beautiful, isn't it?"

Taking the flower from her hand, I replied, "Yes, just as you are." I placed the flower in her hair over the ear before the wind picked up, bringing a chilling blast of cold air.

"Well now," she said, pulling on the jacket.

"I thought you didn't mind the cold," I said, pulling on the collar of the jacket.

Looking up at me, she said, "I don't, but rain is on the way." I inhaled deeply and sure enough there was the smell of rain in the air, hoping it was a ways off yet. I took her hand, and we continued up the path.

I found myself lagging back at times, finding her desirable in those tight jeans. They unquestionably looked good on her from where I had been standing to get a glimpse. With my stare in tunnel vision, I nearly walked right into her when she suddenly stopped.

Turning around with a drive in her tone, she said, "Can we maybe stop and have a bite. I'm kinda hungry now." She cut me a glance that was unmistakably inviting, but she softly kissed me instead.

I wasn't sure if she was funnin', but I loved it. "Sure. You have any ideas?" The place was desolate.

"Huh, let's walk till we find something." She took my hand when she looked up with appreciation, but I had an adrenalin rush to be spontaneous.

Without a word, I suddenly picked her up and held firm, never losing a step. She kicked her feet a moment and hugged my neck with a smile. The motions made the urge in me, want to drop to the ground and ravish her, but I pushed it off again, and took off walking.

"What are you doing, Luke Winterset?" she asked in an unnerving tone.

I felt myself shiver. "Just having some fun with you." I kissed her forehead. With her in my arms, we made the walk slowly. But what the hell, we were getting there.

We were in an average conversation when I saw the overhead shadows on the ground. Tuning in my hearing, I heard the flapping sounds that followed. I was looking at Kimmi, who was talking but I didn't hear. I thought it had been the birds when I returned my attention to her.

"Will you please put me down now?" she said, kicking her legs.

"What if I don't want to let go?" I squeezed gently.

"Well then, how about this?" She grabbed my face and kissed me so fast it made my head feel funny. I stumbled to the ground, landing on my knees. Tumbling over onto the wet ground with her on her back, I was lying over her in laugher. We held one another for awhile.

After a few minutes, I got to my feet, helped Kimmi to hers, and made our way to the top where she stopped to stare out over range. She saw things in a way that was unlike anything I had ever seen before. I had begun to see things in a new way since my return home from the fort, and I knew it was because of the beast inside me. Kimmi's eyes had begun to darken when she shaded them with her hands. I took her hand, and pulled her toward a bench made of stone from the mountain and shaded by several trees.

"The overlook is beautiful, Luke," she claimed as she stumbled. "You come here a lot?" she asked, catching her balance.

I reached for her, saying, "Just when I'm hurt or alone." Those eyes for some reason that day just made me love her more.

She half turned when she sat on the bench and said, "Luke, that was then, and this is now. Leave the past back there behind you, and stay here with me." She took my hands into hers as she spoke. She was right once again and I moved closer to her, placing my arm around her waist and pulling her tight. The soft air carried a scent that wasn't rain. It was something strange.

"Bright Eyes." I jokingly looked at her. "You ready to go back down?" I let the name ring off my tongue.

I saw the curve of her lips when she said, "Oh no. Bright Eyes, not yet ready to leave. Please." She giggled like a school girl the same time a gust of wind came up over the side, blowing the loose hair across her face.

I removed the cap and brushed them aside for her, then said, "Okay, Beautiful, we'll stay a bit longer." We watched the day darken with the sun dipping down behind the oncoming grey clouds.

A sudden shot of cold air came around out of the trees, bringing the faint feeling of moisture and smell of rain to the air. I suddenly felt there was about to be a storm coming soon.

I quickly rose to my feet, pulling Kimmi up by the hand. "I think we should hurry back down."

With a shiver, she agreed. "Yes, I felt it too."

"Come, we've not much time." I picked her up, knowing I had not the time to walk. Running down the hill just fast enough, even with a slip or two here and there, was for her to think I was still me. Even the presence that followed, always kept out of sight.

We made the bike just as the first small raindrops hit our heads. I looked at her and her at me, breaking out in a laugh at each other. I put her on the back, then jumped on, bringing the small engine to life. With a quick glance at Kimmi, I rolled off in a race against the rain. I headed down the mountain side, on the narrow two-lane road, toward the small town below. I felt we were being followed, so I kept an eye out... until we fishtailed. I kept it upright, praying for guidance all the way, as I mashed the accelerator.

When the drops began to get heavier and sting my face, I thought I saw something run across the road and into the woods. Not sure of what I saw, I thought it didn't matter as I hurried to avoid the cold rain that had begun to shower us with larger drops. Reaching the small town, I drove down the main street toward the nearest place to get out of the rain, and that was at a hotel that came into view. Stopping at the front entrance, I quickly killed the engine, got off the bike, and helped Kimmi off. Leaving it where it was, I took her by the hand, and rushed into the building, out of the raging wind that had begun to howl.

We stopped just inside the double doors when the rain and wind slammed the door shut. Poor Kimmi was soaked from head to toe, but she didn't have to worry about makeup—she wore none. She looked at me as I looked at her and we began to laugh at each other.

"Well, now what, Luke?" she asked, looking out at the rain hit and bounce off the bike.

I sighed, watching the wet bike and said, "Guess we wait." I pulled her to me while we watched the wind pick up, howling through the cracks of the doors. I shivered a tad when she slipped her arm around me, and we never gave the desk clerk a thought.

Both of us were mesmerized by the rain, so we jumped at the same time a voice asked, "Can I help you?" The voice came from the clerk at the desk.

I looked at Kimmi with a smile, then faced the counter. "I think we need a place to hold up till the rain stops," I said, walking toward the counter. The young man that smiled at me with an if-I-must smile was a young black man, wearing a uniform for the hotel, which was a Clarion. I stopped and placed my hands on the counter when the fella turned and picked up the phone, making me think how rude he was.

While he was busy, I looked back to find Kimmi staring out the door with her arms over her chest as she took a deep sigh. I couldn't believe I felt so much for someone like her. But how I looked forward to so much more and wondered what would our life bring us in the future when the lights go out.

"Well," I heard Kimmi say.

"Pardon me," I said, turning to fumble my way back to Kimmi who was still standing at the front door, thank God, when I placed my hands on her shoulders.

From where we stood, the whole place was dark, the wind had things blowing around outside, and the trees were tossing limbs through the air when lightning flashed in the sky. The sudden storm was raging outside as I watched my bike get knocked over by a trashcan flying through the air.

"Shit," I cursed with sorrow, watching it hit the ground.

"I'm glad we're inside. I fear the wind would blow me away like the debris out there," Kimmi sighed, placing a hand on top of mine.

"Excuse me, folks," the desk clerk said.

"We're here still," I said.

"My manager has offered you a free room tonight."

I looked at Kimmi who faced me. "Sound good to you?" I asked her.

Shrugging her shoulders, she replied with a quiver in her tone, "Yes it does."

"Be right there," I told the clerk. I took Kimmi by the hand, and we found our way to the counter while the man turned on a flashlight.

Handing me a key, he said, "The room is here on the first floor, so you won't have to worry about the elevator."

"Thank you, sir," Kimmi said.

Smiling, he replied, "You're welcome, miss." I took Kimmi's hand and we fumbled our way down the hall on the left, toward room 106.

I opened the door for Kimmi and followed her in, finding an emergency light on. Kimmi went to the window and look out. The room was an ordinary hotel room with two twin beds, a TV, a dresser, a small closet, and of course, a bathroom. I heard a bump on the window when Kimmi placed her head against it.

"Is something wrong?" I asked, going to her side, feeling something was bothering her.

She took off the cap and brushed hair from her face. "I have no dry clothes to put on and I'm not presentable now. I am sorry," she said in a teary voice.

Placing my hands on her shoulders, I said, "Never be sorry. I'm not." Looking down at her rump, I said, "Besides I think you look really sexy in wet clothing." I tried to cheer her up. She looked up at me with sad eyes and hair clinging to her face. I learned that women think they look the worst when things are wrong. But actually, I think that they look the best when they are at their worst.

She turned to face me, sat down on the window sill, and asked in with a feeble tone, "Luke, will you care for me always?" She leaned back the window.

"What do you mean by that?" I asked, sitting at her side again.

She sounded in despair when she said, "I've been sheltered most of my life, and I don't know a lot." She paused as she bit her lip. "More or less, what I'm trying to say is, I haven't been touched by life, I'm new to the outside world, and I need you to guide me, or I'm lost to it. Understand?" she continued.

Leaning against the thick window pane, I told her, "I've not thought of it that way, but you're right, and yes, I'll care for you always." I pulled her to me, wrapping my arms around her and thought why she would ask me such a thing.

After a few minutes and the lighting struck, I realized we were still in wet clothes, so I took her by the hand, pulled her toward the bed, and sat her down. I meant no harm in what I was about to do but the frightened looked she gave me said otherwise and she began to tremble. "Please don't."

Realizing what she meant, I told her, "Oh no, no. I won't do anything you don't want me to, but we need to get those wet things off you. Okay?" I waited until she decided if that was what she wanted. She finally nodded yes.

With a sigh of relief, knowing she knew I meant no harm, I rushed to the bathroom and got a towel from the rack, and went back to the bed. "Put this around your shoulders," I said, handing her the towel. She nodded okay, taking the towel from me. I reached down and took the shirttail, pulling it up from her pants. She stiffened; I stopped. She nodded, and I pulled the thing over her head. Finding a tiny silk undershirt, she pulled the towel around her shoulders. Next, I took off the shoes followed by the jeans which she was hesitant to take off too. She once would not have minded, but that was another story. Under the jeans, I found a matching pair of lady boxers, which I also left on her. She didn't mind the removal of anything. She was just cautious. I put up one finger to let her know I'd be right back, and hurried to the bathroom to get another towel to dry her hair with.

I undid the braid, and timely dried the long black silky stuff with a feeling that was more than I could say. When I was done, I discovered I had no brush. Instead, I pulled her to her feet, pulled back the blankets so she could lay down, and then pulled it to her chin. After kissing her forehead, I grabbed the wet clothes and began stringing them about the room to dry. I could feel her watching my every move. I thoughtlessly walked right past the half-open window curtain in a hurry.

I had just laid the jeans over the small chair when I heard her whisper, "Come lie with me." Then I heard her softly pat the bed next to her. I faced her with interest, and she nodded okay. Feeling good about the situation, I stripped down to my shorts, tossed them around the room, and climbed into the bed on the opposite side of her.

I slid next to her as she rolled to face me. In the silence we stared at one another, until I reached for her. Pulling her into my arms, I wanted desperately to have her and to keep her safe. She put her head upon my bare chest, kissing the soft side of my breast while her arm found my waist. Enjoying the sensation, I pulled her closer.

❧❦❧

With the shock of watching through the window at the two in the bed, I told Pearl, "We cannot let this happen."

Staring in the window through the slit in the curtain, she replied, "Yes I know. Magnyss will surely kill us both."

"Jade, what are we going to do now?" she snarled at me. Watching Luke gently tease the silkiness of the shirt, I raised a fist and hit the window with all my might. It rattled, startling both of them, and they looked toward us just as we stooped below the window in the stinging rain.

❧❦❧

"Must be debris hitting the window from outside," I said, returning to the soft breast awaiting my attention. I laid my head on her stomach, caressing the breast, and listening to her rapid heart.

Placing her hands on the back of my neck, she said, "Come here."

I looked into her eyes, rising up on one elbow. "Are you sure?" I knew the answer before she did, running a devilish hand under the shirt to the cool quivering breast.

Sighing, she said, "Oh yes. I have long waited to make love with you." I leaned over and kissed her tender inviting lips while my hand slid under her back, pulling her under me. I rolled on top her, and gently placed my legs between hers.

❧❦❧

My jaw dropped before I said, "Shit, Jade." I shouted, staring through the glass, "This is not happening, is it?"

"If we don't stop them, it will," she whined with anguish, knowing what would happen if we let that continue. Looking around the flying debris, I noticed a tree limb on the ground nearby. Without a word, I rushed over and picked it up. Being what we were, such things seemed weightless. Tossing the limb at the window, it barely missed Jade's head when it crashed through the window.

"A bit over dramatic, was it not?" Jade shouted, running at me.

"I suppose, but it stopped them, yes?" I replied.

❦❧

Sitting back on my calves, a large tree limb came crashing through the window. The broken glass was enough to see what I thought were white faces in the rain.

What I saw or thought I saw peering in caused me to leap off Kimmi, rushing to the window. "What the hell?" I said, placing my hands on the glass to look out.

❦❧

Those two will hear about this. Knowing who they were and why they did what they did, made my blood boil with anger, even though I knew it was for the best.

"Luke, are you okay?"

❦❧

In the dark, I could see nothing but the raging wind and rain, splattering my face. It was a short moment when the phone rang. I picked it up and found the desk clerk on the other end wanting to know if we were okay.

❦❧

"Pearl, I think we did it," Jade confessed, sitting on the ground under the window.

"Oh I do hope so. She'll be mad at us later, you know." I knelt down with her, leaning on the brick wall of the building.

"Yes, but that mistake won't be made tonight. She can wait until she is wed, and we are still alive to tell about it." We stayed put until it was safe to leave.

Kimmi and I were placed in another room for the night. I pulled the curtain closed and faced her with a bit of anger. She was already lying in bed with the cover over her.

Sighing at the thought, I said, "I thought I saw something out there earlier."

With an undertone, she said, "No matter. Just come lie next to me, and let us sleep so we can leave in the morning." She patted the bed behind her. Removing the clothes that I offered to keep on, I crawled in. Sliding close to her, I had no thoughts of anything else since the moment and mood had been spoiled. When she sighed softly, I gathered she was asleep, and I found myself beginning to drift off.

When I woke up early the next morning, I found it was daylight, and oddly, I had slept all night in a strange place with a woman. Strange but true, I thought our little privacy was a dream, but it wasn't. Light peeked through the window curtain, and I noticed the emergency light was out. While Kimmi was still asleep there beside me, I watched the rise and fall of her breast with every breath she took. For an instant, I didn't wish to leave her side. I eased from the bed and went to the window to see the damage from the storm.

I slightly pulled the curtains apart and adjusted my eyes to the brightness of the day. There were folks out cleaning up debris from the storm. Realizing I was in shorts, I quietly searched the room and located my pants that I had tossed on the back of the desk chair. Standing at the window shirtless with my hands on my hips, I watched the people, wondering what the hell had been in the window. I never told Kimmi so she wouldn't become unset. I didn't hear her rise but felt her cold arms when they slid around my naked waist. It caused me to sort of shiver from the touch, but it quickly passed with the silkiness of her shirt, rubbing my back.

I turned to see a sleepy face yawning at me. "Morning, sleepyhead." I gave her a hug, kissing the hair on her head.

Groggy, she asked, "Hey, is it still raining out there?"

"It's stopped, but there's a mess out there," I said, looking over my shoulder out the window.

"My clothes please," she said, placing her arms over her chest.

"Sure, sweetie." I gathered her things, gave them to her, then turned away, and went into the bathroom while she dressed.

I grabbed a bath cloth from the overhead rack, went to the sink, and ran the hot water to wet it. When I went back into the room, she was sitting on the side of the bed fully dressed.

I sat down next to her on the bed with the cloth in my hand and faced her. "May I?" I asked, raising the rag to her.

With uncertainty, she asked, "What is it first?" She leaned back in fear, and her eyes widened when she said, "Your eyes are changing colors. Why?"

"If she only knew," my head laughed that unnerving laugh.

Shaking it off, I said, "It's a secret, but you'll like it, I promise. Now close your eyes." She nodded, closing her eyes so I could wipe her face.

I started at the forehead then down the left side of the face and worked around the chin to the other side of the face finishing at the nose. She smiled as she opened her eyes.

With a light tone, she said, "It was nice and warm. Thank you." She reached out and placed both hands on my bare chest. I didn't flinch from the cold as she let them rest there. *What was she doing?* I thought. But I was patient while she stared at my chest, wondering what was on her mind. What did she have to say?

Then I thought, *Oh hell, did she know, and was she about to tell me to get lost?* My mind was in shambles with the thought.

I guess I should have told her before she beat me to it with the statement she made, but it released a heavy burden when she said, "Luke, I'm sorry. I don't mean to stare. It's just you're as warm as that cloth was, and I liked it very much." She let her hands slide down to my waist before she returned them in her lap and said, "Please forgive me for wanting something I can never have." I watched a tear fall. There would always be a pain in me when I would be unable to do anything for her but wish as she did.

I took her by the hands and said, "Look at me." She looked up with tiny tears hanging in the corners of her eyes. "Being different is what makes us unique." I curled her hands into mine with a tender squeeze.

Removing a hand, she brushed the tears away and said, "That has no meaning to how I feel when I am with you. I want to be like you, to have the warm soft touch as yours. It pains me not to be warm for you. I know my coldness is difficult to endure, and I see it every time I touch you."

Stunned by her words, I pleaded, "Give me time to become accustomed to you as you are to me."

She swallowed and said, "I'll give you all the time you need. I have plenty to spare."

Right then I didn't know what she meant by that, so I told her, "Settled then. Are you hungry? We never did found that bite we looked for."

Her lips curved at the corners when she said, "Yes. Very."

"Good. Me too," I said, noticing I was famished. Rising from the bed, I found my shirt and shoes to finish dressing. And since neither one of us had a comb, we left the hair as it was—tangled. Finally, we left to find breakfast.

We stopped at the front counter before we headed out to thank management for the room and to inquire of a restaurant. The clerk was a young girl with light brown hair and eyes and a bit heavy on the makeup. I asked about a small place for breakfast and a towel to wipe the bike down with.

"Try the Night Torch, it's decent, "she replied, reaching under the counter. Pulling out a towel, she handed it to me.

"Thank you," I said, taking the towel.

With a nod, she replied, "You're welcome." The phone rang the same time Kimmi took my hand with a tug, and we went outside in the rising sun toward the bike on the ground.

We stopped in front of the bike, and Kimmi snickered while I reached down to set the bike upright. I dried the seat with the towel, checking it over for damages, but to my surprise, there were none. I pardoned myself to run the towel back inside. When I came out, Kimmi was leaning on the back with a lousy grin. I picked her up and sat her down on it before jumping on and starting it. Keeping to the back roads, I headed toward the small diner on the east side of town. I felt Kimmi tighten her grip around my waist and her knees against my legs, so I patted her hands for assurance.

We found the diner, which was a nice place. Breakfast was good, but Kimmi poked at the pancakes that she hardly ate. Talk was small, but soon it was over and time to leave. I paid the check and walked Kimmi back outside to the bike. I kissed her soft lips, then sat her on the back of the bike. Soon we left, heading home to end the tour. Even though my devilish wanting nearly took place, I felt we had been followed and watched. It was late morning when I dropped her off and went home for a shower.

LEGENDARY

OVER THE COURSE of several days after our adventure, neither of us said anything about that night. I didn't feel right with myself for some odd reason, and I hadn't talked to the old man lately, so I thought it was time. I quickly got up and dressed in a floppy shirt and baggy shorts. Zooming from the room, I went down the stairs, and out to meet the day, which was cloudy and cool. I jogged from the front door to the truck on the front lawn, hoped in, and fired it up. After a couple minutes, I faced it toward Luther's with a pit stop at Kimmi's first.

I pulled up into the driveway, parked under the large oak, hopped out and ran up onto the porch. After I knocked on the door, I only waited for a second or two before the door latch clicked. When the door swung open, Kimmi was standing there in a gold full-length gown with a high collar. Her hair was down but pulled to the back, revealing her red eyes from crying. She ran into my arms, burring her face into my neck.

"Hey, what's this? You okay?" I quickly asked, putting my hands on her waist. She nodded yes, but her voice was muffled when she spoke.

"What's the matter, honey?" I asked softly. She pulled back to face me, and I gently wiped her face with a smile, running a thumb across her cheek.

"We should talk or go see Whitecloud." She sniffled.

"About?" I felt I had been hit by a train.

Kimmi composed herself, then faced me smiling. "You recall the time I mentioned something about you?" Then it backed up and hit me again.

"What is it you cry about so? It can't be that bad." I laughed. But her sorrow showed she wasn't sure about any of it.

"I should visit the old man then." I took her hand as she walked out on the porch, closing the door.

"How about you compose yourself and let me go out to see him for awhile?" I told her, stopping at the edge of the porch.

Her lips curled, and her cheeks dimpled. "Only if you hurry back."

I kissed her cheek and said, "I will, I promise. Go inside now, and I'll see you later." Placing a hand to her lips, she blew a kiss, then turned and went back inside, closing the door. I trotted to the truck, then drove out to see Luther.

When I arrived, there was a fire going, and many of the tribesmen, along with Jason, Paulene, and Whitecloud, were sitting around it. By the time I parked the truck and jumped out, I discovered that there were so many I had never seen before.

Jason came rushing over, grinning like an ass in his beltless shorts and tank top.

"Hurry up, you. You're holding up progress," he said.

"Progress? What progress?" I yelled as he dashed away. "Well, I had better check this out," I whispered, walking toward the group.

I had just sat down next to Daniel and Jason on the ground when Luther started to speak.

"Finish the story, Whitecloud," someone yelled from the crowd.

"You missed some, but that's okay, bud," Jason claimed with a jab in the ribs, making me grunt.

Paulene looked at us and, with a snap in her voice, said, "Shut up."

"Yep, that's right. Tell' em, Paulene," someone said.

"Those that hid came back to restart their lives, but over a great amount of time, the pale faces came to reclaim their land but was fought off once again by the tribe. The Great Wolf kept tabs on his people and his land, but the time came to obtain extra help to protect his land and people against the growing needs of those who think they are better. The ancestors had gotten weak and became few, so the Great Wolf came up with taking the first born of all families in the beginning until he realized that those who were needed most must come from a strong family to keep them together. Some of us here today hold such a spirit in them, and they are the most needed and welcomed here. Centuries ago, those from the eastern shore and Canada, the wolves and Indians had evolved into one becoming a great warrior. Of the seven clans of the Cherokee, the largest and most important is that of the wolf."

I was too busy staring out over the range to notice Luther was no longer talking. I was wondering about my true self and why I was chosen for such a thing.

I was deep in thought and hadn't noticed the others until Luther sat down at my side and said, "There has been a gathering taking place out there somewhere, that I have felt but have not seen." He put a hand on my back. "You must take caution for we cannot tell when or where. They move around at night, and we can't get a bearing on them."

"I've felt it too," I said, sitting upright, facing him.

"How do our legends compare to others?" he asked with a glee in his eyes.

Smiling, I told him, "The one I like the best was finding out you were my grandfather." Losing the smile, I asked, "Whitecloud, do you believe a person can carry more than one type of spirit?"

"How do you mean *carry?*"

I realized at that moment that my grandson knew of the companion within him. It reminded me of the night Waya had visited me when I was still arrogant and overbearing. What I needed was for Luke to ask for help.

"Inside one's self," I whispered, so no one else heard.

"Why do you ask such a thing at this particular time?" He turned to me, placing both hands on my shoulders. "How did you come by this?"

"Dreams, I think. They make me foolish, devilish, and, most of all, crazy with resentment. The dreams have showed me pleasure beyond a shadow of a doubt. And yes, I liked it—a lot."

Tom had overheard the conversation when he told Luther, "You must tell him of the Two Wolves." He was standing behind the man with his hands on his hips, towering like a giant tree.

Whitecloud was taken by the request and so was I when he said, "I think we should take this matter up at my home later." He stood up, and the two men left.

I got up and mingled with the crowd but mostly with the joker and Paulene. Daniel had vanished again, and Willa was talking with Mac. I watched many of the women from the tribe watching me from a distance, behind one another, or a tree in the dark. Some of the younger men stared at me but kept to themselves, leaving me feeling that someday I'd understand the ways of the Cherokee. Passing on the stares, it was time to see the old man while people were leaving. I told Jason and Paulene good night, then went into the house with Luther and sat down at the kitchen table.

When Whitecloud was seated, he was at the end of the table toward the kitchen door, whereas I was seated, facing Tom and Mac.

Whitecloud leaned onto the table, propping on his elbows and asked Tom, "Tell me, what is it that made you think of the Two Wolves?"

"Luke I think has a demon spirit inside him," he said without hesitation.

I was taken aback by what he said and asked, "How would you know if it were true?"

"Tell him of the Two Wolves first," Mac interfered.

"It's a legendary thing," Tom said. "It's nothing to be ashamed of." I glanced at Luther, looking into my eyes with a blank stare before he began.

Leaning back in his chair, he placed both hands on the table with the fingers locked together. I settled in to hear about this legend with a grunt.

"Centuries ago, when the True Wolf Sandseff was among the living, he found that each of us held two wolves: one good and one bad. The one of good nature was helpful, friendly, benevolent, faithful, truthful, and compassionate among others. He discovered the ones that created evil among the village, their eyes would change colors with the warm devilish feelings of pleasure, hate, envy, false pride, lies, arrogance, sorrow, and guilt among others."

He named off a couple I had experienced, so I asked, "And this has to do with me, how?"

"If the old books are true, then you are of the legend." I was flabbergasted, tongue tied or whatever at his words.

"Impossible," I stuttered.

"If it is true, then you hold both. The evil will fight to become the master. You need to find the inner strength to hold onto what is good and overcome the bad that is yet to come."

"Bad? What do you mean?" I shouted in anger.

He sat forward and said, "Your temper just now for one."

I snapped without cause and shouted, "How is this?"

In a firm but soft tone, he looked at me and said, "Drop the temper right now. I will arrange for you to see Della. She can tell for sure, if you're willing to."

"If you think it's worth the effort, sure."

"I'll let you know tomorrow. Go home and get some sleep." I rose from the table and bid good night. I went home, called Kimmi, and told her I had to see Della. She replied in her understanding way, then said good night. I hung up and went to bed.

Sleep was shallow through the night, lying there and staring out the window at the darkness, wondering about myself and what was going to happen. What would Della see in me?

Again, I was with the strangeness in me, but how could one person be so different? The night passed when I dozed off. The sun woke me, coming over the horizon and peeking through the tree limbs, into the window and my eyes. I rolled over and got out of bed, found some jeans in the closet and a shirt. The socks I found in the drawer, and my sneakers under the bed. Dressed, I headed downstairs to the kitchen where I found Mae and Joe at the table mumbling over coffee.

"Morning," I said, going to the coffeepot.

"Well, morning. We haven't seen much of you lately," Mae said with class. I reached into the cupboard and got out a cup.

After pouring the hot liquid, I went to the table where I sat down next to Mae. "I hope I'm not intruding?"

"Not at all," Joe spoke up. The phone rang, and Mae got up to answer it, leaving Joe and I with nothing much to say to each other.

Soon she called for me. "It is Whitecloud, Luke." I rose and went to the phone, picking it up off the counter where she laid it down.

In a frustrated manner, I placed the receiver to my ear and said in a most listless way, "Hello."

"Della will see you today. Get out there, and I'll see ya soon."

Feeling pressured, I said, "Thanks." It was short but to the point. I hung up, told Mae and Joe I'd be back later, left the house in a miserable state and got into the truck.

Joey was standing on the porch, waving when I pulled the truck into the drive, and parked by the large pine near the end. He came down the steps, smiling and stopping when I opened the door, leaping from the truck in one move.

As soon as I hit the ground, he shouted with a firm tongue, "You'll get hurt doing that someday."

Being the smartass I was, I replied with a sharp attitude, "Someday maybe. Just not this day."

With a much more testy tone, Joey asked, "Who put poison in your wheaties?"

Stopping at the hood of the truck, we faced one another, and he said, "Be more courteous in your way of speaking to others." I was about to get even more nasty in an uncontrolled manner when a horn blew. We looked to see Luther's old Dodge pickup coming into the drive.

Joey and I walked up onto the porch while he parked the truck and got out. He was pleasantly dressed in a green shirt, overalls, and a straw hat. He waved coming toward us and his boots laid heavily on the wooden steps when he came up onto the porch. Stopping a moment, he spoke to Della in the Cherokee language, and she responded. They talked for a short time before we went into the house. Following Della, she led us down a long hallway, through a black wooden door that squeaked when it opened and down some short stairs. Going through another smaller door, it lead into what appeared to be a holding room.

The place was well lit and looked like a lab with gray stone walls, a long metal table, two tables with utensils, towels, bandages, and so on. A small sink protruded from the wall near an iron cabinet. I soon found the chair in the dark corner cushioned with foam, a headband strapped to the top, straps around the arms and legs. I was busy scoping the place when I heard Della speak, but I didn't know what she said.

Luther said with a pointed finger, "Get up onto the table."

I was hesitant when Joey placed his hands on my back and sort of pushed and said, "Go on. It won't bite ya." I walked over and hopped up onto the cold metal table. Sitting there with my legs swinging over the edge, I felt my friend roam around inside me like a drifter while the two men talked.

After several minutes, Whitecloud came over, and stopped in front of me. I looked up into his eyes to say something but passed on it.

Placing his cool fingers under my elbows, he said, "Raise you arms, Luke." I did as he asked. He pulled my shirt over my head, and laid it on the table by my leg.

Confused, I asked, "What was that for?" With his hands on my shoulder, he laid me back onto the cold table.

With me staring at the overhead light, he said, "Della's going to rest her hands on you so she can see inside you. If you haven't noticed yet, she's a shaman."

I nodded in disbelief that a woman could tell what was going on inside a person. I laid there and waited, looking off to a light over the sink.

Della's thin face came to mine with a warm smile. I thought her hands would have been cold, but they were warm when she placed them on my stomach and closed her eyes. Her eye movement became radical when something rushed through me, making my veins feel like they were on fire. The intensity caused me to cringe from the burning sensation. Feeling tears fall, I closed my eyes and relaxed, feeling Della move her hands over me. When she stopped below the heart, she mumbled in the Cherokee language.

"Well, my friend, we have been found out. Now what?" my companion complained about what was to be between us. I looked at Della, whose eyes snapped open, staring at me.

She suddenly removed her hands from me and stumbled backwards in a near fall. Joey caught her first while she rambled in tongue so fast. Luther was caught by surprise in her motion, but her face showed fear in it. Calming down, she and the old man talked for awhile. Joey kept an eye on me the whole time I was on the table.

"You should really let me out of here. I will show you and them what we can do together."

In a muffled whisper, I asked, "How?"

"Just relax, and I'll show you how."

"Show me." I sighed, staring at the room of people. I inhaled and closed my eyes.

In a matter of seconds, after I had completely given myself to my companion, I felt something move around inside me. Pushing from the inside, here and there, as it made my skin move like ripples in the ocean. Then it ran around in my veins faster than the heart could pump the blood through them, causing intense pain that brought the tears. I was so relaxed by then I had little thought of myself, until I was knocked off the table to the floor. Landing on my feet instead of my knees, I stood upright.

"Nice job," I heard the companion say. "You don't need friends and family when I let go. This is just a tad of the beginning." Whitecloud rushed to me, but I put up a hand to stop him, and he stood staring at me while I was enjoying the feel of my new self.

"Let's grow and test the reflexes now," the companion growled in my head. "Stand still, and let us stretch outward. I have longed to reach for the stars, kid." I was ready to comply with the request.

Inhaling, I raised my hands to the ceiling and stretched out as far as possible. Feeling my companion slide up my arms, it caused ripples in my muscles. Moving into my hands and fingers, they grew in size, leaving no pain to feel, only stronger, better, and happier. The pants I had on felt too tight when my legs began to thicken. I sprouted out in the chest, back and buttocks. I turned and faced Whitecloud, standing on the opposite side of the table with his mouth hanging open.

In a rude manner, I asked, "Now what do you think of me, old man?" I grabbed the table and leaned over it.

He drew back a fist and hit me in the mouth. "That is what I think." Licking the blood from my split lip, I glared at him unable to stop myself when I leaped over the table in one move. Everyone in the room just stood there, staring at me. I could feel their fear coursing through me, making the companion even wilder.

It wasn't long before it left as quick as it came, "Remember, this is just a taste of what I can do for you." It left me feeling weird but wonderful. I was also bitter with myself for being rude to Luther. I apologized, and he accepted my apology.

"I know of the evil darkness. They can be the devil themselves."

Looking over at the chair in the corner, I said, "Am I cursed for this?" I looked into his dark eyes for the answer before he spoke.

But he replied with force in his tone. "No, never say that. But you do bring a whole new meaning to the Tale of Two Wolves." He began to laugh, telling me the story of the legend.

When he was done with the story, I pulled my shirt over my head and asked, "How does one win if they are both inside you?" While he thought about what he was going to say, I recalled the dream when the companion came to me, but I kept it to myself.

Placing his hands on each shoulder, he laughed and said, "It'll be the one you feed the most that shows itself. You truly stand as the man and the wolf. A true legend that must have the strength to embrace the bad with the good, or it will be the death of you." With a nod of the head to him, I stepped aside, thanked Della, then walked upstairs and out the front door into the misty rain. Going to the truck, I decided to go home for a spell where I called Kimmi and told her I'd be there later after I showered.

EGO

I WAS LYING IN bed, staring out the window, thinking about the days that had passed and why Kimmi asked about my visit to see Della. I told her it was nothing to worry about, and she accepted that. I rose from bed, went to the window and opened it to see two squirrels chase one another around the trees. I quickly dressed in sweats, a tee shirt, and sneakers before running down the stairs and out into the morning rain. Jumping into the awaiting truck, I sat there and pondered if my father knew about the thing within me. With that, I sighed and started the truck, then headed out to see Kimmi.

Kimmi and Casey were sitting in the gazebo when I rolled up into the drive. I parked near the garage and Kimmi came running out to the truck in a sky blue sundress. When she stopped at the hood, I noticed her hair was stuck to her head from the rain. Smiling at her wet face and drenched head, I jumped out, ran around to her, and grabbed her up in a hug. Heading back to the gazebo, I found Casey in a red velvet dress that spread out on the floor.

"What brings you out today?" Casey chirped in her kind voice.

"The usual," I said with a laugh, grabbing Kimmi's hand and kissing her cheek.

"What do you have in mind today?" Kimmi sighed softly.

"Just me and you alone at the lake. What do you say?"

"I think you have a good idea." Kimmi snickered. "Let us go right now—in the rain." She began to laugh. About that time,

Spirit raced around the house, chasing a raccoon. The mud was flying from his feet until the raccoon suddenly darted off under some foliage. Spirit, a much bigger animal, came to a sliding stop.

"Let's take him with us today." Kimmi cringed with excitement.

"I agree. It's time he gets out a bit more." I rose to my feet, and Casey did the same. Taking off toward the house, she yelled at us to take care, with a hand waving in the air.

Shaking her head, Kimmi replied, "We will." I grabbed Kimmi by the hand and walked her to the huge truck. I opened the door, took her by the waist with both hands, and hiked her up into the seat, then slammed the door shut. I went to the rear of the truck and let down the gate, whistling for Spirit, who came running just to stop and sit down at my feet.

"Oh, no you don't." I laughed at him. He just sat there, staring with his puppy eyes. Finally, I picked him up and put him in the back. After closing the gate, I ran for the driver side and hoped in. Starting the engine, Kimmi and I smiled at each other, then left for the reservoir.

The lake was vacant mostly due to the rain. It felt great to have Kimmi during the day without the sun and have so much fun together. I parked, got out, then let Spirit out, who shot off like a bullet from a gun. I helped Kimmi out, who took a good whiff of the air as we walked toward the table. I started to sit down on the bench seat, but Kimmi pulled me by the hand. I followed her to a nearby tree. I looked at her, and she winked. I shrugged my shoulders, then sat in the wet sand. I leaned back on the tree truck, so Kimmi could sit in between my legs and lean on me.

"Comfy?" I asked as she settled back on my stomach, laying her head on my chest. I rested my hands on her shoulders and she reached up with a hand and held it for a moment.

"This is peaceful, Luke. I wish so often to be like you."

"Just think. The end is nearing soon. Then the months will fly by."

"Yes, I count the days until then." She rubbed my legs with a gentle touch that bought that familiar feeling of desire I still had.

I was about to mention something when I caught a foul odor and a rustle of feet. We both looked toward the sound in the woods and the red eyes that appeared. Kimmi gasped when two reddish-brown beastly wolves with black eyes come from the darkness of the trees and stopped not more than ten feet from where we sat. I noticed how small they were compared to others, so I watched them, and they stared at us. I also noticed one ruffle its fur around the neck when they sat down on their hunches as if waiting for something or someone.

After several moments, I was about to stand up, but a raspy voice stopped me. "Don't bother. You'll not live through it, kid," said the raspy male voice.

"Been working out some it seems," another voice said. Both were males, but whom, I couldn't tell.

"Who are you, and what do you want here?" I shouted at them, unable to see either one.

I heard the bark of a tree crumble nearby. "I for one have been waiting for you a long time now," the man said, coming from behind a foamy mouth, foul smelling, and matted beasts sitting there. The young man was about my age, rather tall but thin. He stopped alongside one of the wolves, petting its head. Staring at him, I thought I recognized him in the Expedition.

"You don't know me, but I do know you, Luke," he sort of grunted with a deep voice. "I've been waiting and watching. I even had my round with that redheaded woman but not as unique as you were with her." He stared down at me like a towering mountain.

Knowing he was the one that hurt Willa, all I could think right then was "You bastard."

"You are?" I asked while Kimmi trembled so hard she squeezed my knees until they hurt. Before he could answer, I asked, "How do you know me?"

"We were just wee little ones when we saw each other last. So you don't know me nor do any of the others."

"Why?" I controlled my anger that was rising due to Kimmi's fear.

"He's blind to it," the other voice said.

"Yes, he is. We'll let him linger for awhile. Maybe he'll figure it out in time before the curse takes him—maybe," the tall man said, with an evil grin before turning back into the darkness of the tress. I heard a whistle, then the wolves turned and left us. I held Kimmi, who was trembling so, that her teeth began to chatter.

"You know them?" Kimmi whimpered, shaking like a leaf.

"No, sweetie, I don't, but I may have seen the tall guy some time back. Let's get you out of here." I rose to my feet, picked her up, and headed to the truck while calling for Spirit, who didn't come right away.

I looked at Kimmi whose eyes narrowed, glaring at the lake. I took her to the truck and sat her in the passenger seat, before glancing over the beach and lake.

When I didn't see the pup, I closed the door, and told Kimmi, "Stay here." I turned toward the lake, calling and whistling for him as I made my way toward the woods. I heard not a whimper from him as I searched the area we had been in. It was midday with the rain getting heavier when I began to pace faster, looking in the sand for his prints. It wasn't long before I found them with what appeared to be blood in the sand.

I stooped down and touched the sand, and it was damp with the blood. I took two fingers, scooping up some of the red stuff to my nose, sniffed, and found it to be fresh. The scent in the red sand was sweet, so I quickly disposed of it and stood up. Listening, I heard nothing in the silence for a moment. When I did hear a whimper, it sounded like the pup was coming from the far side of the lake. I headed toward the sound, easing through the trees, feeling I was actually afraid for not only myself but for Kimmi.

The though hit me like a fist to the jaw. *Shit!* I thought, turning and hauling ass back to the truck, forgetting the dog.

When I came from the trees into view of the truck, I found Kimmi in the arms of the man named Jess. My anger went through the roof, and my hands curled into fists. So much so, the nails cut into the flesh of my palms. Kimmi was struggling to get free of him, but he had her arms pinned at her sides. Her dress was torn from her left shoulder down to the breast, resembling a dress with one shoulder strap. Looking at her, I caught a glimpse of a bruise beginning to show on her cheek. In anger, I made a move that even took me by surprise.

Never touching the table, I took one step, and leaped over the top toward them. Jess looked up at me as I came down in front of them. I aimed to kill him that day out of uncontrolled anger.

"Stop," he shouted, grabbing Kimmi by the hair and pulling her head back, baring her smooth neck.

My hands were itching to get at him. "What the hell are you doing here?" I asked in one slow tone, giving Kimmi a glance.

"Something I've been waiting and watching for a long time. I saw you two out in the lake that night. You should have finished what she was begging for, boy." He leaned in, touching her neck with his dark lips, and slid his tongue up her neck. His free hand slid down her back and over her buttocks, continuing around the front and up between her thighs. I saw her eyes look to me and I knew I could do nothing right then with my anger rising and my hate growing deeper.

"You fool! You know what's happening to her. Can I watch?" my companion roared.

He took her head in his palm and said with a downright ugly voice, "It's a shame you didn't take it while you could, boy." He made her face him as he held her to keep her from fighting. I had no choice but to watch him press his dark lips to hers in a kiss. I saw her tears fall over her cheek as mine came to my eyes. I was so angry that I didn't hear the pup I had forgotten, until he charged past me, soaked in blood.

Soundless for such a small animal, he leaped over the table toward Jess with his teeth snapping. Biting into Jess at the hip of his right leg, Spirit took the three of them to the ground. Jess let Kimmi go in wailing pain as soon as they hit the sand. But the pup wasted no time when he instantly took him by the throat while Kimmi scrambled to her feet. Shocked by the event at first, I finally gained my senses, and rushed past Kimmi. Just as I reached down and grabbed Jess by the arm, the pup released his throat. Leaving the bite marks and a blood trail, Spirit done something I thought I would never see in real life.

While Jess was on the ground—just before I got him to his feet—the pup took him by the nonads and shook them like a rag, making Jess scream in pain. Spirit was still locked on when I got Jess to his feet. Before I could stop her, Kimmi charged over with a raised hand that opened the man's jaw down to the bone, leaving a gushing line of blood.

Standing back with a shard of glass in hand and falling tears, she yelled at him, "You sorry, no-good bastard?" I couldn't blame her saying that given the hurt he had caused. The pup, well that was most unexpected. Letting go of Jess's private, Spirit left a blood trail when he came around me in silence. Without warning, the pup growled that deep down growl, and suddenly bit into the man's upper left leg, making Jess yell at the top of his lungs in pain.

"Come, Spirit," Kimmi whispered with a snap of the finger, stepping away from me and Jess.

Spirit released Jess's leg and went to Kimmi in obedience, sitting down by her leg at the table. I yanked Jess around to face me with one hand, and only the spirits knew what I was about to do to him when Jason and Paulene drove up.

I had a hand around Jess's throat by the time Jason got parked. He jumped out, running and yelling at me, "Stop, Luke, please, he ain't worth it man." Ignoring the plea, my fingers tightened around his throat. I could feel the pulse of each heartbeat with blood running in his arteries and him struggling for his life.

I hadn't noticed Jason by my side until Paulene yelled, "What did you do to her, you bastard?"

I felt a hand on my arm when Jason broke my thoughts. "Did you two fight?" His finger pointed to Jess's neck and jaw.

Without turning to face him, I replied, "Not me. It was Spirit."

"Luke, please," Paulene whispered from behind us. "Let's take him to Luther's." Watching his face grow redder with each passing moment, I knew she was right.

I eased off the pressure to Jess's throat, but he took advantage and wiggled free. Taking all of us by surprise, he dashed between Jason and me, but he didn't go far. Spirit went after him again, meeting him at the water's edge where Jess stopped and stared at the growling dog. I saw the anger in the dog's eyes that never left Jess's face.

"I guess, we should take him to see the old man," Jason said in a bitter tone.

I faced him and replied, "Yep, looks that way." Jason nodded, then went to the rear of the truck, and got some twine.

With a good amount of twine in hand, he went to Jess. As soon as Jason placed a hand on Jess, he jabbed Jason under the chin with an elbow. Jason's head went backward, making him stumble and fall into the water. Before I or anyone could stop the dog, a hellish, deep down growl, arose before he had Jess by the nonads again, sending him wailing into the shallow water. I hurried over to Jason and gave him a hand up.

"Son of a bitch," he said, rubbing his chin that had a bruise forming.

Angry, I snatched the twine from Jason's hand, then marched over to Jess who was terrified and laid there in the water.

I dropped down next to him, and oddly, the pup released him, and went back to Kimmi.

"You'll pay for this," I said, rolling him over, him over while he held his buddies with both hands and groaning. Not giving one damn about his buddies, I yanked and tied his hands behind him. Jason helped me get him to his feet, then walked him to my truck, and put him in the back. I didn't have to give the pup a lift up when he did it on his own to guard. I looked around for Kimmi, finding her and Paulene, sitting on the seat in Jason's truck. I composed myself and went to her.

She looked up when she heard me approach the truck with the sand crunching under my feet. Her eyes were wet and red, the bruise was darkening, but she smiled that tender I'm-okay smile. Since she was facing outward, I knelt down in front of her, and laid my head on her leg. I felt her place a cool trembling hand on my head, and then it slid over to my neck. When she whimpered, I looked up, and she grabbed my neck, crying.

I grabbed her around the waist in a comforting hug. "Are you okay?" I asked, placing a hand to her head. She shook her head yes without saying anything and I felt a rush of relief.

"What will you do with him?" she asked, sitting back to face me.

"The old man will know what to do." I wiped a tear from her face with a thumb. Paulene pulled a light jacket from behind the seat and handed it to Kimmi which she put around her shoulders.

"You want to ride with Paulene out to see Whitecloud?"

"Oh yes, as long as I don't have to ride with that," she cried, pointing a finger at my truck.

"Okay." I kissed her head, then turned, bumping into Jason. "Come on, Jason, you're with me."

He nodded, then rushed over to Paulene, giving her a kiss before running over to my truck and hopping in the passenger side. I followed Paulene from the lake to Whitecloud's.

Paulene drove up into the drive way and parked at the old oak tree. I parked on the passenger side near Kimmi. When we finally got out, I was surprised to find Tom and Mac coming out of the house. They were laughing like hell when we walked up onto the porch, and I knew why.

Before we stopped to chat, I heard Whitecloud call from inside, "Y'all come on in." The brothers stepped aside, and I opened the screen door for the girls. The rest of us followed them inside where we found Whitecloud seated at the kitchen table, having breakfast. Mac was the first to pull a chair for Kimmi, who quickly sat down.

She pulled forward when I said, "We have a problem outside."

"Thank you, Mac," Kimmi said, sliding to the table.

"Very welcome. Are you hungry?" he asked.

Pulling a chair for himself, Tom asked, "What's that?"

"No, thanks. I just had it scared out of me," Kimmi replied.

"What?" Mac whistled, looking at me.

"Well," I stuttered. "We had some visitors earlier up at the lake in both human and wolf forms. But there was another voice, only I never saw the face to it."

"They spoke of a curse. What do they want?" Kimmi mumbled.

"I have Jess in the truck." I finally seated myself in the chair next to her. The stillness with no one speaking a word brought an eerie feeling to the room.

Whitecloud glanced over the table, lastly looking at Kimmi. With no one mentioning Jess, he slowly got up and walked to the door where he stared out at the truck.

I saw him smile before he turned around and said, "Looks like he's well guarded for now." He returned to his chair, never sitting down. Looking at me then at Kimmi, he said to Paulene, "Ms. Jackson, please take Ms. Creed home. We have business to attend to."

"I would like to stay," Kimmi intervened.

Paulene stood up when Luther said, "Maybe another time, just not now. Please go home, and Luke can see ya later." I rose from my chair to help Kimmi, who was speechless. We walked out to porch where I softly kissed her and told her I would see her later. She agreed, then followed Paulene to the black Ford and they left.

Turning around in the seat of the truck, I stared out of the back window, wandering how I was going to tell Luke about the real me when the time came.

I returned to table and sat down with the rest. Luther sat down, placing his hands in his lap and addressed the table with sadness in his tone. "Luke has heard us speak of a legend we have that resides in all who are of the wolf. He, along with us, will have to take this creature to its death. It is one that he will find that which torments him now. This thing that calls for him is in the depths of his soul and is called 'the Companion'—a devil within each of us." Looking around the table, he continued. "This journey, which I speak, will teach you how to use things to your advantage. The trees will speak to you, and all you need to do is listen for them as they come in a whisper of the breeze." He paused.

Staring at his distant eyes, I asked, "Does it mean that I will be alone to tackle this task, or will Kimmi be in danger?"

"Both. And it comes sooner than you think. They'll come for her when least expected, use her against you to make you weak, and give into the legend like Daniel did. You see, Daniel was forced to face his dark side when a poison was induced into his wolf's blood. Kimmi makes you vulnerable, and they know this as well. I'm sorry to have to say this, but the thing in which you seek is your mother's twin brother, Jay. He somehow found the way to force the legend upon us, upon those where it was dormant. I once dreamed of Waya when I was just turning toward the companion. He showed me things of which I now know the meaning. Son, your wolf is a loving and kind-natured beast, but the companion in you makes you the most powerful and ruthless creature you'll ever want to know."

Before I could reply, Nate came rushing through the door, out of breath and said in between takes, "Come quick. We've company." Stuttering, he said, "Be prepared, y'all." The whole table jumped to their feet and went outside in a hustle.

When we stopped on the porch, I could see there were several men and wolves about the place.

Cole came forward in his rundown human form, yelling at the crowd with every step, "Luke, step out here, boy." His tone made my skin crawl.

Stepping to a pillar and leaning on it, I asked in a smooth daring tone, "Now, what could you possibly want with me?"

I watched Cole from a distance do as I asked, since Jess was busy elsewhere. I had my son standing next to me so he could see what was about to be the fight of a lifetime. I wanted him to see firsthand what it meant to the chosen one. I found it hard to believe he didn't remember Nick back at the lake. I was going to get what I wanted one way or another.

Three of the beasts made themselves visible when Cole said, "You, boy." The rest circled the area like a playground when he commented, "You have indeed been body building these days, haven't ya?" His voice became deeper with vengeance.

I stepped off the porch into the crowd of things to face Cole, who was lingering near a large grey wolf that growled at me. I shouted at him, "What the hell could you want right now?"

I heard Luther whisper behind me, "Do not let it rule the soul."

"It's not what I need but what I want." He snickered. "The same as Jess there." He made the gesture with his head.

"That is?" I began to feel the growing need in me.

"Wait for it," my companion said.

"First, I want you out of the way for that girl is mine, and I'll have her," he shouted.

"How will you accomplish that?" I mocked him.

"You are a powerful beast, and we want you to join our cluster." Laughing, he said while running a hand between the ears of the wolf, "These here are to help you acquire the needed taste." "When they are done, then I'll have what I came for." He looked at me with death in his face and said, "You should tell your lady good-bye for I have grown inpatient with this matter of you." I was dumbfounded when Cole turned and walked off, leaving the three wolves coming at me, growling.

I was so horrified and astound that I shouted at Cole's back, "How cruel are you?"

He didn't reply. I heard Whitecloud yell, "Do it before they are upon you." Looking back at him, I saw him nod with a forward tilt.

Changing to my wolf, I quickly faced the things in front of me. Watching them, I had the oddest feeling it was going to be a domination spar for Kimmi, who was mine, and she'd stay that way.

"Then you should do something about it," the companion growled at me. At that moment, I knew he was right. I prepared for a long battle, thinking I had no help. I saw it in their red, devious eyes when the smallest of the three charged at me first with foam dripping from its mouth. Feeling a guiltless hate with my companion at my side, I ruffled up, and lowered myself into a crouched position with my claws gripping into the earth. I was ready by the time it got to me, snarling and snapping.

The first thing that hit me was the stench of its drool when I lunged at it and we clashed in midair. My long fangs snapped at its back behind the neck, just missing before we hit the ground. When we parted from the force and faced each other again, it came at me, but stopped short of ten feet and stared over my back. Before I could look back, another of the wolves nailed me in the back of the neck with teeth that spread the thick fur. It kept the points of the fangs from breaking my skin while its hot breath entered my ear.

With a fast and snarling shake, I slung it off, to look for the smaller one. I found it crouched in a ready position and waiting. Making eye contact, I went at it with force, but it leaped over me, and grabbed me in my flank. Slicing through the flesh, it sunk its fangs deep into my right rump. In a frantic moment, I dropped and rolled over on it with my massive weight, making it whine and turn loose of my back. Before I could get to my feet, the third one was on me, sinking its teeth along the jaw and taking us into a roll. I felt the stinging burn go through me like a fire. Before we could stop rolling, the first came back, catching my soft skin under my right front leg. Whining in my own pain, the three of us slid over the side of hill. One lost its grip on my flank while the other clung on for life.

When we stopped, I laid there a moment, feeling the blood ooze from my jaw, and realized I was new to the game. My eyes searched for a way to lose the grip of the thing on my jaw. With the power of my body, I rolled over, and quickly got to my feet, looking for something large and sturdy. Finding it, I drug the creature, running across the rocky terrain, leaping over stumps and headed for the forest. Finding the biggest tree, I hit the trunk with the head of the thing hanging onto my jaw. Breaking the hold, I felt my skin, underneath, tear off when the thing came free, yelping. When it fell to the ground, I made a turnaround to see two of them charging for me. On the other hand, the other one never rose from its position.

I gave it a quick sniff to make sure it was either dead or unconscious while a voice in me said, "Wait for it."

"How long must I wait?" I pleaded, unaware of the approaching two wolves, until I heard them growl.

When I swung to face the sound, I was caught by the smaller of the two in the side of the neck when it leaped over the top of me, letting the second one bite into my left thigh. When I felt the warm hatred inside, my jaw grew harder, and the warm feeling grew stronger. It left me feeling like a losing fight was coming on. I was learning the taste of blood, which was strong with a bitter aftertaste, and that I actually liked the sensual feeling it gave me.

"Great Spirit, help me," I cried.

"Waya can no longer hear your cries boy!" my head screamed. Staggering like I had been drugged and in a dream world, I dropped to the ground.

I heard a whisper from somewhere that sounded like Luther. "Don't give in to him. Fight!"

"Almost there, kid. I can see it in the eyes," Cole growled at me from somewhere in the distance. I heard the crowd closing in but felt nothing more than the warm evil growing inside me.

With the world turning around me in a blur, I closed my eyes to it, for Cole was right.

I felt I was losing this battle to him when the companion said, "Shall I help you with these creatures that seem to think you are weak?"

Sluggishly, I asked "How?" Feeling another bite on my rump, I yelped in pain.

"Open up to me and I will grow with you," the voice said. "Let me come out."

"I hope you're right," I whimpered. Lying motionless, I felt the pain rush through me with every heartbeat. The beasts sensed

I was out cold and released their hold. But Cole, I heard his footsteps coming toward me.

In the time that I lay there, a movement in me eased about my veins like fire that began touching the teeth marks and holes the creatures left behind. My friend felt like a drifter wandering around in my body. It was the strangest thing since my transformation into the wolf, but it felt like something had crawled out of me and picked me up to a standing position. Though it wasn't my own accord, I began to change in a way that was nothing I had ever seen as my companion stuck my hands out in front of me so I could watch.

What I saw was the most unnatural thing, when my fingers extended outward, nearly two, maybe three inches, that ended with long, black shiny razors, for claws. My arms were thick with muscles extending to monstrous lengths for a better reach. I felt myself grow to enormous height, leaving the ground far below. I had to be nine feet tall with massive body strength, the slickest fur, and muscles that rippled in my arms and legs like the ocean currents. Looking down, I saw that my once paws were no longer paws. They were monstrous feet with narrow claws for grabbing the earth with. My own eyes watched my snout protrude further while I felt my teeth and fangs hang over the lips like dragon's teeth, and drool dripped from the ends. As my eyes saw red, I felt my chest protrude and my waist caved in. I conformed to the change, but in the end, I realized the legend was right. I began to laugh with great fury that came from deep inside my darkest self. There were no tears when I reached into the sky and howled like the hell I had came from, knowing I was the dominant one, and no one was going to stop me.

Watching the view of what happened on the hillside, Jason came to me and asked in a frantic manner, "Holy shit! Have you seen such a thing like that happen before Luther?"

Swallowing hard, I replied, "Only in my dreams, only in my dreams." I was overwhelmed once again by the truth about the legend of two wolves. "May the Spirits and God help us all."

"Now, big boy, if we don't stop him, he'll take the girl. And you know what he'll do to her with you gone," my companion roared at me, making me more infuriated. Knowing the truth in what my companion said about Cole, I whipped around looking for him, feeling the blood in my veins like hot iron steel.

What I saw take place out there was far more than I could have ever imagined. The height and strength of the creature were magnificent. I was all too grateful I had decided to send Cole in place of my son. Knowing I would have to inform mother to build a stronger clan, I took my son and left Cole to his fate.

Watching others stray from their hidden places, I found that bastard Cole standing alone with his face ghost-white and trembling with fear.

The only thing he could say before he took off running was, "What the hell?" His eyes peered at me from the small mound he was standing on while I towered over him. One of the many brown wolves bit into the calf of my leg, but the feeling was so little, leaving a bee sting sensation, that I shook off like a bug. It landed on the ground nearby with a heavy thud, but Cole, like the fool he was, took off running. And what do dogs do? They like to chase. I just stood there, letting the grin come across my face, watching, waiting, and knowing he could not outrun me.

I waited a few seconds for him to think he was getting away before I took off after him in a full run on all four legs that surged with power. Cole had several hundred feet of space between us when he began to change into his wolf then slowly his beast. I came upon him, reaching out a massive hand that caught him around the waist while the other grabbed the earth just before we rounded the first tree. The massive claws left the earth behind with deep tracks like a crater. When Cole swung around, he opened my side with deep gashes.

Wailing in anger instead of pain, I lost myself to my companion when I half stood up on both hind legs, feeling no sympathy for him or his kind. When I stood fully upright, I released the hold and opened his chest over the left breast. At that time our blows continued until we both began to tire. I often caught glimpses of those sneaking out to join the party, but a beast of my kind intercepted, leaving me and Cole to our fate. Finally the companion realized it was time to end the struggling. He grabbed Cole around the waist with one hand and the neck with the other and bit into him.

With him in my hands, he faded to human form, losing the battle, but he was smart not to use it again. Holding him in the air, he pounded on the hand that held him with force, yelling for help that never came. I listened to him curse me with every breath he took, knowing he was about to die when I leaned to him. Taking a long whiff of the evil he was, I let out a deep raging roar to the sky. It echoed over the valley with evilness behind it. It was all me and no one but me.

Kimmi and I were sitting out in the gazebo, working on some macramé when an evil sound rushed through the woods. Spirit leaped to his feet from the lying position near Kimmi and began to howl in response.

Kimmi jumped with a scream, "What on earth was that?"

Unsure myself, even though I had never heard such a sound, I replied, "I don't know, and I don't think I want to from the sound of it."

Facing the woods while trying to quiet the dog, she asked, "Do you think he's okay out there?"

Facing her, I didn't know how to respond, so I said, "Yeah, he's fine. I'm sure."

In a moment of pure unforgiving hatred and anger, I took Cole by the waist with both hands. With a twist, I tore him in two, letting his red life-giving blood spew over onto my arms and hands. I stood roaring with his upper body in the right hand and the lower in the left, and looking from one to the other to make sure he was dead. Without looking, I tossed the body parts over my shoulders into the woods. With no thought of my own, I turned around, looking to seek out the many others, either in human or wolf form that had ran off. I wanted to make them pay for their evilness. My anger was uncontrollable with the ability of the companion.

Ranting and raving, I quickly stalked the trees until I found them, one by one, as they tried to hide. I could hear their sniffling whines and their pounding hearts. But most of all, I could feel their fear. First was the small black and white one that was hidden in the lightest part of the wooded area. I reached down and picked it up with one hand and had it face me so I could see the terror in its eyes. Only that didn't stop me when my thumb rose up to the furry, soft belly of the wolf, toward the chin of the beast. With no remorse and a flick from a mighty thumb of my hand, I broke its neck. I heard the pleas from the group, but the companion totally refused to hear their cries to stop. I was hurt with anger, and the thing in me was revolting, leaving me feeling no pain, remorse, or anything for those who wronged me.

Furious to the point of no pain no gain, I located the other death-bound things. Taking each one, I grinned to myself every time I split one open with a sharp claw, or by breaking its neck, or tearing it in two. When I thought all of them had been taken care of, my companion and I stood tall, swinging out with both arms, and hit the trees for the hell of it. Clipping several tops and watching them topple to the ground, I felt I was in control with each swing. Soon enough I looked down at myself and found I was soaked in blood. Trying to shake it off, I leaned against a tree with my shoulder, wiping my face with a huge hand and began to cool off. Feeling the deep change, I realized who and what I was and that I had abolished everything in my path. How could I tell them I liked what I had done but yet I was with sorrow? I turned around and faced the group staring at me.

I was squatting behind the tall mound of dirt, watching Luke demolish the things like toys, making me want what he had.

"Your time will come. I promise. You shall have everything that you want and then some," my companion laughed with fury. "But first, you will have to take the life of that one so there will be no one to stop you then."

"How I long for the time to come," I whispered, getting to my feet and leaving before I was noticed.

Blood covered, I forced myself to walk upright, as the thing I was, back to the old man, who was waiting. But actually, all I wanted to do was run and be wild. "What have I become?" I whispered to myself.

"I told you we were undomesticated and would be spectacular together," my head raged with laughter.

Dragging my feet in regret of my actions, I said, "Shut up!" I finally stopped in front of the old man, dropped to my knees in tears, and reached for his hands as mine began to return to normal.

"I'm sorry. I couldn't stop the rage, old man," I cried. "What is happening to me?" I cried in agony. "Please get it out of me!" I screamed, tightening my grip on his hand. "I am not a killer!"

"No time for that now, child. It'll pass with time. Just remember to pray for the wolf."

Tom placed a hand on my shoulder. "It doesn't change the beauty in you. This is the start until Jay is dealt with. You can bet he was watching and he knows what to expect when you two do come face to face."

"This is the true fight of good over evil, Luke. Someday, someway, you'll find the wisdom to know the difference," Luther soothed, sitting on the ground in front of me.

A good while passed in silence between us while Tom and Mac hurried out to clean the area up the things I had destroyed. Tears came to my eyes to watch them and think of what I had done, but then it wasn't me, was it?

"Where is Kimmi?" I managed to say through dry lips.

"Home. Where she should be?" Patting my leg, Luther said, "This companion will be your death if you let it control you like this. I saw you out there, knowing you had the feeling, and I prayed for you. Now you're sitting here with me. Time will come where you'll have to choose between right and wrong."

Mac stooped down at Luther's side and said, "Cleanup is done."

Nodding, he looked at me and said, "Go home or see Kimmi, but leave here and forget about this or what has happened. I bet she's worried about you." He tilted his head, and I got to my feet, brushing off the dirt. Luther stood up with Mac's help, facing me and me looking into his dark eyes. We grabbed each other in hug for a much needed relief of compassion. When it was over, I hurried to the truck, and jumped in. With a turn of the key, it came to life, and I headed out to see Kimmi who was sitting in the gazebo with Paulene when I rolled into the driveway.

With the setting of the sun, I parked, and both girls rose from their seats. When I came toward them, Paulene pardoned herself and left Kimmi with me. Not knowing what to say, I just stared at her, but she seemed to know something was wrong.

She came to me a one swift stride, placing her arms around my neck. "Thank God, you're okay," she cried with tenderness. Placing my hands on her waist, I pulled her closer, knowing I was going to have one hell of a time, trying to tell her my secrets.

I whispered, "Someday soon my family secret will have to be told, won't it?"

Looking up at me, she smiled. "Someday, just not today." She reached up to my jaw where the scar once was, tracing it with a finger, "Yes, someday." Spirit came dashing around the house and into the gazebo with Kimmi and me. We sat down on the bench with my arm around her shoulders, playing with the pup and feeling there was more to come from whoever was watching from the trees.

EPILOGUE

SINCE I HAVE been blessed by Waya's spirit, life has come at me with many struggles and challenges that have led me to alternate paths. As time goes on, I will let him help give me strength to balance the two within. I will do my best to let his intuition guide me in the best possible way when each day unfolds. But I know there will be times I will want to go my own way, expressing who I am, no matter what. There will also be times when my free spirit will hunger for only the company of the full moon.

My life will become that in which I have conformed to and combined with to be the one I was meant to be. While my dark side drifts around inside me, I will not bend as I fight to free myself, but I will embrace my true self from that darkness within. I know my battle rages deep within my soul. Therefore, I will pray for the fight to end before the darkness consumes me. I must let Waya's strength and power fill me in those times, knowing I must stand alone in the days to come.

Bibliography

"Spirit of the Wolf." Last modified 2013. Accessed December 7, 2012. spiritofthewolf.co.uk/wolf-quotes.